The Chosen

The Citizens of Abrielara Book 1

Taryn Sloane

Glossary of Terms

Brielara – A planet not in our solar system. Home to an alien of species called the Brielarans.

Brielarans – An alien species who originated from Brielara but are now integrated into human society on Earth. Brielarans are never seen in their true form after the age of 5, unless they are male and have begun the Passage.

Abrielara – A town in Washington State named after the species of aliens who invaded them.

Abrielarans – Human and Brielaran Hybrid species living in Abrielara.

- The Brielarans integrated into their society, creating a hybrid species of humans and Brielarans. However humans also live in this community.
- Citizen of Abrielara – You don't have to live in Abrielara to be a citizen of Abrielara. It just means that you are a hybrid species of Brielaran and your home is Abrielara.

- Hybrids – Hybrids are humans who carry the Brielaran gene.
- Female hybrids are connected to the Monarch and therefore can leave Abrielara anytime they want, unless they are chosen. Once they are chosen, they cannot leave the community until of their own free will until they are carrying a hybrid offspring.
- Humans living in Abrielara – Were chosen by a hybrid (Abrielaran) or related to a human who was chosen and live in the society but do not carry the gene.
- Human Females are not integrated into Abrielaran society unless they are chosen. Once they are chosen, they cannot leave Abrielara until the offspring of the Abrielaran is delivered. This is because they are not connected to the Monarch because they do not carry the gene.
- Human Males can move around as they please but are never a part of the community.

Monarch – Is the hybrid queen who governs over Abrielara to ensure the safety and prosperity of the community is upheld.

- She telepathically connects to anyone who carries the Brielaran gene once the Passage is initiated or if the Brielaran who is hosted by the Abrielaran(male) contacts her.
- The Monarch can create illusions, speak telepathically, read minds, and manipulate energy.

- The Monarch is always female and although she isn't immortal, she can live for centuries.

Chapter One

Mika

"**S**he's gone, Mika. Momma's gone."

The moment I found out Momma had died replays in my mind repeatedly, like a tired, scratched record. Each time, the feelings come back as if I'm only hearing about it for the first time. I haven't been home in three years and had no intention of ever coming back, but here I am.

I run my hand down the length of my skirt for the thousandth time. I'm itching to take my top knot down so my braids can breathe.

My shoulders and back ache. The impulse to slouch and hang my head may have to do with the length of the service. But it's probably from trying to hold my head up while fielding disparaging looks and comments from the folks in the community. Church or no church, these folks just can't seem to keep their comments to themselves. No doubt they're witnesses to one or all of the screaming matches between momma and me.

"Such a pretty girl, but such an ugly attitude."

"So beautiful she could grace the cover of Vogue but

couldn't lower herself to grace her mother's house more often. Tsk. Tsk. Tsk."

"She got that dark, beautiful skin and those high cheek-bones from her momma. Too bad she didn't get anything else."

"She ought to be ashamed showing up now. Shoulda stayed gone."

I pretend not to hear the nasty comments. I'm ready to go. I shouldn't have come. If I'd put any thought into it, I would've remembered that I don't belong here. Never did. Coming back was a mistake.

Not just because I hate funerals. I don't know anyone who loves them, but the Homegoing is supposed to be joyful, to celebrate life. Which is great and all, unless you weren't a part of their life at the end.

Celebrate what? Especially knowing how Momma felt about me, I'm about as welcome as an ant parade at a picnic. The whispers and the constant stares are almost enough to have me running from the church. Can't say the comments aren't warranted, but I figured since I won't be coming back, I'd sit with my back straight and let the shit all roll off.

Besides pretending to not hear the snide comments, I've run out of things to do at the repass. I'm out of place and not needed. I want to speak to my sisters alone before I leave. I tried sitting with them at the service. But there was no room for me, and I had to settle for a spot in the back. The church was standing room only by the time I got here. I could never seem to catch their attention once the service started.

Even now, they're surrounded by people waiting on them hand and foot. As they should. They never left. I'm not going to lie and say I don't feel guilty about leaving because I do. To learn that momma's cancer had returned and they shouldered her care without me hurts. It's also embarrassing. How bad of a daughter do you have to be for your mother to not want you around in her last hours?

I grab a cup of coffee and sit on the church's back porch. It's a little chilly but warmer out here than inside. It's obvious the people in this town took my rocky relationship with momma personally.

Well, today will be my official last day in Atlanta. So they can get off their salty, intrusive, judgmental high horses and worry about themselves. I won't be around for them to gossip about anymore. I plan to make that declaration stick this time.

I still can't believe she's gone. She's so vibrant. Was so vibrant. Her energy could be felt before she entered the room. Her thoughts were plastered on her face like a billboard if she wanted them to be. She sang like an angel but could rip you a new one in the next breath without thinking about it. She was celebrated in this community. Loved.

Even by me.

I had a funny way of showing it, I know. But when you're young, usually dumb, full of opinions and hormones, you don't think straight. You never think about how you'll feel when life happens and then it removes the chance to make everything right. All you see and feel are those painful memories and how you could have done things differently. It's unsettling how these memories pop up when you're already vulnerable and dealing with other life shit that's unrelated to your past. Even when you thought you'd already made peace with them all.

I'd like to think I've matured since then. I've come to accept certain truths I learned with time. I'm not as bitter, and although I no longer live in the past, being here throws me back as if I never left.

"There you are. We've been looking for you."

The young lady who walks toward me is obviously not a

part of the original community. Her smile is too genuine and her brown eyes are kind. She stands out in her Easter egg yellow dress in a sea of black Sunday best.

"Looks like you've found me. Who's looking for me?"

"The family is gathering in the conference room in the back for the reading of the will."

"Here? Aren't those things usually done in the office?"

"Not if the client says otherwise. I believe your mother was of the mind that if you showed for the funeral, you wouldn't be back for the reading of the will. So it was best we do this here. We thought we should get on with it now that everyone has already eaten."

Despite our differences, my mother knows me backward and forward. She's right in assuming I wouldn't come back once I left. However, I'm positive my mother left me nothing and there's no need for me to attend.

"I'd rather not if you don't mind. I'd like to speak to my sisters alone. Could you send them out here when they're done?"

"I'd be happy to, but unfortunately, it was your mother's wish that you sit for the reading. It shouldn't take long, I promise."

I've come this far. As much as I hate to, I might as well see it through. If it was her wish, then the least I can do is honor it.

"Alright then. Lead the way."

The conference room is too big of a space for what we need it for. With just five people sitting at a table meant for twenty, I'm sure the Deacon's office would have been just fine. My sister, Taliah pats the chair next to her and grabs my hand as soon as I sit down. I squeeze it before releasing it.

For the first time since arriving, tears flood my eyes. I furiously blink them away. I haven't allowed myself to cry since I received the news. I'm not going to start now. I don't deserve to. Deserters have no right to accept comfort from those who bear the wounds of fighting the battle until the end.

Momma's attorney drones on and on about how wonderful of a woman she was. He shares his memories of her and keeps referring to how wealthy of a woman she was. I really wish I'd left when I had the chance.

I zone in and out of the conversation until he finally gets to why we're here. Why didn't I leave? I sit humiliated by the fact I'm receiving nothing but being required to sit and listen all the same.

I was okay with receiving nothing. I never expected anything. There's no reason I need to be here and listen to confirmation of that fact. At least not in my mind. Knowing my mother, she wanted to make sure I know what I'm missing out on.

I mistakenly thought we'd parted on good terms. We'd come to a mutual agreement that being related didn't mean we had to be in each other's lives.

I left Atlanta years ago thinking every throat-cutting word spoken between us was water under the bridge. I guess I misunderstood the entire conversation, which isn't surprising considering our history. But this is intentionally cruel.

"Well, ladies, that's it. I know today hasn't been easy. If you have any questions, please feel free to contact my office. Shanice, can you fix me another plate with the works, please? Sister Johnson put her foot in that potato salad and that fried chicken Sister Favors brought...hmm. I just have to have one more bite."

"Sure. I'll be right back."

"Excellent." He faces us again. He slides a manila envelope to Brianna and Taliah. "These hold the details of your inheritance. Of course, all of this is in a trust, so it'll always stay in the family. Please keep my services in mind should you need any estate help."

"Wait, that can't be right. You didn't say what momma left for Mika." Brianna leans over to catch my eye. The look tells me she pities me.

"Well, I do have to have a discussion with Mika in private."

Shanice places the loaded plate in front of Mr. Phillips and he dives right in. My sisters leave the room as I watch him go in hard on his food. I grow more and more irritated as I wait.

Is he really going to eat while I'm waiting on him to finish? And instead of talking about whatever he has to say in private, he hems and haws about nothing. With an open mouth, no less. Seriously?

I want to slash his meaty throat. Not only for making me wait but also for sitting in front of me and eating while talking. Besides wasting my time, that is my biggest pet peeve of all time.

While eating... Close. Your. Fucking. Mouth.

I can't concentrate as pieces of food exit his mouth in chunky sprays while he continues to gush about how good the food is.

I endure his horrid table manners until he finally gets around to explaining why I'm still here. Taliah received Momma's house, Brianna received the beach house in South Carolina, and each received an equal amount of cash.

"Yes, I was here when you explained all that to my sisters a few minutes ago." I roll my eyes at him. This man is ridiculous.

"Well, you're mother left you a cabin in Abrielara, Washington. No cash."

I can't bring myself to say anything. All I see are images of what I consider a cabin to look like. Since my mother is leaving it to me, it can't look like much.

For once, the blubbering, greasy-fingered attorney is quiet too. Obviously embarrassed for me. I'm embarrassed for myself. If I had any doubt about how my mother really felt about me compared to my sisters, I don't anymore.

She shouldn't have bothered. I don't need the absence of cash or a one-room cabin in backwoods Abrielara, Washington, to tell me how she feels. Obviously, the purpose of all this is to humble me.

The irony is not lost on me that Washington is clear across the country, far from my sisters. My mother always said I was a bad influence on them, so it isn't much of a stretch to conclude why she orchestrated things this way.

"I know this is a bit of a shock, Ms. Burris."

Mr. Phillips' attempt to console me isn't helping at all.

"You could say that."

"Even though it isn't much, you still need to go to Abrielara and claim it. Then you can decide what to do with it."

"Excuse me?" Surely this country lawyer understands we're living in the digital age. Everything's available at our fingertips these days. "I don't think that's necessary."

"Your mother was very clear. You have to see the cabin in person to claim it."

"What if I don't want to claim it?" I cross my arms furiously. "The little dusty cabin in the woods can't be much. Let nature take it back."

He nearly chokes on the chicken he just cleaned off the bone.

"Of course you do—"

The look on my face stops him mid-sentence.

"Even if you plan to sell it, you'll need to go there to do so.

Not to mention you have to spend a minimum of one week there before you can do anything."

"A week?" My voice elevates an octave. "I have a business to run." He doesn't have to know I can run my business from anywhere. But a week, really?

"You'll have to run your business from Abrielara for the week if you can't take off."

"That's ridiculous. Take off. You're out of your mind."

The attorney is unbothered by my scoffing tone. "Maybe. But it's what your mother wanted."

"What she wanted was to stick it to me one last time. That's what this is. She just couldn't help herself."

"Now, don't talk that way. Your mother was a lovely woman."

"If you say so."

"I do."

"Why don't you take the cabin, then?" My snarky response earns me a stern look a parent would give to a naughty child. I may act a touch ridiculous, but it's my honest response. I've always been a bit dramatic. A trait I apparently never outgrew.

"Because it isn't meant for me and you would still have to spend one week in Abrielara, anyway." He wipes his greasy fingers on a napkin.

"Ugh." My head falls back against the chair. I concede. Doesn't seem like there's any way out of this.

"One more thing I need to mention. You can't tell your sisters where you're going."

"Why?" My lip curls up at the question.

The lawyer throws me an assumptive look.

"Let me guess. Because it's what she wanted."

"You're catching on." He nods slowly.

Chapter Two

Mika

I have to go all the way to Washington to claim a cabin in the woods, whether or not I plan on keeping it. Without looking at the house, I can tell you I'm going to sell it. I'll definitely not stay in a country cabin in the forests of Washington state. I'm a city girl through and through and I plan to make it back home as soon as possible.

Hence the reason I'm on this itty-bitty plane that I caught in Spokane from Atlanta, headed to Wilson's Creek Airport. I didn't want to waste any time returning to New York only to catch another flight. So I traded my flight home for a flight to Spokane.

I was told once I reach Wilson's Creek, which is about forty miles east of Abrielara, a driver is supposed to meet me and drive me the rest of the way.

Fine. I've never been to Washington, and I'm not great at directions, so I'll do as I'm told. I'm on a roll with this doing-as-I'm-told bullshit. Hopefully, everything will go smoother than this charter flight has been so far.

My body moves with the plane's vibrations which isn't remarkable. What is remarkable is the plane has yet to find a comfortable altitude and level out. This is how crashes happen. I swear the entire plane creaks like it'll disintegrate into thin air.

I can't see myself making a return trip in this thing. I'd rather hitch a ride on somebody's boat all the way back to New York. No matter how long it took.

The best thing I can think to do is concentrate on anything other than this plane. It was a ludicrous idea to board this decrepit flying machine. I'd laugh at this situation if I wasn't overcome with fear. And closing my eyes brings me immediately back to my mother.

She was always great at getting the last word, as mothers often are. She stuck it to me this time. I'll take it, though. I honestly can't say I don't deserve this.

Of her three daughters, I'm the one with the hardest head and the slickest mouth. But I'm also the one who never needed her help. I've always been independent. You would think she'd appreciate it, considering Brianna needed constant attention, and Taliah was always up under her. Obviously, my mother enjoyed that kind of relationship with them. Wish I'd found a way to have a good one with her too.

"We'll arrive at our destination in ten minutes. Please put your seat in the upright position and make sure your seat belt is fastened. The temperature is now a warm seventy-five degrees, but tonight is going to be chilly."

I roll the shade up on the window and tune out whatever else the pilot says. The sun is bright, and the foliage is beautiful. This would be a wonderful place for inspiration when I need color ideas for my designs. I'm glad I brought my tablet. Maybe this trip won't be a complete waste after all.

As we descend, the plane shakes so fiercely that I'm positive it'll come apart in the air. I can do nothing but squeeze my eyes shut and grab onto the seat cushion for dear life. I believe the flight attendant mentioned something about using it as a flotation device should the time call for it. The vibrating gets worse the closer we get to the ground. My head and my stomach are a jumbled mess. I pray I can plant my feet on the ground soon.

When the plane lands and I exit, I make a mental note not to get back on that plane again. Once I locate my bag, I notice the place isn't empty, but it isn't bustling with people either. I quickly locate a man holding a sign with my name on it. He's tall and thin but young. I'd guess twenty-one at most. I nod toward the sign he holds over his head.

"Do you think all this is necessary?" I wave my hand at his monstrous sign.

He grins as he lowers his sign. "No. But I've always wanted to do that, so I took the liberty. I hope you don't mind."

"I guess it doesn't matter if I do or not since you've already done it." I give a half smile to take the edge off my words. "So, where to..." I glance at his name tag. "Bobby?"

His nervous smile and gangly appearance makes me rethink his age. I wouldn't be surprised if he was younger. "This way, Ms. Burris."

Thankfully Bobby's truck appears to be new. With a shiny charcoal colored paint job and wheels that look freshly washed, it looks to be in better shape than the plane. That's a plus.

"Where're you coming from?" He pulls his truck out onto the main road, and before I realize it, we're already out of Wilson's Creek.

"Do you want the long answer or the short answer?"

"Well, we have a bit of road left, so how about the long answer?"

"I came here straight from my mother's funeral in Atlanta. I live in New York, but I had to come all the way out here before I can go back home."

"That's a bummer. I'm sorry for your loss. If that's the long answer, then you must not be much of a talker."

I shrug. "Not used to sharing my personal business with strangers."

He spares me a quick look, his eyes widening in surprise. "Blunt. I like that. Tell me to back off if I'm too nosey."

"Don't worry, I will."

He grins and turns his eyes back to the road. "Straight here, huh? That couldn't have been a relaxing trip."

"No, it wasn't. I'm not looking forward to repeating it on the way back."

"I can't say I'm surprised." His loud laugh is jarring. "The Cranky Bird is a well-oiled machine, but she's kind of old. There are plans to purchase another one by the end of the year."

I roll my eyes dramatically. "The what?"

He grins. "The Cranky Bird is the name of the charter plane you flew in. We named her that because she's old and sometimes she takes a little while to get warmed up for a flight."

"Don't worry," he says after looking at my face. "She always passes her tests. She's perfectly safe."

"Right. Glad I wasn't aware of that before I got on that death trap. I have to find another way out of here when I'm ready to go back."

"You can always hire someone to drive you. Might take you longer to reach Spokane, but at least you'll be on the ground."

"You can say that again. Think you could drive me back when I'm ready?"

"Depends."

"On what?"

He flashes me a quick grin. "How much you're paying?"

"Name your price because I'll be damned if I board that charter plane again. I don't think I want to press my luck."

"Nah, just yanking your chain. If you're sure you're gonna be leaving, I'll take you. All you have to do is call the Wilson Creek airport and ask for Sandy. She'll get your message to me. The number's listed. Give me a couple of days' notice."

"So, tell me a bit more about Abrielara. I googled it, but there isn't much written about it online."

"That's because there isn't much there. Coming from New York, you might find the place a little too quiet."

I shrug. "I may like it. I don't mind quiet. I'm perturbed because I could do everything I need to do from my apartment without getting on a plane. I hate being inconvenienced."

"Don't like flying?"

"I don't fear it but a rough flight would make anyone nervous. I just don't get why I have to fly here to sell a cabin. It's ridiculous."

"Yeah, I'm afraid that is how Abrielara handles their business. They're particular about sticking to certain laws. Most people who come here either stay for good or leave forever."

"Why?"

"I'm assuming you either love Abrielara or you hate it. I've lived in Wilson's Creek my whole life and have never known it to be any different. You may like it."

I scrunch up my lips in response.

He shrugs. "Or maybe not."

"Just for the record, I'm leaving. In one week's time, to be exact."

Bobby and I settle into a few moments of silence for the rest of the ride. I watch the foliage pass by at a calming pace. My mind is thankfully slowing and digesting the last forty-eight hours. The tension in my shoulders lets up a little. I haven't had a restful night's sleep since Taliah called with those three little words.

"Wow," I say, absentmindedly looking around.

"Beautiful, right?"

I can't remember the last time I took a moment to enjoy the surrounding scenery. Ever since I branched out with my brand, I haven't taken a proper vacation. That was two years ago. This impromptu sabbatical is forcing me to concentrate on something else besides shoe design and next season's color palette. This could be good for me.

The Welcome to Abrielara, population 3500 sign rushes by. The immaculately clean streets and groomed yards isn't what I thought it would be like here. As soon as we pass the welcome sign and turn off the highway, we're pulling into a driveway.

"We're here," Bobby says. "We can turn around if you want?" He asks expectantly.

I shake my head. Why would I want to do that after finally getting here? What an odd thing to say.

As soon as Bobby stops the truck, I open the door and step out.

This isn't what I envisioned when Mr. Phillips told me I inherited a cabin. This is no ordinary cabin.

"Nice isn't it? If I remember correctly, the entire top floor, including the south side of the house, is made of glass. You have scenery for days."

"You've lived here before?" I ask.

"No but I used to spend my summers working for the

main landscaper in this town. I've mowed this lawn many times.

Bobby walks with me to the door, bypassing a sculpted lawn decorated with every color tulip you can imagine. He notices how my eyes linger on the flowers.

"I hope you like tulips. If not, I'm sure Ray won't mind redesigning your lawn with the flowers you like. He has to come out here anyway and change it up before winter comes." He reaches down and pulls a key out from under the welcome mat.

"Oh no. Leave them. Tulips are my favorite. The lawn is beautiful." He smiles and hands me the key.

"Good. I'm sure someone will come around soon. Everything is within walking distance. If not, there should be a list of numbers on the fridge if you have questions. Also, until you figure out your way around here, I wouldn't walk anywhere at night. Safety is always best."

"Understood. Thanks for the ride. I appreciate it."

I didn't want to admit it, but I hated to see him go. He's the only person I know in the entire state of Washington.

"No problem. Let me know if you need anything. Cell service is spotty in this area, by the way."

As if to prove his point, my cell alerts me that I don't have service. "Okay."

"Weird, I know, but you know how it is when you're in a dense forest area. The satellite signal can be a little weak."

"I get it. Thanks again, Bobby."

"You're welcome, Ms. Burris. Catch up with you in a week...or so."

His small smile doesn't seem real or fake. More melancholic and loaded. He obviously wants to say something more, but he isn't going to. Which is fine. I only have a week, and a week will fly by before I know it. Wishy-washy Wi-Fi for a week doesn't sound so bad.

A royal blue truck pulls into the drive directly across the road. A very tall, attractive man hops out. Broad-shouldered, muscled thighs and a head full of clean-cut, straight, shiny black hair. I can't make out his eyes from here because he's wearing aviator sunglasses, but there's no doubt he sees me. He faces my house and only moves when Bobby calls out to him.

"Hey, Dr. Christiansen! How's it shaking?"

"Hey, Bobby. Going well. You?"

"Just drove your new neighbor to town. Keep an eye on her, will you? Her name's Mika."

I can't hear if the doctor answers, but I feel him watching me. I wave at him briefly but he doesn't wave back. Awkward. Okay, some people aren't friendly. I'm immediately aware of how I must appear, standing on this porch watching him and decide to go on in.

Whatever the reason, he obviously has nothing to say to me. And although I'm interested in his conversation with Bobby, it's none of my business. I'll only be here for a week. A week is long enough to get into some trouble, but I'm not interested. Especially not the kind that keeps your knees weak, your heart in tatters, and where common sense is a foreign language. No, thank you. I don't need the added headache and I'm not that bored.

Stepping into the foyer of this cabin, it seems weird calling this place a cabin. It's too big. My definition of a cabin is like three rooms total. This is on par with resort-style lodging. Insane. How my mother came across this property is a mystery. Fortunately, I have nothing but time to work all of this out.

Someone has apparently been taking care of the place.

The beautiful rich hardwood floors gleam as if they had been polished and stained recently. The electricity is on and the temperature is comfortable. The cabin has an open floor plan with a step-up kitchen.

The south end of the property can be seen through the floor-to-ceiling glass walls that complete the second story. Just as Bobby described. The appliances are new. I know because the instruction packets are still attached to everything. The furniture is modern and comfortable. This is way more house than I'll ever need.

And then I spot it, attached to the wall next to the refrigerator and the back door. It looks out of place in this modern kitchen, but I'm glad to see the house does indeed have a phone. A yellow rotary phone. The last time I saw one of these was at my momma's house. I pick it up and hear a dial tone. If I don't have cell service, at least it works. I've got to test it out. I dial my assistant's number.

"Lady M's office. How may I help you?"

"It's me."

"Where are you? You were supposed to be back in New York hours ago."

I can practically see her hand on her hip as she stomps her foot in frustration. Brandi is my assistant, but most of the time, she acts like she's my mother.

"Not in New York or Atlanta, I can tell you that."

"Where exactly? And what phone are you calling from? Where's your cell?"

"My phone is with me in Washington. Shitty service out here, so I'm calling from a landline."

"D. C.?" Her voice sounds hopeful.

"State."

"What in the world are you doing all the way in Washington state? I thought the funeral was in Atlanta?"

"It was, but now I'm in Washington."

"Why, though?"

I look around the kitchen, with its ornate craftsman-style woodwork and state-of-the-art appliances.

"To unload an inheritance."

"Say what?"

"I won't bore you with the details, but I won't be back in New York until next week."

"Hmm. Well, maybe you can use this opportunity to take that vacation you never have the time for."

"You know I don't have time for that right now."

"Are you kidding? This is the perfect time. You've already completed your winter collection. Your contribution to the museum's History of Fashion is done. It wouldn't kill you to take a break, for Pete's sake."

"I'll think about it."

"I've already thought about it for you. I'll hold down the fort like I always do. You'll disconnect and actually smell the roses for a change instead of replicating the colors of them."

The project with the museum was so much fun, and I'd jump at the chance to do something like that again. Replicating and helping produce all those shoe designs was fun but exhausting. And let's not talk about what it took to meet the deadline. I loved every minute, but maybe a vacation would do me some good.

"Fine. Alright. I'll take a break but just for one week. Then it's back to the grind."

Brandi and I talk for a few more minutes. Then I set the phone on the hook and turn to finish my tour. I explore the house until my stomach reminds me I haven't eaten since...I can't remember when I ate last. I didn't eat at the funeral. It had to have been before I landed in Atlanta.

The refrigerator is like the rest of the appliances. Brand new, complete with a list Bobby mentioned and stocked.

Wonderful. The last thing I want to do is find my way to whatever grocery store this town has because all I want is food, a bath and a bed.

A cold-cut plate with a fruit and cheese platter is in the fridge. Interesting. I didn't think anyone knew I was coming. Maybe momma's attorney told someone and they stocked the fridge. I remove the cover and smell it. Smells fresh. I could make a meal of this and then figure out where I want to sleep.

The master is outfitted in muted blues and grays and is triple the size of my entire apartment in New York. I shouldn't be surprised based on the size of the place, but wow. With a master this huge, of course, the bathroom has to be stellar.

I'm not disappointed. The enormous claw-foot tub in the center of the room calls to me. It doesn't take long to fill the tub with water as hot as I can stand it. I pile my braids on top of my head in a loose bun, add some essential oils I found in the vanity and then I'm in heaven. Pure heaven.

After taking a moment to breathe, I cannot for the life of me figure out why mother wants me here, why she gave this place to me. There's a whole lot I have to figure out because my mother doesn't do things for nothing. There's always a reason behind everything.

It doesn't make sense that she'd give this place to me rather than Taliah or Brianna. Not at all. I hope I can figure it all out before my week is up. If not, then it'll have to stay a mystery.

I soak in the tub until the water turns cold, my mind struggling to figure out the why of all of this.

Chamomile tea sounds good, so I make a cup and grab my

tablet. I can read a book I've downloaded. If it's good, it won't help my sleep situation, but it's something to do.

I thought getting into that deep ass tub when I was already exhausted would put me out quickly. But sleep won't come easy if my mind is too busy trying to figure out my mother's motives.

Rather than read one of my books, I doodle for a bit. Drawing helps me de-stress when I can't settle down. But after drinking the tea and designing two new shoes, I'm still restless. I walk the house again, envisioning my mother here.

Did she live here...ever? If she did, when? Why did she leave? How did she find this place? Why buy a house here but never bring your family? Am I the only family member who's never heard about this place? Why so secretive about everything? What's up with the timeline? What can I possibly find out in a week that she couldn't tell me in her will? And why me?

The questions go on and on, but without answers to at least some of them, I don't have an inkling of what to do. Or where to start. Somehow, I don't think asking every one of the thirty-five hundred residents here is a good idea. Maybe I can find some answers in the study. And if not, then surely this town has a library.

Yes. That's an idea. Every town has a library or a historian who can give me the background of this place. And who knows, hopefully, someone knew my mother. If I find out more about this place but learn nothing new about my mother, I can walk away feeling like I at least tried.

I retrace my steps and turn off the lights as I head back to my bedroom. None of the windows have curtains. Not just the windows in the living room, but none of them. I didn't notice that before. But I guess it doesn't matter. No one can see in here unless the lights are on and that's only if someone is interested.

I double-check the locks. I walk to the glass wall and look over the backyard. If you can call it that. I don't know where the property lines end since there isn't a fence.

The thick forest goes on as far as the eye can see. As dark as it is out here, the sky is so beautiful. It's been a long time since I've seen the stars shine this brightly. They appear closer somehow. All I have to do is reach up and touch them.

I walk the perimeter of the room, bringing me back to look at the front yard. The quiet isn't off-putting at all. It's peaceful. I can actually think clearly.

On that thought, the tea kicks in. I turn toward the bed, but I catch movement across the street. The doctor is leaning against the porch post of his house and appears to be staring up at my window. How did I miss him before?

Something is off about him. I'm not sure what, but the goosebumps covering my body are a sign. I guess I could be overthinking it, but I don't think so. The reaction he had to me when he got home earlier, and now this, is strange. I mean, who doesn't greet or at least wave when you meet someone new?

It could be he knew my mother or someone in his family did. Maybe that's it. I'm a stranger in town, and he's curious about who I am. Bobby said there aren't many visitors around here this time of year. I'm sure that's the reason.

Determined not to give it any more thought, I turn away from the window and get into bed.

Chapter Three

Mika

The doorbell chiming wakes me, and I question where I am for a few moments. But the second ring reminds me and I hop out of bed quickly. I didn't think anyone besides my neighbor and Bobby knew I was here. But then again, Bobby did mention that someone might come around.

I wrap my body in my kimono-style robe and head to the front door, hoping whoever it is doesn't press it again. The chime is beautiful but loud. I've got to change the setting.

I open the door up a crack to see who it is. But the four fashionably dressed ladies standing there push my door open the rest of the way and come on in.

"Good morning! We're the welcome committee for Abrielara." The tall blonde lady says proudly. "Welcome!"

Stunned, I watch them put their baskets on the table and make themselves comfortable at the bar in the kitchen.

"Sorry to barge in on you like this, but we have been dying to meet you. Did we wake you?" The lady with the stunning stilettos I would recognize anywhere asks. All the women are wearing the starting lineup from my spring show.

"Uh... well. Yeah, I got to bed a little late last night. You said you were dying to meet me? Why is that?" Everyone stops moving around and stares at me blankly. Embarrassment creeps up my back.

"You are the shoe designer Mika Burris of Lady M Shoes... correct?" one lady asks expectantly.

"Well, yes, but who told y'all? I didn't think anyone knew I was coming, much less my name."

I'm sure my nervous laugh isn't fooling anyone. I'm a little alarmed by this bit of news. I didn't want to unknowingly break some kind of rule or anything. Mr. Phillips definitely did not tell me anything about a welcome committee.

"Oh, as the welcome committee, we are aware of everyone who will spend any time here. We could barely contain ourselves when we found out our favorite designer was stopping by."

Makes sense, so I let it go. Not like I have much choice. I could actually use their help.

"What a sweet thing to say."

"Nothing less than the truth. Now, let me make some coffee. Why don't you sit down next to Becca and I'll get started? Kimberly made you some banana bread. Her bread is to die for." The woman hops up, her blonde hair swinging behind her as she moves around the kitchen like she's been here before.

"Oh, you aren't dieting, on a strict diet or anything, are you? With a stunning figure like yours, I can imagine it's hard to keep it up."

"Um, yeah, no, I'm not on any kind of diet. I love food." She and Kim flit about in the kitchen, grabbing things and unloading baskets.

"While they do that, let me introduce everyone," the beautiful bright-toned lady beside me says. "I'm Dyana St.

John. To the left of you is Becca Crowley, Kimberly Garrison, and preparing our coffee is Jeana Charles."

"Nice to meet you all. But I'm not sure I need a welcome committee because I'm not staying here very long. I'm only going to be here for the week and then, um..."

Jeana buzzes around the kitchen. I'm in awe at how familiar she is with this room. My confusion must show because Becca speaks up.

"Nonsense. We welcome everyone regardless of how long they're staying. We also like to stock the fridge with food made right here in Abrielara," Becca informs me breezily.

"We set your house up for you before you got here. So we know where everything is. Don't worry. We didn't make copies of your keys or anything," Dyana explains. The other ladies laugh and Jeana comes back while the coffee pot produces the magical brew.

"How are you settling in?" Jeana asks, turning to grab some mugs from the cabinet.

"Okay, I guess. I haven't had the chance to look around town. I was hoping I could do that today. I didn't see anyone other than the doctor across the street yesterday. He didn't seem friendly, so I thought I would venture out today."

"We'd love to show you around if you would like." Becca volunteered.

Her idea peps me up, and suddenly I am glad they stopped by.

"That would be great. I would love the company. Bobby couldn't tell me much yesterday." The thought of having tour guides to walk me around town was great. I felt better already about being here.

Jeana sets a filled coffee mug in front of each of us. "So, you said you met Dr. Christiansen yesterday?"

"Well, I wouldn't say we met. I saw him yesterday when Bobby dropped me off. I waved at him but he didn't wave back. Bobby went over to talk to him and I came on in the house."

"Hmm," the ladies say in unison.

I watch the faces of each one, but none of them look me in the eye. If I didn't know any better, I would guess they were enjoying their coffee.

"So, what was that about?" I ask them.

"What do you mean?" Kimberly asks after taking another sip.

"That hmmm, you all just did and don't pretend you don't know what I'm talking about." I take a sip from my cup and, for a second, forget my question. "Wow. What kind of coffee is this?" I take another rather large sip.

"Because it isn't. This coffee is made from beans grown right here in Abrielara. We have our own special blend. The best you've ever had, right?" Dyana grins and sips hers.

"Yes. Wow." For a few more moments, we're silent while enjoying the richness of the coffee. I normally drown my coffee in flavored creamer, but not with this blend. I'm drinking this cup straight black and there isn't a bitter after-taste or anything. My coffee game has stepped up quite a few notches, and this is only my first taste. I make a mental note to tell Brandi to add it to my grocery list.

After enjoying coffee and small talk, I shower quickly and decide on a long-sleeved sweater, jeans, and walking boots. I don't know how the ladies are going to walk around town with the shoes they have on. I can tell you with all certainty those shoes were not made for walking.

A few blocks up from the house, there is a fork in the road

after the gas station on the right. We follow the road to the left and continue deeper into town.

"So, why don't you guys tell me about yourselves since you obviously know more about me than I do about you? Did you all grow up here?" I look to my right and left as I am in the middle.

"Becca and I grew up here. We've known each other since kindergarten."

I look over at Dyana. Sounds like she can help me find out more about my mother.

"Yes, she recognized fabulous even then." Becca boasts and Dyana swings her purse at her.

"If I remember correctly, I saved you from a beatdown on the playground."

"He just didn't know how to show how much he liked me but for the record, he would've been the one to receive a beat down. Not me." Becca huffed.

"Well, he liked you for sure ten years later, but at the time, he was a spoiled rotten—"

"Watch it, sister, if anyone is going to call him a spoiled rotten pain in the ass, it's going to be me. He is my husband, after all."

"Girl and thank god for small favors! I doubt anyone else could put up with you or him," Dyana quips but quickly recovers. "You know I say that with god love."

"Of course I do, darling, besides you're right." She bumps Dyana with her shoulder.

"What about you two?" I turn to Jeana and Kimberly, who seem to be in the middle of a private conversation.

"Oh well, Kimberly and I are cousins. We were visiting some friends in Wilson's Creek about ten years ago and fell in love with Abrielara. We stayed and raised our families here."

Since she mentioned it, I can see the resemblance

between them with their heart-shaped faces and the same green eyes. "Oh, great. You must love being here then."

"Yes, we do. Just wait and see," Kimberly beamed. "The people are fantastic. They may not seem like it now, but they are. We have everything we need here." She looks around at the other three women and then back at me. "We hope you decide to stay. You won't regret it."

I don't quite know how to answer. So, I don't. I focus my attention on the scenery. Like the cabin, these women are a pleasant surprise, but something is still a little off. I can't put my finger on it. I can't figure out if it's the way they mention staying or how a small town of thirty-five hundred needs a welcome committee. And, of course, my neighbor across the street adds to the weirdness.

I push it to the back of my mind so I don't lose focus on why I'm here. I only have a week and trying to figure out the reasoning behind the weird behavior of strangers is not on my to-do list.

Soon the beautifully treelined streets open up to what I assume is the center of town. I've stepped into the downtown area of a Hallmark movie.

Quite a few people are milling around what appears to be a barbershop. There is a coffee shop, a bakery I learn belongs to Kimberly, and a small courthouse. Their schools are all on the same block. Must be hellafied traffic over here during morning and afternoon drop off. Then we come to a rather large farmers' market and a variety of shops.

But most noticeable is that the men are tall. They seemed to tower over us as we passed them on the street. Not only were they tall but they were also big. Like broad-shouldered, cut and un-ordinarily good looking. Any of these guys could grace the cover of a magazine. So weird. What are they feeding them out here? Must be in the food or the coffee. I begin to voice my thoughts but spot a blue truck.

"What's that building over there? The truck out in front of it looks like the one my neighbor drives."

"It's the medical building and you are correct. Dr. Christiansen owns the truck. All the doctors in this town work over there," Becca informs me.

"Yeah, our doctors are expertly trained and are well-known worldwide," Kimberly boasts.

As we walk, a park comes into view with a basketball court and an active game in play. Just like the men we passed on the street, these guys look huge and delicious.

One of them being my neighbor.

Shirtless. Ripped. Tattooed. Sweaty and yummy. Damn. I seriously need to get laid. I've obviously gone without for far too long.

I forcefully remove those thoughts from my head, but I find my eyes searching the basketball court again. Unlike the men we passed on the street, these men stop their game and stare as we pass by. The ladies act as if they don't notice and continue to talk and walk. I couldn't form a sentence if they asked me to. My eyes connect with Dr. Christiansen, and for once, I know without a doubt he is watching me.

Knowing for a fact makes me feel ... claustrophobic? I'm not even sure if that's the right word. He's in my space. Like all up in my personal space, even though he's more than a few feet away. He might as well be breathing down my neck. His close inspection makes me twitchy, and even though I want to move around, I'm compelled to stop and return the favor.

He's obviously agitated. His firm jaw is clenched as tightly as his fisted hands. His honeyed-colored eyes seem to grow darker by the second. Those intense eyes are framed with dark lashes which match his coal-black hair. Despite being spitting mad right now, he is absolutely... magnificent. There is no other word to describe him at this moment. His body, glistening with sweat and pure angst, appears ready to, I don't know... attack. But attack what?

Although all the men on the court stopped their game to watch us, their bodies don't exude anger like Dr. Christiansen's does. Their faces are, at most, mildly interested. But without even opening his mouth, I can see hate is not a strong enough word to describe what he feels for me. Why is his response to me so different from the others and so strong? I have never met this man, yet he acts as though I've sinned against him. It's apparent he hates me on sight.

I don't understand what's so special about him or anyone here, but something is going on that isn't going on anywhere else. When Jeana grabs my hand, I finally break eye contact. I'm aware of the ball bouncing on the court again and the sound of shuffling feet. But I am acutely aware of a pair of eyes burning a hole in my back as we walk to a boutique across the street. Without turning around, I can tell you whose eyes they belong to like I know my name.

"So, tell us, Mika, what is going on with you and Dr. Christiansen?"

I'm learning Dyana has no problem asking whatever questions she has. She reminds me of me.

"Yeah, girl. He was definitely giving you the heat. I have never seen him react that way, and I've known him since grade school."

And Becca obviously doesn't hold back either.

We are having gelato after eating a light lunch. Abrielara is a beautiful town. I don't understand how this place stays hidden from the rest of the world. I'm sure everyone is nice once they meet you. Well, almost everyone.

"I was hoping you guys could tell me. I've never met him, but he's reacted strangely every time I've seen him, which has been all of two times, by the way."

"Just two times?" Jeana leans in.

"Well, if you don't count last night." I swirl my lemon and lavender gelato around in the cup.

"What happened last night?" Kimberly leans in too. I look around the table. They are all leaning toward me as if expecting a juicy piece of gossip. They're going to be disappointed.

"It was nothing. I noticed he was watching my house last night before I went to bed. Kinda hard for him not to watch my house if he's standing on his porch. You know, since my house is directly across from his."

I hear myself rambling while rationalizing why it's okay for him to watch my house, but I can't help my nerves. To witness someone watching you or your house with such intense animosity is unnerving.

"Watching your house? Oh, honey, he wasn't watching your house. He was watching you." Becca flips her long, straight, glossy brown hair over her shoulder and waves her hand.

"Thanks for that, Becca. I doubt she needed to hear that." Dyana gives an exasperated sigh.

"Sorry, Mika. I let my mouth run without thinking first." She looks sorry for a hot second anyway.

"No worries, but do you guys have any idea why he reacts to me the way he does? Kinda weird, right?" They nod in agreement but don't seem quite committed to it.

"Solomon is usually not nearly as intense as we just saw," Jeana offers, but who the hell is Solomon?

"Who is Solomon?"

"Your neighbor, silly. Dr. Christiansen's first name is Solomon." Becca tosses her empty gelato cup into the trash and pulls out her compact to look herself over.

"Oh. Well then, there is obviously something about me he can't stand. I'll stay out of his way while I'm here." I dump the rest of my gelato into the trash. Although it is good, I no longer have the appetite for it.

"I wouldn't worry too much about him, Mika. Everything will work itself out. I promise. Now what I want to know is, what do you have lined up for next season? I already purchased your new knee-high winter boot before it sold out. Thank god!"

The ladies quickly jump on the bandwagon, but Kimberly's quick change in subject was not missed by me. These ladies were obviously not willing to talk about whatever was bothering Solomon. It could be it isn't any of my business. I need to focus on what I am here for, which has nothing to do with him. I only have so much time to find the answers I need.

With a renewed focus, I concentrate on learning what the ladies offered to tell me about Abrielara. It isn't often I can enjoy the company of women who have nothing to do with my work. God knows my sisters never did, and it wasn't like I could reach out to them now, anyway.

The rest of the day with the ladies, who I call the fab four, is nice but uneventful until I learn the town has a library and a historian. Which was the best news I had heard all day until I was also told the study in my house has an impressive library of its own.

"I didn't see a library when I toured the house last night."

"It's easy to miss. There's a hidden door underneath the stairs. A cozy little library perfect for uninterrupted reading," Kim explains.

"I'll check it out when I get home."

I can definitely start there to learn more about Abrielara before hitting up the town library or historian.

The night sky falls and I'm ready to go home. The fab four walk me back to the edge of the woods until I can see my house and promise to check on me again the next day. I enjoyed their company, but I'm glad to make my way home. I plan to scour the study from top to bottom for any clue why my mother wanted me to come here.

When my colorful lawn comes into view, I notice a visitor waiting for me. When he turns around to face me, I stop in my tracks.

Solomon. I mean Dr. Christiansen. Still wearing the basketball shorts I saw him in earlier, but he put on a shirt.

That's unfortunate.

He doesn't move, and he doesn't say anything, so neither do I. His honey-colored eyes could be so inviting and warm if he didn't scowl so much. His poor teeth must be ground down to stubs from the way he grinds them so viciously.

He's so yummy to look at. Quite a shame I haven't had the chance to see what he's like when he isn't so irritated.

We continue to stare each other down until I can't stand it anymore. This is ridiculous. I sigh heavily, realizing what I have to do. Obviously, he isn't going to make the first move and I can't stand out here all night. I walk up to the porch but not up the steps. I'm not comfortable getting that close to him.

"Is there something I can do for you, Dr. Christiansen?" I cross my arms across my chest. Even though I made sure not one ounce of fear could be heard in my voice, it didn't stop it from trickling up my artificially straightened spine.

Although we are far from each other, I'm smothered by his imposing presence. I can't take a full breath. I continue to hold his stare, even though I want to tuck my tail in and run.

My neck is aching because of the angle I have to hold it to maintain eye contact.

Just when I think he's going to ignore my question, he walks toward me and stops so close I have the urge to take a step back. But I don't. I raise my head more to keep my eyes on him. No telling what will happen if I don't.

The first thing I notice is his pupils are dilated. My mouth goes dry with fear. I lick my lips to stop them from trembling. His eyes follow the movement and then his nostrils flare. His lips curl into a snarl. Anger, hate, disgust—none of those words adequately describe the look covering his face. I don't know what's going through his mind, but I can tell you what's going through mine.

Danger. I am in real danger.

After several moments, his face has transformed into a calmer version of what I just witnessed.

"Yes, there is. You can leave."

"Why? I just got here."

"You don't belong here."

The matter-of-fact way he says it pisses me off. Who is he to decide where I belong?

"Why do you say that?"

"You have twenty-four hours."

"What the fuck do you mean?"

He doesn't respond. He stomps off across the street like a five-year-old being sent to bed with no dinner. So, he doesn't like my last question. I'll try another one.

"Or what?" He doesn't answer me.

"Or what?" I ask again, yelling louder this time. The only response I receive is the sound of his slamming door.

What a prick. He's got some nerve telling me to leave. Who the fuck does he think he is telling me what to do? I shower and dress in my comfy pajamas as I continue to grumble to myself.

His warning is set on replay inside my head. His voice was deep and rough—gravely. I imagine what he could do with that voice if he used it for good rather than evil. With a voice like his, I'm pretty sure his phone game is in the major leagues.

I force myself to put his voice and his warning aside. No matter how many distractions come my way, I have to focus.

I decide to give Brandi a call just to check-in. It's late for her, but she's a night owl like me. I know she's holding it down, but there's no harm in calling her.

She picks it up on the first ring.

"I thought I told you to take a vacation?"

"Well, hello to you, too. How's it going?"

"It's going just fine. I got Marguerite off our backs, at least for a couple of weeks."

"How'd you do that?"

"I told her you were out of the country."

"Ah. How'd she take it?"

"Same as always. She acted put out, but she'll be fine. She has to learn that her stores aren't any more special than the other stores that carry your shoes."

I snort at her comment. There is no love lost between Brandi and Marguerite. They could never stand each other.

"Well, as long as you have everything handled."

"Don't I always?"

"True. Don't keep her dangling for too long. Let her know we'll connect as soon as I come back."

"Sure thing. Now tell me about Abrielara. I've never heard of it."

"Neither have I. But it's a super small town, so not much to tell. The people are nice." I guess.

"Just make sure you relax. Get some spa days in. Don't think about anything. And if I so much as suspect a design is being created, I will fly down personally and take your tablet. I'm serious, Mika."

"I hear you, Brandi. I do. I designed a couple of shoes last night but nothing else since. Honestly, I'm too engrossed in learning about my mother and this town. I haven't thought much about shoes."

"Glad to hear it. So you are for sure coming back next week?"

"That's the plan."

"Cool. Let me know when you're ready, and I'll solidify your travel plans."

"Will do. Call you in a few days."

"Toodles."

After my call with Brandi, I make a light dinner and check out the study. As soon as I open the door, I'm at home. The floor-to-ceiling shelves are filled with books. I have the tiniest urge to break into song and swing from shelf to shelf.

A comfy rose petal pink settee sits in the corner and a window seat graces the front of the picture window over-looking the flower garden. The distinct smell of books always comforts me. My body automatically relaxes because it has been trained to think being surrounded by books means I am settling into another world, undisturbed for the night, surrounded by friends. Who wouldn't be comforted by that?

My first stop is the desk in the middle of the room. The desk, like the house, is beautiful. The dark wood is polished to perfection and faces the window. I can't wait to look over every book on every shelf.

My shoulders droop at the thought, shoving it away from my mind. I won't be able to look over every book, much less read more than a few. There's only so many hours in a day and only so many in a week.

On top of the desk is a white envelope. *Read this first* is written on the top and a book titled Abrielara is underneath it.

I open the envelope and recognize my mother's handwriting immediately. Before I read a single word, my hand covers my heart and my eyes fill with tears. The pain rears its ugly head again, but as always, I take a deep breath and force the tears away.

Focus. This letter is the first communication I've had from her or anyone in my family. This is what I'm here for.

Mika, I'm so glad you've done as I have asked. I'm sure you are confused and have a lot of questions. I promise all of your questions will be answered. Asking you to come here is not the only request I have. There are four things I want you to do for me. You must do them in the order I say and as quickly as you can. I'm aware you like to do things your way, but this once, please follow my instructions.

1. As soon as you can, pay Judge George Christiansen a visit. He is expecting you.
2. Take the book he gives you and the manila envelope. Open the envelope first. George will instruct you on what to do.
3. Do what George tells you to do immediately.
4. Read the book he gives you from beginning to end. You must read the book before leaving Abrielara.
If you have questions, please ask George.
~ Momma

That's it? No words of encouragement, apologies, life wisdom, or answers to any of the questions I have?

I flip the letter over to confirm what I have is all there is. She took the time to write a letter that gave me nothing. Maybe not nothing. She did give me a place to start, at least.

George Christiansen. I wonder if he's any relation to the doctor?

Well, the mystery continues. She sent me here because she needs something done. But she didn't say why she chose me. When it comes to following her directions, I'm pretty sure I was not the first person who came to her mind. But whatever the reason, I'm glad she asked me. I have failed her so many times before.

This time I'll do as she asked simply because she asked. No back talk, no grandstanding to prove a point. Just simple obedience. I'm determined not to let her down. It may be a little too late, but it's all I have right now.

Armed with instructions and a plan of action, I'm back on track. Dr. Christiansen could go fuck himself and his twenty-four-hour timeline. But as I make my rounds, turning off lights before going to bed, I look out across the street. As expected, Dr. Christiansen is standing on his porch, staring up at my window. I swear his anger can be felt from here, radiating off his body like the searing heat from leather car seats in the summertime.

I don't linger there. Instead, I'm compelled to hurry and turn the bedroom light out, then slide into bed. As if the heavy luxurious comforter can hide me from his hate-filled eyes. Try as I might, I could not remove his words from my head. His warning irks me. If I hadn't already planned to be out of here when the week was up, I would plan to stay longer for the hell of it. But as it stands, I think staying for the week will get my point across. When he realizes I'm not leaving in twenty-four hours, what happens then?

Chapter Four

Solomon

"**K**nock, knock. Anyone home?" I walk on in and head to the breakfast room. My dad is nothing if not a creature of habit. Every morning at eight a.m. sharp will find him in the breakfast room, smoking a cigar with his first-morning cup of coffee.

"What in the world happened to you, son? You look like hell." I sit across from him and pour myself a cup.

"Nothing has happened to me, per se. Just having trouble sleeping is all."

"Sleep in your office again?" He puffs out a huge plume of smoke from his cigar, looking at me over the top of his glasses.

"Well, I very well couldn't sleep at my house, now could I?"

"A distraction, is she?" He laughs boisterously. I ignore him. I don't have the energy for our usual morning banter today.

He chuckles at me, obviously still enjoying my discomfort. My dad is my best friend. I can tell him anything, and I pretty much do. He enjoys hearing about my bachelor lifestyle, although some days he gives me a run for my money.

"I don't understand why you're fighting this so much, son. This is what you need to do." He snuffs out his cigar and lays it on the table.

"*See? He understands.*"

"*It's not that I don't understand, Lux. It just doesn't have to be this way.*"

"*There is only one way.*"

"*There's got to be another way.*"

The weight on my shoulders is so heavy it's almost visible.

"I'm sorry to say there is no other way, son. You know that."

"*I told you.*"

"*Shut up.*"

He butters a biscuit and then tops it with jelly, sausage and cheese. I watch as he takes a hearty bite. His eyes roll in ecstasy, as they always do when he has biscuits for breakfast. I can't help but shake my head and smile. Another thing my dad is famous for is enjoying his food.

"I swear Melissa puts crack or something in these biscuits. If I never eat anything besides these biscuits again, I will die a lucky man." He takes another giant bite and finishes his sandwich.

"Yeah, and you've gained twenty pounds in the last ten years because of those biscuits too," I remind him.

"Yep, and I have enjoyed every last one of those pounds." He proves his point by grabbing another biscuit.

If only all of life's problems could be solved with a plate of biscuits.

My mind returns to what has me all fucked up right now. Agitation claws at my gut like food poisoning. My mouth waters, preparing itself for another round with the toilet.

"I hate this. Had I known—" I say to myself.

"Had you known, nothing would have changed," he interrupts. "I understand your dilemma. I do. But the consequences—"

"I understand, Dad." Despite the roaring in my stomach, I swallow the rest of my coffee and pour more into my cup.

"Just give in. Things will go much easier for you if you do." He pushes his plate away and leans back into his chair.

"Alright," I concede.

"All you have to do is follow the process. Sit back. It will all be over before you can blink." He doesn't even pretend to hide the grin on his face. He picks up his cigar again and rolls it between his fingers.

"As a doctor, it's hard to reconcile with that reasoning, Dad."

"I understand it, son. I do. But remember, in this case, the end does justify the means. You've got to follow this through. Trust me."

The grin on his face slips and I believe he does understand my problem with just going along with the process. Especially not something I don't believe in. Because of my stubbornness, I'm being tortured and can barely control myself.

The needling in my brain has started again, and it's getting more and more uncomfortable with each episode. The bouts of anger are getting stronger and lasting longer too. I'm hot all the fucking time.

"I can't even see my patients right now because I'm too unstable. Fuck, I hate this."

The agitation makes me antsy. My leg bounces vigorously as I find it hard to sit still.

I run my fingers through my hair and squeeze my eyes shut as the pricking in my brain starts again and travels down my neck and over my shoulders. I visibly try to shake it off. My father watches me closely.

"Open your eyes and look at me, son."

When I open them, he is walking toward me and looks into my eyes. He nods his head.

"Yes. I can see Lux has been taking you through the wringer. He's obviously impatient. The probing DNA is apparently already working you over. You're running out of time, son. Pretty soon, you won't have a choice at all. I suggest you do what you need to do while you still can." He returns to his seat.

He's right. To be honest, the choice has never been mine, to begin with. But I was hoping for a different outcome.

"Have you made the necessary preparations?"

"For the most part, yes. I've alerted the council. I have an appointment with the Monarch this afternoon."

Dad nods as I speak.

"Excellent. Once she has given her blessing, then there will be no stopping the process. That's the only thing slowing everything down now. I can promise you. I suggest you stay here until it's time to go to the palace. When you finish with your meeting, come back here."

"Why?"

"For your safety and anyone else's who may get in the way before you're ready." He wiggles his eyebrows suggestively.

"Right. I understand. It's probably for the best, anyway. If you don't mind, I think I'm going to go to my room and try to catch some sleep."

"Of course I don't mind."

He stops me before I pass him on the way out of the room by clasping his hand on my shoulder. I turn to look at him expectantly.

"I hate to see you like this, son. You're fighting the inevitable. This is not supposed to be a bad thing. This is supposed to be a happy occasion, a rite of Passage.

"Your story doesn't have to end up like mine. I actually think yours will be quite different. Enjoy the transition. It will do you a lot of good. You will come out stronger on the other side because of it. Get some rest. I will check on you later on today."

I nod but not believing a word of what he's saying.

"A nice sentiment, and I wish it were true, but the statistics are not in my favor."

I set my alarm for one o'clock since my appointment is at two-thirty. The stress eases out of my body as I slip between the cool sheets. The anger is gone...for now, but my mind is still whirling with my predicament and impending doom regardless of what I do.

I don't recall Perry's experience being this way, but it could be because I was away at college for the most part at the time. But Perry chose an Abrielaran. Of course his experience will be entirely different.

Perry is my brother. We don't share parents, but my father adopted him when his father died, and he has been my brother ever since. Now we both work in medicine. Perry's life now is one I secretly envy but never believed I could truly have.

I loved my life the way it was before. No real attachments to any one female and no expectations. I answered to no one. I took care of my patients and lived my life unencumbered. But now, because of this rite of Passage bullshit, I'm a totally different person already, and I haven't even completed the transition yet. Never in my life have I ever reacted to anyone the way I have to her.

I should have realized something was wrong because

before she even got here, I started having dreams, intensely graphic dreams. Even thinking about it now, the images popping up in my head make my dick harder than granite.

But even worse was going to her house last night. Damn, she smelled so good. She's so beautiful with those full lips and high cheekbones. I didn't dare look any lower than her face. I was struggling enough being so close to her. As soon as she walked up to the porch, I knew I had made a mistake going there. But I had to warn her. Otherwise, I would never forgive myself.

However, when I stepped to her, so close... I thought my lungs were collapsing. How in the hell can you live and die in the same breath?

Her eyes are so dark and fierce. As soon as I saw how deep they were, I wanted to fall at her feet. For some reason, I felt she could save me. If by just falling into them, I could be rid of this excruciating tophet I've been living in for the last week.

I wanted to fall into them and never come out. When her tongue nervously swept her lips, I had to bite my tongue to stop from claiming her mouth with mine. And with that, I was instantly aware of another hell I would now have to contend with. The knowledge she exists but that I'm going to have to live without her.

The sound of a groan escaping my throat at the memory finds my hand stroking my hard cock, already throbbing and slick with desire for her.

Fuck. I have to think about something else.

If I don't, the urges and then the anger will come next. Then I definitely won't get any sleep and there is a good chance I won't make my appointment. And I have to make my appointment. I don't want to disappoint my dad. He's gone through enough in his lifetime without me adding shame to the list. If I go through the transition and complete the cycle,

Dad will feel he did his job as a father, as an Abrielaran. To me, he already did a long time ago.

When I told him about my symptoms, I knew what was happening. But I had to tell him because I told him every-thing. You would think Perry and Dee were having another baby he was so excited. According to him, he has been waiting for me to go through this so he can rest easy in his later years. His words, not mine.

I, on the other hand, have dreaded this ever since I found out how all this would happen. The worst part of all is I'll have no control over any of this and will probably enjoy it no matter how much I don't want to. I finally drift off to the image of her dark eyes pleading with me for answers. Answers I can't give to her now, but she will find out soon enough.

My alarm wakes me at one, and I'm rested. Lux must have been tired too since he let me rest. I slept straight through without waking up, which is a record for me lately. I shower and dress in one of my favorite suits I keep here just in case, and then I am on my way to the palace.

I haven't been there since I was a kid. The entire town was there to celebrate the marriage of one of her children, and I haven't been back since. I don't keep up with the family or their comings and goings. For the most part, they are consumed with their own lives as we are with ours. Or at least it seems that way to me.

Most people don't come here unless they need something or are summoned. I don't have to have her blessing to commence with my rite of Passage, but it shows respect when you do. Every man in this community has done this or will, and I have never heard of a time when they did not receive her blessing.

I wish I could be the exception.

After driving for about thirty minutes to the other side of town, the road up the mountain to the palace comes into view. I forget how beautifully majestic this place is until I see it again. The mountainside is breathtaking and is only outshone by the palace. The entire building looks like it's made from Opal. White and pristine until the sun hits the building just right, and then it shines with translucent colors. Exactly like the stone. It's why they call it the Jewel of Abrielara.

The appointment is held in the throne room, and the room is everything you would expect a throne room to be. Opulent, grand and ostentatious. The floor is white marble and the walls are all glass, bringing the outside in. The platform has three throne chairs, with the Monarch's being the biggest and in the middle. Her chair is white and gold, while the two beside her are red and gold. When handling normal business, all three chairs would be occupied, but because this is a rite of Passage appointment, she is the only one present. A rite of Passage appointment is considered an extremely personal experience. Discussing this with the Monarch one on one is a sign of respect to the person going through the Passage.

As is customary, before walking into the throne room, I remove my shoes and bow my head as a sign of respect until she gives me permission to enter. I keep my eyes down until then. She doesn't keep me waiting long.

"Dr. Christiansen, so nice to see you again. What's it been? About twenty-five years? Of course, you were just a boy then."

I raise my eyes, and although I shouldn't be, I'm shocked to see she hasn't aged a day. She looks as beautiful as she did then. Regal and captivating, her dark features are ethereal. There is an otherworldly presence about her, radiating from her amber-colored eyes and glowing like a halo around her. Even her hairstyle is the same. Long cornrows braided straight back from her face and falling to her knees. Her face is clear and free of makeup but yet she is flawless.

She holds her hands out for me to take, and I do, kissing each one before responding.

"Yes, it's been a while. I believe we were celebrating the marriage of one of your children."

She nods, a full smile gracing her face. "Come closer so we can talk."

I move closer and stop when I can't go any farther. She pats the throne chair to her right belonging to the one she's chosen. She notices my hesitation.

"Sit. He won't mind. I promise." She grins softly. I do as she bids, even though I'm incredibly uncomfortable in a chair meant for her husband.

"Now, why don't you tell me why you aren't looking forward to completing your rite of Passage?"

My eyes go wide. I had no intention of mentioning my misgivings about the whole Passage thing. I don't want to be disrespectful, especially since she has the power to obliterate my existence. I happen to like my existence, such as it is.

"Am I that obvious?"

She gives a curt nod. "You couldn't be more obvious if you had written your thoughts on a billboard across your forehead. Of course, Lux has filled me in too." Her soft smile barely reaches her eyes but is sympathetic. "But I want to hear it from you. Now tell me."

"I...uh." I'm at a loss as to what to say here.

"Be candid. I promise you there is nothing you can say that I either haven't heard before or something you will be punished for. Don't think of me as your Queen. Think of me as a temporary nonjudgmental sounding board."

I hesitate again. How can I not think of her as anything but the Queen? And to speak candidly about something that causes me to lose sleep at night isn't something I'm prepared to do. Honestly, I didn't actually have any plans.

"I won't hold anything you say against you. Go ahead. Be blunt if you need to." She pats my hand she holds between hers softly.

Her maternal aura relaxes me enough to open my mouth and speak about what's troubling me. Surprisingly, her maternal nature is what calms me, considering I've never been on the receiving end of one in my life.

"Alright." I swallow the lump in my throat and take in as much air as I can. "I'm struggling with the initial process. I understand the breeding part, which I don't have an issue with. But to..." What word should I use..? "Um..."

"Involve?" she suggests.

"Yes. Thank you. To involve someone who isn't a part of us or aware of our customs is ...uh." Again with the loss of words...how embarrassing. I clear my throat.

"Archaic?" she offers, a playful smile on her lips.

"Um...yes, ma'am." I look down sheepishly. Even though I have somewhat expressed my concern, the heaviness of dread at doing so has sunk like a rock, even lower in my chest. Suddenly my tie is a little too tight and my jacket a little too hot. Sweat pebbles on my forehead. I work my finger around the neck of my shirt, hoping to loosen it up a bit.

"I see. Well, I understand your concern. It is a concern I've heard before, believe it or not. It is noble of you to be worried about the plight of the innocent. Unfortunately, we have no control over that part of ourselves or the decree written centuries ago. Even if I told you to do whatever you need to make your Passage easier, Lux would not allow it to happen.

"It is his right and duty to complete this. You can understand why he would be a little forceful in making sure you followed through."

She touches my shoulder and then brings my eyes to meet hers by lifting my chin. "The only advice I can give you is to do your best to let go and let Lux do what needs to be done. Then and only then will you be able to take some of the edge off. Keep the overall goal in mind. Hopefully, you will be given the opportunity to make it right afterward."

I nod in agreement. I knew nothing would change, but I can't help but be disappointed.

"You were expecting to hear something different, but to deny you this experience is to deny you the opportunity to learn who you are, where you've come from, and what you are truly made of.

"The initial phase of the Passage is archaic. You are right to say so, but our ancestors did not want us to forget what it means to be a Brielaran. Sure we could celebrate your rite of Passage more conventionally, but it wouldn't be true to who we are. They knew how hard things would be for the human in you to accept the process. Let Lux fulfill his purpose. When your cycle is complete, you may be surprised by the outcome."

"I guess. I wish we could go about this in a more humane way," I admit.

"Yes, but the initial phase of the rite of Passage is not to celebrate the human experience."

As she says it, things become clearer. Even though dad has said this before, it didn't click before now. To have the experience Lux is entitled to, I must let go and let things happen. There is no other way.

"I'm glad you understand." I turn to her sharply. I'd forgotten about her ability to communicate so effortlessly with Lux.

"Lux is quite anxious to begin." She smiles in the calm wisdom-layered way she has.

I stand and step off the platform. I kneel in front of her and drop my head.

"Thank you, my Queen, for listening to me today. I appreciate your wisdom and will take your advice."

"You're welcome, Doctor. I have enjoyed our time together and am proud of the young man you've become, a true asset to Abrielara. I wish you a safe Passage and a successful cycle. Please do not wait so long before visiting me again."

I nod again and rise to leave.

"Dr. Christiansen," her soft but commanding voice echoes through the room. I turn to face her.

"Yes, ma'am."

"I want to remind you to keep the consequences in mind should you choose not to follow what has been decreed by our ancestors."

"Yes, ma'am. I will do what is expected of me. Thanks again." She nods and I leave the palace as quickly as I can.

Before I even reach my truck, the heat in my gut begins to boil again. As soon as I'm out of sight of the palace, I strip my suit jacket, shirt and tie off. I roll my head around on my shoulders, doing my best to loosen up. I'm not ready, and besides, it isn't time yet. If I can make it to dad's, I'm sure I can last at least until the magic hour.

I'm still several miles away from dad's but the medical building comes into view. This is as good a place to stop as any. If I'm lucky, Perry will be in the office and can give me some oxygen and a sedative. I'm getting lightheaded and sweating like Patrick Ewing in the fourth quarter. I can damn near hear myself wheezing like I'm breathing through a tiny straw. My nail beds have started to change color and my mouth is fucking dryer than the Dry Valley in Antarctica.

"Calm down, Lux. You're fucking killing me."

"Stop fighting me and I will."

"I'm not fighting you anymore. I just wish we could do this the humane way."

"I'm not human."

"I know that but there has to be a better way."

"There is only one way. This is my right. My duty. Nobody, not even you, can take that from me."

I stumble toward the building. This is by far the worst episode I have ever had. Maybe speaking to the Monarch flipped some kind of switch in me. And now everything is happening so fast that my body cannot keep up. The sound of my heart pounding is getting louder and louder. The pressure in my ears is near to bursting, and I'm afraid of what this means when it does burst. The dark cloud in my peripheral vision closes in. I yank open the door to the medical building, determined to make it to the hostess desk. But before I can say a word, the cloud overtakes me.

The pounding in my head is crushing my skull, but at least I can't hear my heartbeat anymore and can breathe normally. I open my eyes slowly so as not to start another chain reaction to something I have no idea how to deal with. I'm tired of this shit.

"Well, nice to see you come around, princess. I was worried about you for a minute there." I turn to Perry, whose feet are propped up on his desk.

"I didn't realize I made it to your office. The last thing I remember is seeing the hostess's desk."

"You don't remember it because you didn't make it. I had to put your big ass on a gurney and rush you to the ER. You've only been up here for about thirty minutes. I had to grab the crash cart because you coded, man. You were out cold."

"What the fuck is happening to me?"

"You know what's happening. Stop fighting me."

"I'm not fighting you."

"You told her to leave. You're the enemy. Until you give in, you're going to suffer."

"I would say your time is up. You're beginning the transition into the Passage. The probing DNA is at full strength. By tonight you'll be official." His dimpled smile irritates me. "Why didn't you tell me you were beginning the Passage? I could have prepped you so you weren't surprised by all this."

I slowly sit up. "I was hoping there was some way out of this. If you can't tell, I'm less than thrilled about it."

"Hmm. So I'm assuming by now you're aware there isn't a way out of this. The easiest thing to do is to go with the flow. The more you fight, the harder the Passage will be on your body and..."

"Yeah, yeah...I got it, Perry. I got it." My stomach grumbles loudly.

"Sounds like you're hungry. Let me tell you, eat as much food as you can now. Your metabolism is about to triple. You'll be starving to death and hangry will be a picnic at Disney World." He picks up the phone. "Hey, Carlotta, order three daily specials and have the trays brought to my office."

"How long before the food comes up?"

"I don't know. I didn't ask. Why? You got somewhere to be?"

"No." I lay back down. "I'm tired. I'm gonna rest my eyes for a little bit longer. Just until it gets here."

Perry leaves me be and I drift off quickly. I wish I could stay here like this until this is all over. However, it's an unreasonable request. In the grand scheme of things, what I want doesn't matter.

"Yes, sir. Will do. I'll keep him here as long as I can."

Perry's voice wakes me and I sit up as soon as there is a knock on the door. The food service employee sets the trays down, and I begin lifting the domes and diving in without hesitation. I can't remember when I had anything other than coffee these past few days.

I know better. Especially as a doctor, I know I should take better care of myself. But I've been a bit preoccupied. After finishing off the first tray, I sit back to take a breather before going in on the next one.

"So who were you talking to earlier?" I suck down two bottles of water before he answers.

"Dad. He called to see how you were doing. I texted him after I got you settled earlier."

"Hmm. What was that about keeping me here as long as you can?" I start in on the next tray.

"He has an impromptu meeting this afternoon and will be a little late getting home. He doesn't want you to be alone. He would prefer you wait here before you head back over there. I told him I would keep you here as long as I could. You're still in no shape to drive anyway. After you finish off that tray, I want you to rest for a bit longer and then I'll recheck your stats. Under normal circumstances, I would keep you much longer. I'm still contemplating hooking you back up to an IV. You are severely dehydrated."

I stop shoveling food in my mouth. "Why? I passed out. All I needed was some oxygen, food and water, and I'm good." I stop talking because Perry is shaking his head at me.

"No, man. You were so far beyond needing just food and oxygen. For all intents and purposes, you were in the middle of having a heart attack. Your body was shutting down. Thankfully, I was able to deduce you're going through the transition at an expedited pace and not actually having a heart attack.

"Your body couldn't keep up with all the cellular changes happening at once. I gave you a shot that should hold you for another five hours at most. But after that, you're going to have to go with it. Don't fight it. The Passage is less painful that way."

"Thank you." The situation is completely out of my control, yet I'm responsible for all this. I wish I could be like Perry and roll with it. Instead, I have to make things extra hard by questioning every single thing.

"Come on, man. No thanks necessary. You're my brother. I would do anything to save you. I wish you had told me earlier. I could have saved you so much pain." He watches me finish off my food.

"How were you able to concede to Xens so easily? I don't remember hearing you go through anything like this."

"You're right. My Passage was nothing like this. Xens is so docile it was almost like I had to tell him how things would go. By the time he was ready, I was well past ready. Of course, Dee knew what was happening, so there was no surprise there. We were eager to get the show on the road, to say the least.

"Your experience is completely different. The number

one reason is Lux. He and Xens are total opposites, so of course, your Passage will be different."

"Yeah. I wanted my experience to be easier than this since I had to go through the whole thing anyway. Even though I questioned how it had to be done, I understood it would happen. I don't understand why it has to be so... extreme for me."

"If I had to guess, I would say because you're fighting him so hard, Lux probably sees you as the enemy. Also, the probing DNA is what it is. It's gonna light you up no matter how you feel about the Passage. If you weren't so against it, I'm sure Lux wouldn't be so forceful. It was the best thing to ever happen to me. I think the Passage can be the same for you too."

I recover the trays and set them aside. "Perry, as you so eloquently stated a few seconds ago, your situation was completely different. At least Dee knew what she was up against and she knew you. My situation is not like yours."

Perry sits in front of me with the blood pressure cuff and prepares to take my blood pressure.

"True, but because everyone is aware of the process doesn't mean there's a guarantee they will go along with it or even enjoy it. The possibility of rejection is still there." The machine beeps, signaling it's done.

"Still a little high, but it's better than before. Tomorrow morning when the chase is done and over with, it will return to normal. At least until..."

"Until what?"

"Until it's time for stage three. But at least by then, you won't be going through it alone." He tosses me a t-shirt.

"Right. I'm not even thinking about stage three right now. I'm trying to survive stage one."

Perry laughs, rubbing the back of his head. "Shit. That's

the best time right there. Trust me. Nothing you have ever experienced before will compare. I'm telling you."

"Oh yeah? Have you not paid attention to any of the stories I've told you before?" My lascivious smile is answered with a snort.

"Dude, those stories will look like child's play by the time you finish the cycle."

"I don't know, man. It's gonna be hard to top Tokyo," I remind him.

"It's gonna be hard, but it can be done."

I'm shaking my head before he even finishes.

"Wanna bet on it? You got to be honest, though. We'll reconvene when you finish the first half of the cycle." He holds out his hand for me to shake.

I take it, although I doubt anything can top Tokyo.

"Now, why don't you tell me what's been going on with you these past few days? From what I understand, you have a new neighbor."

"How did you find out? Weren't you at a cardiology conference up until yesterday evening?" I forget how fast news travels in this town sometimes.

"Did you forget my wife is on the welcome committee and tells me everything?"

"Oh, right. I forgot." Dyana has been on the Abrielara Welcome Committee since she graduated from college.

He points his pen at me. "Yeah, and you also forgot to tell me what happened at the basketball court yesterday too."

"I can't keep anything from you, damn."

"It's only because you keep trying to. Just keep me up to date and we won't have to have these discussions. Now, start from the beginning. You're not leaving here until I've heard everything."

"You're worse than a woman, you know that?"

I prop my feet up on his sofa and lean back, my hands behind my head.

"The last time I checked, you were a cardiologist, not a psychiatrist, unless something has changed."

"I've got to get the juice somehow. I live a very boring married life with the woman of my dreams. Nothing in my house is juicy except whatever the kids left on the kitchen table this morning or in the pockets of their jeans. Now, quit stalling." He twirls his fingers around and settles back into his chair.

"There's not much to tell."

Perry checks his watch. "We can be here all day. I ain't got nothing better to do."

I flip him off. "Fine."

If entertaining him keeps me from thinking about Mika for at least a few minutes, I'll take it.

Chapter Five

MIKA

I park in front of the courthouse to see the judge. I called ahead to make an appointment. I didn't want to take the chance on missing him. I brought Momma's letter with me so he wouldn't think I was some kind of a lunatic.

If I hadn't already come this far, I would turn right back around and go home. But Momma asked me to do this. As her last request, I will honor it no matter how crazy this all sounds to me. I hope I can find some answers because, at the end of the week, I'm going to leave all of this behind me.

I think.

Yes, definitely.

Maybe.

Stop waffling.

Yes. I'll be leaving at the end of the week. I'll need to get a realtor at some point, I guess.

To run my errands today, I rented a car. According to Momma's note, I have things to do after talking with the judge. Since she seemed to stress how important it was for me to finish as fast as possible, I'm going to assume a leisurely walk through town while I'm doing it is not what she had in mind.

The courthouse is in the center of town. There aren't many people milling about, but I'm still nervous. Why? I have no idea why I should be nervous. It could be I'm afraid of what I'm going to discover. I hope Momma is right in saying the judge will know exactly why I'm here. If he doesn't, I won't have an inkling of the right questions to ask. Worse, if he looks at me like I've grown two heads, then I'll have gotten nowhere. And since Momma didn't enlighten me with any details, I'll leave here with nothing if he doesn't have a clue what she's talking about.

I step out of the car and smooth my short red pencil skirt down with my sweaty palms. I may not have any idea what the fuck I'm doing but I sure as hell look the part. I grab my matching red short jacket to cover my black ruffled chiffon blouse in case I get cold. My stilettos are black, pointy and high enough to cause a nosebleed. My cat-eye eyeliner is sharp and my lashes are dramatic. My lips are moisturized with my favorite red lipstick, and my braids are in a high knot on top of my head. I look like I mean business, but I'm nothing more than a child playing dress-up.

Any other time, you wouldn't be able to tell me shit. I could read you, write you and then forget all about you. But not here. Obviously, I am the odd woman out. I've felt out of place ever since I arrived.

No. Even before that.

My intense neighbor doesn't make things any better. The welcome committee is great, but clearly, they're harboring secrets. My mother finally leaves me a clue, but even she's speaking in code. I don't understand how I'm supposed to find out anything if no one answers my questions.

But I'm determined. I hope the judge is the talkative type because I'm in the mood to hear some answers.

I walk in and take the elevator up to his floor indicated on the map. When I reach his office, no one is in the waiting area. I inform the receptionist who I am and turn around to take a seat.

"No need to find a seat, Ms. Burris. The judge is expecting you. You can go on back." She smiles and points me in the direction of his office.

"Oh—thank you." I return her smile and head in the direction she indicated. When I make it to his office, at the end of a long hallway, his door is open. As soon as he sees me, he jumps up and meets me. A smile as big as Texas on his face and a cigar dangling from his fingers.

"Ms. Burris. It is nice to finally meet you." He gives my hand a vigorous shake. "Please sit down." He closes the door behind me and walks back around to sit.

Judge George Christiansen is like the rest of the men in this town.

Big and attractive.

But where they are stern and to themselves, he is wide open and boisterous. His sable-brown eyes are light and happy. From what I've seen so far, he is as out of place here as I am.

"Nice to meet you as well. Are you related to Dr. Christiansen, by chance?"

"Why yes, he's my son," he says proudly.

"Oh." They favor each other physically but the doctor definitely did not get his personality from his father.

He doesn't say anything else at first as I take my seat. He looks me over as if he is looking for something in particular. I lift an eyebrow to ask if something is wrong but he beats me to the punch.

"You look so much like your mother." His soft tone, minus inflection, implies he spoke more to himself than me, but I respond anyway.

"Thank you."

He nods and taps a finger on the stack of paperwork.

"I was saddened to hear about her death. I was hoping to see her again sometime soon."

It was obvious he did indeed remember my mother and had known her personally.

"Me too. Did you know my mother well?" I ask gently.

"Yes. For about, oh... almost forty years or so."

"Wow." I sit back in my seat. "She never told us about this place. I was shocked when the attorney told me I had to come here. I don't understand. Why all the secrecy?" I implore him softly.

"Well... you'll find out. I promise you. But first, we must do as your mother wished. After we complete her instructions, if you want to come back here and sit down with me, I'll be happy to answer all of your questions. Today, however, is not the day. There is too much at stake to go over everything right now. But you do deserve to receive answers, and you will have them. I promise."

"Okay. I'm going to see you keep your promise. I hope we can finish everything within a few days. I'm only here for a week."

He stops shuffling through a stack of envelopes and his head pops up in surprise.

"A week?"

"Yes. I have a life back in New York that I must return to. I'll have to get back to it at some point."

"Hmm. Well, it looks like we should get started then, shouldn't we?"

I smile the first true smile since I arrived here. Finally. "Yes. Yes, we should."

He picks up a large manila envelope and hands it to me. The heaviness of the envelope sparks my curiosity.

"I'm going to jump right in with no chaser. Is that okay with you?"

"Yes. That's how I prefer it." I run my hands over the envelope with my mother's name on top.

"Forty years ago, your mother lived here for several years. She had a son. For reasons she wrote down in this diary, she chose not to stay. She left her son here in Abrielara when his father died. He is a grown man with a family of his own now."

All of my questions stick in my throat like a big block of ice. A son? I have a half-brother?

Why didn't she ever say anything?

"When you read her diary, you'll find out why. But for now, let's follow her instructions. Her son has heard all about her and the circumstances she left here under. He fully understands she had her reasons for doing what she did.

"Why wait until now to spill the beans? Because ultimately, she wanted you to know you have a brother, and she thought this was the best way to make that happen. Again, when you read the diary, you'll find out why. But for now, you should take all the information you hold in your hand along with this diary and go straight to the medical building.

"Your brother is a world-renowned cardiologist named Perry St. John. I spoke to him moments before you got here. He's going to stay put until you get there."

My throat is closing. I can't utter a word. My mother had a son. A son named Perry St. John. I lay the envelope on the desk and close my eyes. I work at taking slow deep breaths. Letting this new information seep in for what it is.

When I'm calm again. I look back at the judge. His eyes are sympathetic and kind.

"There's not a lot you need to explain other than to tell him about you and your life with your mother."

The sudden realization of what I have to do stops me short. I have to tell a son about his mother. A mother I barely knew myself. That's why I'm here. Of course I know my mother...I know who she is, but we didn't get along. What can I possibly tell him that will put my mother in a good light?

"Whatever you say, good or bad, just be honest. He knows you're his sister. He's anxious to meet you." His big smile from earlier returns. "This is a good thing, Mika. There is nothing to be afraid of. Perry is a happy-go-lucky guy who under-stands the situation even if he isn't aware of all of the details. Your mother didn't want to leave him and wanted you to connect with him. That's all."

"Okay." I gather my things and stand.

"Don't forget to take the diary."

I reach over and take the diary from him. He walks around and gives me a hug.

"Sorry. I'm a hugger. I liked your mother. She was a good woman. You and I are going to get to know each other better. When you meet Perry, you'll see you have nothing to worry about. You never know. You may want to stay."

There's that talk again about staying. I purse my lips a little and he laughs at me.

"At least I hope you'll want to stay." The judge walks me to the door and opens it for me.

"I put my number inside of the diary in case you need me or have questions."

"Thank you, Mr. Christiansen. I mean, Judge Chris-tiansen. I appreciate your help."

"Just call me Judge. Everyone else does."

"Okay, Judge. I'm sure we'll talk again soon."

I walk out of the office building with hands heavy with answers I'm sure will only generate more questions and with a heart equally as heavy.

Did my mother dislike me so much because she wished I were Perry? Did she think she made a mistake by going back to Atlanta rather than staying here in Abrielara? I need to read her diary to find more answers. And I will, but I can't help but think maybe I should reconsider delving any deeper. Whatever the reason for leaving a child behind, she evidently felt she made the best decision possible. Not my place to judge, and definitely none of my business, right? I mean, I have no right to question her actions.

That's not what I'm doing. Obviously, I'm scared. Scared of painting a picture of a mother who would be a completely different mother to him than she was to me.

Not for the first time, I wonder why she chose me for this. Taliah would have been so much better. She could articulate beautifully what kind of mother Momma had been. How she loved to bake and was always the backbone for anyone in the neighborhood who needed one.

She could easily recount how she, Momma, and Brianna would sing the roof off the house and the church when they got together. I could tell all of those stories too. The difference is that Taliah could tell them from a firsthand point of view.

All of my stories would be from the spectator's point of view. Taliah could speak about the talks they always had in secret. Whereas I had none. None of my talks with Momma were in secret. They were screamed loud enough for the world to hear. I wouldn't be surprised if Taliah knew about Perry but was sworn to secrecy. I wouldn't be shocked if I was the only one who didn't know about him or Abrielara.

Well, whatever the reason why Momma wanted me here

for this, I'm here. I park outside the medical building. It's still alive with a lot of people regardless of the hour.

The sun is setting and a chill can be felt in the air. But I didn't need my jacket. I actually feel a little feverish after speaking with the judge. My stomach is tied all up in knots, proving my attempt at playing dress up is just that...all play.

I know what the judge said, but how can I be sure Perry isn't going to act like my neighbor does every time he sees me? Who's to say that kind of intense hatred doesn't inspire him to put his hands on me?

I've never met Perry, but I only have two people to possibly compare him to. The judge and my neighbor. God, I pray he is like the judge.

I grab the diary and the thick manila envelope and make my way to the building. The outside of the building is impressive. The mostly glass exterior changes every few minutes with a different beautiful image. The courtyard is decorated with fountains, flowers, and reflecting pools. Any other time, I'm sure this place is very peaceful, but all I can think about are all the possible ways this can blow up in my face.

Before pulling open the door, I take a deep breath. Here goes nothing. I give the door a good yank while someone pushes it open. I feel myself falling backward and all I can think about is how to keep my mother's envelope and diary from being dumped into the fountain behind me.

Fortunately, a pair of strong arms catch me in time from falling into the fountain. I grab onto his arms for dear life. The heat from his body is familiar, as is the muskiness of his cologne. He pulls me up, making sure I can stand on my own before putting distance between us.

I recognize him immediately and judging by the way his eyes narrow and glint with agitation, he evidently recognizes me too. My sharp gasp of surprise at the level of vexation radiating from his eyes spurns him to lean toward me.

"I'm so sorry," I begin, holding my hand palm out. Hoping it will calm him down.

"Why don't you do what you're told?" He scowls at me with his laser-powered eyes. I continue to move backward until the back of my legs hit the edge of the fountain. He paces back and forth, his obvious outrage at my presence is pronounced in every step.

"For the love of God! Leave!" He points toward the parking lot. "Just leave!"

A small group of onlookers stop to watch. I'm thoroughly embarrassed. However, he evidently doesn't care one bit.

"I don't get what you mean. Why? Why do I have to leave?" I ask quietly, not wanting to draw any more attention to our exchange. I sit on the edge of the fountain.

"I told you to leave, and now you've waited too late."

"Too late for what? I'm not bothering anyone. What is your deal? I don't even know you, and every time I've seen you, you act like some kind of crazy psychopathic lunatic."

My voice escalates with each word. I no longer care who hears me. This guy is pressing on my last nerve.

"You should have left when I told you to leave. Now it's too late. Maybe if you get the fuck out of town now, you might have a chance."

"I'm lost. I don't understand." I cross my arms stubbornly.

He is leaning over me again. I lean back, bracing my hand behind me on the concrete ledge of the fountain to steady myself. His face is red and his lips are so close to mine I feel every word he spews from them.

It must be the lights from the fountain causing his eyes to glow. Seriously glowing. The one thing that hasn't changed is how thick those veins are popping out of his neck like he's got roid rage or something and the level of hate he has for me.

"Look, I don't understand what your problem with me is, but obviously, there is something about me you can't stand. So let's make a deal, shall we? I'll stay out of your way if you stay out of mine. Just because we're temporary neighbors doesn't mean we have to like each other. I'll be gone by the end of the week anyway. Excuse me."

Finding an ounce of gumption, and I do mean an ounce, I stand and walk around him and the small crowd gathered in front of the door.

"Are you slow or something? The end of the week will be too late. Is it sinking in yet?"

I refuse to answer because he isn't making any sense.

He stands there as the disgust written all over his face changes to resignation.

"It's already too late."

He throws his hands into the air before stuffing them into his pockets. His muscles fight to find a way out of his tight white t-shirt. His chest moves up and down vigorously as he pants through each breath. Is it possible he's gotten bigger since the last time I saw him?

I shake my head in confusion because I'm not getting any sensible answers.

"If it's already too late, then what the hell are you barking so loudly for?"

"You're in danger. Don't you see?" he rasps at me. His words are strained and struggle to pass his clenched teeth and tight lips.

"In danger of what, though. You never say." My voice reverberates throughout the courtyard as my frustration leaks out of each one of my pores. Answers...why can't anyone give me any clear answers? I'll take anything at this point.

"Me," he grounds out viciously. My head snaps back as if he slapped me.

He makes an about-face and storms away. Him? What the fuck does he mean?

I'll never understand that man. I don't understand how anyone can. Maybe he's not quite well. It happens to the best of us.

I stand there for a few minutes, willing my hands to stop shaking. Does he mean I should be afraid of him? Does he plan on hurting me? If he had spoken to me calmly, maybe I could make some sense of what he was saying. His communication skills are sorely lacking. Surprising, considering he's a doctor. Which I'm finding harder to believe.

I choose to stay on task. I can't waste any more time thinking about my neighbor. Who, by the way, is the poster child for the necessities of a straitjacket if I ever saw one.

I take a deep breath and walk through the door. My nerves from earlier are mysteriously absent. Probably because the real threat is outside and not in this building. I guess he was good for something.

Dr. St. John's office is on the sixth floor, and it's a little creepy up here. There are only enough lights on to see where you're going but that's it. Evidently, everyone else had the good sense to go home for the day.

I pause only for a second before knocking on his door.

"Come on in!" he bellows. I pause for at least a full minute. The reminder from Momma to do this quickly is what forces me to push the door open and walk on in.

Not surprising, Perry St. John is like the rest of the men in this town, but not. His face breaks into a grin as soon as I walk through the door and he rushes over to hug me. My eyes well up as soon as we step back and I see he shares some of Momma's features. He has her wide nose, her dimples, and they have the same mouth. That's all, but it's enough.

"Sit down. Please." He motions to the sofa and he sits at the opposite end. We sit in silence for a few moments.

I'm sure we're thinking of the same person. Momma.

"I'm not sure where to begin," I admit. I remember the envelope. "This should help."

"Wait." He lays a hand on mine. "I want to say I'm happy to meet you. I have a fairly good idea of why she left me here, and honestly, I've made peace with it. I wish I could have spent more time with her, but since I can't..." He shrugs. "I'm happy I got to meet you. Meeting you connects me to her again."

"That's sweet of you to say. I'm happy to meet you too. I'm not gonna lie. This is something of a shock. We've never heard about you and I'm having a little bit of a problem wondering why she would leave you here. I don't understand why she wouldn't tell us."

I'm baffled, but then again, I would be the last person to say I understand the workings of my mother's mind.

"I will be happy to enlighten you on what I believe could be the reason, but now is not the time. I think there is something a little more pressing we need to discuss."

More pressing than a monster of a secret falling into my lap? Not likely.

"We just met. What else would we have to talk about besides Momma and our family?" I prod gently.

"I think you should leave." His face, stern and dimple-less.

No way. No fucking way. My shoulders drop dejectedly. The joy I felt earlier disintegrates faster than it would have had you zapped it with a phaser from a Sci-Fi movie.

"Not you too."

Perry grabs my hands. "It's not what you think. I would

love to sit here and spend all night and day talking about Momma and you, but I think you should leave. Or at least try."

I stand up sharply. My back all up in a dither, preparing to let him have it. I can't believe this. First my neighbor and now him. I thought he was different. That's what the judge said. Apparently, that's not the case.

He jumps up with me. "Before you get upset, let me explain. I think it's too late, but I would like you to attempt to leave. If you can make it to Wilson's Creek, then you are scot-free. But if you find yourself right back here, then the choice has been taken from you. I can always come find you once you leave, but you can never come back here. I don't want you to lose the ability to choose if you still have it. If the choice has been taken from you, then you won't be able to leave here for a while."

"What are you talking about?" I'm astounded. He sounds crazy, but I don't want to insult my brother when I've just met him.

He grabs my elbow gently and guides me to the door. "Drive straight out of town. Don't stop at the house. Don't grab anything. Just go. I will find you if you can make it. I'm going to follow you until you pass your house. I'll wait there for an hour. If you come back to the house, we'll have our answer. Now, please. We've got to hurry."

Perry's wide steps are hard to keep up with as we exit the building. I barely manage to not twist my ankle in my higher-than-a-kite heels. I pull out of the parking lot with him close behind me. I'm not sure what to think. I'm totally confused. I don't understand the urgency of leaving, but okay, I'll do as I'm told and ask questions later.

Again, so not my character.

Once I pass my house, I raise my hand to say goodbye to

Perry as he pulls into my driveway. Hoping I can make it to Wilson's Creek and will have the chance to see him again someday.

An hour later, finds me circling my house again for the third time. I'm positive I'm not lost. I can't be. There's like one road out of this strange town, yet I've managed to miss an exit somewhere. Then I remember what Perry said. If I end up back at my house, then the choice has been taken from me.

But by whom? On whose authority? And how? How is this even possible?

I park my rental beside Perry's SUV as he steps off my front porch. The look of resignation on his face does not bode well for me at all.

"Looks like you're staying a while."

"I don't get it. I don't understand how I can make a loop around Abrielara but not see an exit for Wilson's Creek. I can't grasp how I can be here for less than a week and already I've had two people tell me it's best I leave. I can't make heads or tails as to why Momma had me come here. I definitely don't understand why she would have a son and then leave him behind. I don't get any of this."

I flop down onto the couch and toe my shoes off. Then I pop back up as if the couch is hot.

"Or—" Hope fills my chest. There may be a way I can leave. I run to the kitchen and head for the phone.

"Or what? What are you doing?"

"Bobby said he would come and pick me up if I wanted him to. He probably isn't in the hanger, but I'm sure I can leave a voicemail, and he can be here in the morning to pick me up."

I pull open the drawer nearest to the phone and grab the small phone book. I leaf through it until I find the Wilson's Creek Hanger's phone number and call the number listed, but I receive the voicemail.

"I thought airports stayed open all night," I say more to myself.

"Most do, but you are in a part of the state that functions on a different set of rules. Besides, you can't go anywhere anyway."

"Why the fuck not?" I'm so tired of people telling me what I can or can't do.

"Because you've been chosen. You can't leave until the rite of Passage has been completed."

"Chosen? Rite of Passage?" None of this makes any sense.

"I can't tell you anything more. But I promise you'll find out everything soon."

"Why? Why can't you or anybody else tell me anything?"

Now I'm getting angry. This is utter nonsense.

"It is not for me to say. I have to obey the laws of the land, so to speak."

I roll my eyes and plop down on the couch I vacated moments earlier. More secrets. More questions. That's all I'm getting. I never receive any true blue answers from anyone. I'm doing nothing but running around in circles like a dog chasing his tail.

"I wish I could tell you more but I can't."

He sits across from me. The look of resignation on his face earlier slightly morphs into something else. His dimples make periodic appearances, his lips seem to have difficulty sitting still, and his eyes have caught the wandering bug. I cock an eyebrow at him.

"What's wrong with you? You look like you're up to no

good. Spill it." He leans his head slightly to the side and shrugs his shoulders.

"I know you wanted to go home. I know you have a life in New York."

"How did you find that out?"

"Small town and I happen to have an inside track to the goings on around here."

"Ah...that's right. Dyana." I motion for him to continue.

"I'm sorry you've had your choice to leave taken from you. But I can't help but be happy you're staying because I'm blessed with being able to spend more time with you. My kids will have the chance to meet you. I don't have to hunt you down. I know exactly where you are. This is great."

The grin he was fighting so hard to keep under wraps is now out, loud and proud. Dimples on blast and his straight, sparkling whites would make a toothpaste giant proud.

"You still haven't told me what all of this is about." I remind him.

He checks his watch and stands. "Unfortunately, tonight is not the night. Besides, it's not my story to tell. But I promise you'll have a better idea of what this is all about by this time tomorrow or, at the most, in a few days."

I don't believe him. I'm so tired of this shit. I shake my head and put it in my hands. Everyone is giving me the runaround. Including Momma. If her objective was to drive me crazy, then she has succeeded. I've only accomplished racking up more questions rather than finding answers. This has to be some kind of joke. A joke the whole town is in on.

"This is ridiculous. You told me we would talk. I did what you told me to, and now you're telling me you can't tell me what's going on because it isn't your story to tell. This a load of shitty hogwash and I'm sick of it. I'm tired of seeking answers and only coming up with more questions. I'm surrounded by people who have the answers but no one is talking."

Perry watches me rant and pace but I can already tell he isn't going to tell me shit.

"Please don't feel that way. I promise you'll learn everything but not tonight. Now, I've got to get on home. I promised my kids a bedtime story. Maybe tomorrow you and I will do lunch and we can talk about what's in the envelope."

"Fine. I'm a bit tired anyway." I follow Perry to the door and open it for him. "Thanks for coming by," I say dejectedly.

"No worries. Don't forget, sometime this week, we will have a nice brunch. You'll tell me about you and Momma, and I will answer some questions you have."

I squint my eyes at him because I don't believe him.

"I will. I promise. Then we will take a break, and I'll tell you all about Abrielara."

"Promise?"

"I promise." His dimples make another appearance and then he damn near skips to his car. He gives me a quick wave over his shoulder and drives away.

After forcing down some food, I take a quick shower and dress in a silky white nightgown. I go back downstairs, grab a bottle of wine, open the manila envelope, and pour all its contents onto the coffee table. I drink straight from the bottle and look through the pictures.

Some pictures I recognize of Momma as a teenager. There are some of Taliah, Brianna, grandma and me. Some other pictures I don't recognize at all.

From the scenery, it appears some were taken right here in Abrielara. She doesn't look all that happy in some of them. There was one of her and a tall, good-looking man, I assume is Perry's father. And then there's another one with her and the judge, his arm around her shoulders. Both of them smiling and obviously happy.

I wonder what happened between her and the judge. He clearly felt something for her. At the very least, they maintained their friendship even after she left.

Perry said he understood why she left but I don't. The mother I knew would have never left her child behind, no matter what. Yet here I am, having met the son she did indeed leave behind.

These pictures only create more questions. No answers. But that's par for the course. Then I remember the diary. I put the pictures back into the envelope and grab the diary. Leaning back into the couch cushions, I settle in for a long night.

Chapter Six

Solomon

The Transformation

I'm hot. Not like, let me turn on the air conditioning hot. I mean fire and brimstone hot. Like I want to claw my skin off hot. Like my skin is smothering me. I can't breathe, can't take in enough air, and I'm sweating from the inside out—hot. As if there is any other way to sweat.

I strip out of my clothes and lie back down. I can't stand this. I've got to do something. Just lying here dripping all over my sheets is driving me mad. Maybe a cold shower will help.

"I told you what to do. Give in."

I'm done arguing with Lux. We don't see eye to eye. We never will on this. No use in talking about it anymore. I block him from my mind. I can't think when he's doing all that talking.

Under the cold spray of the shower, I find myself nodding off. I half-ass dry off, throw on some basketball shorts, and lie back down. And for a while, I can breathe. My skin isn't on fire and peeling from my bones... until it is.

The pain is so intense that at any moment, I'll be incinerated by it. And wouldn't that be a blessed mercy right now? All I can do is grit my teeth and bear it. My skin crawls and my vision darkens the way it did earlier today. Fuck me. Not again. I focus on controlling my breathing. The last thing I want is a heart attack. I try my best to hold myself together, allowing my mind to drift, hoping to avoid all stimulation. I crawl as deep into myself as I can without letting go.

In through my nose.

Out through my mouth.

Repeat.

Slow, deep and steady.

The pain finally eases and I can breathe. I almost feel sane again. I keep at it until I'm almost convinced I've got it beat. My eyelids are finally heavy. The fever is gone, and I'm not being smothered to death. But when I begin to drift off, the dreams filter back in. I'm sweating again. Liquid fire flows through my veins, lighting me up like some evil Christmas tree.

"Fuck, it hurts."

"It wouldn't hurt if you would just let me out!"

A tortuous scream echoes through the night, unlike anything I've ever heard. An overwhelming adrenalin surges through me.

I jump up, fully awake now, and pace the floor. I expect to see someone in my room, but no one is here. Only me.

A growling rises and it's only when I feel the vibration in my chest that I realize it's coming from me.

I am the growler.

The screamer is me.

With that knowledge, I let it rip. From the lowest depths of my soul, I growl. I howl. I scream. It feels so good. I've never felt this alive before or this free.

The need to jump out the window and run until I pass

out vibrates throughout my body. I'm shaking uncontrollably. Lux isn't going to let this go. I knew that as soon as we saw her. I've held out as long as I can. Dad and Perry told me the best thing to do is relax. It will be easier on me to let go and let it happen. Easier said than done but that's what I'm going to do.

I lie back on my bed and close my eyes. Lux's will overshadows mine in a thick dark cloud. For the first time, Lux pushes himself forward. My skin stretches, my fingers, tongue, and hair lengthens. I panic and question my decision not to fight it. Lux pushes me further back. Now my option to choose is completely gone.

"You never had a choice," Lux reminds me.

I wish to God my beautiful neighbor had left town. It's quite evident that she hasn't because I smell her sweet aroma from over here. She's calling to me. Asking me to come find her, to take her and make her mine.

God, I can't wait to make her mine.

She's ours and we've waited long enough.

The urgency hits me like a big red fire truck with its sirens blaring, and I'm running. I'm running out of my house and toward hers. Not once taking into consideration what is supposed to happen when I get there.

Mika

I flip through the pages of Momma's diary again and then chuck it off to the side after I finish off the wine. I read her diary from cover to cover but it doesn't give up the goods. It reads more like a love story than anything. Okay...maybe I didn't read it cover to cover, but I did skim it. That was enough to get the gist of it. I want real answers, but the diary isn't going to give it to me and the focus I arrived here with is gone.

So is my patience.

Since everyone has worked so hard to keep the answers hidden from me, they can keep them. Fuck it. I give up. At this point, I see no evidence Momma had any intention of telling me anything worth noting. I fully anticipate that I will still have questions if I read her diary from cover to cover. The funny part of it all is since arriving, I have done what I was told to do. Well, besides leaving when I was screamed at to do so. But aside from that, I have done what was asked of me without argument.

For me, that's saying something. I'm known for arguing for the hell of it. If my mother said the sky was blue, I would say it was purple because it was different than what she said. Of course, now, as an adult, I'm not quite as contrary, but I don't just do as I'm told. I always make decisions based on what I want to do, think, or believe.

But not this time. This time, I didn't push back much, if any, and where did that get me? I can tell you where I didn't get me, and that is out of here. I followed Momma's instructions only to be told to leave when I never had a chance to begin with.

I have to face the facts. My relationship with Momma cannot be explained or rectified. It is what it is. She'll remain a mystery to me just as Abrielara will, I'm sure. You cannot tell me there is no way out of this town. Aside from holding me captive, how can anyone keep me from leaving?

If nothing else, maybe I can walk out until I can hitch a ride. So, until then, I guess I'm stuck here. And if I can't leave, then there is no reason why I can't suck down another bottle of wine.

If I'm lucky, I'll pass out on something soft. Maybe tomorrow, I can pick up Momma's diary and read it again when I'm sober.

I trip over my feet, getting up from the couch. Obviously, that time is not now. I giggle to myself. God, I'm so pathetic. How did I allow myself to be swindled into coming here and now I can't even leave? If something were to go down, who would I call? The welcome committee? I am completely fucked.

Perry says I won't be able to leave for a while. What kind of tomfoolery is that? And how long is awhile? I don't think so, sir. I'll be leaving here tomorrow.

As soon as I sober up.

I grab another bottle of wine from the chiller and release the cork. I don't even notice if it's red or white. It doesn't matter. Alcohol is alcohol. It'll get the job done. As I tip the bottle up and take a healthy swig—an unnatural chill covers me from head to toe.

You know, since arriving here, I've always felt something wasn't right about this town. I couldn't put my finger on it.

Whatever that something is only felt like a twinge before, but it isn't a twinge now. My body is on full alert. That twinge has turned into a full-blown body alarm.

I don't want to turn around.

But I must.

I'm afraid to even move a muscle, but I must.

I count to ten and slowly turn around.

On the other side of the room is... I have no idea what it is. Nothing I have ever seen before. What in the actual fuck?! It's not an animal. It's humanoid and monstrous. I have never seen anything that big with my own eyes before besides a bear. This is definitely not a bear. The eyes are red and cat-like, but it doesn't look like a cat. The lips are very thin. The nose is also thin, with several holes on each side. He has black talons where his fingers should be. The hair on its head is black and long, falling past its shoulders. Its skin shimmers, copper-like, but holographic, a chameleon—changing colors in the light. The skin has the texture of a marine animal, maybe a whale.

Maybe it's a man in a suite? It's one hell of a suit if it is.

In either case, this is a flight and not a fight situation. There is no way in hell I would ever win against that thing.

I can't move. I can't breathe. I want to believe whatever this is, is a figment of my imagination. Maybe I should cut back on the wine. Actually, there's no maybe about it.

In a brief moment of sanity, it does cross my mind to think of a way out of this. But my internal screaming is so loud I'm surprised I can conjure a single thought.

What do you do in situations like this?

Play dead?

Reason with it?

Threaten it?

Grab a knife or a fire extinguisher?

The longer I stand here, the more time is running out. What the fuck do I do? Panic finally rises to the top of my throat after being delayed by alcohol.

"Run," it says in little more than a guttural command. The wine bottle slips from my fingers and although it doesn't shatter, wine spills everywhere. But I don't flinch. I'm still frozen with fear. Its head tilts to the side, maybe in confusion over my lack of movement.

"Run. Now," it commands again.

Tentacles sprout from his back and swirl around him.

Not a man in suite. Definitely not a man in a suit.

The internal scream lodged in my throat finally escapes. I don't need another warning. My legs find themselves and again, I do as I'm told. I run straight through the living room and out the front door. I do not grab my shoes, cell phone, keys, or my purse. I do not pass go, nor do I collect two hundred dollars.

I run. I have no idea where I'm going, but I can tell you two places I'm not going.

I'm not going back into my house and I am for damn sure, not going across the street. I'm pretty sure my angry neighbor would not take pity on me but would instead say he told me so.

Lux- The Chase

Watching the emotions play across her face as she tries to figure out what I am and what to do is interesting and irritating at the same time. Interesting because I can guess what she's thinking easily. Irritating because I'm ready for the chase to begin. Standing there in her sexy, thin nightgown did not help her situation one bit. I see her nipples protruding from her nightgown from across the room. Her breathing is erratic, forcing her breasts to rise and fall underneath it.

Fuck yeah, she is scared, and that makes me want her more. She'll need the adrenalin for the chase.

Exhilaration fills me. The vibration in my blood hums at a low frequency but is enough to stimulate me. The thrill of going after what I want in this way is enthralling and the ability to fulfill my purpose is gratifying. For once, I'm in the right place at the right time. And without a doubt, I will catch what I'm chasing. I was made for this.

As soon as she hits the tree line leading into the woods, I start counting down from fifty. If I catch her easily, it's no fun. I stretch my neck and roll my shoulders. This won't take too long, but I have to give her a good head start.

Run Chosen One. Run. Because once I catch you, I'm never letting you go.

When I make it to the tree line, her scent couldn't light the way any better than if she had sent up flares.

Euphoria billows from the pit of my stomach to my throat, manifesting into an unearthly yell which echoes through the forest. Nothing responds to my call. The forest is completely silent except for her panting shallow breaths. I will let her have a few moments to catch her breath before I continue the chase. I want to taste her fear in the air before I allow myself to catch her. Making my victory that much sweeter.

Mika – The Probe

The yell echoing through the trees spurns me to run faster. It's a warning. I run as fast as I can, but even in my alcohol-induced state, I can only keep this up for so long. I truly have no chance of outrunning whatever that is. I have to find a place to hide.

If I had been in the right frame of mind, I wouldn't have run into the woods. I would have grabbed my keys on the way out and gotten into the damn car. If horror movies have taught us anything, it's that nothing good ever comes out of running into the woods. But here I am, running deep into the woods like a dumb ass. But oh well, I'll be damned if I turn around and go back the way I came.

I risk a frantic look over my shoulder to see if whatever it is still follows me. I expect to see his hair blowing in the wind and his eyes glowing in the night. But I see nothing. Time to find a place to hide.

I finally stop running only because I don't have the lung capacity for it anymore and it's fucking dark. I can't see where the hell I'm going. I need to work out more. I promise you after I find a way out of this mess...I am gonna have my ass in the gym every day.

After grabbing a few breaths, I start running again. I can't run indefinitely but I have no idea what else to do or where to go.

I finally stop because I have to. I don't have it in me to keep going. I hide as best as I can behind trees with thick limbs and bend over, gasping for air. I should be quiet, but it's impossible when you can't breathe.

When I can breathe without wheezing, I look around. A few yards away is what looks like a small cabin. I assume it's for storage. Whatever it's used for, I hope it's unlocked.

It isn't.

I circle the building, and there isn't a way in without a key that I can see. I walk back toward the back side of the cabin, hoping I can sit and hide. I pray whatever is chasing me will keep going.

No such luck. As soon as I turn the corner to the building, I sense him behind me. I don't want to turn around. The last time I did, I was faced with something nightmares are made of. I don't want to know what happens next.

I step forward, but a hand clasps my shoulder and then shoves me hard against the side of the building. My face is smashed against the cold jagged wood. The hand moves from my shoulder to the back of my neck, immobilizing me. My body is forced so close to the building I cannot take a deep breath, even speaking is almost an impossibility.

"Please don't hurt me," I manage to whisper.

The hand behind my neck moves to the front of my neck. Tears fall silently from my eyes, and for the first time since all of this started, I realize this could be it. This could be my last night on earth. Watching hours of the ID channel did not help me prepare for this at all. This is not how I thought it would end. I begin to shiver and shake, both from the temperature and fear.

What I can only assume is a tongue, slowly sweeps the side of my neck, the side of my face and up to my hairline. I squeeze my eyes tighter. I don't want to see it. I don't want to feel it. I don't want any of it.

"Please don't hurt me. Please," I whimper.

He wraps an arm around my waist while his hand at my neck holds me still. Then two more hands, I think they're hands—one behind each knee—spread my legs and then lift them off the ground. My legs bend and press into the wood. How can he subdue me this way with only two hands?

"No." I sob quietly even though I'm sure it doesn't care about me, and crying won't do me any good whatsoever. I can do nothing but cry as something slithers up both of my nostrils and into both of my ears. He attaches his body to mine somehow. Like suction cups to my thighs, stomach, and back. His body is plastered to mine like a vacuum forcing us together.

Heat rushes through my body like lava, filling in the cracks of the earth after a volcano erupts. It's scorching hot. There is not a place inside of me he does not touch. He's even rummaging around in my head. And then he stops, his arms tighten around me.

"You are one of us," it growls, holding me tighter.

I have no idea what he means, and I don't care. I'm on fire. On the inside, I am literally on fire. I continue to wail loud enough that everyone in Abrielara should hear me. They are unsurprisingly absent, however, but it doesn't stop me from bellowing anyway.

When another rope of sweltering magma burns through my body, the agony is too much. Entirely too much. Darkness threatens, but I fight it off. My voice is gone from the screaming and crying. Why did I bother? No one coming to my rescue. No welcome committee to bust in when they're not invited. My nosey-ass neighbor is conveniently absent when, any other time, he would be sitting out on his porch watching me.

I'm alone like always. No one cares what happens to me. I will die out here and no one will know about it or care. Except for Brandi. She will. My sisters won't notice anything different.

With that, I give up. I give in. There is no way I can fight what is happening to me. And even if I somehow survive this, no one will believe me if they even care to ask.

When another rope of white-hot liquid broils its way through me, I let go. I can't take the pain anymore and there is no reason to keep fighting it. This time when the darkness comes, I welcome it. Hoping if I ever do wake up, this is some awful dream. And that I have never heard of or set foot in a place called Abrielara.

Solomon

I'm aware of the moment she passes out. The stiffness in her body leaves likes she's giving up the ghost, and I have a moment of regret, but it passes quickly. When the probe is completed, the all-consuming heat I felt before goes with it. Lux allows the suckers on his tentacles to relax. He fades away to rest and I take over.

I feel like myself again but not. Lux is calm and I'm no longer on fire. I'm human again, but I'm worn out. My muscles ache but I feel alive. More than alive. I feel elevated. Transformed. Lux has receded, but I am still seeing the world as he saw it during the chase. Everything around me seems sharper and more vibrant.

I know it's because Lux and I are merging into one. It's one of the side effects of the Passage. If we complete it, Lux will earn the right to walk around in his true form when he wants, with my permission of course. That's never happened before. The Brielaran side of us never sees the light of day after the age of five until the Passage begins. He's always been with me. Always had his own mind and personality. But there was never a time when I felt that he and I were the same. He's been a part of me my entire life but this is the first time when I've felt a part of him. I can feel him beneath my skin, as if all I have to do is peel off a layer and I'll see him there.

This transformation is something I'm going to have to get used to and I'm not sure how it's supposed to go. I'm happy for Lux to complete his duty and earn his right to walk in society as a complete being. I'm just not sure how things are supposed to go from here. We are nowhere close to completing the Passage and if the Chase was anything to go by, it isn't going to be easy.

The act of probing is exhausting for both of us. Actually,

for all three of us. This whole transformation thing has taken its toll on me. I can't say I'm not ready to see this phase come to an end.

I walk us back to her house, knowing my duty isn't over yet. Now that Lux has done his part, it's my turn to do mine. I still need to clean her within the next six to twelve-hours or the burns left by the suckers will become so much more painful for her.

The shocking part is that she is one of us. I didn't see any signs, nor did anyone else she had been in contact with. How did we miss it? The Brielaran in me should have recognized the Brielaran in her. Was her mother aware or did she just decide to not tell anyone when she sent her here?

It begins to drizzle when I make it to her house. Days seem to have passed since Lux told her to run when it has only been a couple of hours. She hasn't moved a muscle since passing out. I lay her on her bed, and for the first time, I notice her legs and feet are cut up from running in the woods. Some of the cuts are pretty deep.

Her once pristine white nightgown is gray and brown in spots. Her poor knees are all scraped up, and she has the beginnings of a bruise on her face and neck.

Lux was too damn rough.

"I did what needed to be done."

"A little finesse wouldn't have killed you."

Lux is uncharacteristically silent. Keeping quiet is for the best. I was already aggravated with him, but to manhandle her that way wasn't called for.

I'm sure her body holds more evidence of what happened out there if I could look closer, but I need her permission first. For some reason, I don't want her to wake up and see Lux. Not yet. Not after everything that just happened. I can't bear the shrill of her screams anymore. The best thing I can do is go home, shower, take a nap and then come back here and clean her up. I hope by then she'll be happy to see me and then I can tell her the whole truth.

I find a first aid kit, take care of the deeper cuts, and then pull the covers over her. I kiss her forehead lightly and then make my way downstairs. I straighten up the living room a little and clean the sticky evidence of the spilled wine in the kitchen. Then I have earned the right to go home and rest.

Before I even make it across the street, I am completely myself again. At least physically. I barely remember taking a shower, but I remember my head hitting the pillow and how her body fit perfectly in my arms.

Exactly six hours later, I wake completely rested and on a mission. I have to get to her. I take a look inside from the windows and don't see any movement or evidence she has been up. I let myself in.

I've heard it's perfectly normal for the chosen to sleep like the dead after the chase and the probe. I hope she gives me a chance to explain things so I can complete the aftercare.

Before going upstairs, maybe I should at least bring her some water and orange juice. If she's up to it, I can cook her some breakfast afterward.

I tap lightly on her bedroom door and then peek my head in when I don't receive a response. She's awake, reclining in bed and facing the window. It's obvious she's been awake for some time. I take a few tentative steps toward her.

"Mika, I hope you don't mind my coming in. I knocked but since you didn't answer, I wanted to make sure you were okay."

"I'm fine," she says without sparing me a glance. "Is there something you need? Or let me guess, I didn't leave fast enough, so you're here to scream at me for my disobedience... again." Her tone, though soft, was no less snarky had she said them any louder.

"No. I'm not here to yell at you. I need to talk to you. I'd like to explain some things, and then there are some things I need to do to make sure you're taken care of..."

Her laugh is deep and course. She shakes her head. "Isn't it a bit too late for that?"

"No. Actually, it isn't. I need to look you..."

"You don't need to do shit but get the fuck out of my room. I don't understand why you're even here right now. You were so adamant I get the hell outta town. I'm inside my own fucking home, minding my own fucking business, and now you seek me out. Where were you last night, huh? Conveniently not at home, I'd guess."

"Mika..."

"I don't believe I've given you permission to call me by my first name. As a matter of fact, I'm positive I didn't. Another thing I'm sure of is I told you to get the fuck out of my room. So I don't understand what you're still doing here."

"Mika..." This is not how this was supposed to turn out. She hasn't looked at me once since I walked in here, until now.

"Get out." When I hesitate, she repeats herself, only louder. "I said, get out. Get out. Get out. Get out," she yells hysterically, emphasizing each word with a slap to the bed.

"Fine. I'll give you some space but I'll come back later." I keep my voice calm because I understand. I deserve her anger and frustration.

"Don't fucking bother."

I don't answer. I close the door behind me and head toward the kitchen. She doesn't want me now, but in a few hours, she will. And when she does, I'll be here.

Chapter Seven

Solomon

I t's been three days.

Three full days since I probed her and she won't let me come near her. She is in so much pain I can hear her crying but she locked the door. She locked it two days ago when she realized I wasn't going anywhere. Today is different, though. Today, the crying has changed into screaming, which means the pain is unbearable.

I've been sitting outside her room, begging her to let me in, but she refuses. It kills me to listen to her go through this alone. I understand her aversion to me. I totally get why she wants nothing to do with me. I take full responsibility for that.

However, if I don't do something, she can die. I can't let that happen.

"We have to do something."

"I think you've done enough. This is all your fault."

I have to call someone. I don't want to, but I have no choice. I need help. I call Perry. Since he has already gone through all of this, he'll understand the severity of what's going on.

As soon as he picks up, I feel like an idiot. I should be able to handle this on my own. Listening to her cry leaves me utterly useless, helpless, and weak. I've got to do something.

"Hey, man. You've been MIA lately. You got some good news for me?"

"No, Perry, I wish I did. I need your help. Please grab Dee, Dad and whoever else you think can provide some assistance and come to Mika's as fast as possible."

"What's going on? Are you okay?"

"No, I'm not, but most importantly, neither is Mika. Just hurry."

Perry, Dad and all four women of the welcome committee show up within ten minutes. Their worried faces turn to me simultaneously. By this point, they can hear Mika's agony and know I'm to blame. Before they can question me, I tell them briefly what's going on and my plan to remove the door and provide her with the help she needs whether she wants it or not. But Dee disagrees.

"No, Solomon." She holds up a set of keys. "Let us go in there first before you go barging in. I'm positive she feels like her life is completely out of her control. The least we can do is to help her have some say in it. Breaking down the door and exerting your power over her will not help your case later. You'll just make it worse. We'll make her see reason."

"And if you can't?" I stand, somewhat relieved someone else has a plan.

"Then we'll help you do what you need to, even if we have to tie her down ourselves."

Mika

As soon as I hear the doorknob jangle, I grab the lamp, preparing to hurl it at Dr. Christiansen's head should he make an appearance. I don't understand why he won't go home. He's had absolutely no interest in me since I got here other than to tell me to leave, and now he suddenly wants to be a friend.

For what reason?

When I woke up three days ago, I thought for sure I had a horrible nightmare. Until I had to go to the bathroom and noticed the whelping on my stomach and thighs, the handprint on my neck and bruising on both legs above my knees. I was even further confused when Dr. Christiansen showed up here wanting to take care of me. I don't understand what he means by that, but I don't need or want his help.

But now, those whelps are sores, cracking my skin wide open and seeping some kind of greenish fluid. The pain is excruciating and getting worse by the hour. My stomach contracts painfully every few minutes and it's distended. The nausea is horrendous but renders nothing but dry heaves.

I can only assume the infection is also inside my body and not just on my legs. At first, I kept the fact I was in pain to myself. However, at this stage, I don't care if he hears me or not. The pain is worsening and mirrors the pain of whatever happened to me in the woods. I prayed for death then, and I am screaming for it now.

Yes, I could use a doctor, but I don't want Dr. Christiansen anywhere near me. Yeah, my pride may be the very thing to kill me, but at least I won't be in pain anymore and I won't be a pawn in my mother's sick game, either. I've tried to clean the sores myself, but now they are getting so infected and swollen that it's impossible. I can't see all of them and it's getting harder for me to walk.

When I see Dyana, Kimberly, Jeana and Becca, I want to weep with joy. Even though I'm angry at them, I need their help more than I need answers right now.

"Honey. what are you doing to yourself?" Dyana rushes over and hugs me as the others surround my bed.

"What do you mean, what am I doing to myself?" I ask defensively.

"It's obvious you're in pain, honey, and Solomon can help you. Why wouldn't you let him help you?" Jeana asks, removing the sheet off of my legs.

"Because I can't." I don't meet their eyes. If I say it out loud, it will sound childish, and I'm not in the mood to be pitied any more than I already am.

"Let's sit you up so we can get a good look at you. We need to see how much damage there is and then go from there." Becca grabs both of my hands to help me out of bed. When the sheet falls away, and they help me to the bathroom, their gasps are audible and simultaneous.

"My God, Mika," Kimberly exclaims, her hands flying to cover her mouth. I can't look them in the eye. I see what they see. The nasty open whelps seep with something that feels like acid.

I should have told someone before now. How did I let this happen to me? How did I let this go on for so long without seeking some kind of help?

Shame is why. Shame and disbelief.

The liquid seeps down from one of the sores and burns a path down my leg. I have no shame left. My body shakes with the intensity of the pain. I lean against the sink for support as tears run down my face. I don't have the strength to stand up unassisted.

"Please just kill me. Put me out of my misery. I can't go on like this one more day," I whisper, hoping someone hears me. I look into the mirror at each of them. Their eyes are red and running over with tears too. Dyana is shaking her head at me.

"We understand Dr. Christiansen is your least favorite person, but he is the best person to take care of this," she explains.

"You mean to tell me there is no one else in this town besides Dr. Christiansen who can help me? Absolutely no one else?"

"Well, any doctor can help you, yes, but you'll be scarred for life. Why not have Solomon help you? He's already here," Jeana explains.

"He can make you feel better quicker, Mika. Just let him do it. We'll be here to make sure nothing happens to you, but we cannot continue to sit here and watch you suffer like this, and neither can he."

I'm confused.

"How do you know he's the only one who can help me? Are you guys even curious how this happened? What do you mean by neither can he?" I ask Kimberly.

My heart pounds at all the questions rumbling around in my head. If these ladies knew the danger I was in and didn't tell me...

"He's the one who called us over here. He asked for our help since he couldn't convince you to let him in."

Jeana ignores my first two questions. Now I know they know something more than what they're letting on. I don't believe for one minute he cares anything about me. Only he knows the true reason why he's stuck around these few days. If he couldn't stand to watch me suffer, why wait until now to send for help?

Apparently I can't trust anybody in those town. Not the

judge, not Perry, not the Fab Four, and certainly not the doctor. Since I'm in no shape to debate the facts, I keep my thoughts to myself. Not hard to do when you're being eaten alive from the inside out.

"So don't go anywhere. We're going to get Solomon in here. He'll know exactly what to do. Just promise us one thing," Becca asks.

"What?" I say with agitation in my voice.

"Let him do what he needs to do. You may think it's crazy or weird, but it'll help you in the end. Okay?"

She reaches over with a Kleenex and wipes the tears from my face, and then hers. At this point, I'll agree to anything as long as the pain will stop.

"Fine," I agree through gritted teeth as another pain burns through my abdomen. My stomach contracts so fiercely it almost brings me to my knees, but the whelps are so bad, it hurts to bend them.

Jeana and Kim grab onto my arms to keep me from falling to the ground. All I can do is hang onto them, cry out in pain, and pray for death. More echoing cries, hoarse and thick with tears, tear from me.

"I can't take this anymore."

Dyana leaves me, and soon the others follow. I'm not sure what to do, so I stand there facing the mirror as acid continues to eat away what skin I have left on my body. Sweat travels in little rivers down my face, mixing with my tears. My body shakes uncontrollably. I'm afraid I'm in the early stages of shock.

I can only pray for something so merciful.

I hear the door creek open, and I chance a glance at the door in the mirror. Dr. Christiansen stands there, eyes dark, bloodshot and sunken. His eyes catch mine. I drop the hold they have on me before they have the chance to sear through me. Heat powered by anger trickles down my back. I clench my eyes shut, trying my best to keep this whole situation in perspective. No matter how much I hate to admit it, I need him right now.

Whatever he sees in my eyes or on my face moves him to rush over and gently turn me to face him. His eyes sweep me from head to toe quickly. There's something familiar about the heat in them. I don't have to look him in the eye to recognize it. I keep my eyes down. Even though I'm afraid he has already seen the pain in them, I don't want him to see me raw up close. I figure he'd seen enough when he walked through the door.

His voice sounds caring and is barely a whisper. "I am going to bend down and take a look at your legs, your back, and your stomach. You can lean on me if you want. I just need to see the extent of the injuries. Okay?"

His voice is calm and all doctor-like. I'm surprised at how much better his presence begins to make me feel. The idea of relief in my not-so-distant future I am sure, has a lot to do with it.

I nod, closing my eyes in anticipation of his reaction I'm positive will mirror the fab four's. I allow him to put my hands on his shoulders as he kneels in front of me. Some of the sores can be seen easily, but he cannot disguise his shock when he lifts the hem of my gown.

His breathing becomes heavier and faster. His hands start to tremble slightly as his fingertips glide ever so softly around the sores. A tortured moan escapes him. It brings me out of my haze of suffering long enough to wonder why he appears to care so much. Maybe it's a part of his identity as a doctor. Either way, I'm not sure what reaction I expected, but it wasn't that.

He stands without giving me notice. I'm not prepared for

how close he is to me. He is much closer now than when he first knelt in front of me. I smell the coffee he had this morning for breakfast. I see each of his eyelashes and how they curl up at the ends.

God, I would kill for lashes like his.

His eyes are agitated, but it doesn't take anything away from the unusual color. The irises are dark red around the pupil but gradually lighten and turn into a warm golden color resembling honey toward the edge. The arrangement of colors reminds me of ...fire. I've never seen eyes that color before. If I recall correctly, they didn't look this way the last time he was this close to my face. They are so bright and intense as he watches me look him over.

Despite the anger boiling deep in my chest every time I look at him, I haven't had enough. I could gaze into the warmth of his eyes all day, but I look away anyway; completely disgusted with myself.

I am at odds with these conflicting feelings where he is concerned. The outrage is fire-hot but so is the attraction toward him too. I don't understand it, but maybe my brain is trying to find something else to focus on other than pain.

Nothing I've experienced has made any sense from the moment I arrived in this town. He is here to help me, and as soon as I'm better, I'm outta here. I take a tentative step back to give us some space.

At that moment, I'm reminded of why we are both in this bathroom when another gut-wrenching spasm hits me in the abdomen. I bend over, leaning on him for support as another tortured cry erupts from me.

As soon as the spasm ends, Dr. Christiansen takes my hand and slips one of his around my waist.

"Aren't you going to ask me how this happened?" My whispered question obviously sounds pained but it's pleading tone should tell him I want him to ask me. I need him to ask me. At least then I could pretend he doesn't know what's going on here. But just like the welcome committee, he doesn't answer my question but the clench in his jaw tells me he wants to.

"Okay, this is the plan. I am going to pick you up and carry you back to bed. So hang onto me so I can get you there." He continues to talk to me softly and gently. I'm not sure how he expects me to react, but I can assume, based on the very animated conversations we've had in the past, calm is not what he is expecting out of me.

Unfortunately, calm is the only reaction I have enough energy for right now.

I obey without comment. He carries me carefully to bed. He sets me on the bench in front of the bed and then steps away. He strips the sheets from the bed. After laying down some towels, he helps me lie down.

"Okay. What I'm about to do will seem strange, but I promise you I have to do this. There is no other way.

"I will explain everything to you later. Right now, we need to take care of this because if we continue to wait, it may be too late to fix it. I need you to trust me on this, okay?"

"I don't have a choice." I concede. As it was told to me four days ago, the choice has been taken from me.

"Right." He nods and spreads my legs open as wide as he can without hurting me. He slides my panties down slowly, careful not to scrape them against my legs. Any embarrassment I may have felt has been totally removed by my level of pain. His eyes meet mine for a brief second before he kneels between them. But then, as an afterthought, he raises his head.

"I'm sorry. This is going to hurt at first. But it will eventually feel better. I promise." His eyes resemble glowing embers.

I swear they did not look that way moments go. He bends his head down between my legs again. My only response is to close my eyes tightly, preparing for the worst.

Solomon – The Aftercare

The moment I see her injuries, I hate Lux for doing this to her and I hate myself for not breaking down her door. I should have completed the aftercare at the sixth hour. Better yet, I should have taken the consequences and not involved her at all. I never wanted to hurt her. That was my whole problem with this process in the first place. I wanted to avoid the chase, the probing, and the aftercare altogether. But no, I had to follow through because that was what was expected of me, and now, I've gone against the oath I took when I became a doctor.

First do no harm.

The only good thing is I can fix this. She is going to hurt like hell in a minute, and when she finds out how, why and who did this to her, she will hate me even more than she already does. But at least then, she will have all the answers she's been searching for, plus some.

I take one last look at her before I command my tongue to morph into the forked one that can heal her wounds. Her eyes are closed tight as tears continue to flow silently from them.

I make the first lick, a long but tentative one across the thickest whelp on her inner thigh. Her body arches sharply off the bed, her hands coming to cover mine on her knees. She screams so loud I'm surprised she didn't shatter the windows of my house across the street. It takes considerable strength to keep her from closing her legs and crushing my head to death.

As much as I want to check on her, I don't stop licking. I lick faster. I lick longer. Up one leg and then start on the other. I lick her stomach and behind her knees. She continues to bawl and wail.

Seeing her in this much pain and knowing I'm the one who did this to her is killing me. I feel her agony as if it were my own. For every pain wave racking through her body, one equally as powerful ravages its way through mine.

I swallow the pain with the guilt and focus on licking away the evidence. I pause only for a second before licking her hairless mound. My acidic probing DNA eating away at it too.

I make two more passes over both legs and her mound before my tongue works between her lower lips and then delving inside her. My long tongue dives deep and sweeps every surface it can touch. I take my time because I want to make sure I don't leave any probing DNA behind to do more damage.

I'm not sure when it happened, but Mika has passed out. I turn her over to take care of the wounds on her back. I've done all I can do for now. She screamed and cried so long that I had to tune her out, or else I wouldn't finish the job. At least she isn't screaming anymore, but the tears still flow like rivers from her eyes. I grab the first aid kit I brought in and begin dressing her wounds, not realizing I have continuous flowing rivers of my own.

When I exit Mika's bedroom, Dad rushes over and hugs me.

"How is she?" His eyes are full of worry too. Everyone heard her screams of torment as I did.

"She's sleeping. I need to put her on an IV of antibiotics and pain meds. She's also dehydrated. I'm going to put her into a medical coma. The pain is too much and we have several more days of this before it gets better. The injuries are so bad, Dad. So bad." I shake my head in shame.

"Well, you're fixing it now. Perry will grab what you need to set up the IV. I want you to grab a shower and take a nap."

I start to protest.

"No. I mean it. You aren't going to do her any good if you can't even hold your own head up. You can sleep here in one of the other rooms. Run to your house, grab what you need, and then come back here.

"The ladies and I will get some food going and listen for Mika. I'll stay here with you just in case you need support. The ladies need to get home to their own families."

I hesitate only because I've kept watch for several days. I don't want to leave her.

"She'll be fine for now, son. Go pick up your stuff." He pats me on the back while guiding me to the door.

I do as told and grab some things from my house. However, I wait for Perry to return with the supplies so I can get her settled before I lie down for a while. I won't be able to rest if there is a possibility she'll wake up in pain.

"I think putting her into a coma is a good idea. From the sounds coming from her bedroom, I can about imagine how bad the burns are."

Perry sets up the IV. While I was at my house, the welcome committee came in and put fresh sheets on the bed, cleaned the bedroom and bathroom, and opened one of the windows to air it out a little.

"Yeah. If I had known how bad it was going to be. I would

have been more aggressive in making sure I took care of her despite her hostility toward me."

"You did the best you could at the time, Solomon. Don't beat yourself up. You're taking care of it now. Hopefully, you'll have the chance to explain everything before her heat cycle is in full force. Right now, you can at least slow it down since you're putting her under."

"That doesn't make me feel any better. This whole time she has been several steps behind what is happening to her. She still doesn't have an explanation for what she went through. And now I have to tell her what it means to go through a heat cycle that will have already started manifesting itself. She's going to hate me more than she already does by the time everything's said and done."

Perry shrugs while he continues to work. "I know, man. When explaining the heat cycle, you'll have to explain it all. Judging by her reaction so far, I don't think this will bode well for you but I have faith it'll work out." He flashes me a smile.

"I hope you're right."

We finish up our work. I watch her for a few more minutes after Perry leaves the room. Even with the bruise across her cheek, she's still beautiful.

I kiss both of her cheeks. I look down at her slightly parted lips, tempted to sneak a taste, but then I think better of it. When I do taste her lips, I want her eyes open. I want her to be fully aware of what's happening and who's doing it. I want her to choose it, to choose me. Until then, I'll have to wait.

When I make my way downstairs, Dad is flipping through T.V. channels, and Perry is sifting through the photos on the coffee table, reminding me of what I wanted to discuss with him and Dad.

"So, I need to talk to you guys about something I discovered during the probe."

Dad mutes the T.V. and Perry stops sifting. "Is everything alright, son?" concern written all over his face.

"Yes, or at least I think so. During the probe, I found out she's one of us."

Perry cocks his head to the side. "What do you mean she's one of us? If she were connected to us, we would have realized it by now."

"I think there's more to it. There is no doubt she carries Brielaran DNA. Lux recognized it immediately."

Perry and I look over at Dad.

"What do you think, Dad? What are the chances I am not mistaken and she does belong here?"

Dad only pauses for a second. "One hundred percent."

What the...?

"Are you serious? Why didn't you ever say anything?"

"Yes." He looks over at Perry. "Mika is your full-blooded sister. I wanted to tell you, but I wanted to follow Dolly's wishes as much as possible if I could."

"That would mean that she—"

"Has the same father you do. Yes. Her mother had her come back here for that reason. She wanted Mika to understand where she came from and to know you."

"Why couldn't she let you tell her? She didn't have to come here at all." Frustration and anger take turns clawing at my insides. "She went through all of this for nothing."

"Son. As you said, she belongs here because she is one of us. Her mother wanted her to have the opportunity to decide for herself. And being one of us and chosen means she has a Passage to complete of her own."

Perry starts pacing, trying to wrap his brain around this new development. "If all of this is true, why didn't we detect her before the probe?"

"Sit down, Perry. I've got a tale to tell you, and it will take a while."

"Judge, I don't have the mental capacity for the long version. Give us the cliff notes. We'll work thru the details later."

"As you know, your father was a geneticist secretly working on a way to alter our DNA so some of the pain we experience during the Passage could be avoided. He did not have permission to do a sanctioned study, so he tested on himself in secret. When Dolly came into town, he chose her. But instead of allowing the Passage to happen naturally, Dane forced his body to go through the symptoms to simulate it so he could test his latest DNA-altering medication on himself."

Perry and I exchange glances.

"What happened? I don't recall ever hearing anyone mention anything like this. This would have been nice to know before I damn near died in the lobby of the fucking hospital." I can't keep the angry tone out of my voice.

"Nothing. He experienced the Passage like normal and Dolly got pregnant with Perry. Dolly decided to stay and committed to Dane and Perry. A couple of years later, Dane believed he successfully created a variant that would help with the pain of the Passage. He also hoped it would hide certain characteristics that make us different from the rest of the world. This would also keep the Brielaran comatose if we chose. So, if the host did not want to go through the Passage, they wouldn't have to and wouldn't be penalized for it. He wanted to keep the Brielaran in us dormant indefinitely if we wanted."

"Sounds cruel." I can't imagine Lux or any Brielaran being okay with that.

"What happened then?" Perry asks, even though we've been told the story doesn't end well.

"He injected himself with the newest variation and then forced himself to go thru the Passage again. The pain was still there and the aggression was a hundred times worse. He was able to complete the probing phase again with Dolly. But later that night, he could not phase out of the Brielaran as he should have been able to. He became so violent and unstable that the Monarch had no choice but to put him out of his misery."

Dad rises from the chair, heads to the kitchen, and returns with a bottle of vodka and three glasses. He pours us each a glass before continuing.

"So, since he was taken out before completing the entire rite of Passage, Dolly was in danger."

He looks at me. "Your mother had already left us, and besides Dane, I was the closest to Dolly. When I went to check on her after hearing what happened to him, I found her in a similar situation as Mika. I didn't know how long she suffered with the burns, but it had to have been a while because she was hallucinating when I got there."

"Dad..." Even though this happened years ago, I felt for my dad in a way I can only appreciate now having gone through what I have. He waved me off.

"I had to take care of her. So even though I was not the one who probed her, I couldn't leave her like that. It was a good four days before she came around and the wounds began to close up.

"She seemed happy to see me. She asked about Dane and was upset when she found out what happened to him. But when I explained the whole situation, she was beyond pissed. She couldn't believe he would jeopardize their marriage and their lives."

He stares into his glass, obviously watching a replay of the past.

"As you are aware, after completing the aftercare, the heat happens naturally. I fell in love with her." He chugged the rest of his drink and poured another. Perry and I followed suit and chugged ours too.

"We were beginning to start the consummation stage. It was just a formality because I had already committed to her in my heart and I believe she had committed to me as well."

He chuckled and poured another drink. "There's something to be said for having your head between a woman's legs on a consistent basis."

"Oh yeah?" I give him a half smile.

Perry nodded and grunted in agreement.

"Yeah. You'll become accustomed and addicted to a particular taste no other woman can satisfy. Trust me on this, son. Keep that in mind when you take this journey with Mika."

"I will," I respond, fully aware it's already too late for me. The Brielaran in me was not the only one who chose Mika. I did too.

"So, what happened next, Judge?" Perry tries to keep us on task.

"Well, the night of our official consummation, I was doing what I discovered I loved to do best when I tasted something different. I realized she was pregnant. I don't believe she knew it yet.

"Apparently, when Dane completed the probe, they had sex at some point. That is something that has never been heard of here. We decided it was best Dolly and the baby leave Abrielara while they could. She technically held up her end when she had you, Perry. Since Dane was dead and didn't complete the process the second time. She was free to go. Obviously, no one else knowing about her pregnancy helped."

Dad got up and walked over to the window. He was obviously back in Abrielara thirty-five years ago.

"I wanted her to stay, and for a little while there, I thought she was going to." He turns and looks at Perry.

"She didn't want to leave you, Perry. She didn't, but if she wanted to keep Mika safe, then she had no choice."

"Safe from what? No one here would hurt a baby, even if she didn't carry the gene."

"True but because of what Dane had done, Dolly didn't want her or her baby treated as outcasts or experimented on. So until she knew for sure if her baby carried the gene, she had to get her out of Abrielara. She knew she couldn't take you out of Abrielara until you were of age. You were still a baby. I told her I would take care of you and keep in touch with her so she could keep tabs on you."

"So why didn't she say anything to Mika about who she was?"

Dad turns back toward me.

"Well, because after Mika was born, it appeared the Brielaran gene had missed her. She was born human. There was not a trace of Brielaran in her anywhere. At least not the ones the eye could see. Although it was apparent early on, she had an aggression problem, was overly dramatic, and reacted strongly to being told what to do. But other than that...nothing. It appeared the gene Dane tried to mutate was successful when being passed organically."

"And she never told Mika?" Perry topped off my glass and then Dad's.

"No. She wanted Mika to discover this place on her own. If she got here and nothing happened, then she didn't want it to impact her life. If she was chosen or felt at home, she would tell her or leave it to me.

"But life gets in the way sometimes, and before we knew

it, Dolly found a normal guy and got married. Mika never showed any sign of having Brielaran DNA. She had two more daughters and settled into a normal life that did not involve us." He places a hand on Perry's shoulder. "Don't misunderstand me, son. Your mother loved you. She was so happy to receive the updates I provided about you and spend the time she was able to with you. She was very proud of you."

He returns to the chair he'd vacated moments ago. "Since you've chosen Mika, you must educate her beyond the general info about who we are. She has the right to understand who she is. Of course, we'll help you. But make sure you are thorough. Even if you think she's going to leave. She deserves to be told the complete truth before she leaves here if that is still her choice. But there is one thing that I would like you to keep in mind when you do discuss this with her."

"What's that?"

"She is a totally different kind of hybrid, and we don't know what that means yet. She could be exactly like us or nothing like us. We have no idea what the Monarch would say if she found out who she was. We also don't know if she is susceptible to the same consequences that we are if she decides not to complete the rite of Passage. Make sure she fully understands before she makes a decision."

We have no idea what kind of hybrid she is, but then neither does she. She does deserve the right to know the truth, and I intend to tell her. But she isn't going to like any of it. What scares me the most is that even if we complete the Passage, she will not choose me. She's going to leave like human females usually do. Even if she isn't completely human, human is all she knows. After I explain to her what happened and that I'm the cause, how will I ever convince her to stay?

The next few days are spent exactly the same. I rise early, go to her room and check her vitals. I change out her IV bags and lower the dosage of meds keeping her under. After removing her bandages, I give her a sponge bath and then kneel in front of her and take care of her wounds.

For three days straight, Mika's phone rings incessantly. After a message from her assistant stating she was going to book a flight down if Mika didn't answer, I was motivated to reply on Mika's behalf.

I kind of implied that I, Mika, had decided to extend my vacation for a couple of weeks. Luckily the assistant didn't question the text. In fact, she seemed ecstatic at the idea. She was happy to leave Mika to her vacation and hasn't called back again, thankfully. I've had other pressing issues on my mind.

Like making sure Mika gets better.

It has become quite the ritual for me. I learned the entire aftercare process generally takes an hour, depending on the extent of the injuries. But I like to take my time and make no less than three complete passes each visit. So I usually spend about two hours alone with her in the morning and evenings.

Dr. Franks is covering for me until my Passage is over but he's only able to handle the mornings right now. I'm fine with it. I appreciate his help. Without him, I would have difficulty taking care of Mika the way I want to. After spending time in the office, I grab a bite to eat for Dad and me and head back to Mika's. Dad stays with Mika while I'm gone and spends the evenings and nights with us.

After taking a nap after dinner, I brush my teeth and head to Mika's room. It's eight o'clock and time for her second round of aftercare today. Last night was her final low dose of anesthesia. She should come around soon. I'm looking forward to moving on to the next step in our Passage, but at the same time, I'm a little saddened that my time with her will be ending. Especially if she chooses not to complete the Passage with me. It probably sounds sick, but I enjoy this time with her. Even though she's not awake, what I'm doing is helping her. She no longer cries in her sleep, which broke my heart every time I witnessed it.

I check her over. Her vitals are fine. She's getting stronger every day, thank God. I remove the sheet off of her legs. Most of the cuts have healed and will soon be undetectable. I carefully remove the bandages and I'm happy with what I see. Some of her wounds have closed up and healed completely. It looks like she'll need no more than three additional days of aftercare and then she should be good to go.

I bend her legs so they are arched on both sides of me and her feet are planted on the mattress. The deepest and most hideous wounds start above her knees and go all the way up to her stomach. I start below her knees and lick long and steady strokes. I do my best to be as gentle as possible. Some sores are still a little swollen, and I bet they're still painful.

I've seen this done by others in the clinic here after I graduated from medical school. There are skills that Abrielaran doctors need to have that your typical medical school does not teach. Some doctors have had to complete the aftercare for patients because the Brielaran who did the probing could not complete the cycle for some reason. In these cases, the aftercare is completed by administering simulated DNA so the wounds would heal and the life of the chosen one could be saved.

I can't imagine anyone other than me doing this for Mika.

I'm the one who put her in this situation, so I should be the one who fixes it. Of course, I have ulterior motives.

I chose Mika completely. There's nothing I want more than to complete the Passage with her. I want her to choose me like I've chosen her. I want what the Brielarans have told us we should expect when the Passage is complete. Even if my life experience tells me I should expect something entirely different.

Chapter Eight

Mika

Sensual strokes of something warm and wet caresses my legs, getting closer and closer to my aching core. My entire body is lit up, alive. More alive than I can say that it ever has. I want to reach out, touch what is touching me, and express my gratitude. Each touch gets me closer and closer to cresting but not close enough.

I want more.

I'm aching for more. I need more. I crave more. Without more... I will lose myself, my mind, and the ability to connect to something greater. The strokes are unhurried. Stroking me into a languid fevered frenzy. A scream of frustration builds in my throat.

Then the warm, sensuous strokes finally find my throbbing core. It weeps with joy and relief that finally, it gets the attention it craves. The touch is so familiar, as is the scent. But I can't place it.

I fight through the muddy fog, reaching toward the touch. I finally break free. Forcing my eyes open and blinking rapidly to clear my vision. That scent stirs something in me.

The strokes continue, breaking my focus from identifying

the scent until the strokes hit a spot inside me that reminds me of who it belongs to.

"Mine." My voice rushes out in a hoarse proclamation as my orgasm shudders through me. To say that out loud is liberating. I have no idea why I felt the need to scream out mine, but whatever the reason, it felt damn good to do so. I gather myself and then look down between my legs to see the iridescent golden eyes of Dr. Christiansen watching me.

"Dr. Christiansen?" My hoarse voice is not quite as boisterous as it was a moment ago. He raises enough for me to see his forked tongue sweep across his lips.

Wait. Forked tongue?

"Solomon," he informs me.

Surprisingly, seeing his forked tongue does not shock or repel me. If anything, it heats me up that much more. With what? I'm not sure. I'm not given much time to think about it. His head dips again, and the stroking continues, intensifying the tide of another impending orgasm. My hips move with the tempo of the strokes. The vibration of his moans escaping his lips as he licks me is stimulating and almost too much. My hands grasp the sheets hoping they will keep me grounded. At any moment, I'll be carried off in a cloud of orgasmic euphoria.

And I am. After announcing the arrival of three more orgasms by screaming his name at the top of my lungs, I can float down in exhaustion to catch my breath. My legs and hands are shaking. Dr. Christiansen... Solomon removes my legs from his shoulders and gently lays them on the bed. He goes to the bathroom and returns with a warm towel to wipe me down. Then he sits beside me. His monstrous erection outlined in his shorts is not missed by me. Seeing it confirms what I am missing out on. I turn my face away from him, suddenly hit with embarrassment at my exuberant display of approval.

"Now why are you acting bashful all of a sudden?" His teasing voice sounds so good. His scent is intoxicating. I don't understand why I have never noticed it to this extent before.

"How are you feeling? Do you hurt anywhere?"

"No, I'm fine. Thanks."

I clear my throat and refuse to look at him. I don't want him to see the embarrassment and frustration rising within me. Although I had multiple orgasms, I still feel jilted because I didn't get to experience what he is so proudly showing me now. Or it could be something else. Something brews in the pit of my stomach and I'm not quite sure how to process it.

"Well, if you're up to it, I would like to talk to you. There are some things we need to discuss. The sooner, the better."

I swallow my pride and turn my eyes back to his. His eyes are back to that warm honey color again, making me question whether I saw the color change at all.

"Okay, well, I would like to take a shower first."

"I would recommend washing off instead of a shower. The bandages don't need to get wet. I think I'll do the same."

He steps back as I sit up and swing my legs over to the side of the bed. I quickly remember why I was in bed in the first place. I move the edge of my gown up my thighs a little bit more to see my inner thighs.

There is still evidence of my sores, but none of the pain. As a matter of fact, the majority of the sores are completely gone and so are the stomach spasms. I look up at Dr— I mean, Solomon sharply.

"The whelps, the sores...they're almost gone."

Solomon leans his head to the side, looking down at my legs.

"For the most part, yeah. Pretty soon, all evidence of the

burns will be gone. When you're done with your rinse, why don't you meet me in the kitchen? I'll make us something to eat. You have to be hungry."

"Okay."

I rise from the bed, and he moves to stand in front of me. His eyes no longer glow but are still vibrant.

"Thank you for your help with the whole seeping whelp's thing." I look down as I say it. The vision of his head between my legs reminds me exactly how he helped me.

"I hope you still feel that way after our talk. I'll meet you downstairs."

He runs his hands through his hair and walks out the door.

I wait until he closes the door behind him before making my way to the bathroom without pain. I can't imagine what he could say that would change how grateful I am that he helped me.

Solomon

As soon as I close her bedroom door, I release the breath I've held since she woke up with my head between her legs. I thought for sure she was going to start screaming bloody murder. I'll admit that I wasn't exactly thinking my clearest when I showed her my forked tongue, either.

But fuck me, I couldn't be any happier hearing her scream "mine" or, even better, my name when she came. I should have stopped when she woke up but I couldn't. It was bad enough that once she woke up, the aftercare became less about aftercare and more about satisfying her. Then, of course, it's even worse when I couldn't stop rubbing my dick while I ate her out. Even if I didn't cum, at least I could make her cum several times. I hope she'll be able to forgive me after hearing everything.

I wish I could do all this over, including the first day I saw her. I should have thought this through. Who in their right mind would want to be with someone who was rude and downright abrasive toward them from the first moment they laid eyes on them? Instead of trying to find ways to skip out of this whole rite of Passage thing, I should have been thinking of ways to make sure that it was a success. Instead of being an ass, I could have been nice to her. Gotten to know her.

"You should have followed my lead. I knew what was best."

"Shut up."

"If you had, this would have been so much easier."

"No. Because you were so forceful, I'm shocked this didn't turn out worse."

"I had to force your hand. If it were up to you, we would never complete the Passage."

"Just fucking be quiet so I can think, Lux."

I can't think when he's running his mouth. I need my wits about me when I talk to her. I can't afford to fuck this up. I'll have to grovel or, at the very least, talk fast. If I'm lucky, she won't spit in my face. It'll be a miracle if she decides to continue the Passage with me.

"With us," Lux *corrects me.*

I'll be truly blessed if she decides to complete all the stages with us, but I won't get my hopes up about that.

I completely understand what the judge was talking about when he explained his experience when completing Dolly's aftercare.

I'd already chosen Mika before I completed the aftercare.

Completing the aftercare for her made me fall that much harder. Dad was right. Tasting her over and over again only fine-tuned my taste buds to crave only her. Every day my mouth watered with anticipation of tasting her. She has become an addiction that I may never taste again.

As soon as she had her first orgasm, I almost transformed into Lux because I was disobedient to his wishes to complete the next phase. As much as I wanted to, I couldn't. I need to talk to her first. I have to make sure she understands it all before taking one more step. I want her to be my partner in this going forward instead of an uninformed participant.

As the cold water pelts my hot skin, I brace a hand against the cool shower wall. My mind replays the images of Mika screaming my name and the taste of her on my tongue as she comes into my mouth. The undulation of her hips as she rode my tongue was the sexiest thing I've ever seen. So beautiful.

The cold water does nothing to calm my dick down. I can't ignore it any longer. I grasp it in a tight grip and stroke, mimicking the strokes my tongue was blessed to give Mika. It only takes a few and my angry cock erupts like Mount St. Helen. My dick jerks as it releases all of the pent-up desire I have for her.

I have to convince Mika to finish this process with me. I'm afraid to find out what will become of me if she doesn't. But I better start thinking about it. I need a plan B. Unfortunately, I don't have a lot of time.

The heat for me has already started. I cannot trust myself to do the right thing if faced with an opportunity without explaining everything first again. Lux will take over and do what I'm having a hard time doing if I don't complete this. And judging by the last time he took over, it wouldn't be anything pretty.

Mika

A shower would have been great, but a wash-off was good for now. Unfortunately, it did nothing to refresh my attitude. All it did was give me more time to think about what happened. I'm grateful for what Solomon did for me but I also remember what happened that required that I receive help to begin with. I'm not blaming him for what happened in the woods. That wouldn't be fair, and to be honest, I can't tell anyone how it happened. Who would believe me?

But the Solomon and the welcome committee obviously avoiding my question says they know something. They may not know who did this to me but it isn't the first time they've seen these types of injuries. How else would they know that Solomon could heal them? Heal them by licking them, no less.

Licking them. Like an animal would lick a wound.

I still don't understand why Solomon was insistent that I leave town. I don't understand why Perry wanted me to leave even though he was sure I couldn't. Did they know what was going to happen to me? What was that...thing that attacked me that night?

I know Solomon has something he wants to address tonight, but I've got my own agenda. I'll insist on getting all of my questions answered tonight. If Solomon can't answer my questions, he's gonna have to tell the judge to come over and do it for him. I refuse to go another twenty-four hours without answers. I believe having my body scorched to death allows me the right to have this request.

I make my way downstairs to the kitchen to find a shirtless Solomon in a pair of low slung grey sweatpants, putting some food on the table. You cannot tell me that he doesn't have a clue how good he looks in those sweats. Why else would he wear them?

A large tattoo covers his right pectoral muscle that I remember seeing when he was at the basketball court. He turns around to show a beautifully sculpted back. The man has a nice ass too. I suppress a moan. The desire that was only slightly quenched earlier is renewed by looking at him. My nipples harden and the damp heat returns to my core. I grit my teeth to stave off the intense urge to hump him like there's no tomorrow.

Where in the hell is this coming from?

"You made it back here fast." Another fact that was not lost on me is how familiar he is with the contents of my kitchen.

He turns toward me when I make it to the table. He smiles, which isn't something I've seen before. He looks like a totally different person. I can't help but give him a half-lipped smile in return.

"I showered here. I've been sleeping here too, so I could keep an eye on you. I didn't have that far to go."

Ah...that explains it, then. He shoots me a quick grin. "Have a seat." He sets a glass of water in front of me. "I wasn't sure what you liked, so I made a little of everything. Help yourself."

"Thanks." I grab some fruit and continue to watch him as he makes his way around the kitchen. It isn't long before I'm more interested in watching him than cleaning my plate. His bulging muscles are putting on a gun show that I would gladly pay money for. You know how they do it.

A little pec bump here.

A little bicep flex there.

A soft, slow finger drag down the abs ...wishing he would do that... everywhere.

I wonder if he's doing it on purpose. With a body that beautiful, he and men like him are the sole reason why gray sweats were invented. The only possible way his pants are staying on at all has to be his round, hard, juicy ass. I wet my lips with the thought of seeing it up close.

I need to look at something else. Think about something else, or he's not making it out of this kitchen without being licked down at least once.

He finally sits and goes in on the food he piled on his plate. I try to keep my eyes on my own, but it's impossible. My vaginal muscles are pulsing. Every time it contracts and releases, my pussy gets wetter, my nipples harden, and it's increasingly harder and harder for me to concentrate. All this because he's sitting in front of me, practically naked, eating fruit and licking the sweet juices from his lips. I would love to lick the juice off his lips or anywhere on his body, for that matter. I want a small taste. Just a little one should sate me for a little while.

I force my eyes back to my plate. I squeeze my thighs as tight as I possibly can. I have questions that need answers. Salivating over this man is not going to give them to me.

What the fuck is happening to me?

My appetite for food has evaporated, and all I can think about is riding that thick, hard dick I saw earlier. The image of his head between my legs and the sensations he generated inside me is enough to keep me wet for hours. I'm so fucking turned on that I swear I could fly to the moon under my own power and still have the energy to fuck him senseless.

The real fucked up part is that he doesn't seem affected by me at all. You would think he ate pussy for a living and it was no big deal for all the attention he's paying me. I grit my teeth as anger and aggression begin to fester inside of me.

How dare he sit there and eat as if I'm not at the same table? How dare he sit there and eat after everything I've gone through? On top of that, he's treated me like shit ever since I arrived in this town. I can't believe I was sitting here salivating over his body. Damn near about ready to come in my chair. So damn close to begging him to drill that dick into me with everything he's got that I lost focus. Just. Like. That.

I shove my plate his way and cross my arms.

"Here, why don't you go ahead and finish my plate too. You appear to be starving. When you're done, I would like to talk if you don't mind."

I don't even try to keep the irritation out of my voice. I mean, come on. He's the one who insisted we talk, but now he's more interested in shoving food into his mouth as if he'll never eat again.

He cocks an eyebrow and washes down whatever he is eating with water. "Sorry, I didn't realize how hungry I was until I sat down. I'm done now. Aren't you hungry?"

"I'd rather get some answers first and then eat if I still have an appetite."

He nods and then stacks my plate on top of his and moves them both to the end of the table.

"Understandable."

He looks me over for a bit. Probably contemplating if he should tell me what is on his mind or not.

"I don't want you to be alarmed but I texted your assistant while you were incapacitated."

My lips form around a question but he continues speaking before I can ask it.

"I didn't think you would want her to worry, so I told her

you were extending your vacation for a couple of weeks. She seemed to like the idea."

"O-kay." True, Brandi would like the idea.

"I did not correct her when she assumed I was you. I thought it was easier that way."

I nod again, watching him as I do so. "Is that all?"

He pauses as a look of apprehension settles over his face.

"No way are you backing out now. Spill it. When you're done, I have some questions I need answered. So, you might as well start talking. In the morning, I plan on hightailing it out of town as fast as possible, so let's get to it."

His lopsided smile in response is almost my undoing. I'm not sure if it's because he's sexy, and I want to hump him to death, or if I'm just angry at his obvious disrespect of my time. The fact that I'm holding it together at all is a wonder in itself. He holds his hands up in surrender.

"I promise you, I'm not backing out or anything. I'm going to tell you the truth and I will be happy to answer any and all of your questions. I'm not hiding anything."

"Fine." I keep a steady gaze on him that I secretly think he likes. He doesn't appear to be threatened by my show of anger or irritation at all. He actually looks like he's enjoying it.

I watch his eyes cover every inch of my face, pausing at my lips before returning to my eyes. I'm still a little confused by the complete change in his attitude toward me.

The animosity he had no problem showing before has been nonexistent since I woke up from that horrible night-mare. There is an awareness that was not there before. Even with anger brewing in my gut, when his eyes meet mine, it's like time slows down for a minute before desire blows through and wreaks havoc with it all.

"You must have a lot of questions. I think we'll be more comfortable in the living room."

I wait a second longer before taking his hand. There is undeniable strength but gentleness as he grabs onto mine.

He waits until I sit on one end of the sofa before sitting on the other. He crosses his large arms across his equally large chest. I suddenly wish that he had put on more clothes before sitting down to have this talk. But I'll be damned if I say anything. All I need is one more reason or excuse to prolong getting the answers I need.

As if he hears my thoughts, he reaches over and grabs a t-shirt from the laundry basket in front of the couch. After dragging it over his head to put it on, he takes a deep breath and then holds my gaze.

"I'm pretty sure you've noticed that Abrielara is not your typical small town. For well over a thousand years, this area has harbored a secret. Your mother stumbled upon this secret years ago, and that secret is what brought you here." He looks away from me and runs a hand through his hair. He leans forward and looks at his hands before looking at me again. "That same secret is what attacked you a few days ago," he says softly.

Tears spring to my eyes. I knew it. My throat starts to close and I force myself to calm down by slowing my breathing. I won't get any answers if I pass out.

"I'm going to address the most pressing issue, and then I can go into everything else if you still want to hear it afterward." He watches me as if he's expecting an answer, so I nod to tell him to continue.

"Abrielara is a town of alien hybrids."

I snort loudly at the ludicrous story he's trying to tell. Aliens indeed. I don't believe it, but then I remember what I saw in my kitchen that night. However, it's still hard to believe. I'd half convinced myself that I was attacked by a man in a suit.

"Everyone here is a hybrid or chosen by a hybrid. I was less than courteous when you arrived here, and I apologize for that. I was concerned for your safety. Which as it turns out was needless because you had already been chosen."

"This is some kind of a joke, isn't it? You put something in my wine before I got here and I hallucinated everything."

"Mika..."

"Chosen, Solomon? Chosen for what?"

"I'm going to explain that..."

"You said that everyone here is either a hybrid or is chosen by a hybrid. What does that mean?" I couldn't wait any more to ask.

"Chosen means that an alien hybrid here in Abrielara has chosen you to complete the rite of Passage with him."

"Rite of Passage?"

Solomon scoots toward me a little.

"Yes. A rite of Passage for a hybrid is kind of like someone going thru puberty, except it isn't like that at all." He rubs his eyes and shakes his head a little.

"I'm confused," I admit.

"What I mean is that a rite of Passage is when the alien DNA in a hybrid is completely matured and is ready to complete their duty to society by choosing a female. Which basically means to choose a mate and procreate."

"Ah." Then what he said hits me. "Oh." My eyes widen at the realization. "No way. No fucking way." No fucking way he could mean me. This is not happening.

Absolutely not.

This is too much.

I did not come here for this.

"Yeah, so you were chosen by a hybrid to complete the rite of Passage. The Passage is completed in stages. First one is being chosen or choosing. The second stage is the transformation. The third is the chase. The fourth is the probe. The fifth is the aftercare. The sixth is the heat. The seventh is the consummation."

"Seven stages, huh?" I'm trying to keep all of this straight but it's hard when I have to watch him scoot closer toward me again. Now he's sitting in the middle of the sectional, looking like he swallowed something sour.

"Yes." He takes a deep breath and clears his throat. "We have completed five stages and are at the beginning of stage six."

"I'm sorry, did you say we?"

His face is about as red as a beet.

"Yes. We." He says after a moment. "I am the hybrid who chose you and the hybrid who probed you. Which is why I had to be the hybrid to complete the aftercare."

The only words I hear are chase, probe, and aftercare. There is some information missing that is keeping me from fully grasping what this situation is. But when my brain finally catches up to the meaning of what he said, rage, as I have never felt it, swells up from my belly. Blazing a path up to my head to the point that I feel like it is going to explode.

I sharply rise from the couch and put some more space between us. The relative calmness that blanketed me is quickly disintegrating. I turn to look at him again, straight into his beautiful golden eyes.

"What did you just say to me?"

Chapter Nine

Solomon

I knew I was going to fuck this up. I knew the moment she understood what I had said and how it related to her. Her eyes flare with anger and brighten with an awareness that causes Lux to recognize the Brielaran in her. Which, of course, excites him to no end.

Scared? No. Anxious? Hell yeah. I'm anxious to see where this leads. It's promising to be something interesting. At the same time, the longer this is strung out, the more evident the probability of this not going my way. I cannot afford for this conversation to get out of hand. From the look in her eyes, I only have a few seconds before that happens.

"Mika, please let me explain before you jump to conclusions." I stand with my hands in surrender.

"Jump to conclusions? I wonder why I would do that? You've been spinning a whopper of a story since we started this conversation. Do you really expect me to believe this shit?" She leans her head to the side. Obviously not a good sign.

"I meant to say before you form an opinion. Please. Just let me explain it, so you know everything before weighing your options." I do my best to keep my voice calm and desperation free, but I doubt I'm succeeding.

She crosses her arms in front of her. I see a vein pulsing at her temple. She's struggling to hold it together. At least she's trying.

"Please sit down with me." I motion toward the couch she just vacated.

"No. I prefer to stand when I hear you tell me again that you were the one who hurt me."

I'm not going to win this battle, so I let it go.

"Okay. Well—"

"I don't believe you," she interrupts. "You look nothing alike. His hair was long, for one thing. Yours isn't."

"Because we are two separate beings sharing one body," I try to explain.

"Where are they?" She circles the couch, staring me down.

"Where are what?"

"Your arm thingies." She waves her hand at me, obviously at a loss for words.

"Arm thingies?" I have no idea what she's talking about.

"The alien—thing that attacked me had arm thingies for hands. I don't see them. So if you're him, where do you keep them?"

"Do you mean tentacles?"

"Is that what you call them?"

"Yes."

"Then yes, that's what I'm talking about. Where are they now?"

"I only have them when I shift. Even then, I may only have two unless I need more; they extend out from inside my body. I don't walk around with all of them out in any form. Only when I'm not human and when I need them."

She doesn't do more than nod as she continues to watch me. Questions clearly running rampant in her mind.

"Would you like me to finish, or do you have more questions about my arm thingies?"

My attempt at humor doesn't amuse her at all. She straightens her shoulders as if steeling herself against hearing the worst. I hate that I am the reason she feels she has to.

"The rite of Passage is not a choice that we have. We are forced to transition and the Brielaran in us has control. I wanted you to leave because I know this is not an easy thing to go through."

"When you realized it was too late for me to leave, why didn't you just tell me what to expect so that I wasn't scared out of my mind?" she practically yells from the top of her lungs.

"I couldn't. It is against the rules. I could lose my life for violating the rules," I say calmly. "If I could, I would have. Besides, do you think that once you laid your eyes on me, you would not be as scared had you known I was going to show up? I highly doubt it."

She just rolls her eyes in response, so I continue.

"The next day, when I came back to check on you and begin the aftercare so you would not suffer the burns, you wouldn't allow me to."

"Are you saying the burns are my fault?" she whispers, tightening her arms around her chest.

Although she spoke softly, I better tread lightly here. It's the calm before the storm I see brewing in her eyes that's even allowing us to continue this conversation. Soft, in this case, does not mean weak. If I say the wrong thing again, I won't be surprised if she takes my head off.

Literally.

"Absolutely not. You had no idea what was going to

happen. And given our previous run-ins, I can see why you wouldn't want me anywhere near you."

She walks back to the couch and sits. Neither of us speaks for a few minutes. I can almost hear her brain ticking away, going through all of the information that I just told her.

"That was you standing in my kitchen that night?" Her voice is still soft, controlled, and not at all timid.

"Yes," I answer without hesitation. I move closer to her, now sitting right next to her, needing to offer whatever comfort I can.

"Can you turn into the alien any time you want?"

"Now that we've started the Passage, yes."

"So does that mean you can choose not to?"

"Well, yes...sometimes. I mean, it's complicated." What is she getting at with this line of questions? I'm afraid to ask.

"Complicated how?"

"Depending on the situation, his will can overpower mine. When I'm no longer human, I also have no control over whatever he does. I'll not have any control over him until I complete the Passage now that it's begun."

She nods slowly, appearing to come to some kind of conclusion in her mind. Before I can ask what it is, she tells me.

"I need an apology before doing anything."

Her matter-of-fact statement was not a request. Her chin is lifts defiantly. I understand the control she speaks with belies the rage bubbling inside her. Her eyes penetrate mine with force, demanding obedience.

Her request isn't unreasonable. I'm happy to give it to her if that means we can move on. I lean over her, placing a hand on the arm of the sofa.

"I'm sorry. I'm sorry for the hateful way I treated you when you got here, and I'm sorry for scaring you to death. I'm sorry for hurting you. If I could, I would do everything differently."

Her face doesn't change. I guess she didn't like my apology.

"That was sweet and nice to hear and all, but that was not what I meant. I believe you would have done things differently if you had a choice. So no, I don't need an apology from you. I need an apology from the person or being that scared me to death, who chased me through the woods, and who pushed me up against that cold wood building. The same one who surrounded me with his go-go gadget arms and scorched my body with his lava-like DNA. That's who I need an apology from before I even think about going any further into this insane mind fuck of a nightmare."

"I apologize to no one for doing my duty. To no one," Lux roars in my head.

I sit back in my seat. She would ask for the one thing I cannot guarantee that I can give her. "I'm not sure if I can give you what you ask."

She turns toward me. "Why? You already said that you can turn into him whenever you want."

"Yeah, but I also said I cannot control him once he's out. I can't make him apologize. As a matter of fact, there is no guarantee that he won't hurt you again. He's already in the heat stage. There is nothing stopping him from making you complete the consummation stage whether you want to or not. I don't want to risk that if I don't have to."

"Then I guess we are at an impasse."

She removes herself from the couch and walks toward the window as if being near me is just too much for her. It's apparent that she's giving up but I'm not. There is way too much to lose.

"There is something else you need to know before you dig your heels in any deeper."

"What's that?"

"You have been chosen, but during the probe, it was discovered that you do in fact belong here."

She turns to face me. "What does that mean?"

"Remember when I said that everyone here in Abrielara is either a hybrid or chosen by a hybrid?" She nods. "Well, you are also a hybrid chosen by another hybrid."

"Excuse me, what?"

"This happens all the time. The difference is that you are a different kind of hybrid. Something that we are unfamiliar with."

"Solomon, you're not making any sense right now."

"During the probe, do you remember hearing that you were one of us?"

"Well, yes, but I thought it was just the ramblings of a lunatic. Not anything I should buy stock in, and besides, I was too consumed with being burned alive from the inside out to pay much attention to anything he said."

"No one detected you when you arrived, so that could only mean one thing. It means that Perry is not your half-brother but your full brother. Your father, a geneticist, experimented on himself and passed an undetectable gene mutation onto you. That means we have no idea if what happens to us if we do not complete the Passage happens to you too. You are unfamiliar to us. We cannot afford to waste time going back and forth in case your consequences are worse than ours. Ours is bad enough."

Fear and more questions are clear in her eyes, and I know I just dumped a bunch of information on her, but I need her to see as much of the picture as possible.

"What are your consequences for not going through with it?"

"If we do not consummate and procreate, we may not be able to phase out of the Brielaran. Depending on how violent we are, we will either be eliminated or removed. We cannot risk exposing Abrielara or putting anyone inside Abrielara or out of it in danger."

She inhales sharply. Her hands shake a little as she listens and computes the information. Maybe now she'll understand the seriousness of our situation and concede.

Without realizing it, I have walked over and now stand inches away from her. Her rapid breathing tells me what I needed to know. She's scared. Good. But the clench in her jaw tells me something else.

She's stubborn. Stubborn as fuck, and in this moment, I know she isn't going to change her mind.

"I understand your concern but I still need an apology before moving forward," she says softly but sternly.

"Mika, I don't think you understand what's at stake here."

"Damn right I don't, but you evidently do. According to you, we are a ticking time bomb but I still need an apology."

"Fuck, Mika—" I shake my head, getting more frustrated by the minute.

"How would you feel if you were attacked by someone and still had to complete all these stages with them as if nothing ever happened? Maybe you don't understand the pain I endured when the whelps seeped down my legs and how I blamed myself for it happening. Or how I had to seek help from the one person who seemed to hate me the most if I wanted any kind of relief.

"I can see how you may not understand how I felt so out of place when I arrived since you were born and raised here.

The only truly friendly people I have met were the welcome committee, Bobby, Perry, and the judge.

No one else has made a point to get to know me. Not even you. All I was trying to do was honor my mother's final wishes by coming here, and instead, I'm faced with rude ass people, no answers, pain, and more mysteries. It appears she just wants to continue gaslighting me from beyond the grave. Why else would she want me to come to this godforsaken podunk town?

"I've had minimal contact from my family since I left home years ago. I guess they don't give two shits what happens to me either since they can't ever seem to find the fucking time to answer a fucking text once in a fucking while.

"I'm in some kind of B-rated horror movie. All I'm asking for is a fucking apology. I'll do my best to fall in line with the rest of that bullshit you spouted a few minutes ago. But I mean, damn, is an apology too much to ask for? I understand you can disassociate from the entire situation since someone else controls you sometimes. But personally, I need to be able to let this shit go so I can move the fuck on."

"I understand more than you think. I promise you I do," I say calmly. I'm trying my best appeal to the reasonable side of her. I'm assuming she has one.

The transformation was no cakewalk for me. The probing DNA burned me just as it had burned her. But this isn't about me.

"You sure as fuck don't act like it."

Her voice had gradually gotten higher and louder with each sentence, and now we're nose to nose. Her eyes flash with so much beautiful white-hot rage. All it's doing is turning me on that much more.

The irises of her eyes start to glow a beautiful light blue. Again, proving the presence of Brielaran DNA in her blood.

Lux rejoices at the passion in her eyes. My dick is hard as a brick right now. Our panting breath mixes and mingles in a way I wish our bodies would.

However, irritation counters by clawing up my body like an itchy rash. My teeth grind as I fight off the aggression already setting in my bones, ready to make an appearance to show her who's boss. We don't have time for this. I want to get on with the shit.

"Why do you have to make this so difficult? Did you listen to anything I just said? You could die tomorrow, and you're worried about a fucking apology."

My voice has risen. Anger now beats a drum in my chest like a war cry.

"You are such an obstinate, pigheaded asshole," she screams back just as loudly. Her hands clench in tight fists at her sides.

"Well, sweetheart, you're no picnic yourself. You're...."

I suddenly lose the words I was going to say. Her eyes are still glowing, hypnotizing me to do whatever she wants. I don't even know why I'm arguing with her. She has the upper hand. And I can only think of one thing right now.

".....beautiful."

The light fades from her eyes, taking the anger in my chest with it. Her face softens and her lips morph into a bashful closed-lip smile as she ducks her head, making her that much more beautiful.

"Thank you."

Her softly spoken words travel across my body like a lover's touch. But when she looks up at me, her eyes don't match the sweetness in her voice. The usual dark warmth of her eyes has turned stark cold.

"So, what's it going to be then?" she asks stoically.

"Fuck my life."

I do a quick about-face and walk out the door, slamming it before I do something stupid, like fuck some sense into her. Aside from that, there is evidently nothing else to discuss. She can keep wanting her apology, but as much as I want to give it to her, it isn't up to me.

Mika

I watch him stomp his way back to his house from the window. I don't understand what's so hard. I want a fucking apology. It may seem unreasonable to anyone else, but not to me. Of course, I understand what he's trying to say but it doesn't change my mind at all.

When I see his light come on, I turn away from the window and damn near have a heart attack.

"Judge. I didn't realize you were here. You could have said something."

"Sorry. I should have announced myself. I just didn't want to interrupt the discussion between you and Solomon. Seemed to get a little bit heated for a minute there."

The judge stands in a maroon smoking jacket with an unlit cigar hanging from his lips.

"I'm sorry if we woke you. I didn't realize anyone else was in the house."

I rub my eyes and head toward the stairs. According to the clock, it was going on midnight. My eyes are heavy, and after latching onto those golden nuggets that Solomon dropped tonight, so are my shoulders.

I have more questions, of course. No surprise there. My mother never told me I had a different father than Taliah and

Brianna. She never let on that I had a brother or was a totally different person than I thought I was. She never said anything.

Maybe that is why she was so angry with me all of the time. Maybe I reminded her of what she left behind. At this point, I'll have to ask the judge or consult the library. Those are my choices. God knows her diary didn't tell me shit. I can't ask Solomon anything and I'm not sure if Perry has any answers or not.

"It's fine, my dear. Solomon and I were taking turns watching over you. I'm glad you're better."

"I wasn't aware. Thank you so much, Judge."

"No thanks necessary. I'm here for you. You look pretty exhausted, so why don't you go to bed. I'll make sure everything is locked down."

I turn to face the stairs again, only to stop short. Maybe there's no time like the present to get some questions answered.

"Actually, if you don't mind, I would like to talk."

The judge moves into the kitchen and pours what I assume is whiskey into a glass. He holds up the bottle of liquor.

"Join me for a glass of kick-in-the-ass to start your day?"

"Well, I don't think I want a kick-in-the-ass to start my day per se. I think I've already had my ass kicked enough. However, I would like a drink of something to calm my nerves. So maybe not whiskey but a little wine?"

"Coming right up." I sit at the bar and wait for my glass.

This week has not gone the way I planned it. At least I'm getting some answers, if you want to call them that. Answers begetting more questions but answers, nonetheless.

Why in the hell had I agreed to complete the Passage if I got an apology? An apology from an alien, no less. An alien! Where is my head these days? I'm just asking for trouble.

"Is life that bad?"

"I'm sorry?" I pop my head up. The judge sits across from me and my glass of wine sits to my right.

"You've been sighing quite deeply for the last several minutes. Not to mention you'll wear a groove into the bar if you continue to trace your invisible image into it."

I force my hands off the bar. "Sorry. I just have a lot on my mind. I'm not sure if I should even bother trying to understand any of it."

"Well, of course you should try to understand it. Understanding it all will have a direct impact on your life and at least a couple more. I'm sure you're talking about what you and Solomon discussed before he left?"

I take a healthy gulp of my wine and nod in agreement. "Yes. Some of the things he told me are confusing. At least now I understand why Momma sent me here instead of Taliah or Brianna. There is no way she would endanger them the way she has me." I take another mouthful of wine and swallow it in several gulps, slowly.

"Your mother didn't send you here to hurt you. She sent you here because you belong here and you deserved to know the truth about yourself."

"But I still wonder why she never said anything or, at the very least, why did she treat me differently than she did everyone else? It's not like being born was my fault, nor was it my fault that I had the father I had."

"I can't answer those questions for you, but I think the longer you search for answers, the more likely you'll find them. Be patient. That's all I can say about that."

I understand that no one can speak for my mother but my mother. Unfortunately, she's dead, so all I have to go on are the words of other people and her diary. My mind returns to Solomon and our argument.

"May I ask you something?"

"Sure."

"Did you know what was going to happen to me when we met in your office?"

He pauses before taking another sip of his drink. "Yes I did."

"Why didn't you tell me?" I implore softly.

"I couldn't. It's against the rules. Even now, there are details about the Passage that Solomon is supposed to tell you. It's his right to do so."

"I don't get it. I almost lost my life in those woods. And you all just move about your lives like it's a common occurrence."

"Around here it is."

His statement stops me cold. How many others have gone through this and ended up at a bar similar to the one I'm leaning on and asked these same questions?

"Did everyone know? More specifically, did Perry know?

I know the answer of course. I'm just having a hard time believing it.

"Yes, he also knew. I'm sorry, Mika. I really am but this is apart of who we are. Give Solomon a chance. You won't regret it. Besides, you kind of have to complete the Passage anyway since you're a hybrid too."

"Yeah, Solomon mentioned something about that before he left. So I asked Solomon for an apology from the alien who attacked me. Do you think he'll give it to me?"

The judge tops off his glass. "Did you now?" His lips twitch slightly.

"Yes. I'm still not sure why I insisted on it. I just knew right in that moment, it's what I wanted."

The judge's rumbling burst of laughter echoes throughout the kitchen. If I wasn't such a mess, I would be laughing too. He wipes the tears of mirth from his eyes with a handkerchief he pulls out of is pocket.

"Your request is not as odd as you or even Solomon thinks it is. You should ask the welcome committee what their demands were when they were going through the Passage. I would dare say your request is quite tame compared to theirs."

"Really?"

"Yes. This part of the Passage is different for every throuple who's going through it. Humans who are chosen usually don't have any demands. But Abrielarans certainly do. I haven't heard of anyone who hasn't. However, keep in mind that although demands are common, apologies are not. If it were up to Solomon, you would have your apology in a heartbeat. But Brielarans are sticklers for tradition and will not apologize just because you think you are owed. I wish it were different, but that is the way it is."

Figures.

"Solomon told me as much. All I can do is try, I guess. I told him I would complete the phases with him, but first, I needed an apology. But you're saying the same thing, which means I most likely won't get it and will have to complete the phases anyway."

"Well now, that's not exactly true. It may be hard to get, but not impossible. Just in case you don't though, you'll need to come to terms with it so you can move on. I'm proud of you for asking for an apology. You deserve one but just understand that is not how our culture works."

"I'll try."

Although I say the words, I'm not quite sure if they are true. What does it mean to be a part of this community? If it's sheltered from the outside world, how am I supposed to function outside of it?

The judge and I stay up until early afternoon discussing my mother and how I came to be. I realize that I never knew my mother at all. Not that I thought I ever did, but I did think coming here was going to enlighten me just a bit.

Maybe it has but now I'm positive I don't know myself either. Some things are beginning to make sense, such as my penchant for aggression and my tendency for the dramatic. According to the judge, these are Brielaran traits. Of course, humans have them too, but Brielarans usually take it to a whole new level. At least until they complete the Passage and calm down.

After all the talk about Abrielara, Brielarans, and the possible consequences of not completing the cycle, I still want my apology. I may not get it, but I will not stop insisting I have it. It's in my best interest to complete the phases, even if I don't have all the answers or can't stand the Brielaran or the human I must complete it with.

By noon, I can't keep my eyes open anymore and I make my way to bed. I convinced the judge I was fine and he could go home whenever he was ready. Solomon isn't coming back to apologize or continue our argument. What's surprising is I'm not quite sure how I feel about that.

Chapter Ten

Mika

The next few days pass in relative peace except for the daily call I receive from Solomon at four o'clock. No pleasantries or update requests about my health. Just—

"Have you changed your mind?" he asks gruffly. Obviously still all up in his feelings.

"Nope." My response is clipped and quick. His rapid response to my answer is a dial tone.

This goes on for the rest of the week. He doesn't come by. He just sits on his porch from nine p.m. to midnight, watching my house. I'm not sure what he expects to see. But I can promise you, nothing is going on over here but pure sexual frustration with a triple shot of rage.

Every night I either relive the chase and the probe in my nightmares, or I dream about Solomon and his forked tongue between my legs. Sometimes he does more than lick me, and sometimes, I don't dream of Solomon at all.

Sometimes I dream of that... thing that attacked me. This confuses me because I don't understand why or how that creature can generate reactions of heat and desire in me when it hurt me so badly.

Cold showers don't help and neither does the alcohol. I'm just about ready to give in because I can only take so much more of this shit. But my stubborn pride won't allow it. I become more agitated and antsy by the day. I can't sit still to save my life.

I find myself mindlessly pacing the house. I'm not sure if it has anything to do with the phase Solomon talked about or if I am just having a fit of cabin fever. I've got to get out of the house. I could use a distraction that doesn't involve Solomon or his Brielaran. Maybe I can enlist the girls to go curtain shopping with me tomorrow. Maybe, if I can't see him, then he'll stop haunting my dreams.

"I can't believe you want to cover those gorgeous windows with curtains." Jeana shakes her head in disbelief. "Do you realize how many yards of fabric you're going to need?"

"It doesn't have to be curtains, Jeana. It can be shades. I was thinking of getting some of the automated kind. What do you think?" I hold up some color swatches.

"Personally, I think you should just give in and then you won't have to worry about covering your windows." Becca shuffles through the swatches, obviously bored with the selection.

"You do have a point, but if I give in, then it means he wins, and I can't have that."

Dyana looks at me like I've lost my mind.

"Um, you do understand you'll have to give in at some point, right? This is just how this works. Leaving without completing the Passage impacts you too. At least, we think it does." She returns the curtain swatch to the wall display.

"Yeah, that's what I'm told. By the way, I have a question for you guys. I asked it before but ya'll ignored it."

I look at all four of them, placing my hand on my hip. "Why in the world did you all not tell me what was going on...or what was going to happen? Are you guys held to the same laws of the land that Perry and the judge are?"

I put air quotes around *laws of the land*. I look around at the welcome committee expecting definitive answers.

"You could have at least said—hey, nice to meet you but you may want to high tail it out of town before some crazy alien decides to choose you. That bit of knowledge would have been helpful."

"We would've if we could have, Mika. Jeana and I understand more than anyone what you're going through. Becca and Dyana at least knew it was coming. We didn't. We're human chosen by hybrids." Kimberly looks at Jeana and she nods in agreement.

"Yeah, but you're right. I think it would help you if you heard our story too. How about we head over to the Cork and suck down a couple of bottles of wine while we do that?"

"Ooh. I can definitely get down with that." Becca is already halfway to the door before the rest of us get our feet moving.

The Cork is a very chic winery in the center of town. Today is a gorgeous sunny day and we chose to take advantage of the patio garden. After placing our order, I wanted to get right to it.

"So, I'm interested in hearing about your experience when you first got here."

I want to find out if it was anything like mine. I'm having a hard time believing that no one thought to drop a hint or anything.

"Well, Jeana and I didn't have a welcome committee or guidance whatsoever. We stumbled upon Abrielara by accident and absolutely fell in love with the place even though no one would talk to us. But I guess since we had each other, we didn't notice all that much."

"Yeah, Kim and I were always somewhat oblivious to our surroundings. Trust me, coming to Abrielara removed that habit pretty quick once things started happening." Jeana looks at me with empathy. "We totally understand where you're coming from, being hit with all of this out of the blue. Thankfully, Kim and I were chosen at the same time, so we had each other to talk to about it. Even though we experienced the phases separately, we still had each other. I can't imagine going through this alone...like you have." She takes another sip of wine and then immediately refills her glass.

"The night of our chase, we were staying at The Pettigrew, a little bed and breakfast near the center of town. We were up late, watching movies and eating popcorn. I got up to go to the bathroom, and when I came back, there were these two beings in our living room. Jeana was completely oblivious. She had no idea they were there. At first, I was frozen and unsure of what to do. They didn't realize I was behind them. But once they did and turned to look at me, I let out a scream, yelling at Jeana to run."

"We weren't thinking all that straight and ran in separate directions. One went after me, the other after Kim." Jeana whispers, pretty much to herself.

The table is quiet. I'm reliving my experience. I'm sure the ladies are doing the same.

Kim clears her throat and gives a short laugh. "When I

saw them, I thought for sure that they were vampires. The word alien never entered my mind."

"What did you think they were, Jeana?" Her eyes pop up to mine.

"Honestly, I didn't think that far. I was hoping it was all just a terrible dream or I had gotten a hold of some bad alcohol if that's even possible. Instead, we woke up in our rooms, in our respective beds, as if nothing had ever happened. Except the burning was definitely real." Her face scrunched up, remembering the pain.

"Yes. But we did not suffer as badly as you did," Jeana says sympathetically. "We were in our beds with two strange men in our suite. As soon as the pain hit, they were right there. They didn't wait for us to ask or for permission. They just got right to work."

"Thank God." Kim shakes her head at the memory. "I can say that we didn't take too kindly to the idea that we couldn't leave and were bound to someone we hadn't even laid eyes on. But once the heat hit, we didn't care. We just wanted it sated. We didn't have much time to give it a whole lot of thought."

"Yep, ultimately, when everything was explained, we were very forgiving. We had already fallen for them by then. And here we are."

I feel a little foolish for being so stubborn in my insistence an apology.

"Do you regret any of it?"

"I don't. I hate that we had to be scared to death and experience that awful probe, but overall, I'm happy because I have the man of my dreams. I have my kids. I would never have found him had we not decided to take that detour outside of town." Jeana shrugs her shoulders.

"I agree. For me, the end result justified the means. We absolutely love it here. The people, the atmosphere, the sense of family and connection it's hard to find anywhere else. I think you should give it a try. Give Solomon a shot. You may find you like him and that you like it here." Kim offers a small smile.

"Perry told me you're one of us already. Your family is already here, Mika. All you have to do now is complete the phases so you can have the full experience. I promise you, if he could have, Solomon would have done things differently. He knew the time had come for him to fulfill his duty. He was just waiting on you. You guys would make such a good match. Where is your head right now with everything?" Dyana asks gently.

"Yeah, Solomon told me I was one of you. The judge explained a lot of things to me. My mother told me nothing but we never got along, so no surprise there. I know I have to complete the phases. I have no choice. What about your experience, Dyana? What was the Passage like for you?"

"Well, we're taught about the phases, but the true experience is never explained in detail. They want the process to seem as natural as possible, and they want us to have our own experiences. An experience not influenced by other stories.

"The Brielaran likes to incite fear, likes to experience the adrenaline rush that comes from fear. He wants to physically run after what he wants and take from it. Showing whatever he's chosen that they're in charge. They're animalistic that way. The act of conquering something they want or crave is engrained into their psyche," Dyana explains.

"I gave into it quite easily. I already knew Perry chose me. He just couldn't say the words to me before the chase. But it didn't stop me from being scared when he showed up at my house out of the blue. He just stood there, on the front lawn staring at my window. It was like the middle of the fucking night and cold. I yelled at him to take his crazy ass home and he said nothing. Of course, up until that point, I'd never seen Perry's Brielaran before, but I knew it was him as soon as I saw him. He just stood there. Creeped me out. Once I realized what was happening, I kicked it into high gear. H was still standing in the front yard when I snuck out the back and started bookin' it. I wanted him to catch me but I knew he wanted the chase. To make it easy for him was to disrespect him, so I gave it all I could until I couldn't run anymore. I'd been so intent on my run that I didn't notice I was headed straight for the lake."

She stops talking and smiles at me a little. "By the time I realized it, he was gaining on me and the fear had me treading water. I couldn't swim. I sank like a big thick rock."

"Dyana," I whisper.

"Yeah, thankfully Xens, Perry's Brielaran, knew I couldn't swim. He drug me out of the lake, and once he confirmed I was okay, he started the probe. Nothing asked, nothing explained. It is quite alarming, even when you know what's going to happen. But we were taught not to fight it so you could get through it quicker. So, I didn't."

She looks across the table at Becca. She shakes her head and points at her. "But this one over here though, she did exactly what we're told not to do."

"Hey, what can I say? I never did what I was told, and I didn't plan on starting then either. My story starts similarly to Dyana's. I knew what I was taught in school and no more. Michael and I had a rocky relationship at that time. I liked him. He liked me but neither one of us was going to admit it. I was pretty positive that he had chosen me, but I didn't have solid proof officially until he showed up for me. I'd just come in from a day at the spa with Dyana when I saw him. I had settled into my hammock and was two winks away from calling the hogs when he said run. I looked up at him and told him no."

"And he let you?" I ask, astonished.

Unbelievable. I ran through God knows what on command and this chick just told him no. I never thought to say no.

"Sweetie, there was no *letting* me about it. I told him that I don't run, especially not after I had just finished a full day of body pampering. He kept repeating himself, saying run every chance he got."

She starts laughing. "He was getting so pissed. I was laughing at him and he just got angrier. I finally decided it was in my best interest to run when he screamed at me. It sounded like something straight out of the depths of hell. Whatever was associated with that dream, I wanted no part of it. So I said, fuck it, but you're paying for a whole new mani-pedi as soon as I was able to make it back to the salon. Then I took off."

"It never occurred to me to say no," I admit.

"Oh, trust me. Fighting like that was not smart. He made me pay for it by not going easy on me as soon as he caught me. I left my mark on him too, but he was beyond furious. In case you haven't noticed, Brielarans are uppity creatures. We are warriors by god!" She says, shaking her fist in the air. "Feared by the ruthless! Exalted by the small ones beneath our feet and strong because of the numbers of our army!" Becca pounds her fist on the table in time with her little speech. I am shocked. "No one dares question our motives because only we know best!"

Evidently, that little speech is one they have heard before. Her story was a little hard to believe, considering my experience, but I also wasn't born and raised here.

"Hey, it's true. There are two things you never tell a

Brielaran. Never tell one no and the second is to tell him what to do. Remember those two rules and your life will be peaches and cream from here on out. It just so happens I hate peaches, so I don't care if things get a little rough sometimes." She pops a grape in her mouth, satisfied with her explanation of the Abrielaran race.

"Well, I know it seems silly, but I asked that his Brielaran give me an apology. He pretty much told me it wasn't going to happen. He hasn't spoken to me since, other than to ask me if I've changed my mind every day. Which I haven't. So here we are."

I suck down the rest of my wine.

Becca lets out a whoop. "Seriously?" I nod to confirm and then she lets loose. "That is fucking awesome! You're an Abrielaran, alright." She is so tickled. It isn't long before the rest of the table is cackling right along with her.

"How are you so sure?" I ask curiously.

"Think about it. A big alien chases you, scares the breath out of you, and now you are demanding that same alien apologize. Brielarans and Abrielarans alike have a flair for the dramatic. Especially when they feel they have been done wrong. That backbone you have is all Brielaran, sweetie. Just saying." She shrugs unapologetically.

"I have to admit. That is pretty awesome. What did he say when you demanded an apology?" Dyana leans toward me, chuckling over her glass.

"He stomped out like a child. He calls me every day at four, asking if I've changed my mind. I say no, and he hangs the phone up in my face."

I snicker a little and the ladies continue to laugh that much harder. "I guess it is kind of funny. All I want is an apology. Is that too much to ask for?" I look around the table.

"That is too much to ask from a Brielaran who thinks he's

done nothing wrong. What you have to understand is that Brielarans don't apologize for their behavior when what they've done is in the name of duty. Especially for something that they see as a necessity. If you get Lux to apologize, please record it. I've got to see it for myself." Becca explains.

"Lux? Who's Lux?"

The ladies calm down and stare at me strangely. "Lux is Solomon's Brielaran," Jeana says.

"He has a name?" It never dawned on me that creature would have a name.

"Yes. All hybrid males have a Brielaran that's a separate being. Females are different. For males, when the Brielaran takes over, the hybrid has no control. At least not until the phases are complete. Males are physically stronger than females. Their bodies are built for protecting and physical labor. Females are mentally stronger. Their gifts vary, but the tentacles you see in males will eventually be absorbed back into the body long before the female hits puberty."

I'm stunned into silence. So much information, I'm not sure how to even respond.

"Every male is born into this world fully aware of the Brielaran they host. They are separate but one. The Abrielaran never physically transitions into the Brielaran until the Passage begins. Until then, the Abrielaran is in control and the Brielaran is present in personality only. Brielarans have personalities separate from their host like any other male on this planet. They make decisions based on the Brielaran way of life. Keep that in mind any time you are dealing with Lux."

Dyana's soft explanation gives me a lot to think about.

"Are you saying my request for an apology was unreasonable?" I look at each woman around the table.

"Not if you honestly feel you need it. There's a reason

why you felt the need to demand it. So now that you have. Stick to it. Don't waffle. Lux will feel like he's won," Becca advises. "But let me warn you now, Lux can be a straight-up booty hole when he wants to be. That's what makes this whole thing funny. I hope you receive your apology, but don't be surprised if you don't get it."

"Yep, that's the tune that's being sung on the regular around here," I mumble to myself.

"However, you asking for an apology isn't entirely farfetched. Every Abrielaran female that I know of has demanded compensation for the pain she was put through," Dyana explains.

"Such as?"

"Well, during the heat stage I demanded that Perry take care of me. After being in the lake, I got a chest cold. Perry was about to go away to college and then medical school. So I insisted he get a little bedside manner practice in. He had to feed me, change my sheets, basically wait on me hand and foot until I got better. Then he had to find a way to treat me twice a month while he was away. I didn't care what it was, but he needed to do something."

"What did he do?"

"She was getting something every day. Chocolate, flowers, jewelry. It got to a point where she didn't even have to ask for anything. He was bringing her something every time he came around."

"Wow."

"Yep. I eventually got tired of it and told him to stop. Believe it or not, there is only so much chocolate you can eat before you've had enough. Becca was much more demanding than I was."

"I deserve every bit of luxury that man can afford and lucky for me he can afford a lot."

"What were your demands?" I ask.

"Since he ruined a perfectly good mani-pedi, he had to pay every time I wanted one. At first he tried to give me one himself but the man can't color in between the lines of a coloring book. Forget about keeping polish off my toes."

"Isn't your husband like an architect or something?"

"Yep but a painter he is not. Anyway, since he couldn't give me one himself, I insisted he pay out the ass for it. I wanted to be treated in different spas all over the world. The first one was in Paris, Madrid, then Johannesburg, London, Rome, Dubai...those are the ones I can think of off the top of my head. He was treating me until I got pregnant then picked it back up again after I had my babies. The man is still paying for choosing me today. Making me run in the woods and ruining a perfectly good pedicure."

"That sounds expensive."

"Oh it was. I was trying to see if there was a bottom to his pockets, but I haven't found it yet. I wanted to find a way to inflict some kind of pain on him and I knew burning through money was the best way to do it."

Trying to smother a giggle, wine goes down the wrong pipe and I choke a little on it a little. "Sounds like Solomon is getting off light with my request for an apology."

"Yes but you are asking for something that's hard to give." Dyana reminds me.

"I think that's what makes it good. I should have thought of that," Becca says.

"I'm sorry we couldn't tell you what was happening. We weren't completely sure if you were being chosen until we saw how Solomon responded to you that first day we took a walk around town." Dyana squeezes my hand.

"And even then, we still couldn't say anything because once we realized that you were chosen, we knew it was the right of the one who chose you to explain things," Kim explained.

"I wish it could have been different but I understand," I admit and smile at each of them. "You guys have been a big help to me."

God knows my mother wasn't. Naturally, I'm not going to admit that out loud.

"We're glad you're staying, at least for a little while. And now that everything is out in the open, we can talk about whatever we want." Becca gives me a half smile.

"I'm beginning to understand secrecy is the name of the game around here. I'm just glad I have a welcome committee to talk to about these things...now that we can talk about it."

I rub the back of my neck, the agitated restlessness is creeping back in. This shit is getting old. My hands shake and I ball them up in my lap.

What in the hell?

Trying to ignore it, I ask the group another question.

"Well, it looks like I'm already off to a rocky start." I look around the table. "I guess everyone's situation is unique but the same in some way."

"Yep. That's a nice way to think about it. Just remember that the sooner you complete the phases, the sooner you can get on with your life. Like designing more shoes. I'm going into the final stages of withdrawal. You've got to start a new line or add some to the ones you already have."

"Okay, Becca, I got it." I smile at her.

My scalp is crawling again and although it is a nice warm day, chills run up and down my body. I look around nervously. Not sure if I should ask the ladies what's going on around here. But luckily, I don't have to, I look up and all the ladies are watching me with curious intensity.

"Mika, are you okay?" Kim reaches over and puts her hand on my shoulder.

"I honestly don't know if I am or not."

My stomach takes a sudden turn, not enough for me to empty it, but just enough for me to clutch it aggressively.

"Tell us what you're feeling. I bet we can already guess what it is, though," Becca remarks nonchalantly as she pours more wine into her glass.

"Agitation and I'm antsy. Restless. I'm not sleeping well. And just now, my stomach started cramping—"

I watch the ladies look around us as if expecting to see someone. I start looking around too, curious as to what I might find. They turn back around to me.

"Well, you're in your heat cycle. You're cramping, most likely because Solomon is around here somewhere. You've been agitated and restless because you should be consummating right now," Becca enlightens me.

She turns around again just when heat licks up my body like flames from a bonfire. I've gotta get out of here.

I grab my purse and lay some cash on the table.

"I'm gonna head home. My head is starting to pound something fierce. I'll give you guys a call tomorrow."

"I highly doubt it, but it's nice to have goals." Becca grins and finger waves at me as I turn and head for the gate facing the street. The rest of the ladies say their goodbyes, but I barely notice.

I don't have the energy to respond. I just want to go home and lie down. I don't even have the energy to enjoy the abundance of colorful climbing rose bushes I pass on my way out. I make a right on the sidewalk and slam right into the formidable chest of Solomon, smacking the breath right out of me.

Chapter Eleven

Solomon

I grab her arms to steady her and place her a good arm's length away from me. I had no idea where I was headed. Lux is pretty much guiding my steps these days. I shouldn't be surprised. Now that I'm face to face with Mika, I understand why I was led to the center of town when I don't have any business here.

It's getting harder and harder to hold Lux back. He's pretty angry with me right now. By his book, we should have already consummated our bond several times over.

Standing this close to her now has me clutching the fence with one hand to make sure I don't touch her again. But god, how I want to. I've missed seeing her. Especially after forming the habit of licking her down twice a day to now not even seeing her at all. It's eating me alive.

One look into her eyes tells me she is in no better shape than I am.

"Mika." I stuff my hands in my pockets.

"Solomon." Her aloof tone kind of ticks me off.

I watch her eyes roam over me, and mine do the same to her. My tongue hungrily runs over my lips, craving a particular flavor I haven't had in several days. A flash of the last time I had my head between her legs lights up my mind. I suppress a groan hoping to stuff the memory away. But my dick refuses to let it go, thickening, hardening, and aching for her.

"Consummate," Lux says.

Like I need a reminder of what the next step is. It's all I can fucking think about. I take a deep breath and another step back. I drop my hands in front of my erection.

"Are you here to give me an apology?" she asks haughtily.

"No," I answer without thinking about it.

Her only response is to sidestep me and continue down the sidewalk like I was no more than a wad of bubble gum on the pavement. How dare she dismiss me like that.

I follow right behind her, fuming as her fine ass sways in those tight-ass jeans she's wearing. Lux keeps pushing forward, and I keep pushing him back in a steady shoving contest. I'm running out of time. I plan on following her home and hoping I can talk her into forgetting the apology for now. I'm sick of dealing with the consequences of prolonging our inevitable consummation.

Instead of keeping to the sidewalk, Mika makes a sharp right into the farmer's outdoor market. She grabs a bag and floats from booth to booth, filling it with fruit and vegetables. My arms stay crossed to ensure I can keep them to myself. I try to keep a safe distance behind her.

Naturally, I'm stopped by patients and their families to talk, or just people of the community. But my eyes always keep her in my line of sight. Every so often, she rolls her head around her shoulders or clutches the side of her stomach. I see the agitation on her face; she is undoubtedly fighting the heat. Just as I am.

I don't understand why she won't give in. Well, actually, I do understand, but if she considered what was at stake here, she would just get this part of it out of the way. Then she can have her apology. I thought for sure she would make the right decision if given the choice, but instead, she is dragging this out when we don't have the time to spare.

"Hello, Dr. Christiansen. I haven't seen you around our local haunts lately. What's been keeping you?"

A hand reaches out and touches my arm. I look down at the sculpted nails painted bubble gum pink, and I follow the arm until my eyes meet up with a face of a girl I don't remember seeing. Ever.

"We do not have time for this shit!" Lux growls.

"Don't tell me! Tell her!"

I remove her hand from my arm. "Have we met?" I ask, doing my best to be polite but not interested.

I look around her for Mika and find her standing by the canned jelly booth. The look in her eyes can only be described as murderous. For once, I don't think she wants to murder me. This, of course, pleases me to no end but we can't afford that complication right now.

"Of course you know me, silly. Don't you remember last summer at Brady's? You and I spent a bit of time in the hot tub?" She gives me a slow seductive smile and moves her painted nails up my arm. "If you don't remember me, then I'm positive Lux does. Maybe you should ask Lux if he wants to come out and play." Her hand lays flat on my chest and she leans into my ear. I don't give her time to say whatever she is about to say because I don't care to hear it.

"No, I can't say that I do, and I can promise you that Lux isn't interested either. In case you haven't heard, we've chosen someone."

I look over at Mika, who is now at the seafood booth, pretending not to watch me. I return my attention to whoever this chick is and remove her hand from my chest. "So, if you don't mind, I'm going to get back to her."

"Oh—"

When I make it back to Mika, she doesn't say a word or acknowledge my presence. I continue to silently stalk her, and she continues to ignore me.

We make our way around the market. She grabs a bouquet of tulips and pays for them on the way out. Not sure why she's paying for tulips when she has a yard full of them.

We continue to walk in silence. I don't walk too closely behind her, but I can tell I'm not far enough behind to suit her. She's eating up the sidewalk like she's walking on hot pavement barefoot. But my legs are longer than hers, so I'm having no problem keeping up.

One block from our neighborhood, she crosses the street and walks into the pharmacy. I decide to wait this one out. Just in case she's picking up personal items that she would rather I not see.

I lean my back against the brick building and watch the shoppers make their way in and out of the shops. After an eternity, I check my watch and see only ten minutes have passed. I decide to go in and check on her. We need to quit pussyfooting around.

"Today is the fucking day!" Lux roars inside my head.

"Calm the fuck down.. All in due time, my friend. All in due time".

My voice is calm but I'm hanging on to my humanity by a solitary thread.

We are out of time.

I walk into the pharmacy and head straight to her. I can't see her from the door, but I sense her. She's in the back by the body wash. I turn down the aisle she is on to see her back facing me.

"It's time to go." I can hear Lux's gravelly voice laced with mine. It isn't going to be long now before he forces the issue and shifts completely.

"Then go. I'm not ready yet. No one told you to follow me anyway."

She doesn't turn around to look at me. She returns the bottle to the shelf and picks up another one.

"Where you go, I go and right now, we're leaving." I reach over and grab her arm, only for her to yank it from my grasp.

"I'm not going anywhere until I'm ready. If you want to go, then go," she says a little more forcefully.

She walks down another aisle, and I follow her, somewhat aware of the concerned stares we're receiving. Urgency pricks my skin like tiny needles, injecting my body with agitation.

"I'm done with this shit!"

"Lux, hold it in, man!"

"Mika—please do not make me do this here. Let's go. Now."

I work hard to keep my voice calm. She walks down another aisle, ignoring me completely. Leisurely shopping as if she has all of the time in the world. This infuriates us both. Lux is pressing down on me and I'm trying my best to keep us both in check.

"Chosen One."

Lux's voice carries a lot farther than I thought it would, and I don't hear myself anymore. She jerks her head in my direction. Fear radiates in her eyes and she turns and runs down a different aisle, closer to the back of the store. I follow with purposeful steps. When she runs out of space to go, she turns and watches me approach.

However, when I am only two aisles away, fear is no longer in her eyes. Determination is written all over her. I see the edge of her irises shimmer with the same iridescent blue I saw the other day. But this doesn't slow us down. In fact, it makes Lux that much more anxious to get to her. Excitement is boiling through our blood just at her scent. I feel her heat from here.

At this point, Lux takes over completely, and my humanity is shoved into the backseat. I barely notice the change because my focus is completely on her face. So much so that I barely notice that she raises her hand in front of her. She doesn't say anything but it's obvious she wants us to stop. Of course, we don't stop because Lux takes direction from no one, especially not from the female he has chosen.

Coming from her palms are waves of energy that I can only see because Lux is in control. Before I can ask what it is, we are put to a dead stop less than a foot in front of her. Lux's head bounces back and I feel the vibration through my body as he makes contact with the energy field and he's thrown onto his back with force. Lux doesn't even groan but my face feels like it's shattered into a million pieces.

I can hear Mika's feet as she runs away from us. Lux doesn't waste another second. He runs after her. A tentacle extends, ripping a hole in my shirt, and wraps it around her waist. Tugging her back toward the arched alcove in the back corner of the room.

"Let me go, you asshole," she wheezes out, grabbing at one of Lux's tentacles that found its way around her throat. When we're in the alcove, he shoves her up against the wall.

"*Come on, Lux, this is not necessary. Let her go. She was just protecting herself. I doubt she even knew she had the power to do that.*"

"*Doesn't matter, Solomon. I'm tired of waiting. Today is the day we consummate, whether she wants to or not.*"

"*Lux, I will not allow you to force her.*"

"It isn't up to you." He snickers. "You've had plenty of time to convince her to agree. Now it's my turn."

"I said, let me go!" She screams out when Lux loosens his grip on her throat and presses her shoulders and her hands to the wall. Her feet are flailing around, trying to kick him but not making contact or at least not hard enough to make a difference.

"No."

I don't think I have to say Lux took great joy in telling her that.

"I hate you so much, you cowardly low-class—"

"Don't care," Lux interrupts her with a sing-song voice. Taunting her.

He's such a smart ass.

To emphasize his point, Lux leans into her, ripping my shirt completely open as he wraps an appendage around her waist. He wraps another one around each of her legs, spreading them and bringing them up even with his waist.

"No!" Mika yells at him with bass in her voice. Her nostrils flare as she exhales. Her chest moves up and down as she pants out weighted breaths. Her pebbled nipples tell me that her emotions are not all based on fear.

"I don't take orders from you. I chose you. I've been patient enough," he grinds out.

Lux presses his body into hers until he is nose-to-nose with her. Their eyes are drilling into each other with so much anger it's palpable. Rapid, raspy breathing is the only thing that can be heard. The moment the thirst waters my tongue and the heat between us burns white hot, there's no doubt what is coming next.

"Not here, Lux," I yell in an attempt to put a stop to this madness.

Lux ignores me, shields his teeth, and dives in. His mouth

meets hers and she welcomes it. I know she welcomes it because she moans with what sounds like hunger and relief. She kisses him back. Lux grinds on her, and she grinds back.

The aggressive energy laced with frustration surrounds us but combusts into heated desire. Her eyes are completely blue now, glowing in the height of her heat. The grinding turns into frantic dry humping, only I'm not sure you can call it dry humping.

She is already hot and dripping wet. She feels so good, and I can just imagine how she feels inside. The scent of her heat drives Lux to almost a manic state. He's close to losing his damn mind.

Lux growls loudly and is ready to come in our fucking pants. Mika is so deep into her heat she's high. Literally high. Her moans are lascivious and loud. Lux doesn't have to hang onto her anymore because she is hanging onto us for dear life. Her fingers are entangled in his long hair. Her legs are wrapped around his waist. His hips jouncing to a rhythm only she and Lux are aware of.

If I don't do something quickly, Lux will have her naked and fucking her against this wall in front of everyone in this pharmacy. More importantly, after it is all said and done, Mika will hate me most of all. As much as I want to complete the consummation, it cannot happen now. Not here.

"Stop this now Lux. This is not the place. We need privacy to do this right."

Lux doesn't respond but removes his lips from hers only after removing the shield from his teeth and biting her lip first. He continues to grind against her wantonly. The anger returns to her eyes, and I can see she's angry at herself for giving in. Lux turns her head and licks her from her neck to her hairline. She grits her teeth and tries to move her head away from him.

"All this should just teach you that I am in charge. Not you. If I wanted to, I could complete the consummation stage right here, right now, and you couldn't stop me. As a matter of fact, you wouldn't want to. You would beg me to keep going and scream my name by the end of it. Keep that in mind the next time you want to give me orders."

Lux finally lets go of her and walks away.

"You just had to be a dick about it, didn't you? Damn it, Lux. You're making this harder, not easier."

"She will submit to me."

Walking out of the alcove, I see that we are surrounded by a crowd and we have to walk through them to exit the store. The stares are full of questions and obvious concern for Mika. So, to put their fears to rest, Lux gives them one word that can sum up this situation.

"Heat," he announces with his head held high. Obviously not feeling one bit of shame for the spectacle he made of himself.

"Oh." The crowd responds and nods as one collective unit and then disperses to go about their shopping. Apparently, just knowing what all the commotion was about was enough for them to move on with their lives.

I, on the other hand, want to turn around and see about Mika. I'm sure this is the sole reason why Lux won't allow me to gain control and insists on heading home. He thinks he's doing me a solid by walking away. If it were up to him, he would already be balls deep inside of her right now, getting ready for round two.

"Tonight, Solomon. Tonight she's ours. No more waiting."

"Fine, but she wants and deserves an apology from you. I think you should give it to her. Especially after the stunt you just pulled."

"I apologize to no one for doing my duty."

His emphatic contemptuous refusal to do what he should angers me.

"Well, while you're doing your duty...keep in mind we would like to complete the process. Which for me means wanting her to choose us in the end. She isn't just anybody. You keep acting like a dick, she won't choose us and then what? Just doing your duty could cost us everything. Get your fucking life together. I care about her. You care about her. Quit being a dick and act like it."

I didn't realize that we had stopped walking. It's been a long time since I've talked to Lux in this way. We normally get along well, but he's pushing my limits lately. Lux may still be in control but I have him thinking. For once, at least.

"You're right, Solomon. I was overcome with heat. We will make this right tonight."

"You're serious right now? You aren't planning something sick, are you? Because I swear, Lux—"

"I told you we will make this right tonight, and that is what I mean. You plan your part, and I will take care of mine. I'm tired. We must rest."

Lux may be a pompous dickhead, but he isn't a liar. If he says we'll make this right, then we will. I feel better than I have since before Mika even showed up here. Now, if we can convince Mika to forgive us, there may be hope for us after all.

Mika

Embarrassment is not a word that even comes close to describing what I'm experiencing right now. My braids hide most of my face and the hot seething tears running down it. I kneel on the floor, trying to gather my dignity and the items I dropped. Most of the crowd that gathered to watch has disappeared, but it didn't stop the intense mortification from pressing down on me.

I can't believe I gave in to the urges that have consumed my thoughts every day and night since I woke up to Solomon and his forked tongue. I'm angry with myself for proving to him how right he was about who's in charge.

I've insisted on getting an apology before completing the consummation stage. However, there I was only moments ago, humping the alien who hurt me like he was the last person I was gonna fuck—ever.

Of course, I'll most likely give in long before I get my apology. The word heat does not adequately describe the chemical-like feeling that courses through your body with the images that float through your brain.

No matter how much you say you don't want to...you realize that, more than anything...you want to. You can't help yourself. It must be what an addict goes through. Constantly needing and wanting something you know isn't good for you but can't wait to get your hands on it anyway. It becomes a necessity in your life that you never knew you needed before now.

Just coming to terms with all of that does not remove the questions I have about myself. The energy field that I conjured up without conscious knowledge of how to do so adds truth to the notion that I am one of them. But how in the fuck did I do that? The only thought in my head at the time was I wanted him to stop. And I was fucking angry. I could feel the rage boiling in my body. Reminded me of how I felt during the probe. Liquid. Hot. Rage.

I look at my hands, wondering where did all that power come from. Was it natural instinct that caused me to put my hands up the way I did? The force at which he hit whatever I pushed out was formidable but he got up like it was nothing. At least it slowed him down for a hot second. A lot of good it did me, though. Too bad I didn't know I had this power before the chase. I could have done something about that awful probe.

Even still, knowing there is something unusual going on with me and maybe Solomon was speaking the truth about belonging here, doesn't make me happy. I don't understand any of it, and neither does anybody else. Finding out that I'm a hybrid no one has ever heard of makes me feel more alone. I don't belong, and quite possibly, I'm being controlled. I have no answers about myself, and evidently, no one else has the answers either.

I'm exhausted with all of this. This time in Abrielara has taken my former life and turned it into a dream, a fantasy. I haven't sketched a shoe design since the first night. Yes, I know I'm supposed to be on vacation, but I'm always thinking about design. I dream about design. I live and breathe design. This behavior is totally not like me. I have been consumed by the life here and the mystery of my existence.

It's like the world outside of Abrielara doesn't exist anymore. Not even my sisters. Now I'm being guided by urges I don't want and didn't ask for. I have to make it through this so I can leave. If I can rush through this final phase, I can go back to my life as it was before and thank God for its predictability.

Yes, that's what I'll do. Finish the phases, then as soon as the exit for Wilson's Creek comes into view—I'm taking it. Fuck the apology.

From what I've experienced of Lux, I'll be waiting until Doomsday to get it. It wouldn't be a real apology anyway. Obviously, he isn't sorry about what happened and would do it again if given the opportunity. He made that quite clear in the pharmacy.

"Here, honey, let me help you with that. In the meantime, why don't you clean up your face a little bit." A hand wrapped in Kleenex shows up in front of my face.

"Thank you."

I take it graciously, turning my head and discreetly blow my nose. The motherfucker bit my lip. I run my tongue over the tiny puncture wounds. They'll heal quickly but that isn't the point. He fucking bit me.

When I'm sure my face is presentable, I turn back and all of my stuff that was splayed out on the floor has been picked up. Even my purse is gone. I look around frantically for my purse because that is the only thing I would recognize since I didn't see the lady who gave me the Kleenex.

"Over here, Mika."

At the photo center is a petite distinguished woman with gray hair in a pixie haircut. She has a pair of green reading glasses, with a peacock on the edges, perched at the end of her nose.

"How do you know my name?" I ask when I make it to her counter. Even though I am somewhat new to town, I still haven't met that many people.

"Oh, everyone knows who you are," Nancy, according to her name tag, says flippantly. "That heat is something else, isn't it? As soon as we heard that Lux finally chose someone, the entire town was ecstatic. It's about time that wild child calms down. It is about time he fulfills his duty. We cannot wait until you two complete the Passage." She grins at me.

"Um..." All I can do is watch this nice lady bag up my purchases.

"Oh, and don't worry about that incident earlier. You are

in a town full of folks who had to go through something similar."

"Well, it didn't seem like it considering everyone was staring like we were the afternoon matinee," I mumble awkwardly.

"Well, it would be one of the hottest matinees we've seen in this pharmacy, I can tell you that. We hadn't seen Lux before, so we were curious. I should have known he would be as sexy as the day is long." She winks at me, smiling broadly.

I stand there blinking like an idiot as a fresh batch of embarrassment heats up my face.

"Honey don't take it so seriously. It's okay, I promise. There's not a lot of exciting things that happen around here for those of us who have already completed the Passage. So any time we can see some action, we tune in. But in your case, we wanted to make sure you were okay too. You seemed a little distressed...at first."

I insert my credit card into the POS system and wait for the beeping to start so I can yank it out. I'm still frustrated and embarrassed. I just want to get out of here. That apparently has become the mantra for my life.

Nancy hands me my receipt. "Listen, hon, Lux is egotistical and has more swag than common sense, but once you complete the consummation phase, he'll be putty in your hands. I promise you. Right now, he's sitting pretty with all of his demands because he thinks he has the upper hand. But it's you who has the upper hand. For you to harness your power, complete the consummation and make him pay for all that high-handedness. If you can make him grovel, please get it on video. I would love to see it."

Nancy's smile is contagious and I return it, feeling a little better.

"But that Solomon, though..." She shakes her head and

closes her eyes as if she is savoring her favorite piece of candy. "That Solomon is a sweetheart and a genius with children. You've scored a pot of gold with that one."

Obviously, she has not met the Solomon I have, but I'm not gonna bust her bubble.

"Thanks for your help, Nancy." I hope my smile is convincing. I grab my bags and walk out.

Thankfully, Lux nor Solomon are waiting outside, and I can walk home in peace. I daydream of possible escape plans after the consummation has been completed. At this point, I don't care to learn anything more about being a hybrid. I've gone this long without knowing anything about it and I think I've done just fine. I don't want to delve into any more possible reasons why my relationship with Momma was so horrible, either. From what I understand, I should be able to leave here free and clear once the phases are done. That's exactly what I'm going to do.

The sun sits low in the sky but not enough to darken it. I walk up my driveway and see my bags from the farmer's market waiting for me. I'd forgotten all about them. Solomon must have grabbed them and brought them here. God knows Lux would not lower himself enough to do it. You can bet on that.

I look at Solomon's house but don't see any signs of life over there. I pick up my bags and head in. I spend the rest of my evening doing household chores like laundry, cleaning out the fridge, mopping the kitchen floor, and cleaning my bathroom. By the time I'm done, I have worked myself into a state of exhaustion that should put me out for the night. At least, I hope it does.

Since that night when Lux showed up in my kitchen, I make sure not to fall asleep in my living room. I have developed an aversion to being on the first floor after dark. Yeah, I guess you can say I'm now somewhat afraid of the dark. I make sure to lock up and head upstairs. When I finally make it to bed, I'm reminded of why I went curtain shopping earlier today.

Those beautiful wide open windows, bringing those stars in so close now, just remind me, for a fact, that we are not alone in the universe. In all the places in the universe I could be, I wish I could be anywhere else but here.

I wake to an unnatural quiet that immediately makes me pause. This isn't good. The alarm clock on the nightstand says it is only eleven p.m. I've been asleep for about three hours.

I lay still so that I can listen, but I don't hear anything. I don't trust it. I firmly believe in listening to my gut, and my gut tells me that I'm not alone in this house. The only person who would have a reason for breaking into it is Lux.

I sit up in my bed and turn the lamp on, and sure enough, there sits Lux near the window. His bronze muktuk-like skin glistens in the moonlight from the window. His amber eyes flicker and glow like a fire in the hearth. It takes everything in me not to appear startled.

He evidently chose to forgo the ripped t-shirt from earlier and donned a vee-neck black t-shirt and dark wash jeans. I get a better look at his two tentacles, serving as arms. On the ends of them are four thick finger-like appendages with talons.

I cross my arms over my chest. I learned my lesson about sleepwear since the chase. No flimsy nightgowns for me. At least not while living here in Abrielara. I have on a short t-shirt and pajama bottoms. I have a pair of sneakers right here next to the bed in case I have to do some strenuous cardio...like running for my life.

I don't address him. I don't have anything nice to say, so I'm just gonna keep my mouth shut. His eyes roam what he can see of my body so many times that I feel the need to cover up.

I roll my eyes and head to my dressing room to grab a robe. It's not like what I have on is revealing, but the way he looks at me, I might as well be naked.

I don't realize he's following me until I turn around after grabbing my robe. I take a step back.

"What the fuck? I'm gonna need you to back up. How did you get in here?"

He shrugs. "The door."

"Then you can find your way back through it."

I put my robe on and tie the sash. I wait for him to do as I said, but he remains rooted in his spot. No way am I moving anywhere near him. I don't trust him as far as I can throw him.

"We need to talk, C.O."

I squint my eyes together in disgust.

"We don't need to do nothing. You need to get the fuck up out of my house. I don't understand why I have to keep repeating myself. I don't want anything to do with you."

He steps toward me and my hands bunch up into fists at my sides. Anger boils in my stomach again.

"We will talk. We have not completed the phases." He takes a few menacing steps toward me.

I smirk. The phases. It always comes back to the phases. I'm so tired of hearing about the fucking phases.

"We don't have to speak to complete the phases."

A lustful grin cracks his face open, his sharp teeth glinting maliciously. "You are right, Chosen One. We do not need to talk for me to fill you up." He takes a couple of more steps toward me.

Images of us in the pharmacy float through my mind and the feeling of finally completing the consummation warms my blood with heady lust. Knowing this is not all me helps me admit to myself that, yes. I want that. Hate is exactly what I feel for Lux. But it isn't the only thing. It also pisses me off that I have no control over how I feel.

What I feel in this moment is an incessant need to make him pay for what he did to me. I wonder if I can do more than just throw up some kind of a wall to make him back up off me.

"You disgust me." I raise my right hand without knowing fully what I want to do with it, except I want him to feel what he made me feel the night of the chase and today in the pharmacy. I push my hand toward him, palm out in the stop position.

"Before we do anything, there is something I want you to know."

The grin on his face just gets bigger. "What is that, Chosen One?"

I imagine my hand is around his throat, and I see my hand imitate what I'm thinking without touching him. The grin leaves his face and his hands go to his neck. I walk toward him, pushing him backward. When his back hits the wall, I move my hand upward, which moves him up the wall with his feet dangling.

Oh my god it's working!

"I want you to know what it feels like to have someone crush your windpipe so you can't breathe." I squeeze my fist a little tighter and hear Lux gasping for air. His legs kick.

"Don't know what to do with your legs? Let me help you with that." I imagine his legs spread with his knees up, and sure enough, his legs do what I imagine.

Oh my god, oh my god, oh my god!

I am freaking the fuck out right now but I refuse to let Lux see it.

"Isn't that better?" His response is enlarged eyes and raspy breath.

"I appreciate you laying down the law in the pharmacy. I was obviously confused about who was in charge. But just so we are clear, when I let you go, I don't ever want to see you again."

I drop him, just as he dropped me in the pharmacy, and he hits the floor. He uses the shelves to help pull himself up. His breathing soon returns to normal. We have a stand-off...just staring at each other. His eyes are glowing amber-red. I don't care what he's thinking, but I want him out of my house. Out of my life and away from me.

"I came here to apologize," he says without malice.

"I don't believe that for a second."

Lux drops to his knees in front of me.

"It's true. I apologize for hurting you. For scaring you. I am sorry about how I treated you in the pharmacy. Please do not punish Solomon for my actions. He asked me not to go after you in the pharmacy. He asked me to give him time to explain and you time to understand. I did not want to. He does not deserve to pay for my mistakes."

I'm not sure if I should believe him or not, but I'm more inclined to do so just based on the discussions I've had with Solomon, the judge, and the Fab Four.

"Fine. I have to see Solomon to complete the Passage, but I'll only see him during the day unless previously agreed upon. No more dropping by my house at night, uninvited." Lux gets off his knees and walks slowly toward me, his hands up submissively.

"We will do as you ask. I understand why you don't want to see me again. I hope you change your mind one day."

He watches me closely. I still don't give him any indication of what I'm thinking. Maybe I don't know what I'm thinking. I have a lot of confusing emotions going on inside me right now with him so close and submissive.

He walks until he is directly in front of me, within touching distance.

"I want you to know that I am sorry for a lot of things, but there are some things that I am not sorry for. I am not sorry for initiating the chase. That is my duty. I am not sorry for choosing you. I would choose you over and over again. And in case you weren't aware, Solomon chose you, too."

Chapter Twelve

Solomon

I guess the meeting with Mika went better than expected. She's angry and hurt but hasn't changed her mind about completing the Passage. Lux has been quiet since we got home. Hearing her say she never wanted to see him again hit him hard. It hit us both hard. The only thing he has said since getting home is he should have listened to me.

Yes, I agree. He should have listened to me. But there's no point in discussing it now. We have to move forward. We have to make it through the consummation, and then I'll have to beg and plead with her to commit to us. It was a hard enough feat before, but since Lux fucked up royally, it will be damn near impossible to convince her now. It also brings to light a scary scenario I didn't consider before.

"She wouldn't do that," Lux speaks up, fully aware of what I'm thinking.

"We don't know that. Anything is possible at this point. She's mad at us."

"We must make it up to her," he replies with determination.

"If that can even be done."

I'm not giving up, but I must be realistic about our options and outcomes. Mika is not your typical girl or the typical C.O. For one, she isn't fully human. That fact alone means that if I impregnate her during the consummation, she will be able to leave Abrielara with our baby. Humans who are chosen cannot do this, until they complete the Passage. Abrielarans or hybrids can move about however they want once a baby has been created. However, they must state their intention to the Abrielaran if they don't want to suffer the consequences. Of course, the fact remains we still have no idea what rules apply to Mika if any.

I'm not sure if Mika understands that or not. I'm positive she doesn't know after the consummation, there is one more phase. The commitment. To me, this is the most important of the phases. I intentionally didn't tell her about it. It's the phase I fear and want the most. It's also the phase that most humans don't complete. They run for their dear life once they've had the baby and don't look back once the door opens. Lux sealed our fates with that fuck up at the pharmacy.

Second, Mika is a hybrid we are unfamiliar with. I would like her to meet with Brady to run some tests, but I'm not sure if she'll be down to do that. We've been so caught up in this Passage stuff we haven't been able to look into her DNA. I wish I could go back and redo today.

"I will make this right."

"We will make this right, Lux. Both of us fucked up. Just at different times."

I should have been nicer to her in the beginning. I should have attempted to get to know her so that when I had to explain the Passage, she may have been more inclined to follow the rules.

There's a lot of work to be done. No matter how long it takes, I'll let her control the time frame. We can be in the heat stage for however long she wants. We're going to suck it up and deal with it. During that time, I hope I can change her mind about Lux.

Lux and I are the same, even if I'm mostly human, and he is all Brielaran. It's a sad life for a Brielaran if he cannot shed the human skin every once in a while after completing the Passage. There are activities that Abrielara has for its citizens that allow the Brielaran in them to act true to nature and celebrate completing the Passage with the one they've chosen and the community. We have a chase reenactment that's done on a community-wide scale. It's a three-day event that usually results in an increase in our population by a large margin.

I've always wanted to participate but couldn't because I hadn't chosen anyone. If Mika doesn't want to see Lux again, we wouldn't be able to take part. Never mind that she looks on our chase as a nightmare, not a segue into a life of fulfillment and happiness.

Of course, if she leaves with my offspring, then that will be the least of our worries. I cannot afford to let that happen. Then there is the other option. She could leave our offspring here and never come back.

"We will make this right."

"Yes, we will."

I step out of the shower and crawl into my bed after drying off. Tomorrow I'll begin my campaign to date her. She has already agreed to complete the Passage, but I want her to choose us because she wants us...and for no other reason than that.

"Did you see her when she put me up against the wall in her closet?"

"Yeah, Lux, I did. Beautiful, wasn't she?"

"Magnificent. The Brielaran in her shined brightly in her eyes. She is still feeling the heat."

"Yes, I noticed. But you and I both know she doesn't have much control over that."

"Yeah. I understand. She was beautiful, though, wasn't she?"

"Yes, Lux, she was."

I finally drift off to sleep with the vision of Mika in the throes of heat that we witnessed in the pharmacy.

She was beautiful indeed.

Getting back to work forces me to focus on my normal day-to-day. Seems like ages since I've been here. Although my return to work hasn't quite gone as smoothly as I would have liked. With all the Passage references I keep dodging, it may have been best that I stayed at home.

But seeing my patients reminds me of my goal. To have what every Brielaran dreams of having. A family of my own. Created with the one I've chosen and who's chosen me.

"Well, hello there, little Trixie. Have you been good for your momma?" Trixie looks up at me with her Brielaran eyes and then grins widely, lifting one of her legs in the air. "How's she been doing, Momma? She finish the meds Dr. Franks put her on last week?"

Before her momma can answer, Trixie lets out a rather loud fart and then giggles. I chuckle at her.

"Looks like she's feeling a lot better."

"Yes, it was a fight to get the meds down at first, but we finished them."

"Good. No more fever or rash?" I pick up the six-month-old from the carrier and lay her on the exam table so that I can look her over.

"No, she's all good now."

"Excellent."

Trixie adds in her input of baby gibberish as I look her over. I love kids. I can't wait to have some of my own. I hope to God I still have that opportunity.

I've tried to shove the whole fiasco with Mika to the back of my mind while I'm working, but it's hard when surrounded by kids. Kids who may have been created during the consummation stage of their parents' Passage. A Passage I'm struggling to complete.

"How is she relating to Johnny? Or should I ask how Johnny is relating to her?"

Mrs. Gillis chuckles and shrugs one of her shoulders. "Okay, I guess. He asked why she looked so much different than he did. I thought it was too soon to give that talk, but Paul said it was the perfect time and explained it to him." She laughs again. "He took it so nonchalantly I was shocked. He just said okay and then ran out to play like it was no biggie."

I smile and nod my head. "That's why I love kids. I'm glad he took it well."

After my assessment, I place Trixie back in her carrier. "Everything looks good. Continue to monitor her. And I'll see you at her nine-month appointment if nothing else comes up. See you later, Trixie."

I hand Mrs. Gillis the sheet to give to the appointment setter on her way out. Trixie throws her toy to the ground in agreement and spouts more gibberish.

Mrs. Gillis picks up her toy and her daughter and walks toward the door.

"Oh, Dr. Christiansen, I wanted to congratulate you. It's good to see you finally choose someone, so you'll have some little ones of your own. You're such a good doctor. I'm sure you're going to make a brilliant father."

I take a deep breath and plaster what I hope is a friendly

smile on my face. That's all I've been doing this morning. Looking over babies while trying to avoid the whole Passage conversation. Another reason why I didn't want Lux to confront Mika in the pharmacy.

Now everybody knows who I've chosen. That news spread faster than gossip on Sunday morning after church. I'm sure the news had already made it around town several times over before I even made it home. I wouldn't mind, except that I don't know what state my Passage is in.

Yeah, Mika said she would complete the phases, but she knows nothing about the last phase. She can't agree to something she has no knowledge of.

"Thank you, Mrs. Gillis. I appreciate that. I'll see you in three months."

I update Trixie's chart and then head to my office. I need a minute. I've been busy today or I would have taken a nap in my office. I didn't sleep that much last night. I ended up crawling out of bed at about three a.m. only to find myself standing on my front porch watching Mika's house...again.

All day long, I've tried to put my day in perspective, which normally isn't a hard thing for me to do. But today, almost every patient I've seen has a parent, who heard about my pharmacy drama, attached to them. Most of them have been tactful, but a few sounded a little salty in their comments about Lux.

Lux has a bit of a reputation in this town. Not all of it's good. But as soon as the consummation is complete, Lux will calm down and our shenanigans will be a thing of the past.

I hope.

A quick rap on my door brings my head up off my desk. "Yes."

"Your last appointment before lunch is in exam room

seven when you're ready, Doctor." Charlotte, my charge nurse, informs me.

Charlotte is a pretty little thing with doe eyes and a dirty mouth when you dick her down just right. She and I used to fool around about a year ago. Word was that she was sure I would choose her because she had gotten so used to me bending her over my desk every day during my lunch hour. As soon as I heard that, I put a stop to it. I didn't know who or when I would choose, but I knew for damn sure it wasn't going to be Charlotte.

"Thanks, Charlotte. I'll be there in a minute."

I pull out my tablet to check my calendar for today. After lunch, I have two more patients and then I'm done. They were regular checkups and shouldn't take that long.

"You got it, doc." Charlotte ducks out and closes the door. I walk over to my office window. I have a clear view of the reflection garden from my office. It's a nice peaceful place to sit and reflect, have lunch, or just slip away for a few minutes. I have taken advantage of the garden's peacefulness on quite a few occasions.

But now, all I see when I look at it is that day I ran into Mika on her way to see Perry. Another shining example of how I could have acted better. She looked ravishing but frightened.

I remember stuffing my hands into my pockets to keep from touching her. When I almost ran her over coming out of the building, I wanted to kiss her so badly. Her soft, plump lips made me want to shove my dick in her mouth. The vision of her red-painted lips around my dick stayed with me for days afterward.

God, I was so rude to her. How am I ever going to make it up to her?

When lunch finally rolls around, I'm ready for it. I'm not hungry, but I want to step out and take a walk and get some fresh air. I grab my sunglasses and take the stairs to the first floor rather than the elevator. I make my way across the lobby to the front door and push it open with gusto.

"Oh!" The exclamation is soft and feminine. My natural impulses take over and I grab whoever I bumped into to keep them from falling over. I've got to stop doing that. I set them on their feet and take a step back.

"Are you—"

Mika. She's looking down, running her hand over her short, slim skirt, not unlike the one that she wore the night I ran her over in this very spot.

"Mika. Are you okay? I'm sorry. I didn't mean to run you over again."

She looks up with startled eyes and then looks away. Her eyes avoid mine and I'm ashamed.

"I'm okay. Thank you." She says politely and then tries to walk around me, but I stand in her way.

"Mika, please look at me."

Her eyes take a slow trip from the ground to my eyes. Judging by the dark shadows under her eyes, I think she had the same night I did.

"I'm sorry for everything. I hope you can forgive me." Her shoulders drop at my apology.

"Solomon, you have nothing to apologize for. Lux is the one who embarrassed me in the pharmacy. Not you."

"True, but I'm apologizing for how I initially treated you. I was rude and hateful, and you didn't deserve that. I want this to work, and to do that, I have to admit my part in all this."

Her eyes lighten and seem to relax a little more.

"Okay. I accept your apology." She smiles just a little and I smile a huge one, but it doesn't give my true feelings justice. A weight lifts off my shoulders.

"Good. I would like to take you out on a date tonight. A picnic. I understand if it's still too early yet."

My excitement has taken over my tongue and I'm rambling.

"Sure. I'll come." She giggles and then her smile falters. Uncertainty settles into her eyes. "It's going to be just you and me, right?"

"Yeah...if that's what you want. Sure." Lux's ego sinks deeper. I run my hand through my hair, my nerves getting the better of me.

"Keep your head up, Lux. It's going to get better. She just needs some time."

"I will make this right."

"We will make this right."

"Okay, great. What time?" Her voice softly breaks into our conversation.

"I'll pick you up at eight. Wear something a little warm. The evening will be chilly and we'll be outside."

"Okay. I'll be ready."

She smiles again and walks around me to open the door. This time, I step out of her way and open the door for her. She doesn't look back after her whispered thank you, but my eyes follow her until she enters the elevator and I can't see her anymore.

My walk completely forgotten, I decide to sit at the fountain and contemplate our date tonight and all the ways I can make this right.

Mika

I feel Solomon's eyes follow me until I step into the elevator to Perry's office. I wasn't expecting to run into him today, and it kind of unnerved me a little. He looked good but tired. His black scrubs with his name written on the front breast pocket reminded me he was a doctor. I had forgotten that minor fact. Had I remembered it, I would have had Perry meet me elsewhere for lunch.

But now I'm glad I did. We need to finish this. The sooner, the better. I can't help but be sad about that, but it's for my own good. Obviously, Lux only wants to humiliate and dominate me based on his behavior in the pharmacy. He has no interest in this becoming a long-term affair. The way he's treated me so far proves it.

For once, we are on the same page. I'm not interested in a long-term affair either. As soon as this heat and consummation business is over, I am so out of here.

The elevator dings and opens onto the sixth floor. This time, the floor is alive, with many moving parts going in all different directions. Its bright atmosphere, courtesy of the enormous windows letting the sun in, makes me...happy.

Relaxed for once.

Perry and I finally got around to planning that lunch we talked about. I'm supposed to tell him about Momma and me, and he's supposed to enlighten me a little about him, his family, and Abrielara. I'm just happy for any kind of distraction that doesn't involve Lux or Solomon and allows me some time out of the house.

I enjoy my time with the fab four but right now, all I can

think about is how they knew what would happen to me but didn't say anything. Not a damn thing. Not a whisper, nothing. Yeah, they told me they couldn't because of the so-called rules, and I believe them, but I still can't help being a little salty about it. I'll move on, eventually. It's just a lot to take in and, in the grand scheme of things, is rather minor considering the other things going on in my life. Which is why I refuse to make a big deal out of it.

I walk into Perry's empty waiting room and past his receptionist's desk to his office. He told me to come through the waiting area this time instead of the side entrance like I had the first time.

"Knock, knock." I tap on his office door. It swings open, and without wasting a second, he pulls me into a bear hug.

"You made it." He puts me down, takes off his white doctor's coat, and hangs it neatly on the coat rack. "Are you hungry? Because I'm starving." He leads me out of the office and then turns to lock it. "What are you in the mood for?"

"I don't know. What's good around here?"

We decide to grab lunch from a roadside taco stand that Perry says I just have to try. Who am I to turn down tacos? Nobody, because this girl never turns down tacos. We sit at the tables not far from the stand and dig in.

"Wow," I say in between mouthfuls. "These tacos are amazing."

"I told ya." He grins and takes another bite of his taco, smacking loudly. "So, what do you think of Abrielara so far? Is it a place you can see yourself settling down in?"

Although food wasn't flying out of his mouth, I am still disgusted by his lack of table manners. His mouth opens again to say something, and I reach across the table and grab his lips with my fingers.

"Could you not do that?" I ask as politely as I can.

"What?" he asks when I remove my fingers from his mouth.

"Talk while you're eating. Chewing with your mouth open to name a couple."

He grins and leans his head to the side. "Pet peeve?"

"Yeah, one of my biggest."

He chuckles. "Sorry. There is no other way to talk while eating, and since we only have an hour, I want to make the most of it. I'll do better."

"Thank you."

After chewing and swallowing, Perry asks, "So, back to my question. Ever think you could settle down here? Raise a family here?"

I stop eating and stare back at him blankly. "Settle down? Here? The only plans I have right now are to complete the consummation stage and then get the hell out of Dodge. Besides, I have work I need to get back to. I've slacked off enough."

Even though he tried to hide it, I still caught the disappointment that crossed his face for a hot second.

"What?"

He shrugs and crumples up his taco wrapper. "I was hoping you were going to stay. I take it you and Lux didn't hit it off?"

"That's putting it mildly. Lux is an entitled, self-serving bully who hasn't had any home training. I already told him that I didn't want to see him again. I know that I have to see Solomon, which is fine. But I don't have to see Lux, which is how I prefer it."

Perry doesn't do more than huff.

"What's your Brielaran like?"

Perry gives another shrug and wipes his mouth with a napkin before balling it up and throwing it on his now empty plate. "My Brielaran's name is Xens, and you can say he is quite different from Lux. Completely laid back and never in a hurry to do anything. I have to push him sometimes because he isn't the aggressive type. Except during the Passage. However, unlike Lux, Xens has not been put in a situation to see what he hungers for but can't have it. Especially when that something, for all intents and purposes, belongs to him."

I give him a look of disgust and he chuckles at me, throwing his hands up in the air.

"Okay, I admit it. Lux is very charismatic. He's a very black and white, no sugar coating, shoot from the hip, old-fashioned kind of guy. Yes, he has a reputation of being a flirty prankster with asshole-ish tendencies. But ultimately, his heart is in the right place."

I cock an eyebrow at him. I don't believe any of that bull.

"Usually," he offers. He leans forward and places his arms on the table between us. "That stunt in the pharmacy was a little much. He went too far but look at this whole thing from his side. Xens and I have always known that Dyana belonged to us and we belong to her. She has always known it too. So even though we still had to go thru the rite of Passage, we always knew the outcome. Lux, he has never known who he was going to choose. He's always been in limbo. And now, to finally find you but still have no idea how it is going to end is straight torture. He's in the worst kind of limbo. He's found you, he's chosen you, but he's not had the chance to claim you."

"Okay, so I can see why he is a little frustrated. But to manhandle me? I understand how the burns are caused by the acidity in their DNA. Brielarans can't help what they are, so the burns aren't Lux's or Solomon's fault. But to..." I can't even bring myself to say it. I shake my head and sit back in my seat.

"To humiliate you in public? To force you to face the feelings you're having rather than to pretend they don't exist?" he asks, leading me.

"Yes." I take a deep breath. "Yes, I can admit that. It wasn't his place to do any of that. Not just the choking part, but I'm new to this. There's so much going on here for me. A lot of it I just don't understand. I'm just now slowly getting a grasp on some of it, yet I'm expected to just roll with it.

"What started all of this was me requesting an apology. That's all I wanted. He refused to give it to me. I already agreed to complete the Passage, so what is so bad about asking for an apology? And just because I'm requesting an apology that he had no intention of giving me does not mean he had the right to do what he did. I can't see how that's fair."

"It isn't fair. You're right, but as you're aware by now, life isn't fair. Things have to be done whether you fully understand them or not sometimes. Asking for the apology may have been the spark for the whole fiasco in the pharmacy, but ultimately, it was because of the heat cycle and how long you have been in that stage that was the catalyst for what happened. By now, you two should have already worked through all of that and possibly have you pregnant already. And by the way, every Abrielaran female asks for some kind of payment or retribution for the chase and the probe. It's kind of your right to ask for whatever you want, and as the Abrielaran who chose you, he is obliged to give it to you. Lux got off light by you asking for an apology. My fool ass was flying in chocolate from all over the world." He shakes his head. "I digress. The issue Lux had was the fact that you were asking him to apologize for doing his duty. If you had asked for anything else, he would have given it to you without a second thought. You asked for an apology and you are delaying the consummation because of it."

I hang my head. I haven't allowed myself to even think about the possible outcome of the consummation. He speaks about pregnancy like it's no big deal.

"Look, Mika, I completely understand where you're coming from. I've seen enough humans come through here to understand that what's being asked of you isn't something your logical brain can reconcile. But remember, you are not completely human. You're a hybrid. Your days of walking away are over. Not unless you want Lux to probably die and your brain to have to fight the insanity that will infest it until you also die. Assuming that you're exactly like us, that is."

He reaches over to touch my hand, bringing my eyes up to meet his. "Choosing a life here among your people and completing the Passage with Lux is not as bad as you think it will be. I promise. Ultimately, he needs you, and you need him. Why not make the best out of the situation instead of focusing on the worst?"

"I've already decided to consummate. I've also decided to allow Solomon to take me on a date. I'm not sure what it all means but I'm trying to play nice. I promise not to make any sudden moves yet. Just one day at a time."

"Good." He takes a sip of his lemonade. "Let's not forget that I'm here...so that idea should solely influence your decision to stay."

I throw a piece of lettuce at him that fell off of my plate. "You have a point there." He bows his head in response.

"So, not that discussing my experience with Lux isn't fascinating but I want to learn more about you. Had you honestly not heard about me before I got here?"

"Well, to be honest, I did. When I was about eighteen, before I went off to college, I decided to go hunting around the judge's office for information about our parents." He rubs his smooth-shaven chin. "I got tired of hearing the same answers I always got when asking questions. It's like people around here are trained to answer the same way. It was infuriating."

"Around here? You don't say," I chide. He chuckles at me.

"Yeah, so I found Dolly's diary. I read it from beginning to end. She mentioned the pregnancy, of course, and that she had you, but the diary entry date was more than a year after your birth. I didn't know you were my full sister. I never connected those dots. I thought we were half. That little nugget was left out of her diary."

I nod along. "I didn't learn anything earth shattering when I read it either. What would have happened if someone here had found out about me?"

"The Monarch would have had someone pick you up and bring you back. By any means necessary."

"Hmm. Are you happy to have a full sibling or how do you feel about it?"

"I'm happy to have a full sibling. Even though neither of us knew about our dad other than what is in the history books, at least you can tell me the things about Dolly that I didn't read or the judge didn't tell me."

My eyebrows take a hike and I look away. Guilt hits me and I hope whatever I tell him doesn't make him think negatively about her.

"What? Your face took a turn there."

"Honestly, Dolly and I did not have a good relationship. I don't want to color your idea of her based on my life with her. If there comes a time, I would like you to meet my sisters...our sisters. They had a wonderful relationship with her, and I think their version would be better for you to hear than mine."

Before I even finish, he's shaking his head. "No. I want your recollection. You and I are more alike than the sisters and me. I want to meet them because we all share some of the same DNA, but I want to hear what your experience was like specifically."

"Well, I can promise you it'll take more time to tell than you have in your lunch hour. So maybe another time we can talk. Just promise me that whatever you thought of her before does not change based on what I tell you."

"I'm Switzerland. I won't take sides. I promise." He smiles his dimpled smile again and then stands. "Back to the office I go. I'm glad we had this chat. Maybe we should make this a weekly thing."

I dump my trash into the can. "I'd like that. Now that's out of the way, why don't you tell me about your beautiful family on the way back?"

"I thought you would never ask," he says, pulling out his phone. His dimples are so pronounced I'm sure we're on camera somewhere. He goes right into telling me stories about the shenanigans his kids manage to engage in on the regular. He tells me how he and Dyana met and a little about his life with Solomon and the judge. It's a fantastic way to keep my mind off my date tonight. Even if for only an hour.

After my lunch with Perry, I decide to spend my afternoon reading. If I can keep my mind occupied with other things, then maybe I won't stress about tonight. And maybe, just maybe, I'll be able to keep the heat at bay when I see him. I change my clothes and get comfy in the library with my mother's diary.

I still don't understand why she wouldn't have said something to me about my lineage. At the very least, she could have told me my father was not Brianna and Taliah's father.

I honestly don't understand why she couldn't tell me what was going on in her last letter to me. I mean, what could have happened to her after I found out the truth? Would she get hurt or die? She was already dead when I received it. There were no repercussions that she would suffer once I read it. She wasn't Abrielaran, so I don't understand. I just don't get it.

Even while growing up, a few facts about me would have gone a long way to making my life just a bit easier to navigate. A lot of things would have made much more sense. It would have forced me to look inward instead of looking elsewhere for answers.

Fred Burris was a nice man and didn't treat me any differently than my sisters when he was around. I guess my mother felt that was her job. Both of my grandmothers treated me the same too. So, if people not of my blood could treat me fairly, why couldn't she?

I look down at the cover of the closed diary and realize this will not answer that question or any of my questions. Her letter and first few pages didn't enlighten me at all. If anything, she had me go to others for answers. So it doesn't make sense for me to continue searching her diary for them.

I can sit here and ponder why a dead woman made the decisions she made or find the answers I need on my own. I just have to move forward. Pretty sure that any answers I do find will just foster more questions.

On that thought, I set her diary aside. Maybe one day, when I'm okay with what I find, I can pick up her diary again. Maybe just read it for entertainment value and nothing more. The more I think about it, the more I like it.

So instead, I walk the short aisles of the library and pick up what looks like a dystopian romance novel. It makes me wonder, and not for the first time, who put this library together. This is usually not the genre of romance I like to read but since stepping out of my comfort zone is the theme since I've arrived here, I figure why not.

I'm deep into the novel when the grandfather clock chimes the seven o'clock hour. I begrudgingly rise from my place on the window seat to get ready for my date. The novel did its job keeping my mind preoccupied, but with the chiming of the clock, my mind goes right back to Solomon and Lux.

You're going to make the best of this.

You're going to get through this because you have no other choice.

Solomon isn't so bad. He promised it would be just us.

God, I hope he can keep a promise.

Chapter Thirteen

Mika

Remembering what Solomon said, I dress in dark jeans, waterproof boots, and a thin t-shirt underneath a long-sleeved fitted sweater.

I pick up a heavier jacket to bring in case it rains or gets cold. I let my braids hang loose and decorate my face with light makeup. I wasn't sure if I should bring anything since I don't know where we're going. He said a picnic, but that doesn't tell me much. I let it go based on the fact that he asked me out. If he wanted me to bring something, he should have told me.

A light knock on the front door accelerates my heartbeat and I find myself rushing to it. I stop and command my heart to slow down and to breathe. When I've done that, I open the door.

Solomon looks good but isn't dressed warmly at all. He's wearing a t-shirt with Jimi Hendrix on the front of it, jeans and working man's boots.

"Hi." His eyes are that warm honey color, proving to me that Lux is hopefully far, far away.

"Hi."

"You look nice."

His eyes sweep over me and the warmth travels my body. That makes me nervous because it reminds me of the heat in my blood that I've been trying to ignore.

"You look nice too. You aren't going to be cold wearing just a t-shirt?"

"I have a sweater and a jacket in the truck if I need them. I don't think I will, though. I've been running a little hot lately."

My mouth falls open with the sudden revelation as to why he's been running hot. That's a conversation I would rather not have, so I choose to ignore that too.

"I need to grab my keys and I'll be ready to go."

Solomon steps off the porch as I lock up. I turn to find he has opened the passenger door for me.

"Thank you." I step up into the truck.

"You're welcome. Let me take your coat."

I hand him my coat, and he hangs it behind me in the cab before coming to the driver's side.

"Are you warm enough?" He throws me a quick look.

"I'm fine. Thank you."

"I hope you're well rested."

He backs out of my driveway and it isn't long before we are driving through town.

"Why?" I look at him as the lights from the street illuminate his face. The shadows play with the sharp angles, giving him an otherworldly appearance.

"Well, the drive is about thirty minutes away, and then we have to hike up the mountain for like fifteen minutes."

"Hike? Up a mountain?" I lean forward, about ready to tell him to take me back home.

"Well, it's not a true hike, exactly. But because we're going to be walking up a slight incline, I call it a hike. The incline is so slight, most people don't even notice it."

"Oh, okay." Thank God I love shoes and bought these cute hiking boots on my tour of Abrielara my second day here. I had no idea I would actually have to hike in them.

I turn my attention back to the road. My eyes take in the scenery in a part of town that I had not yet visited. It is getting more rural, so I assume we're already on the other side of town. The night sky gets darker and darker because the lights of Abrielara are getting farther away.

"So, what did you do today? Did you finish your mom's diary yet?"

I jerk my face in his direction.

"Yes, and it told me nothing worth noting."

"Sorry to hear that." His wrist rests lazily on the steering wheel, his fingers tapping lightly on the dash. The pointer finger of his right hand taps a beat on the center console. It suddenly dawns on me that maybe he isn't as relaxed as I assumed him to be.

"I had lunch with Perry and then I spent the afternoon reading a book from that wonderful library inside the cabin."

"Ah...yes. That library is pretty special. I used to sneak in there when I was a kid to find the books I wasn't allowed to read."

"You sneaking into a place where you shouldn't...can't say I'm surprised by that," I say without thinking. The indirect reference to Lux was unintentional, and I immediately wish I could take it back.

His fingers tap a rapid beat on the dash again. This time the taps aren't light but heavy and loud.

"Are you nervous?" I ask when I can't take it anymore.

It's now his turn to jerk his head sharply toward me. His

fingers stop tapping, and he removes his wrist from the steering wheel and instead allows his fingertips to guide the wheel from the bottom.

"Um...a little. I guess." He offers me a quick smile. He clears his throat. "I don't want to fuck this up. If I do, you'll probably never speak to me again and then it's over for me."

He looks at me again and I give a little shrug.

"I can't say you're exactly wrong."

"See. I knew I had a reason to be nervous. That's why I brought an extra shirt in case I sweat through this one."

I snort out a laugh. "I hope you brought deodorant with that shirt."

He gives me a shocked, offended look. I shrug again.

"Just saying." I watch the smile on his face and decide that I like it. Just as I thought when I first saw him, he looks good when he smiles.

"You should do that more often."

He glances at me with a puzzled look. "Do what?"

"Smile."

"Oh. Why is that?" His eyes return to the road, and he slows down as he takes a sharp turn down a narrow, unlit road.

"You look nice when you smile."

"You think so?" He sounds honestly surprised that I would think so.

"Well, doesn't everyone look better when they smile?"

He shakes his head as if trying to decide if my statement is true or not.

"I don't know. I went to college with this guy who looked creepy when he smiled."

The befuddled look on my face must say it all. He laughs at my reaction.

"No kidding. If you could look up what a serial killer's smile looks like, it would have his picture in the dictionary."

I scoff at the notion.

"I promise you, if I'm blessed enough to spend more time with you, I'll show you my graduating class photo. I bet I won't even have to point him out."

I'm still shaking my head in disbelief even though I concede.

"I guess it's possible that he looks that bad, but I would have thought that as an adult, he would have grown out of that."

"Nope. I told him during our graduation party once that there were only two pieces of advice that I could give him. They were to never smile in pictures and to never buy a windowless van...of any color."

I bark out a laugh at that one. "If his smile is that bad, then that was probably the best advice he has ever received. What did he major in? Do you remember?"

"He was going to med school to study gynecology."

"Oh my god." I cover my eyes and shake my head. "That is awful."

"I know, right." His smile transforms his face into one I instantly wish I could see more often. I look away before I get caught staring. Instead, I opt for the scenery outside the truck as it comes to a stop.

"We're here."

I see nothing but darkness and I'm hella creeped out but I get out of the truck anyway. He hops out, opens the cab, and grabs our jackets, a picnic basket, and a small backpack.

"Do you mind taking the blankets? I can carry everything else."

"Sure, no problem." I reach over and grab the blankets. He opens the toolbox in the back of the truck.

"I need to grab a flashlight out of here and then we're set."

The hike is just as he said. Not really a hike, but it was a good fifteen-minute walk. It's hard to see out here in the dark and the thick brush. I am by no means a country girl, so the sounds coming out of these woods on top of knowing Lux isn't that far away is unsettling to say the least. It's darker than pitch out here. I'm glad he knows where we're going because I can't see shit, even with the help of the flashlight.

Despite putting my trust in Solomon, my mind can't help but reference all the movies I've seen when scenarios like this one end badly. Someone always ends up dead.

Always.

As we get closer to what looks like an entrance, my curiosity gets the best of me, and I have to ask.

"So, where are we exactly?" He unlocks the huge garage-like door and pulls it up to let us in.

"We're going inside this mountain. I thought you would like to know a little about how the Brielarans came to be here."

I take a step and then stop. "Um...one more question before I walk into more darkness."

"What's that?" He looks concerned.

"You're not going to try and kill me, are you? I mean, who all knows that we're here?" I ask, trying to cover up how nervous I am. I don't think he's out to kill me or else I wouldn't be here but this is the weirdest date I've ever been on.

He looks shocked that I would even suggest a thing.

"No. Of course not. Why would I want to kill you? That's crazy."

I throw my hands up. "I'm kidding, but it doesn't hurt to ask." I continue walking toward him.

"So do you want to know about the Brielaran side of your-self? Or was I just hoping that you were curious?"

"Oh. You know...I never thought about it. I've been kind of preoccupied with other things. But of course, now that I'm presented with it, I'm interested in learning more."

I follow right behind him as he closes the heavy door and then heads down some stairs that were obviously put there in recent history.

"Well, prepare to be pleasantly surprised."

We go down farther, and it's dark as all get out in here. If it weren't for the flashlight, I wouldn't be able to see him, and he's directly in front of me. After some time, he finally stops walking and turns to me.

"Okay, so this is the tricky part. We're going to have to jump down from here. There aren't any stairs. I'll jump down first, and then I'll need you to jump after me."

"Uh, what?"

"Don't worry. I won't let anything happen to you. I promise I'll catch you. Okay?"

"Do I have a choice?" I ask, crossing my arms in disgust. Why do I always end up with the crappy dates? Does anyone do a nice dinner and a movie anymore?

"Yes, you could always go back the way we came, but I hope you don't because I want you to see this. I promise you it's worth all this walking."

"Okay, as long as I don't run into any bats or anything."

He laughs softly. "No bats."

He turns and then jumps off the ledge. He shines the light in my direction.

"See? The drop isn't too bad."

He puts the basket down and puts the flashlight in his pocket. He leaves it on so that I can still see him. He holds out both hands to me.

"Throw down the blankets and then jump. I promise not to drop you."

I'm not feeling this at all. This is not going to go well. I can already see it. I'm positive I'm going to end up with my own episode on the ID channel.

"Solomon, this isn't a good idea. I could land on you," I say after throwing down the blankets.

"Sweetheart, that's kind of the point." He chuckles.

Did he just call me sweetheart?

"Now jump." Uncertainty hits me but he doesn't look worried. I've come this far. I might as well see it through.

"On the count of three. One. Two. Three."

I say a quick prayer that I don't break either one of our necks and jump. He catches me as he said he would. His arms wrap around me tightly without so much as a grunt. Heat emulates off his body. I fully understand why he wanted to forgo wearing a jacket. He's a furnace all on his own.

He continues to hold me. Our faces are so close that I can melt into his honey eyes even without the help of the flashlight.

"You alright?" His rough whisper draws my eyes down to his lips. My mouth remembers what it felt like to have those lips on my body.

I inhale deeply, forcing myself not to moan out loud. He smells so good, so yummy, so...I furiously blink those thoughts from my brain. He's too close to allow thoughts like that loose.

"Yes. Thank you." I remove my hands from his neck and he slowly lets me go.

"I told you that I would catch you." He bends to pick up the jackets and the picnic basket.

"Yes, you did."

He watches me for a few seconds more, then turns his back and starts walking again.

"We're almost there."

I take a deep breath and follow. I hope I do a better job of keeping my distance once we get where we're going. Being in his arms brought the stirrings of the heat cycle past the low simmer I've kept it at so far today to almost a full boil. I've got to do better.

We walk for another ten minutes or so and I begin to hear what sounds like water dripping. We turn a corner and it's like someone flipped the light switch on.

I look up, and there is a hole at the top. The moonlight shines through, lighting up the entire cave. The cave's walls look like it has jewels shining in the rock.

What in the world?

In the center of this cave is a pond with crystal clear water. I can see straight down to the bottom.

"It's the moonlight hitting the crystals and minerals exposed in the rock just right."

"It's beautiful." I gasp in wonder.

"Yeah, it is."

"Where are we? What is this place?"

I continue to turn as if I am on a carousel, in complete awe of the beauty here, hidden inside of a mountain.

"This is actually a crash site. When the first Brielarans came here, they crashed into this mountain. They didn't survive. But their ship continued to send out a beacon and a search party from Brielara came to recover their bodies. Some of the search party stayed behind."

"Where's the ship they came here in?" I look at the clear water, hoping to see something at the bottom.

"It's with the Monarch, inside the mothership."

"Monarch? Mothership?" *Get the fuck outta here.*

Solomon outright laughs at me.

"Yes. We are governed by a Monarch. Her palace is a big ass mothership, capable of taking us all with her in case things don't work out here. The palace is also cloaked so that it can never be found by the rest of the world unless she wants it to be."

"Interesting."

"Well, if you decide to stay, you'll get to meet her. She knows and connects with every citizen who lives here. It's part of the reason why all hybrid children must stay with an Abrielaran in their formative years."

"Hmm. So, why were they coming here at all?"

I've tried not to put too much thought into my hybrid roots, but now that I'm here, I might as well learn something.

"Let's set up our picnic first. I don't know about you but I've worked up an appetite. Do you see a spot where you'd like to settle down?"

I find a spot behind us that looks like it has a good view of the total scene. Solomon lays down the blankets and then plops down to unload the basket. When I see the chicken, my stomach growls loud enough for Solomon to hear it. He chuckles but doesn't comment further.

"Guess I am hungry."

I suck down some water and watch Solomon fill a plate and then hand it to me. I smile when I see what's on it.

"Typical picnic, huh?"

He shrugs as he fixes his plate.

"I didn't want to push my luck. I thought if I kept it simple, I would surely pick at least a couple of things you would eat even if it wasn't everything."

"Looks like you did pretty well because I love everything

here. Fried chicken, potato salad, macaroni salad, homemade rolls, baked beans and is that peach cobbler?"

"Yeah, you guessed it." He grins proudly.

"Did you make all this? There isn't a store container in any of this."

"I wish I could take the credit for all of this, but no, I did not. I asked the lady who cooks for my dad to fix this up for us. She was more than happy to do it."

"That was nice of her."

"I thought so." He grins at me and digs in.

We eat and talk compatibly about nothing too heavy. Just things about his practice and Abrielara. He asks me about my career and life in New York. We steer clear of relationship questions. Even though it wasn't discussed, it feels like an unspoken rule. Fine by me. I don't want to hear about any escapades I'm sure he's had.

When we finish eating, we clean up but I'm not quite ready to leave yet. It's peaceful here with the water, the moonlight and the colors ribboning thru the walls of the cave. It has my designers brain going wild with possibilities. It's also been great having a normal conversation with him for once.

"So, tell me the story of Abrielara."

"I did promise you that, didn't I?" He grins at me.

"Yes, you did." I return his smile. Maybe we can at least be friends after all this is over.

Before now I would never have imagined that I would enjoy spending time with him, but I do. He's funny, he's sweet. He cares about people. Now I understand what Nancy in the pharmacy meant when she described him...to a degree. How in the hell did he end up with Lux? Since I refused to mention Lux's name, I couldn't ask him, but maybe one day I would get the chance.

"Before coming here, the Brielarans were a scavenger race

on the verge of extinction. They were lawless and had no boundaries. They were basically killing each other off to the point that there would be no such thing as a Brielaran within one hundred generations if they continued as they had been."

"Ruthless."

"Yep. To say the least. It reminds me of the wild west. You know, there's the law, but there weren't a whole lot of people strong enough to uphold it. Brielarans were impulsive, gluttonous, and lacked willpower. Their behavior was like a disease running rampant among them. They had only survived as long as they had because several colonies managed to leave and look for other places to live."

"That's sad. I can't imagine having to leave your home just so you can survive."

"Yes, it is. Brielara was literally dying because it wasn't being taken care of. They knew they lacked certain qualities that other societies valued. They wanted to be accepted, and more than anything, they wanted the Brielaran race to survive. They wanted the universe, the creator, to know they were worthy of life and love. They wanted to prove their existence was not a mistake and were willing to sacrifice a part of themselves to make it happen.

"So when a colony found Earth and Earth appeared to be inhabited by a race of beings far weaker than they were, they thought it was the perfect place to start over.

"Assimilating into the culture here wasn't as easy as they thought it would be. After several failed attempts at integrating into the way of life here the clinical way, they decided that changes were in order. They realized the probe was not as thorough as it needed to be."

"I'm a little lost. What do you mean it wasn't thorough? What are they probing for?"

"Compatibility. We still probe for that reason only. Basically, when our DNA matures, the Brielaran seeks someone who could help him fulfill his ultimate duty. Which is to procreate. Remember, the Brielarans are seeking ways to ensure the race lives on.

"In the beginning, men were probed as well to see if their bodies could host Brielaran DNA without harming anyone. For women, it was to see if they could be inseminated and carry a Brielaran to term and deliver it."

"Oh."

"They learned fairly quickly that they were going about this all wrong. Although the subject's overall health was important, it wasn't the only component that mattered.

"I won't bore you with the details. But in the end, they realized that the males would have to be born from an inseminated human female, making hybrids. There was no other way to force them to host them. Secondly, not all women can carry a Brielaran successfully and deliver them. So the probe needed to be thorough enough to make that determination. Running blood and urine tests weren't enough. At the risk of sounding crass, they did not want to waste DNA on a host who couldn't complete the Passage."

He stops talking for a moment and my mind quickly rehashes what I experienced. Of course, I've heard of alien abductions and humans being experimented on before. I never really put much thought into the validity of those accounts. I mean, there are lots of stories out there. Who knows what's true and what isn't? But here in Abrielara, it's true.

Aliens are real. Abductions are real. Experimentation is real.

"If you would rather not hear this, I don't have to finish. I don't want to make you uncomfortable or anything."

His words are gentle and I appreciate the thought. But

I'm learning more about these people than the entire time I've been here.

"No, it's okay. I want to know. I actually need to know. Since I seem to be a part of all this."

I meet his eyes. The more I learn about this place and these people, the more I understand Solomon. God, I hate to admit it, but I'm even learning a bit about Lux...a little.

"Only if you're sure. We were having such a nice time. I don't want to ruin it."

I smile this time, and he gives me a quick one, but it isn't genuine. His words in the truck come back to me. He's nervous and worried about fucking everything up. Fucking what up exactly, I'm not sure, but I don't like seeing the worry on his face. I put a hand on his knee.

"You won't ruin it by telling me about the past. What I would really like to know is why the chase? Why does it have to be that way? I understand that the Brielarans didn't know squat about humans when they got here. So there were a lot of failed testing and trials that forced them to find a way that worked. How did they get to where we are now?"

He sighs deeply, seeming to relax a little.

"Well, after all those failed attempts, they realized that humans are fragile. People died. And instead of trying to turn them into a version of a Brielaran, they realized they needed to be more human. They considered just taking over the planet, but they already knew Earth would just end up like Brielara.

"Despite their behavior, Brielarans are not completely heartless but they had to keep trying. So they decided to run their test more naturally. Of course, being a little uncivilized, they made a lot of mistakes. But thankfully, they learned early on they just couldn't go around attacking people."

He takes a swig of lemonade.

"As we know, Brielarans love the art of conquest. This and the fact that they knew adrenaline moves the blood through the body quicker than anything else. It made sense to them to implement a chase with the probe.

"The Brielarans and the men of this area came to an agreement. The Brielarans promised to make sure these people prospered, that the women would be taken care of and respected as well as the children. The town's women were never told of the agreement so the chase was real for them."

I sit up straight. He can't be serious.

"Are you kidding me? There is absolutely no other way than to scare women to death and damn near kill them in order for the probe to be successful? And the men in this town agreed to that? Telling them what was going to happen would not change how scared they would be, I can tell you that. And what about the women who were probed and not chosen?"

Anger begins to fester inside me but I feel Solomon's fingers lightly touch my shoulder. He lightly caresses me, obviously, to calm me down.

"This was a long time ago. Things were different back then. Even the way humans saw each other. You're assuming that the Brielarans were civilized. They had their moments of clarity, but ultimately they were not. They had a lot to learn. Still do, as a matter of fact. The women who were probed but not chosen had their memories wiped of the event so they could continue living as if nothing ever happened."

"I would have loved to have my memory wiped," I say more to myself.

"If you were human and chose to leave here after completing the Passage, or weren't able to complete it, you could request it, and it would be granted. But you are not all human, and as far as we know, you have a Passage to complete as well."

That didn't make me feel better at all.

"Also, keep in mind the natives of the area at the time of the crash revered the Brielarans. If you look closely enough around this cave, you'll see some of the hieroglyphs that the tribes drew to commemorate the crash.

"Eventually, as years passed, the natives of this area were aware of what they were. Hybrids were being created and living alongside the humans. Then, of course, the entire Passage and how it happens was passed down through DNA. Females knew something was going to happen. They were educated about their duty to society by their mothers. The rite of Passage became something to be celebrated for all. The females weren't afraid. They were excited. The chase with the excitement helped accelerate the DNA through the blood. Which meant that the probe could do its job. And the Abrielaran race continued to flourish."

I release a breath I didn't know I held. Knowing that the citizens of this town came to know what was going to happen and looked forward to it makes me feel better. Can't say that I don't think it's a bit crazy, but it was better than I originally thought.

"But when people who were not native to the area began moving in, they didn't understand. In order to keep the peace, they came up with this plan. So yeah, they wanted the Brielarans to continue to protect them and keep the land rich. If the women knew and decided not to participate, the Brielarans could turn violent and take them anyway or kill them all.

"Of course, the female hybrids knew they had a choice, but to this day, I have never heard of a female hybrid who decided not to stay after completing the Passage. Doesn't mean it hasn't happened. I just haven't heard about it."

Hmm...food for thought, I guess.

"Why are females unable to leave once they've been chosen if they don't want to stay?"

"Because, above all, the success of the Brielaran race is the most important. If women were chosen and allowed to leave, then there is the possibility that others would find out and put the race in jeopardy. Brielarans were and still are not interested in drawing attention to themselves or this town. They want to continue to live in peace and they want the creator to be proud of them.

"They wanted to experience what true love was. Not just mating to extend the race but actually caring about someone else just because. They had traveled the galaxy many times over and witnessed other species do it. So why couldn't they? Something had to change or they would die. No question about it. They were able to accomplish that here. They didn't want anything or anyone jeopardizing that."

"Okay, but how was I unable to leave when I tried, though? The exit for Wilson's Creek did not show up, and I know it's there because I saw it coming into town."

"Because Lux let the Monarch know who we chose and where you lived. She cloaked the exit so you couldn't see your way out."

"How?"

I'm flabbergasted.

"She has mental abilities that you would expect an alien to have. This entire area is under her protection and control. She's here to make sure we continue to follow what was decreed years ago."

I nod but I'm still working on wrapping my head around all of this. It'll take more than a single night to make sense of it all.

"Brielarans understand the value of life because theirs was almost snuffed out. From the moment they came to that conclusion, they were on a mission to change their destiny. Nothing gets in the way of that."

"Is that why my father Dane was killed? Because they valued life so much?"

My words are soft but the edge I feel is in the spaces between them. Solomon's hand is now caressing my shoulder, not just his fingers. I don't understand why I'm taking this so personally. Well...actually, I do.

I spent my entire life with a woman who basically hated me, and all along, I had a father who may have been the person I needed. Instead, because the Brielarans value life so much, they killed a man that was only trying to help them.

"Actually, yes. Dane knew what the consequences were for testing on himself without permission. We are connected. What affects one, affects us all. He knew there was a chance that his genes could not take the mutation he introduced and that he could literally lose his mind. But the cause was important, so he did it anyway." He leans in and softens his voice. "The Monarch only took his life when she was positive that he was already gone. She didn't want him to do any more damage to himself or anyone else. She did not make that decision lightly."

The moment he leans into my space, I forget what we are even talking about. His scent gives me a heady experience I recognize. His voice is as warm and seductive as his honeyed eyes. The continued caress of his hand on my shoulder is not calming me down in the least.

Instead, it's stroking a fire I thought I'd put out before sitting down to this picnic. The need to sit back and add distance between us is great, but I can't. I crave his touch too much. I don't want him to just touch my shoulder. I want him to touch me everywhere. I want the heat I've been feeling to finally consume me, exhaust me. I'm so close to begging him to ruin me that my body vibrates from the power of it.

I don't dare look up. If I do, I'm done for. There will be no turning back after that. I close my eyes tightly and concentrate on breathing in and out slowly. At this point, I don't care what I look like. I need this heat to either go away...or deplete me. Whatever it chooses, choose something and do it.

His fingertip on my chin forces my face up. I keep my eyes closed. I know he has leaned in closer because I feel his soft breath on my face.

"Let me look into your eyes, Mika." His voice, smooth as honey a minute ago, is rough and almost hoarse now. I do as he asks because I have to. Whatever he asks, whatever he needs, it's my job to give it to him. To supply it.

Where the fuck did that come from?

The thought didn't stop me from obeying his command. I open my eyes and look straight into his warm glowing ones.

"So beautiful. I need you. I can't wait anymore." His whispered words make me unbelievably happy.

"I don't want you to," I whisper back.

Heat radiates throughout my body and pulses to the beat of my heart. I want him more than I want anything else.

His glowing eyes flare like fire when another log is added to it, sparks flying and heat billowing out. His lips connecting with mine is the most satisfying thing I have ever tasted.

He must agree because a desperate moan escapes his lips when his tongue caresses mine. He pulls me closer, lifts and plants me so I straddle his lap. I feel his hardness through our jeans and all I can hear in my head is...

mine, mine, mine...

...over and over again. I work at moving his shirt up so that I can touch him. I have to feel his skin underneath my fingers. His lips eat at mine frantically, but I know what he's thinking when his hands cover mine. I pull back a little, but he doesn't let me go far.

"Are you sure this is what you want? I don't want to misunderstand what this means." His weighted breaths are audible and are felt more than just on my face.

"Yes. This is what I want."

The uncertainty in his eyes tells me I have to convince him with more than my words. I remove my sweater, my t-shirt, and my bra. That should make things perfectly clear. I watch his face as he looks me over.

"Well damn."

A slow grin animates his face before his lips cover my nipples, his tongue wetting them as his lips suckle them into hardened peaks. My head falls back and a euphoric moan escapes me. This is what I've been waiting for. This is what I've been waiting my entire life for. The feel of his touch on my body is what I've been missing, what I need.

My hands cup the back of his neck as his suckling continues to pull the cord connected to my core. The chill I felt in the air earlier has dissipated. Now, I'm burning up with an exigency I didn't know I had before coming to Abrielara. None of the worries that flooded my mind before matters now. He is all that matters; him, his lips, his body, and this heat between us.

Without warning, Solomon lays me on my back. He removes my boots and then covers me. His lips never leave my body but they do travel.

They follow his hands. He licks my stomach as his hands work at freeing me from my jeans. I try to free him, but he moves my hands above my head and holds them with one hand while his other finishes the job.

When he succeeds, he looks up at me. His eyes still glowing brightly.

"Before we go any further, I have to quench a thirst first."

The first brush of his tongue on my lower lips electrifies me, arches my back. My enraptured voice echoes throughout the cave. I've missed the feeling of his tongue there. He knows how to lick me—the right pressure, the right frequency. Why did I ever think that I could live without this?

Chapter Fourteen

Solomon

The Consummation

My first taste of her after such a long time is a rush...straight to the head. Every cell in my body feels electrified and revived. It's as if somebody hit me with the paddles and jump-started my entire body, not only my heart. By tasting her, the effects of the many nights of no sleep and worry disappear as if they never existed.

I've missed her. I've missed this. I've missed taking care of her and seeing her every day. Any kind of interaction was better than nothing but I absolutely hate it when she's mad at me. I move my tongue between her sweet folds, swirling around, seeking the little swollen bud hiding underneath her clean-shaven hood.

When my eager tongue finds it, my lips surround it and suck the juices from it. Mika grabs a handful of my hair, grinding against my lips. Her illegible ramblings are exactly what I want to hear. Her body trembles and I increase the suction of my lips. I flick my tongue against that little bud in rapid succession until her body opens up for me and showers my tongue with her sweetness.

I don't stop. I know her. She has another one in her, so I continue to lap up her honey and not miss a drop. From top to bottom, I take my time. My languid strokes keep her right where I want her, totally entranced but hanging on the edge.

Her body continues to ride out the waves on my tongue. Her hips, gyrating against my face, are building to another orgasm. Without removing my lips from her pussy, I look up to see her face. Her eyes are closed. Her mouth is open, expressing her utter enjoyment of what my mouth is doing to her. Her back is bowed, and her beautiful breasts point toward the hole in the mountain. The moonlight dances on her chest, providing a spotlight for my private show. My hand goes to my extended dick, still inside my jeans, rubbing it to keep it happy for a few more minutes. With a few orchestrated flicks of my tongue and increasing suction of my lips, her body shakes again with pleasure. Her hips rise off the cave floor as her voice sings another orgasm. The sound of my name being wrenched from her lips and echoing through the cave makes my dick pulse with pride.

She called my name.

I lick up her juices and she grabs my shirt, yanking it over my head. She goes right for my jeans and wastes no time getting me out of them. I would love to slow this down but I can't. I'm on autopilot and everything, down to my movements and how fast I move, is not determined by me.

Lux.

Her eyes are glowing brightly in the moonlit cave. As soon as I'm naked, she looks me over. Her head lowers toward me as her hand reaches for my throbbing cock. Her mouth opens when she gets closer, her intention clear. I press a hand to her shoulder to stop her.

"No. Not yet. Later you can. I promise."

She looks a little embarrassed for asking. I press my hand on her shoulder, and she lays back down on the blanket-covered ground.

"I want my dick to get wet, make no mistake about it. But I want your pussy to wet me up first. I've waited forever for it."

I kiss her lips while I settle my body into the warmth of hers. In the minutes I spent eating her pussy, I'd forgotten how intoxicating her mouth is. Her lips are succulent and it's easy to get lost in them. My body naturally rocks into her sweet clit while we feast on each other's mouths.

My head is about to explode...both of them. And with that thought, I stop moving. The absolute last thing I want to do is explode all over her stomach. I don't want to waste a drop. I want every bit of it inside of her.

She looks up at me in wonderment, the light in her eyes pulsing to the beat of our hearts. I don't ask permission. I don't need to. I see the hunger in her eyes and I'm sure she can see it in mine. I move the head of my dick through her soaked folds to spread my precum on her and to collect her juices on me. She wraps her legs around me and lifts her hips to tell me she's ready.

She is oh so ready.

I sink into her intoxicating heat with one thrust. Her elevated sigh runs through me.

"Oh, baby..." I whimper.

The headiness of being inside of her is the greatest high I've ever experienced. I feel like I'm floating, weightless and unencumbered. I move inside of her, her delicious pussy closing in around me. A groan breaks free from deep in my chest, breathy yet heavy as it echoes against the cave walls.

Her keening sighs complement mine. We move in steady,

fluid movements. Our hearts are transported and lifted beyond where I ever thought they could go. I know she feels the same because I can feel it.

I catch her eyes in intermittent intervals, glowing so brightly that they are almost neon. The tightly pulled rope between us urges me to keep going. To not lose focus. We are almost there. Almost over that hill we've been climbing since we started the Passage.

My hips rotate on the way in and out. I make sure to rub against her sensitized nub on the way in every time. Her soft mewls add more air to my lungs and girth to my dick. Her pussy squeezes me as I make my way in and then releases me on the way out. My body begins to shake and I know I'm being wound tight.

I let go a bit more and quit controlling the tempo of my hips. I let my body decide, and gradually, my hips pump faster. Going deeper, our hips bumping harder. I grab her waist as mania overtakes me. I feel her let go so I can completely take over. I slam into her without mercy. She whimpers but her pussy continues to milk me in vice-tight clenches. The pace nor the intensity changes until that rope finally snaps.

"Solomon!" My name evaporates from her lips in elated exhaustion. Her body quakes underneath me and her pussy baptizes my needy dick with her sweet cum, setting me off.

"Mika...Mika." My head lays next to hers, my lips on her neck. Her name is exalted and floats out from the depths of my soul as my seed shoots anxiously into her.

My hip movements are softer now, reminiscent of the fluid ones of earlier. Her body continues to extract every last drop out of me, the grip of her pussy not letting me go.

I hope to God she takes note and truly never lets me go.

As our breathing resets, I watch for any signs of regret or pain. I don't see any. I haven't moved since spilling inside her. I'm afraid if I move, then I'll break this unbelievable bubble we are in. My semi-hard dick is inside her, reeling from the aftershocks of her still-pulsating pussy. Her fluorescent eyes warm the deepest part of me while they strip me bare.

Completely and utterly bare.

But I don't mind. I'm actually happy about it. I want her to continue to expose every pothole and burn that has scarred my heart. I want them to finally see the light of day. I don't expect her to heal them, but I do want her to soothe them, love me and commit to me in spite of them.

Because I already love her. I'm already committed to her, even though she doesn't love me and probably will never commit to me.

Those thoughts bring Lux to mind. I want her to feel this connection and understand that Lux is already a part of us. Forgive him and allow him to participate in our relationship if she allows us to have one. Now that we've consummated, he will only add to our life together. No matter how short it may be. However, now is definitely not the time to bring up Lux. I have to tread nice and easy if I want her to change her mind.

I lean down and kiss her lips while removing my flaccid dick from her heavenly body. I can't help but moan at the sensation. I prop myself up beside her, resting my head on my hand.

"How do you feel?" Does she feel this connection between us?

"Aside from being a little chilled now, I'm good."

"Yeah, the cave is not known for its tropical atmosphere."

I grin at her, and she offers a shy grin back. "Do you know your eyes glow blue when you're angry or turned on?"

She gives me the side eye. I shake my head at her. "It's true. They do. Let me show you." I reach over and pull my cell phone from the pocket of my jeans. "Smile. You're on camera."

Her closed-mouth smile is a little bashful but I take the picture anyway and show her. "See?"

"Wow." She continues to stare at her picture. "It's never happened to me before. Why now?" She grabs my phone to get a closer look.

"I think it's because the probe awakened your Brielaran genes." She gives a slight nod and hands my phone back to me.

"It's my opinion, but I'd like to make an appointment with Brady to see what his thoughts are. Besides, we need to run some tests on you anyway so we can better understand what kind of hybrid you are. Do you mind?"

"No, I guess not."

"Cool. I'll call him tomorrow and set up an appointment for you. I can come with you, you know to give him some info to help put the pieces together for you."

"Yeah, sure, that would be great. Thanks." Her eyes move around the cave, but unlike before, I can tell she isn't just taking in the scenery. She's got something on her mind.

"What's wrong?"

"Nothing. Just taking it all in."

She doesn't look at me. I reach over and grab her hip and tug on it to force her body to face me. She finally looks me in the eye.

"Now that I have your attention, why don't you tell me what's on your mind. Did you enjoy our date?" I ask her softly while massaging her hip. I move my hand down to palm her round ass. My fingers are itching to get back into her moist heat.

I can't help but be distracted by her. My scent on her stirs my dick even though I want to know what she's thinking about. My body is overcome with reminders of how it felt to be inside her body. My eyes roam over her, taking in her beautiful full breasts and her chocolate kissed nipples. My head already leaning down to take one into my mouth, but her voice reminds me I did ask her a question.

"Yes, I did. The date was great or is great." She smiles a little and continues to look around the cave.

"Well, if it isn't the date, then it's something else. You are obviously distracted by something."

I kiss the tip of her nose and then her lips. I don't mention that I'm distracted too...by her.

"What is it, baby?" Her eyes widen a little at my endearment. I have no explanation for it. They apparently come naturally to me while I'm with her. Go figure.

"It's um, a couple of things, actually."

I pull her closer, hoping to do away with her distractions so that I can get back inside of her. My dick is already pointing toward her, ready to go again.

"Tell me," I mumble, putting my lips to her neck, sucking her skin into my mouth.

"You have to stop that first. I can't think or talk when you're doing that."

She braces her hands against my chest and pushes me back a little.

"That's kind of the point," I inform her but I do what she asks.

"What happens next? With this Passage thing? We completed the consummation phase, right? Does that mean that the heat is over?"

"Wanna get away from me already?" My heart trips up at the thought.

"No, I was wondering how this works. I don't know what to expect now. Just curious."

She looks around the cave again, worry distorting her features.

"Well, now that we have succumbed to the heat, it is technically over, but the consummation phase isn't over until I impregnate you."

The thought that she was already looking for a way to skip town thunders through me, and suddenly I'm not interested in having sex anymore. If she leaves, then it's over. The exact thing I've been afraid of happening is done. I'm repeating our family history. I lean away from her and lie on my back. My eyes on the ceiling.

"Oh, okay."

I look over at her and watch as she goes between watching me and looking around the cave.

"How does that make you feel, to know that I have to impregnate you before you're free?" My question is almost whispered because it's a question that isn't based on fact. It isn't over when I impregnate her.

"Surprisingly, I'm okay with it. I wanted to make sure I understood correctly. Perry kind of mentioned it when we met for lunch but he wasn't clear. He tried to explain the difference between his Brielaran and yours and the hopeful outcome of this phase."

The life finally returns to my ultimate dream. There's still hope that this could work out.

"Okay. Good. I was afraid you were leaving me already."

The joking tone in my voice is misleading. I'm not at all joking. I'm totally serious but I don't want to scare her away.

Not when I've finally gotten a taste of what it means to connect with the one I've chosen.

She smiles at my joke and shakes her head. "Not yet."

I turn my body to face her again. "So, what was the other thing that's bothering you?" Her eyes return to the walls of the cave. Whatever she sees captivates her.

"Do you see that?" Her voice whispers as if she is telling me a secret. I follow her eyes, but I don't see anything.

"What exactly should I be seeing?"

"Hieroglyphs. Words. I see them all over the walls of the cave. I didn't see them when we first got here, but I do now. I don't know how I could have missed them before. They're glowing so brightly." She looks back at me, her eyes wide with fear and worry. "Tell me you see them too?"

Mika

I know his answer before he speaks just by the look on his face. It's proof that I've utterly lost my mind. By agreeing to go thru this Passage, I've signed up to be the head of the crazy committee. What other reason could there be for me seeing all of these glowing symbols everywhere?

I stand up, throw my t-shirt on and look around. They're everywhere. Not only that, but I understand what they mean. I can read them. It's the weirdest shit. Maybe there's some scentless psychedelic gas in here making me crazy.

"I don't see them, but that's only because it's dark in here. But if we walk around with the flashlight, I'm sure I'll be able to. They're all over the cave. I do know that." He stands and watches me.

"But I can see them now. They're glowing different colors depending on what they used to write them with." I turn around quickly to look at him. "Don't ask me how I know that. I just do but that isn't the weirdest part of it."

"What?" he asks, worry now on his face.

"I know what they mean. What they're saying." His eyes widen.

"How? This is written in a dead language we've never been able to read. Only the Monarch can." His astonishment was not unfounded, nor was he alone in feeling that way.

"I don't know."

"What do they say?" His eyes are full of concern but at least he's not looking at me as if I fell off the crazy train.

"Some talk about a visitation from the sky people. But the symbols are accounts from the Brielaran point of view." I point toward the wall underneath the biggest hole where the moon was shining through earlier. "There's a group over there that details the crash and the visitors who came after them. Others talk about their appearance, what was found with them and what happened years later." I look back at him again, feeling his eyes on me rather than the places I pointed out. "Do you think I'm crazy?"

"No, not at all. I'm sure there's a logical reason for it. This is more evidence of why we need to get you tested to see what your genetic makeup is."

He wraps his arms around my shoulders and pulls me to him. "Don't worry about it." He kisses my forehead, his hand lowering to my hip. "We'll get you some answers soon. But in the meantime, how about I get you home? We can continue this discussion when we visit with Brady."

"Okay." I feel better knowing he didn't think I'd lost my marbles. At least that's what he said and I'm going to run with it. I shouldn't be surprised. Strange shit has been happening ever since I was dropped off in Abrielara. I wasn't expecting this. No one said anything about the Passage bringing on strange talents. Hopefully, this doctor can make some sense out of all this because I can't see sense in any of it.

The ride home is peaceful and quiet. I guess Solomon understands that I needed it because he doesn't pressure me to talk. He looks over at me periodically and squeezes my hand that he's been holding on to since we got into the truck. I don't know what his intention was when he asked me out. I hope it wasn't solely to get into my pants so he could get on with this Passage. I freely admit now that I like him. He is a genuinely nice person. And I'm more into him than I'd like to admit. Even to myself.

Something happened to me during the consummation. It felt like it was much more than sex. He touched a part of me I didn't know was there to touch. I felt a connection with him that far surpassed the connection I felt during the heat stage.

I don't know what all of this means. I do know that I owe it to myself to learn more. What does this mean for us? I don't even know what Solomon wants. Or if there's an us. Hell, I don't know what I truly want. We haven't discussed that, only what the Passage requires.

Maybe I'm thinking too fast or too far in advance. I guess I shouldn't worry about what either of us wants until the Passage is complete. Which he confirmed meant that I had to have a child. I haven't given that fact any thought whatsoever because I can't do anything about it. I have to complete the Passage or risk dying. It apparently doesn't matter if I want it or if I'm ready for it or not.

"We're here."

So engrossed in my thoughts I didn't notice that we'd made it home. He turns off the truck, let's go of my hand to grab my jacket from the cab and exits the truck. I follow behind him. He takes my keys, opens my door, and follows me inside.

"I hope you enjoyed our date. I sure did."

His face is hopeful as I take my jacket from him and hang it on the rack. "Yes, I did. Thank you for inviting me. It was quite eye-opening."

"In a good way, I hope?" He takes my hands and kisses them.

"Yes. Definitely in a good way."

The relief in his eyes makes me laugh.

"Hey, I had to ask. I was concerned with messing up, if you remember."

"Well, you can rest assured. You did not mess up."

His beautiful smile lights up his face. "Great. Then does that mean you'll go out with me again? Like, tomorrow, maybe?"

"Sure. I would love to."

He picks me up off my feet and squeezes me tight, burying his face in my neck. "Thank you." He sets me down but doesn't let me go.

"No need to thank me."

He kisses my cheek and then kisses the other one. I figure what is good for him is good for me, and so I kiss both of his cheeks too. His lips twitch just enough for me to see it. It makes me smile. I'm still getting used to seeing him happy rather than angry all the time.

He lets go of my hands and pulls me roughly against him by my waist. His eyes burn through mine and I feel the heat down to my bones. A light haze covers my vision and I feel myself succumbing to it.

"I thought the heat was over," I murmur before his lips cover mine. He runs his tongue over my lips, corner to corner, then inserts it between them. I run my hands up his chest and around his neck. My body trembles with anticipation and excitement. His hands cup my ass and he presses his erection into me. Feeling how hard he is makes me hot. Wet, hot, and hungry.

"Technically," he mumbles.

Our kisses become more frenzied the hotter we get. Our moans and sighs are felt more than heard.

I don't know much about me, Abrielara, the Passage or my mother. But I can tell you one thing I do know.

I want him.

Like yesterday. At this moment, I don't think I can possibly ever not want him. Insatiable is the only word to describe how much I want him. Being close to him removes any thoughts from my mind other than how to have him inside me again.

He lifts me and I wrap my legs tightly around his waist. He grabs my ass and grinds his dick into me again, causing a gush of heat to spread through me and wets my panties. I know he can feel it. He grinds harder into me as if feeling how wet I am for him turns him on.

We make it to the couch, and he throws me down on it, going right for my boots and tugging them off. Next, my pants and panties go, and his face is planted between my legs like he couldn't wait to get there. His tongue sweeps at all of the juices that have leaked out. His tongue taps against my clit and I come. I can't hold it off because I didn't see it coming.

I scream his name like my life depends on it, my fingernails clawing at his back and my hands yanking at his hair. He doesn't stop. He keeps eating me as if he hasn't had me in years instead of an hour ago. I haven't even calmed down from the first orgasm before he nips at my clit and I see stars again. He grabs me by my waist and trades places with me, but instead of removing his clothes, he sets me right on his face and resumes eating me again.

"Solomon!" I try pulling at his head to get him to stop. He finally lifts me up enough so he can talk.

"What is it, babe?"

"You've eaten me out plenty of times. When is it going to be my turn?" He grins at me, his eyes already glowing.

"After you come for me one more time. Trust me. I'm gonna get mine. Now, fuck my face."

He pulls my hips over his face again and works that tongue so expertly I have no choice but to do as he says. I'm afraid of hurting him, but when he keeps pressing his mouth into me and my hips down onto him, I figure he's okay, and I let my body do what it wants. I ride his face until my body shutters, my juices fill his mouth until I can't hold myself up anymore.

He lifts me up and sets me to the side and strips down.

"Hands and knees, baby. On the couch. Face down."

I do as he says, arching my back so he has more to work with.

"Just the way I like it," he whispers with approval.

I feel him behind me and then he kisses my lower back, creating shivers up and down my spine. He rams his dick inside me so fast and hard that a gasp tears through me. My pussy squeezes him in response to his roughness, instigating another wave of damp heat to smother his dick before he even begins to move. I brace my hands on the arm of the couch, ready for the pounding I'm sure he's about to unleash on me.

He doesn't disappoint. It's painful. I'm not going to lie. But it hurts so good. I want more of it.

"Mmmm...Solomon," I whimper.

He rams into me over and over again, bringing tears to my eyes. My swollen pussy lips take the beating and weep for more. His fingers imprint on my pelvic bone as he grinds into me. He pushes my hips down a bit as he thrusts up into me, hitting a new spot inside me.

"Fuck, Mika, take that dick, baby. You feel so good."

It's happening again. Bright lights and colors, stars, lightning...you name it, I see it. He continues to ram into me without any semblance of tenderness or mercy and I come harder than I ever have in my life. As soon as my pussy clamps down on him, he leans over my back and hugs me tightly to him as my pussy bathes his dick with my hot cum —again.

My pussy continues to milk him and then he finally lets go. He showers my eager pussy with every drop he has to give, and there's a lot of it. I feel every rope he releases and it goes on forever.

I love it.

I love the way it feels when he comes inside of me. I love how he spreads me and fills me up so much that I feel as if I can't even take a full breath.

That acknowledgement astounds me. Just hours ago, I was hoping I never saw him again and now I'm waxing poetic on how much I love the way he feels.

What is wrong with me?

We lie there in relative silence. Our heavy breathing is not so quiet. I can't move a muscle. Not because I'm exhausted but because Solomon is lying on top of me and he's heavy. But I like it. Just one more thing I love about him.

Not surprised.

His dick is still pulsing inside of me and my pussy is contracting around his still thick dick. I feel him begin to ease out of my body, but then he suddenly surges back inside me as if he changed his mind. His dick twitches inside of me and I feel it growing thicker and hard again.

"My god, Solomon!" I moan in ecstasy and automatically spread my legs so he has more room to move again.

You know...in case he wants to.

And he does. His hands slide underneath my body to latch onto my breasts. His body moves slowly, tenderly, and seductively in and out of mine. A startling contrast to how he just took me. My body tingles all over, right down to my toenails.

"Holy shit." I groan in wonder.

The lethargic way his body moves is in no way lazy. It's methodical, intentional, and skilled. His body plays mine so beautifully. He hits all the right spots to generate the right notes. He knows how to touch what, when and where. My body has never been this responsive to anyone before. Ever.

"Baby, you feel so good. It's like you were made for me." His voice groans in my ear.

The reverent way he moves and touches me brings tears to my eyes. He moves one of his hands from my breast down to my pussy and finds my clit to tease. I'm so wet that you can hear it, even though he isn't pounding into me like before. He is torturing me, killing me softly with each and every stroke. He's filling me up again. My pussy is sore and swollen but it is praying and pleading that he doesn't stop.

Please don't stop.

He maintains the same pace. He doesn't speed up. He doesn't slow down. He's driving me insane as he tenderly strokes my sensitive nerves. I'm filled to the brim. Any minute now and I'm going to...

"Come for me, baby," he growls in my ear.

He pinches my clit, my body trembles, and my pussy milks his dick, convulsing all over it at the same time. His thrusting hips never change speed or intensity. He lets me ride him through it.

Then he follows me. He growls my name as he empties into me, still fucking me through it. My head buzzes with electricity and it spreads through my body. He pumps and I squeeze. I don't want it to end.

I never want this feeling to end.

Chapter Fifteen

Solomon

"That was pretty slick," she mumbles. I raise up on my elbows so I can hear her better.

"What was that babe?" I kiss her cheek and she looks over her shoulder at me, which I'm sure is hard to do since I'm still lying on top of her.

"I was saying that was pretty slick what you did there. You told me I could taste you after I fucked your face, but I never got to."

"Oh, you caught that?"

I hesitantly slide out of her body. I knew when she asked I wasn't gonna let that happen tonight. I was too hungry for her. Selfish? Maybe. Okay yeah, but trust me, I'll let her wrap those beautiful lips around me at some point.

"Yes, I caught that," she replies airily as my dick plops out of her.

"I'll make it up to you. I promise. Just not tonight. I know you're tired and I'm tired. I thought maybe we could shower together before going to bed."

I step away from the couch and pick our clothes off the

floor. She turns over and hikes an eyebrow at me and I raise my hands.

"I'm not saying that I have to sleep over here. I'm saying I don't want the night to end and would love to shower with you."

"It's okay and you can stop worrying about messing up. I think we're past that. Don't you?"

"I assume nothing. You're the boss here, remember?"

She shrugs and slowly rises from the couch. I can see that she's sore and that somehow makes me feel proud. I step back to watch her creep around the couch a few steps before I swoop in and pick her up. I like seeing the evidence of my work but I hate to see her in pain.

She squeals, her arms latching onto my neck.

"Does this mean that you agree to shower with me?"

"Yes, and you can sleep over. At this point, that would be plain ridiculous for you to go home after the night we had."

I chuckle at that. "You have a point."

I set her down to sit on the bathtub and turn the shower on.

"How hot do you like it?" My fingers test the water.

"As hot as it will go."

I smile over at her. "My kind of girl." I close the glass shower door. "I'm going to run to the bathroom I used when I stayed here. I think I left some shower gel in there. Be right back."

If I had the energy, I would have skipped all the way there and back, but I don't have the legs for it after the marathon we had. By the time I get back to the bathroom, Mika is already in the shower with her pretty pink shower cap on, all soaped up. Her shower gel smells like lavender and warm vanilla.

Believe it or not, my dick perks up at the smell of her soap. As if I didn't just fuck her within an inch of her life a few minutes ago. I was damn near positive that I only had enough energy to take a shower and fall asleep.

Evidently not.

Her back is turned toward me when I open the shower door and step inside. I wrap my arms around her and press my hard dick between her soap-slick thighs.

"Oh!" Her tiny gasp does something to me. Fuck. She does something to me. I take her loofa sponge and rub it all over her body but I become frustrated. I want to feel her skin with my hands. I drop the sponge and pour a little soap into my palms. I then rub my hands all over her body. I rub her nipples, and the peaks harden for me. Her whimpers drive me to continue.

My hands run down her body to the apex of her thighs. I run my fingers thru her folds, making sure to be gentle, and she leans into me. Her head falls back on my shoulder. I kiss her neck and rub her into a quivering frenzy. All while stroking my own fire by continuing to rub my hard cock between her thighs.

Fuck, I want her. I can't believe how badly I want her and how quick my recovery time is after beating that pussy up earlier. I can't help myself. I rub my hard cock against her fat pussy more urgently. I gotta have her one more time. One more time and that's all for tonight.

"I know you're sore, baby, but I need you. Last time tonight. I promise not to be too rough." I growl in her ear.

I turn her around and lean her back against the shower wall. I lift her up and sink into her before she can wrap her legs around me. She whimpers, wrapping her arms around me and laying her head on my shoulder.

"Fuck, you feel better than anything I've ever felt in my life." I groan out.

"You do too." She pants softly.

She clinches around me and I know that this one is going to be a short one. I already feel my balls draw up at her admission. I grab her ass with both hands and move her up and down on my dick, nice and easy, hoping to minimize the impact of invading her body when she is so tender.

"I can't get enough of you." My voice shallow and raspy.

She quivers around me as I keep my long deep strokes steady and gentle for her. I'm already shaking. I don't know how much longer I can hold out. I move one finger to press on her tight asshole and I grind into her. The tip of my finger slides in and she comes for me. Shaking all over me and squeezing my dick and my finger like she hasn't had multiple orgasms already.

I let out a roar from the pit of my gut as my balls empty for the fourth time tonight. I hold her for a few more moments, enjoying the feeling of her surrounding me. I'll never get enough of this.

Never.

I slide out of her as soon as I can catch my breath and set her on her feet, but I continue to support her. She has absolutely no legs at this point. I soap her down again for good measure and then do the same for myself. After rinsing off, I shut off the water, and we stumble out of the shower to dry off. By the time we make it to bed, I doubt we have one eye open between us. I'm so fucking tired and I think she's already asleep. If she wasn't before we left the bathroom, she definitely was before her head hit the pillow.

I'm awake enough to turn off the light and snuggle up behind her. When sleep floats in, the last thought I remember is...

she's mine. She's all mine.

Mika

I'm in heaven. I couldn't lift a muscle if you paid me, but I'm in heaven. I know Solomon dicking me down last night is mostly to blame for this wonderful feeling. However, I know his heavy body partially lying on me is responsible for some of it too. As my brain wakes up a little more, I realize something is different. I don't move as I try to make sense of it all.

The fact he's lying on top of me isn't what's strange. It's what's between my legs, around my waist, and on my shoulder, giving me pause. I inch away from Solomon as best as I can without waking him up and turn to look over my shoulder. It's as I suspected.

Lux.

It's his appendages that are wrapped around each of my legs and around my waist. It's also his hair that is fanned across my shoulder. I reach over, turn on the light, and scream at the top of my lungs.

His eyes are open but are completely black. I can't see his pupils at all. He doesn't budge at the sound of my scream. Not even a little bit.

I extract myself from his tentacles and scurry off the bed. I'm so fucking pissed and creeped out right now that the heavenly euphoria I woke up in is long gone. I run to my closet, grab a t-shirt to throw over my naked body, and storm back into my bedroom.

"Lux!" I scream at him but he still doesn't move.

"Lux! Get your fucking ass up!" I shove his shoulder as hard as I can but it barely moves. He's as thick as a cement wall.

"Lux, get up. I swear I will donkey kick your ass off my bed if you don't get up."

I slap at his chest, back and arms and finally see a difference in his eyes. His eyes aren't cat-like at all, as I first thought. They're closer to crocodile. As he awakens, I see the film covering his eyes move, and then I can see his red pupils shine through.

He looks around as if he isn't quite sure why he's here and slowly gets off the bed, his appendages retracting back into his body. He runs his hands through his hair and then cups his hands around his hard dick. Too late for all that. Not only have I already seen it, but I also woke up to it nestled between my ass cheeks.

"Solomon must have been tired last night."

I cross my arms across my chest, getting more agitated by the second.

"I don't know what that has to do with you being here."

I know my words came out more harshly than I intended when I see his shoulders drop. I've never been an intentionally cruel person. Even to someone I feel has been cruel to me, so seeing that I hurt his feelings doesn't sit well with me. Unfortunately, I don't get the chance to apologize.

"I think it would be best if Solomon explained."

Before my eyes, the Brielaran disappears and Solomon stands before me. I've never seen them change before. It's like witnessing a seamless magic trick.

"I'm sorry, Mika. I should have explained. We haven't had the chance to talk about what it means to be a hybrid male. Everything happened so fast yesterday. It didn't dawn on me to explain that this could happen."

"I understand. So explain it now." I get back into the bed and cover my legs with the sheet. He follows me and covers his naked body.

"Well, you know, when you're exhausted, you kind of sleep like the dead. For male hybrids who have begun the Passage, that same mechanism that puts you in a deep sleep is similar to the one we use to change between human and Brielaran. It isn't intentional. It happens naturally. The more tired I am, the more likely I'll wake up as Lux. If I go to bed as Lux and I'm super tired, then I'll most likely wake up as me. I hope you understand, and please don't think Lux planned this because he didn't. I promise you."

Now I feel bad. Lux obviously was as shocked as I was to see himself wake up here. It's becoming more obvious to me that never seeing Lux again is going to be impossible if I plan to continue to spend any kind of time with Solomon. Which I do. With that thought, I know what I need to do.

"Okay, so obviously, not seeing Lux again is unrealistic."

Solomon looks down but shakes his head.

"Not if we want to continue to see each other." He looks at me, his warm eyes looking deep into mine. "Do you want to continue to see me?" He grabs one of my hands and kisses it. "I definitely want to continue to see you."

"Yes. I do."

He smiles and leans over and kisses my lips.

"Good. Then we need to figure out how to make things right between you and Lux."

I nod in agreement, but I don't know how. I know part of it is a pride thing for me. He hurt and embarrassed me. Yes, he apologized, but how do I know he isn't going to strong-arm me again? How do I know he isn't going to exert his will over me when I've made it clear that I don't want it?

"Right. So what is the typical relationship like between the Brielaran and the women they choose? All of us have a similar experience, so how did they get past that experience to have a compatible relationship?"

"I'm not exactly sure. I've never gone through this before, but I'm sure we can figure it out." He looks at me as if he's afraid I'll change my mind.

"I know we will. Don't worry, I'm not going to leave because it's hard. I told you I would finish this and I will."

"Okay, I appreciate that, but I want you to enjoy the rest of the Passage. I want you to look back on the entire thing and say it was worth it and you're glad you did it. Promise me if you have any questions or doubts that you tell me so we can work through it."

"Okay. I promise."

"I want you to know that I want this to work more than I want anything else."

Hearing him say how much he wants this too, makes me want to fix my Lux issue that much more.

"First I need to talk to the other chosen ones and get their feedback. Then I can talk to Lux, and we can decide what our rules are going to be."

"Rules?" Solomon gives me a wary look. Reminding me how Brielarans feel about being told what to do.

"Rules that both of us agree on. I'm not going to dictate to him what our relationship should be because it isn't only about you and me. I get that now."

His face lightens at my explanation. "Okay." He looks over his shoulder. "Clock says it's five-thirty. You got some-where to be?"

My eyebrows knit together at his question. "No. I'm stuck here, and I know a handful of people. Where would I be going?"

"Just asking." He reaches over, turns the lamp off, and then pulls me down to the mattress. "I need a bit more sleep because I have plans later." He pulls me back toward him in the way we were before I realized I was in bed with Lux.

"What do you have to do later?" I mumble, already feeling sleep weigh down my eyelids. He wraps me up in his arms, and I feel like I'm back in heaven again.

"Eat that pussy and dick you down. What else is there?"

Solomon

Although I told Mika I needed more sleep, I wanted an excuse to get her back in my arms again. I'm sorry that she was upset, but I'm not sorry that we've worked out a plan to improve our relationship.

"I'm sorry. I did not mean to cause you more trouble."

"Lux, you heard her. She understands and it all worked out. You have nothing to apologize for."

"I should have sensed that she was awake and prepared for it."

"Lux, you expect too much of yourself. We were exhausted. You know this is a normal occurrence when we're that tired. We had a strenuous night last night. It was to be expected."

"Yes. I am happy for you, Solomon."

"Be happy for us. She has agreed to find a solution between you. That's huge."

"Yes, I am happy for that too. Although she was upset, I was happy to have the chance to peacefully hold her in my arms."

"I'm happy for you, Lux. If things go our way, you'll have many more nights like that to come."

"That is my greatest wish, Solomon. To have that for both of us."

"Me too. Trust me. I want that more than anything."

I wake up exhilarated and fucking more turned on than if you plugged me into a light socket. When the fog leaves my brain, I know why.

Mika has those lips I love so much wrapped around my dick and sucking the life right out of it. I feel her throat constrict around my hard cock and damn near lose my load right then. I can't stop her. I don't want to stop her but I'm not gonna last. My eyes roll to the back of my head and my hands find her head.

"Mika, baby…" I moan. I'm able to look down at her and see her eyes glowing that magnificent blue and her mouth full of my cock. One of the most beautiful sights I've ever seen. She stops sucking my dick and waits for me to continue.

"I'm gonna come if you keep going." I grunt at her. She raises an eyebrow and continues. She increases the suction of her mouth. It's like she wants me to come down her gorgeous throat.

I try not to…I do, but I can't help myself and I start fucking her mouth. She lets me control her head as I shove my dick down her throat. She gags a little, and I love how that sounds. I make her do it a few more times and then I can't stop it from happening.

I come down her throat as a roar exits mine and I keep coming. She swallows it all and licks me clean. After she cleans my dick with her tongue, she wraps it around my balls and sucks them into her mouth. Chill bumps cover me and I feel my body preparing for another round. My dick begins to thicken and harden again.

Fuck! This shit is unprecedented. I've never had this many orgasms in this time frame before. She's gonna fucking kill us. She rubs her hands up and down my thighs. Runs her tongue along each of my balls and then watches my dick stand up for her right before her eyes.

She smiles triumphantly as I can barely catch my breath. She rises above me but doesn't sit on me. She leans down so that our faces are close. So close I smell myself on her breath.

"This morning, I had a hard time staying asleep. It could have been because everything is happening so fast, or it could have been because your impressive dick was sticking into my hip. Then I remembered how you wouldn't let me taste it last night even though I wanted to. So I decided to do something about it." She licks her lips lasciviously. "You are delicious, by the way."

"I am?" She leans back and swings one leg over me.

"Oh yes. I plan to taste you more often. But right now, I need a ride. Are you gonna give me one?" She doesn't wait for my answer, but did she need to? We both know what my answer would be.

She lowers herself onto my stiff as fuck cock. Her wet pussy leaks all over it. It takes considerable restraint to keep from taking over. I grit my teeth, hoping it will help me keep a rein on my emotions. Obviously, all the pussy I ate and fucked last night did not dampen my need for her.

Her pussy puts my dick in a chokehold.

"Fuck me," I gasp. My hands grab onto the globes of her ass, squeezing them.

"As you wish."

She smiles that smile again and fucks me she does. The rise and fall of her hips compliment the contractions of her sweet pussy around my dick. I run my finger down my dick to catch her juices and then I run my finger down the crack of her ass to lather it up.

Her eyes glow brighter when she realizes what I'm doing.

She leans over me, putting her hands on either side of my head, giving me more room to do what I want to with her ass. She rides me nice and easy, no hurry. Driving me out of my mind.

I move my hips up to match her movements, but mine aren't as smooth as hers. I'm on the edge already, and I want her there with me. I take one hand off her ass and put it between her legs on her clit. I swirl my finger around her cum soaked bud. Another finger from my other hand is pressing into her tight rosette.

"Holy...shit." She sighs and her hips move in tight circles around my dick. Now her movements are a lot less smooth. Her pussy is drowning my dick in her sweet juices, coating my fingers while I rub her clit.

"Fuck. Ride that dick, baby." I pinch her clit and push two of my fingers into her ass.

"Shit, Solomon!" She gushes all over me as she bounces on my dick. I rise and pull her to my chest as the gravity of my orgasm hits me so hard I can't even call out. My jaw clenches as the shudders quake through my body. The pulses of her pussy keep pulling me into her.

As if there is any other place I'd rather be.

Mika

After having my way with Solomon, I slept until almost noon, but now I am wide awake and wired. I can't get Lux off of my mind. So I leave Solomon in bed to take a shower. My mind is crowded with everything that has happened since I arrived here and how things have taken a total one-hundred-and-eighty-degree turn.

Who would have thought after getting off that rinky-dink plane, I would find myself falling for my formally hateful neighbor?

Falling for.

All it took was one date. One date and I am already talking about finding a way to make my issue with Lux right. Does that mean I plan to stay here? Obviously, something is going on with me that will require more thought, but to stay and be with Solomon and Lux?

For how long?

All Solomon said was he wanted this to work. He didn't say for how long or what he meant. I know the consummation isn't complete until we procreate. But then what? We share custody?

These questions bring me back to how I'm going to learn more about the typical relationship between a Brielaran and his Chosen One. While I'm at it, I'll get answers to those other questions too.

As I dry off, I can't help but see the irony in all of this. When I got here. My head was full of questions about my mother and our relationship. I was so intent on finding answers to why things were how they were. Now I have questions of a totally different nature that have nothing to do with my mother. Sure I would love answers to my original questions, but now I have more pressing questions. And I think I know how I want to do it.

When I walk out of the bathroom, Solomon is still out, so I tiptoe out the door, quietly closing it behind me. Once I make it downstairs, I head to the kitchen and start some coffee. The first place I have to start is with the Fab Four. I reach for my cell phone and start thumbing through for their numbers. They'll know the best way for me to put my idea into play.

By the time Solomon makes it down to the kitchen in nothing but a pair of sweatpants, we are just sitting down with mimosas. The ladies don't give him a second look, but I can't take my eyes off him. His black hair is still damp from his shower, making his honey eyes pop. He's wearing black sweats instead of the grey ones I saw on him the first morning we talked. His body is delicious. I saw him like two hours ago and my body is in the middle of completing the pussy Olympics. As if I'd never seen or had him before.

God, I need help.

"Good morning, ladies. I hope I'm not interrupting your brunch."

He speaks to them but doesn't take his eyes off me. Their murmured replies aren't acknowledged by him or me. Becca and Kim do a double take. He walks straight to me and takes my face in his hands.

"Good morning, beautiful," he whispers and then lays those juicy lips on me, damn near sucking mine right off my face. I can't stop the moan that slips passed our lips. He tastes so good and my pussy clenches when he shoves his tongue down my throat.

I can feel the eyes of the four on us, but I don't care. I wouldn't say no if he wanted to spread me out on this table right now and eat me for brunch. He finally frees my lips and gives me a sexy grin.

"Good morning," I reply breathlessly.

He gets on with making himself a cup of coffee and I brave a glance around the table. Everyone except Becca looks surprised. Their eyes wide with questions. No way am I going into any details about him when he's within earshot.

But I will later. It'll help them understand why I'm asking for their help. I give them a small shrug and mouth later so they can at least let it go for now.

"What are you all up to today?" He leans against the counter with his legs crossed at the ankle. Again, his muscles are defined and put on a show with every move he makes. I wonder if he knows how not to do that when he isn't wearing a shirt?

"I think we would much rather talk about what you and Mika have been cooking up," Becca informs him. My eyes close tightly, embarrassed at her bluntness, although I shouldn't be. He laughs at her.

"Ah, come on now, Becca. You and I both know that when I go back upstairs to get dressed, you'll get the details then."

She wags her finger at him. "You have a point there, oh sexy one. So why don't you take that coffee with you upstairs so we can get on with it." He throws his head back and howls at her.

"Not yet. I'm having too much fun delaying your gratification." He winks at her and looks over at Dyana and she smirks at him.

"Hey there, sister-in-law. How goes it?"

"Well, obviously not as well as it's going for you. I'm happy to see it."

He shrugs his agreement.

"If you must know, your girl asked for our help. We think it's a noble cause so we're lending our expertise. No worries, you'll hear all about it soon enough. If you want to be of help, why don't you run by my house and spend some time with your niece and nephew? Ever since you started the Passage, you haven't been around. You've been missed. They've been asking about you."

I grab the pitcher and refill our glasses while listening to their conversation.

"That's actually a good idea. I feel horrible that they've noticed I haven't been around. I'm sorry, Dyana. I should be a better uncle to them than that." His crestfallen face shows how deeply sorry he is.

"Nonsense. The Passage is top priority. They'll forget you were ever gone as soon as they see you. Now, kick rocks so we can get down to the business of talking about you." She waves him off.

He isn't at all offended. He laughs and kisses her cheek on his way out of the kitchen. "Only because you asked so nicely." His eyes look me over. "Come and see me in a minute. I wanna run something by you before I leave." He winks and leaves without waiting for a reply. I have no idea what he wants to run by me, but my panties are already wet with just the idea of getting my hands on him again.

"Well...I guess it's safe to say that the consummation phase is in full effect." Jeana takes a healthy gulp of her mimosa.

"Yes, please do tell." Kimberly picks up her glass with her pinky pointing straight up. "Inquiring minds want to know if the rumors are all true."

"Oh, Kim, I know you had to see him through those sweats like I did. There is no way some of those rumors aren't true. But I second the notion, inquiring minds do want to know." Becca drains her glass and reaches for a bottle of water.

"Well, I definitely don't want to know any details. He's my brother-in-law. I'd prefer not to hear anything about him that I'll have to force myself to forget later. However, before we discuss anything, we gotta get him out of here. So go see what he wants, even though we already know, so he can leave. We have things to do."

"If you insist. Be right back." I try not to rush my way up the stairs even though my heart has already beaten me there.

Chapter Sixteen

Solomon

I pull her into her dressing room and shut the door as soon as she walks in. I put her back up against the same wall she put Lux up against and shove my hands under her long flowing skirt. I pull it up to her waist and lay my lips on hers.

She's already melting and I'm nowhere near done with her yet. When I let her lips go, she's panting, and her eyes have taken on a hazy appearance.

"What did you want to see me about.?" Her breathy question is rhetorical. She knows what I want. She just wants to hear me say it.

"The first and last thing I want to taste every day is your pussy. I didn't get enough this morning, so I'm going to get it now." I shove her panties down as she tries to stammer out a rebuttal.

"B-But what about the ladies downstairs...mmmm."

I shove three fingers into her tight soaking-wet pussy. I thrust my fingers in and out of her, clearly planning on more than experiencing a tasting.

"They'll be fine. Besides, this won't take long at all."

My dick is already hard as granite and hearing her

panting sighs gets me all worked up. I can feel precum dribbling down my dick as we speak. I remove my hands from her warm pussy and drop to my knees. I force her legs on my shoulders and brace her back against the wall for support. I don't waste any time lapping her up. Her legs are already quivering, and her pussy is dripping wet.

I fucking love this shit. I nibble her clit until she starts to come and then I dip my tongue into her honey pot so I can catch the windfall. She tastes so good.

I stand up, leaving her legs on my shoulders. This opens her up wide for me, not that my dick needs any help finding a way inside her. One thrust and I'm all the way in. Her gasp echoes my groan and I waste no time pounding into her. Initially, I only wanted a taste, but I can never just taste her. I always want more than one taste, and if my tongue gets one, it's only fair that my dick gets one too.

She pants and grinds against me and it drives me insane.

"Fuck baby. Why is your pussy so good?" I huff out as I continue to pummel her with my cock. My balls slap against her ass and I swear she loves it.

"Come for me. Clamp down on my dick and squeeze the fucking life out of me."

I grind my pelvis into her clit and her pussy does exactly what I told her to do. I cum so hard and yell so loud I can't hear anything past the booming in my ears and my name shrieking past her lips.

We cling to each other in silence, willing our bodies to calm down. Her perfect pussy pulsates around me and my dick throbs in response. Fuck I want her again, but honestly...when don't I want her? I know she has things to do, and so do I, but all that matters is this right here. Being with her, even if we aren't fucking, is a dream come true. Now, feeling her around me, milking me dry is the purest heaven I've ever had.

"Solomon?" Her soft voice pulls me out of my head. I move back a little so I can see her face. I drop her legs so they are around my waist.

"Yeah, baby?"

"Is it always like this?" Her eyes slowly dim, and that only means one thing to me. She's got worry on the brain.

"No. It isn't. I've fucked other hybrids and it has never felt like this. Never. What about for you?" It'll break my heart if she says it has. She shakes her head.

"No. I wondered if we are reacting to each other this way because of the Passage. Because this is the most phenomenal sex I have ever had." She giggles at the thought. "I have never had so many orgasms in one day or ever as I've had with you." I kiss her lips because that statement deserves it.

"I'm happy to hear that, sweetheart. Real happy to hear that." I kiss her lips again and pump my dick inside of her again.

"You are insatiable." She sighs. Her pussy relentlessly squeezes onto me tightly. It's the sweetest torture. As much as it pains me, I make myself stop. I kiss her neck and whisper in her ear.

"If you didn't have company I would keep pounding this pussy, but I don't want to be rude. Just remember tonight, it's on."

She smiles sweetly and kisses my lips. I feel her pussy latch onto me one last time and then releases me.

"I can't wait," she whispers and then drops her legs from my waist. She walks out of the closet and into the bathroom, closing the door behind her.

I'm already craving her again. I bring my fingers that were just inside her to my nose to smell her sweet aroma and then into my mouth to lick them clean.

Mika

My fingers shake as I clean up in the bathroom. That man is going to be the death of me. I know he is. No one can have this much sex for a long period of time without consequences.

But what a way to go.

The thought makes me laugh. I catch my reflection in the mirror and the smile on my face makes me happy and sad.

I have to keep in mind that this won't last. Yes, we're enjoying ourselves now. But when the Passage is over, I don't know what's going to happen. He likes me. He likes having sex with me but he hasn't said anything more than that, so I can't expect anything more. In the meantime, I plan to enjoy it while I can so I have memories to hang on to when I leave here.

The ladies are right where I left them. A new pitcher of mimosas is sitting on the table. I dump what was left in my glass and make myself a fresh one.

"So, I think it's safe to say that we got one question we had answered." Jeana smiles so big I'd think she was the one doing all the hollering if I didn't know better.

My eyes drop to the table and my mind quickly reviews what Solomon and I did in my closet. I'm embarrassed that I was so loud because I have no doubt that they heard us.

"No point in pretending you don't know what we're talking about. We heard you. I actually think the entire state of Washington heard you. Can't say I blame you, though. You lucky girl you." Becca purses her lips and winks at me.

"Mika, you don't have to entertain her. I'd like to say her behavior is because she was raised in a barn with wild dogs. Unfortunately, I can attest to the fact that she was indeed raised in a house by very respectable parents." Dyana mean mugs Becca who in turn shrugs her shoulders at her, totally unbothered by her comments.

"I'm not pretending I don't know what you're talking about. I thought we were going to wait until after he leaves before discussing him?" I'd rather not have him hear me recount my experience with him. Not that he doesn't already know, but still, it's good to pretend that we aren't going to talk about him, at least.

"He already knows we're going to talk about him. Might as well get to it," Becca states matter-of-factly.

I look up, mid-sip, and giggle because Becca is relentless and soon the ladies are laughing with me.

She apparently is as interested in knowing more as everyone else. I nod, my mouth holding a gentle smirk. "Fine. The rumors are definitely true. He is blessed and is exceptionally talented in how he uses it."

"Told ya. You all should listen to me more often," Becca gloats.

A throat clearing at the foot of the stairs has our heads swinging in that direction with our mouths open. Solomon's half-lipped smile proves he heard us and is proud of what he heard. He walks over to me wearing another classic t-shirt that fits him like a glove and loose-fitting faded wash jeans. He smells so good I want to strip him down where he stands.

"I'm headed over to the Johns. Need me to pick up anything on my way back?"

"No. I don't think so."

"Alright, beautiful, I'm out. See you tonight." He pecks

my lips quickly and then my cheek. All of us, Dyana included, watch him leave.

"I'm married and make no mistake, I love my husband. He's a prince of a man, but Solomon is truly a sight to behold." Kim takes a long sip from her drink.

"He knows it too. Smug son of a bitch," Becca says, rummaging around her purse.

"I'll agree with you there. You know, I used to think that Lux was the one with all the swag but watching him walk from the table to the front door, I'm pretty sure that was all Solomon," Jeana says.

I look at Dyana, and she looks like she's going to be sick. I start giggling because this whole conversation is ludicrous. I never knew that these ladies put any thought into Solomon.

Becca's sly grin tells me she's probably about to top their comments with one of her own.

"Solomon definitely has his own swag. Everyone likes to say that Lux is the wild child but they both are. Solomon got away with a lot of stuff when we were kids because everyone believed it was Lux making him do it.

"But I caught him many times with his pants down and not just at parties. Dyana and I used to spy on him, Perry, Ashe, Brady and Michael all the time. I mean that is pretty much how Dy and I got our sexual education. Those boys took orgy to who new level...at least to us. Some things we didn't even know were possible until we saw them in action."

"Becca could you shut up? I'm sure hearing about the sexual exploits of the male hybrids of this town is not why she asked us over here." Dyana looks mortified.

"Well, it's not the first time I've heard Solomon or Lux was popular with the ladies around here. So that isn't new. The only part that was different than what I've heard is about

Solomon being the wild one and Lux isn't the only one. But that would make total sense to me."

"See. She didn't mind." Becca sticks her tongue out at Dyana.

"Becca, you are my soul sister and I love you but I need you to grow up. You have children of your own for Pete's sake." Dyana rolls her eyes.

"You're mad because it's true." She turns to me and ignores Dyana. She points her thumb in Dyana's direction.

"Dyana has always been the good girl. I was always dragging her off to spy on them because I was curious. They still don't know that we saw as much as we did. She won't admit it but she enjoyed spying on them as much as I did."

The look on Dyana's face has me so tickled and I can't stop laughing and the rest of the table chimes in.

"Okay, okay." Dyana looks at me with a wide smile on her face. "She's right. We did learn a lot about sex from spying on those five but they have no idea. I don't know how we got on this subject but now that we've gotten that out of the way, I want to know how you got from running from Solomon at Corks to him fucking your brains out and living here with you?" Dyana's face is elated. Obviously, she is happy with the turn of events.

"True. We heard what happened at the pharmacy, but I would love to hear your side of it," Kim says.

"He isn't living with me exactly. He stayed over last night after our date. It was kind of late when we got back."

"Honey, you don't have to justify anything to us. We've been thru this before, remember?" Jeana reminds me with a knowing smile.

The smile growing on my face is mirrored by everyone at the table. "In that case, he fucked my brains out and was too tired to walk across the street afterward."

"That's my girl." Dyana laughs.

"I still want to know your side of what happened at the pharmacy. The rumors were interesting enough, but I want to know if they are anywhere close to the truth," Jeana says.

"I can tell you what happened. Lux walked in after her and informed her that they were going to complete the Passage whether she wanted to or not. Mika being Mika told him to fuck off and he chased her down. They were in the heat cycle and burning hot, so when they got into close proximity to each other...that heat consumed them both. That's how Mika ended up against a cold brick wall with Lux between her legs."

Becca's account of what happened is surprisingly good, considering she wasn't there, but she's missing some information.

"As usual, Becca, your assessment is...astounding." Dyana says announces.

"I thought it was quite entertaining and surprisingly, pretty close to what happened."

"Ha!" Becca's scoff is loud and funny to me. "I'm right yet again. You all are gonna stop doubting me one of these days." All eyes turn back to me, completely ignoring her.

"Why am I not surprised?" Dyana's eyes widen.

"Well, some things are missing but she got the gist of what happened."

"Okay so tell us what she left out." Kim gets up and starts another pot of coffee. This wasn't exactly what I wanted to talk about but it can help explain why I'm asking for their help.

"Well, the heat is...coercive, as you know. I wasn't ready to go and still trying to get some shopping done, but Lux insisted that we leave. He kept coming at me and I don't know, something happened, and I put my hands up to stop him and it's like he hit an invisible wall or something, and he fell backward. I ran but he caught me and dragged me to the alcove."

The ladies lean toward me with their mouths open. Their coffee and mimosa's forgotten.

"He raised me off of my feet by my throat and said some stuff about not telling him what to do." I wave my hand between us. "I can't remember it all. I remember being so pissed. The next thing I knew, we're kissing and clawing at each other. He's like all over me, like everywhere, and we were humping each other to the point that I forgot the crowd watching and he didn't seem to care. But then suddenly, he reminded me that he was in charge and that he could do whatever he wanted to me and not only could I not stop him, but I wouldn't want him to."

"No, he didn't." Dyana's statement is not meant as a rebuttal. Her eyes are squinted almost shut.

"Yeah, he did. Then he drops me and leaves me surrounded by everyone in the pharmacy. I was mortified."

"You poor thing." Jeana reaches over and grabs my hands.

"I was also pissed. That night, I got to bed, and sometime after eleven, I woke up and Lux was in my bedroom sitting in a chair, watching me sleep."

"Weirdo," Becca mumbles under her breath. I ignore the comment.

"I got up, grabbed a robe in my closet, and he followed me. I'm still angry but even angrier because he came into my house without my permission—again. So when he followed me and said we needed to talk, I didn't want to hear it. I remember wishing he could feel what I felt when he hemmed me up in the pharmacy. The next thing I knew, I had him up against the wall, legs kicking and squeezing his neck, as he had to me...only I wasn't physically touching him."

"What did you say?" Dyana whispers.

I look around the table and the shock on her face is mirrored in theirs. I don't repeat myself. I go on with the story.

"So when I let him down, he told me he had come to apologize. I didn't believe him but he dropped to his knees and apologized for attacking me in the pharmacy. He told me that Solomon didn't want any of that to happen and to please not hold it against Solomon. He said that he was not sorry for choosing me but he was sorry for hurting me. So I told him fine. I'd continue the Passage with Solomon because I told him I would but I didn't want to see him ever again. He said he understood and left."

"Mika, you do realize that what you did was not normal?" Anxiety laces Dyana's words.

"Yes. I've honestly tried not to think about it. Solomon says he'll make an appointment with some doctor named Brady to run tests. Until then, I don't know what's happening to me or why." I look at the ladies again, trying to decide if I should continue. What if they think I'm nuts?

"There's more, isn't there?" Becca asks.

"When I went to meet up with Perry for lunch on Friday, I ran into Solomon. He asked me out on a date and I said yes. So last night, he took me on a picnic inside of a mountain."

"He took you to the crash site?"

My eyes meet Kim's. "Everything was great. The heat got pretty thick and we connected. But afterward, I kept seeing the signs and symbols illuminated on the cave walls. I didn't see them when we first got there, so I thought it was strange. I asked Solomon if he could see them, and he said not right now. But the weirdest thing for me was that I could not only see them, but I could also read and understand them."

"Holy shit," Dyana whispers, seemingly to herself. She looks over at Becca, and I don't miss the look between them.

"What is it Dyana?"

She looks back at me and shakes her head.

"Go on with your story first."

"That's pretty much it. We came back here, and we can't seem to get enough of each other. I asked you ladies over because Solomon and I decided that Lux and I needed to get along since he and I will be spending more time with each other." The ladies look a little confused, so I explain a little further. "I went to bed with Solomon last night and woke up to Lux this morning. He scared the shit out of me, but he was out cold."

"Oh....yeah, the first time seeing that is quite a shocker," Kim says, completely understanding what I woke up to.

"So, I wanted to know the experiences of the women in this town who were chosen but weren't raised here. I want to know how they were able to get over the whole chase, probe thing and have a relationship with the Brielaran who did it. I want to know what is considered a normal relationship between the two. I could ask you guys, but I thought I could get to know the ladies of the town, and they get to know me at the same time. A dinner party or something would be a great place to do that. What do you think?"

"I think it's a great idea. You know I'm always down for a party." Becca pulls out her cellphone. "I can start a group text right now. How many people do you want here?"

"Oh, I don't know. Just a bunch of women that will be willing to discuss their relationships. I don't want anyone to feel like they have to but it is kind of the point of the party." I shrug my shoulders.

"I think we should make this a smaller group. No more than fifteen total. That way everyone will have the chance to talk. And you can get to know them," Dyana offers.

"Ooh, I know a few people we should invite!" Kim pulls out her phone.

Soon we are engrossed in planning the party but I haven't forgotten the look shared between Dyana and Becca. I'll ask Dyana when I can get her alone. I have a feeling it's something I'm gonna want to know.

Solomon

Perry and Dyana live closer to my dad, near the center of town. Their house is not a log cabin but a large modern home that Perry had custom-built when they got married. When Dyana told me that the kids missed me, I felt terrible. I've been so caught up in the Passage and getting to know Mika that I totally let my scheduled visits with the kids fall by the wayside.

This is not like me at all. Every Sunday afternoon, I made a point to come over and spend the day with them. I haven't seen them since Mika came to town. Which has been damn near a month.

I'm a piss poor excuse for an uncle. Yeah, I know the Passage can consume you, but that isn't their fault, and they shouldn't have to suffer because of it.

I pull up into the driveway and before I even get out of the car, the kids run out to meet me. Perry's mini-me throws himself at me first.

"Uncle Solomon! You came! Can we go to the park now? Ooh, I know! Can we ride go-carts? I gotta a new video game, you wanna play with me?"

"One thing at a time PJ. We have all day. You know, you look more and more like your father every day?"

"That's what mama says. She says that she's gonna have to

beat the girls off with a stick. What does that mean, Uncle Solomon? Why would she want to beat girls with a stick?"

Perry Jr., whom we call PJ, is seven and looks exactly like his father, complete with dimples.

"I'll tell you when you're a little older, champ." I pick him up so he can ride on my back as he likes to do.

Following close behind is tiny four year old Mae, her tentacles swirling around her, like her hair and she's naked. Again.

She hates clothes. Any chance she gets, she's ripping them off and takes off like she's a prison escapee. Then there goes Perry, her warden, running after her and screaming her name like she should be the scared of the sound of his voice, which she isn't. She runs faster. The only thing she hates worse than wearing clothes is getting her hair combed. I call her my wild-haired fairy because her wild hair gives her a feral appearance.

She's adorable and the bad thing about that is she knows it and uses it to her advantage every chance she gets. She already knows how to manipulate people. It's crazy. Perry is the only adult in our family that cannot make Mae behave. My father and I have no issues when we keep her, but poor Perry can't figure her out. He can't even make her keep her clothes on. Dyana makes her wear them and usually does her hair too. Since Mae doesn't have a stitch on and her hair is all over her head, I'm guessing she must have been in a rush to get to Mika's.

"Play! Play!" Mae screams at me from the top of her lungs. She climbs up my body to wrap herself around me.

"If you want to play, you have to put your clothes on and sit still for me to do your hair. Are you gonna be good so we can play?"

She thinks about it for a few moments and then nods.

"Good. Go to your room and pick out an outfit and let Daddy help you get dressed. Then I'll do your hair and we can play. Okay?"

"Okay." She hops down and runs back into the house. Perry shakes his head in disbelief.

"How do you do that?"

"I don't ask. I tell. You ask, beg and plead which tells her that she has a choice. So when given the choice, she is going to choose wild hair and no clothes every time."

"I guess. So you come by for the kids or are you here to pay up?"

I walk through the door he holds open for me and set PJ down. I walk into the kitchen to grab something to drink.

"I have no idea what you're talking about." I feign ignorance, but I know full well what he's talking about.

"You know exactly what I'm talking about. Pay up and tell me about it."

I set down my water and reach in my pocket for my wallet. "Alright. You win."

"Ha! I told you! So how was it?" His know it all grin and pursed lips makes me want to pop him a good one, but he was right. He won fair and square.

"I couldn't get enough of her. I still can't get enough of her. If the Welcome Committee wasn't over at her house right now, I'd still be dicking her down right this second."

"How does it measure up to Tokyo?" He has to hear me say it. I roll my eyes.

"Fine. It was a hundred times better than Tokyo. Surprising, considering there were quite a few more girls to play with in Tokyo. Does it make you feel better to hear me say it?" I hand over a crisp one hundred dollar bill.

"Thank you and yes, it does make me feel better to hear you say it."

"So, besides not getting enough of her, what happened? She told me that you asked her out. What happened next?"

We sit down in the living room and my mind goes back to last night. My dick gets thick real quick thinking about her.

"She's phenomenal. The whole experience was amazing. I didn't know it could feel like that. I've never felt anything like her before. This heat is not just physical, it's emotional, mental, and spiritual too."

"I told you man. So where did you take her?"

"I took her to the crash site for a picnic. We ate and the next thing I know I'm yanking her pants down. But you know what? Something happened at the crash site that shook us a little. I've been thinking about it and I think I know what it is."

Perry watches me in confusion. "What the hell are you talking about? What shook you?"

"She can see and read all of the hieroglyphs in the cave. She was only able to do that after we consummated. It freaked her out."

"What the fuck?" Perry creases his eyebrows.

"Yeah, our thoughts exactly. But like I said, I think I know what she is." Our eyes meet and we respond simultaneously.

"The Librarian."

"Yep. And if she's the Librarian, then that means only one thing."

"You're the Guardian," Perry answers.

I sigh deeply, leaning back into the cushions of the couch. "Yep."

We sit in silence for a little while, thinking it over. This revelation scares me and makes me happy at the same time.

Happy because it adds another fiber to the rope that binds us together. It scares me because Mika may hate the idea.

"She's anxious to leave. What do you think she will say when I tell her about the commitment phase and then about being the Librarian? She's going to fucking hate me." I lean my head back against the couch.

"You haven't told her? Why?"

"We started the consummation phase last night. We've been a little busy."

Perry laughs at me, shaking his head. "Understandable but I suggest you tell her about the commitment phase as soon as you have the chance. You may not even have to tell her about being the Librarian."

I don't know why I didn't realize it. Perry's right. Educating her about being the Librarian isn't my role to play, exactly. As soon as the Monarch finds out that Mika is here and what we suspect, she won't waste time reaching out to her.

"The only real question is whether you wait for her to come to you or if you should take Mika to her. I know what I'd do if I were you."

"Take Mika to her," I answer, even though he didn't ask. I nod, thinking of the possible ramifications if she has to come to us.

"Yep. The sooner the better. Have you set up an appointment with Brady yet? I think that's probably the first thing you should do. You know, just to confirm what you think."

"Yeah, I sent Brady a text before I got over here. We have an appointment tomorrow at two."

"Good."

The sound of thundering tiny feet coming from the stairs ends our conversation for now. Mae is dragging a pair of pink overalls behind her.

My heart warms at the sight of her. To me, she is the cat's meow, the bee's knees, and the crunch in Cap'n Crunch. She launches herself into Perry's lap so he can help her finish getting dressed.

Before choosing Mika, I thought that PJ and Mae were the closest I was ever going to get to having a family. Even though I wanted one of my own, I still considered myself blessed to have them in my life. The possibility of my dream coming true used to be unfathomable. And yet, here I am, getting closer to completing my Passage with the one I have chosen.

Mae wiggles and squeals, anxious to get down. As soon as Perry has her dressed, she runs to grab her hair basket that her Momma keeps all of her hair products in. She brings it to me and then drags her pink kiddie chair over to sit in so I can do her hair. I run my fingers through her tight curls. I must not be moving quite fast enough for her because she yells at me, urgently.

"Hurry!"

I laugh at her and pour some conditioner into my hand to put into her hair. "Yes ma'am."

Chapter Seventeen

Mika

"Okay, so looks like everyone we've invited has agreed to come," Dyana informs us.

"Well, it's not like there's a lot going on here and everybody has wanted to get to know Mika since they found out Solomon chose her."

"Thanks a lot, Becca. Sure makes me feel welcome." I roll my eyes at her.

"Sorry, girl. I didn't mean it like that. I meant that when there is something new to do, we tend to jump at the chance."

"Yeah, I can't even remember the last one who was chosen. We've been in kind of a drought the last couple of years." Kim's eyebrows knit together, deep in thought.

"I would think that you all would have newly chosen ones all the time." I look around the table.

"True. But most of our chosen ones are Abrielarans. They already know what's expected. Having new blood come to town and be chosen is not an everyday occurrence, I can assure you. Come to think of it, I'm like Kim. I can't remember who the last new chosen one was." Dyana put air quotes around new.

"Joanne," Jeana whispers, her eyes wide as she looks around the table.

"Oh, that's right. Joanne." Kim's voice is laced with sadness at the revelation.

"Joanne? Who is Joanne?" My eyes ping-pong between them.

"Joanne was a woman who lived on the outskirts of Abrielara. She and the baby died." Becca's softly spoken words speak volumes about how hard the tragedy must have hit the community.

"That's awful" My hand goes to cover my mouth. "She wasn't an Abrielaran originally?" Each of the ladies shake their head. "How did he find her to choose her? How did that happen?"

"Joanne backpacked around here on the regular. She never came into town. She always kept to the outskirts. I don't remember where she came from but she became an unofficial regular. One night she came across Jake damn near bleeding to death in the woods. He had been mauled by an animal. She was able to stabilize him until she was able to get help.

"In the time it took her to nurse him back to health, he had chosen her. They got married and continued to live outside of town. When she got pregnant, she kept saying that she would stay in town in her last few weeks so that she could be near medical care. Unfortunately, she never got the chance. She'd been out walking, not far from her house, when she collapsed."

Dyana stops talking and no one says a word. "Jake found her the next day when he got home from hunting. By then it was way too late to save them."

"Oh, that's sad." I don't know these people but I feel for them. "So does that mean he has to live alone for the rest of his life or what?"

"No, he doesn't have to live alone for the rest of his life. He chose Joanna and completed the Passage, so he technically fulfilled his duty."

"Which means he will hopefully have another chance if he wants it. If he doesn't choose someone else, he can still find someone to spend his life with and be happy," Kim adds.

"Yeah, but we all know that Jake doesn't want anybody else. He stays out there in that cabin by himself. He comes into town to check in the store, but not often enough to connect with anybody." Jeana's voice is riddled with pity and sadness.

"Well, he isn't exactly by himself. Don't forget that Ashe is out there every weekend too. So at least he has someone to talk to," Dyana offers.

"I don't think they're friends, though. I think they live near each other, so they tolerate each other," Becca counters.

"What a way to dampen the mood," I say with a heavy sigh.

"Sorry. Not sure why we went there but it's okay. Today is going to be a good day. We have a party to get ready for, so I say we go do our shopping before the ladies start showing up." Kim gets up from the table. "I'm going to head over to the bakery and grab a couple of cakes. I'll be back in about an hour."

"Okay. Then I guess I should probably run to the grocery store and grab a few things. Anybody wanna come with me?" I look around the living room trying to remember where I put my purse last night.

"I will. I can pick up some things too. I'll drive," Becca says, hopping off the bar stool.

"Cool. You guys want me to pick up anything while we're out?" I look between Jeana and Dyana.

"No," Dyana says. "I am going to call Perry and let him

know that my plans have changed. Then I want to run over to the liquor store. You've got a nice stock but trust me—this group of ladies will drink you right into the poor house if we don't pad your cabinet a little. " She pulls out her cellphone.

"She's not lying. It's not that often we can get this many ladies together without our husbands and kids. I can stick around here and keep Dyana company if you don't mind." Jeana says.

"No problem at all. Um...Dyana would you mind letting Solomon know that I'm having company over and he should probably wait until much later to drop by?" Jeana and Dyana were already texting away on their phones as Becca and I head to the door.

"He already knows. He's still with Perry. The kids will be keeping him busy. Don't worry." Dyana winks at me and goes back to texting.

"Well, alright then."

As soon as Becca and I buckle up and she backs out of the driveway, my mind keeps rehashing what the day has brought me so far. Some laughs, some fun, and some sad.

I know that sadness like losing the one you love happens all the time to people we know and don't know. But it makes you think about your own life and what it means. I don't know what I'm doing. I don't know what is out there for me.

What I do know is that Solomon is someone who makes me feel. Hell even Lux makes me feel. Although what Lux makes me feel is anger, rage, embarrassment and yes, hunger. But the deeper I get into the life of Abrielara and what it means to be chosen, the more confused I become and the more questions I have.

And it all got that much more complicated when I learned I wasn't who I thought I was this whole time. I'm a hybrid, and that's where the rules and the feelings get convoluted. At least for me. If I'm honest with myself, I would say that the biggest question glaring me in the face is if I choose to stay, what is my place here supposed to be?

Seeing the hieroglyphs and understanding them was a shocker to me. I've never been into languages or anything like that. I mean, where did all of that come from all of a sudden? I'm almost afraid to even ask.

"Hey. I'm sorry about what I said about Solomon earlier. I didn't mean to upset you or anything." Becca's apology brings me out of my musings. I think for a moment to figure out what she's talking about.

"Oh, there's nothing for you to apologize for, Becca. You didn't upset me. I'm thinking about things overall."

She looks over at me quickly before turning her eyes back to the road. "You looked a little sad there for a minute. I wanted to make sure it wasn't because of anything I said. I can be crass and blunt sometimes. I don't mean any harm by it."

"Becca, it's okay. I promise. I've learned your personality in the short time I've gotten to know you. You aren't mean-spirited. I was actually thinking about the story of Jake and Joanne and how sad it was. I was also thinking about my life and how I'm no closer to figuring out what I should do than I was when I first got here."

"You want my opinion?" She parks the car in a parking space directly in front of the store and turns to look at me.

"Knowing you, you're going to tell me whether I want to hear it or not anyway." I purse my lips at her.

"True." She chuckles and shrugs her shoulders. "I think that in your heart, you know what you want to do. You don't know why you feel that way. Yes, there are a lot of questions that need answering. Yes, your relationship with Lux and Solomon is new and weird, but that is to be expected.

"Ultimately, you owe it to yourself to see what all this

means to you. Not what your mother wanted for you or why she wanted you to come here. You are surrounded by people who are like you. You can still design your shoes. You can still have a relationship with your family. But if you leave here, what would you have learned about yourself? Now is the time to find out."

"That sounds nice. But it hasn't escaped me that many of the humans who have been chosen left here as soon as they were able. Nor have I missed the fact that Solomon and I have not discussed what we want, or what this means for us. We've discussed what the Passage requires and our desire to complete it, but that's all. What happens when I get pregnant? Because believe me, at the rate we've been going at it, I would guess that it's only a matter of time before that happens. Are we going to share custody? I mean how does this work? I know Solomon likes me, but we haven't discussed any kind of commitment."

Becca's eyebrows reach for the sky and then scrunch up, confusion covers her face. "Solomon didn't discuss commitment with you?"

"Well, no. I mean, we just started the consummation phase last night. We haven't done much talking, definitely not about anything serious."

"He discussed the rite of Passage with you, though, right?"

"Yes. He told me there were seven phases. Umm, the last one being the Consummation phase, which ends with a pregnancy. But I don't know what happens after that. Everyone seems to get married and settle down and have more kids, at least the hybrids do. We haven't discussed anything else. I mean, what if I'm not ready to have a baby and settle down? Is that the reason why some of the chosen ones that were human left so quickly afterwards? I can't imagine another reason."

Becca's arms are crossed at her chest and her eyes are

squinted. She pinches her lips together in apparent frustration.

"Did I say something wrong?" I grab my purse before opening the car door.

"No, you didn't say anything wrong. But Solomon left out some details that he owes you." She gets out of the car.

"Like what?" I can't imagine that after the talk we had after the chase, he would leave out anything important. That would have been the time to tell everything.

"He has to tell you. It's his right. But you can best believe that I'll make sure he does."

By the look in her eyes, I have no doubt she will.

"However, at the end of the day, I don't think it will make that much difference to you. Remember, you may be a chosen one, but more importantly, you're a hybrid." She smiles at me and grabs my hand. "Now, let's see what we can buy to set this party off right. I'm so looking forward to this."

Solomon

"Looks like we're on our own for a while." Perry stuffs his phone back in his pocket and adjusts the string for Mae's kite. Her ladybug was getting away from her.

"Why do you say that?" I let go of PJ's kite and let him take over. There was a nice breeze today. Not too strong, but strong enough. It was a great day for flying kites.

"Dyana said that they're having a party over at Mika's. They invited some ladies from the community to get to know Mika and vice versa. Sounds like Mika is trying to get the dish on you." He gives me a questionable look under hiked eyebrows.

"Dish on me? There's nothing to tell." I give a haphazard shrug and go back to watching PJ fly his kite. He's running around and the string is a little tight. I cup my hands around my mouth.

"Give her a little slack, PJ. You don't want the wind to snap the string and take the kite away from you." He follows my direction, and the kite goes back to floating in the wind rather than being beaten by it.

"You can keep telling yourself that, bruh, but I know better. Don't forget, I was right there with you. This can go either way for you, depending on who they invite to this party."

I turn my head sharply in his direction. He has a point. Some of the women in this town think I hung the moon. By the same token, some women in this town think I've been sent by the devil himself to turn their wholesome daughters into followers of my cult of iniquity.

"Who are they inviting and why would she want to get the dish on me? She already has the best seat in the house." Maybe I should have stuck around and ear hustled for a little while longer this morning.

"Dee didn't say, man. If we want to find out, there's one place we can go to get a bird's eye view of who they invited."

"Yeah, my house."

I continue to watch PJ and his Superman kite and see him struggling a little with keeping it in the air. I run out and help Superman fly again. When he gets the hang of it, I run back to Perry and Mae.

"You know, there's another way we can find out who they invited." The grin on my face widens as the thought comes to me.

"How?" Perry looks over at me and then back to Mae.

"You can text Dyana and tell her that while they're having a good time, we thought we would invite all the husbands and the kids over to my house for a little barbecue. Nothing special. Just some burgers and dogs. Then I'll know for sure who she invited and can start a plan of defense when this is all said and done."

"That's smart, but you know that we'll have to have a barbecue, right?"

"Of course. Now, text her back. The sooner I know who they invited, the sooner I know what I'm up against."

After flying kites for a couple of hours, we finally have our list of who was invited to their little hen party. We've already texted the husbands of those ladies and are now on our way to the store to grab the food for the barbecue.

"Looks like you got off a little light. This may work in your favor after all." Perry throws several bags of chips into the grocery basket.

"I don't know. She did say that Freya was going to be there. She's definitely not a big fan of mine." I grab some cans of soda and put them on the bottom of the basket.

"I don't remember you having anything with Freya. Refresh my memory." He taps PJ on the shoulder.

"Son, go to the bakery and grab two cookie trays." PJ runs off toward the bakery, and as soon as Mae sees him take off, she wants out of the basket to follow him. "No, Mae. PJ is going to be right back. Just sit tight."

"Noooo!" she screams loud enough to wake the dead. "Down! I want down now!" She kicks her legs and tries to stand in the front seat of the basket. I grab her and take her out, but I don't put her down.

"You know that as soon as her feet touch the floor, she's going to take off, and I won't be able to catch her, right?"

"Don't worry, I'm not going to put her down. I just can't have her standing up in the basket."

"Mae, are you a big girl?" I ask her calmly. She nods at me but proceeds to kick her feet, wanting to get down.

"Well, big girls don't scream and holler like that. If you want to be a big girl. You have to act better than that."

"But I want down!"

"The answer is no. Do you want to go back to the car?" She shakes her head vigorously. Her crocodile tears streaming down her face in rivers. PJ comes back with the cookies.

"Then you will sit back in the basket and act like a big girl. If you don't, we're going back to the car, and when your friends come over, you'll be taking a nap instead of playing. Do you want to take a nap or play?"

Her eyes suddenly stop running. "No naps. I want to play." I give her a big smile and a kiss on her forehead.

"Good. Now sit down in the basket so we can finish this up. The sooner we get done, the sooner you can see your friends."

I put her back in the basket and she doesn't make another peep. Perry looks at me and shakes his head. "What are you? The kiddie whisperer? I see you in action all the time but I can't get over it."

All I can do is laugh. It's always easier when the kid isn't your own.

"So, back to Freya," he reminds me.

"Freya was the chick that came to Brady's last party of our senior year. She threw up in the hot tub."

I prompt him to remember but based on the look on his face, he doesn't.

"She's Annie's cousin. You remember Annie? You hooked up with her in the janitor's closet our freshman year. She followed you around the rest of the year after that."

"Oh yeah. We called her little orphan Annie because of her red hair."

"Yeah, that's right. Her Momma sent her off to live with her grandparents for a year, and when she came back, we barely recognized her."

"I remember her now but I don't know why Freya wouldn't like you."

"I passed out in Brady's bedroom and woke up to Freya trying to...you know..." I motion with my hands and Perry's eyes widen.

"Oh."

"Yeah. I told her to, you know, get out of the room. In not-so-nice terms and she left embarrassed. I know that I could have been a bit more tactful but I was hungover, and I didn't know her all that well at the time. Since then, she pretends she doesn't see or know me. Which is perfectly fine by me. But I don't know what kind of story she's going to tell Mika. You know I'm already working with a deficit here as it is."

"Well, we shall see. I'm sure Mika can listen to these stories and still decide for herself."

"Yeah, I know she can. I just, I don't know. I still feel that our relationship is fragile. Anyone can say anything and put everything I've worked hard for in jeopardy. I don't want to lose her."

The idea of losing her feels like death to me. I refuse to let that happen.

"I got your back. Just stay honest and communicate. That's all you can do."

He makes it sound easy, but it isn't. First of all, nothing with Mika has been easy so far. Except for one thing. And that was falling in love with her.

I'm in love with her.

We are in love with her.

It doesn't shock me at all. It was easy as breathing. From the moment I saw her standing on her porch when Bobby dropped her off. I knew she was the reason I was in the early stages of the Passage. She was the sole reason why I couldn't sleep, and when I did, I dreamed about her.

Now we've finally consummated and I'm falling deeper and harder for her. I can't get enough of her. My need is so strong I literally thirst after her. I know this isn't all because of the Passage, even if it helped me along a little.

And although Lux has been submissive and quiet lately, I can feel his uneasiness. I literally feel him pacing inside my head. He's worried. This party has the potential to change it all for me. I'm almost there. She agreed to work on her relationship with Lux. If that works out...then I believe anything is possible. I can finally see that she may possibly commit to us after all.

But what if she doesn't?

With dogs and burgers on the grill and our guests already showing up, the barbecue is in full swing. Perry and I know all of the husbands and their kids. I'm the pediatrician to most of them. However, some guys who were not formally invited showed up based on the fact that they heard there was food.

It's fine. Actually, the more folks who show up, the better. Anything to keep my mind off Mika and whatever nonsense they're feeding her across the street.

When the women get together, it can become a man-bashing event quicker than I can tie my shoes. The next thing you know, a promising relationship like the one I'm trying to have with Mika turns into a relationship from hell. Or flat-out disintegrates. If they insist on pumping her with a bunch of unrealistic expectations, and she believes even an inkling of that shit, there's no way our relationship can be a success.

I bring my mind back to my party and turn my eyes back to the little kids. Mae is okay for now, but I know it won't take much for her to be overwhelmed. When that happens, somebody better put their running shoes on.

"Hey, Solomon. What's up, man? How's it goin'?" Ashe steps up on the deck. I'm surprised because I didn't invite him and I haven't seen him in several months.

"Ashe. What's up? I haven't seen you in a while. How's Jake?" Ashe has a huge cabin in the back woods of Abrielara, not that far from Jake, whom we only see glimpses of throughout the year. Every time I see Ashe, I think of Jake. Ashe is more social than Jake but Ashe travels quite a bit for work, so we hardly ever see him, either.

"Yeah, I just got back in from a week in Alaska. I've got a new resort opening up in Juneau." He shrugs. "Jake is Jake. He's good. He's getting ready for a hunting trip, so you know he's pretty stoked about that."

"I bet."

"I ran into the judge when he was out checking out checking on a friend. He told me about your little get-together and that I should come on out. Say hi to everyone. Hope that's okay."

"Of course. There's plenty to go around. Grab a plate and Perry will hook you up with whatever you want.

"What's ole Stix up to these days?" I follow Ashe as he grabs a plate and holds it out for Perry to load up.

"The same as usual. Just as contrary as always."

"Ashe, my man. What's been goin' down? Haven't seen you in a while," Perry says as he loads the plate.

"Working man, you know how it is. How've you been? I

see PJ looks more and more like you every day. Where's Mae?" Ashe's eyes trek around the yard.

"Yeah, he couldn't look more like me if I had spat him out myself. Mae is here somewhere. As long as she keeps her clothes on, we're good but don't look for that to last long." Perry fans his fingers out in front of him. "Just giving you a fair warning."

Ashe throws his head back and laughs. "No worries. How's Dee? I'm sure she's just as beautiful as always."

"Oh yeah, course. She wants another baby, but we're going to wait until Mae is out of this running stage. I can't imagine running after two of them. I can barely keep up with her."

"Be honest, Perry, you can't keep up with her at all," I say.

"True. That girl runs like she's training for the Olympics," Perry says. He shakes his head in wonder and grabs a plate. We head over to the edge of the deck and take a seat.

"How's Coh? Has he been keeping you busy or laying low?" Coh is Ashe's Brielaran. I grab a water from the cooler, looking out over the yard to put my eyes on Mae. She still has clothes on, so we're good.

"Coh is good. He has his moments, of course, but for the most part, he's taking a back seat for now. I heard that you've chosen someone. Congratulations."

"Yeah, thanks. Still going through it, though. She's the reason why I'm even having this barbecue."

"Oh yeah? What's her name? Do I know her?"

"Mika and I wouldn't think you would. She wasn't raised around here with us."

"How'd she end up here?" Ashe stuffs several chips in his mouth.

"Her mother used to live here a long time ago. She died and asked her to come here. Turns out Mika is a hybrid but that isn't even the most interesting part. She's Perry's full-blooded sister."

"Wow. No kidding?" He looks over at Perry for confirmation. Perry shrugs his shoulders.

"Yep. Amazing, huh?"

"Yeah, what are the odds?" Ashe turns back to me and points a finger. "You got lucky." He shakes his head in wonderment. "At the rate I'm going. I'm never gonna make the Passage. How did it go for you?"

Perry says nothing while shaking his head and stuffing his mouth with food. Keeping his mouth shut for once, in a manner of speaking.

"Honestly, the transformation was the worst experience that I've had in my life. I was like one of those hotdogs over there, except I was being burned from the inside out. Add in the fact that I felt like I was having a heart attack too." I sigh heavily. "Let's say I'm glad that part's over."

"Well, I can't say I'm looking forward to that shit. Damn." Ashe chuckles dryly.

"Yeah, I wasn't either but trust me when I say when people tell you to let go and let it happen—for the love of God, let go and let it happen. Otherwise, you'll barely live through it. Trust me."

"Listen to him," Perry chimes in, thumbing at me. "You know Solomon always has to take his knocks the hard way."

I flip him the bird and keep eating.

"I'll keep that in mind on the off chance I happen to be blessed with the opportunity." He rolls his eyes and now it's my turn to chuckle.

"I will say, though, after all that, I'm glad I did it. I'm happy with who I've chosen. Now, if I can convince her this is a good thing and to stay here..." My shoulder lifts wishfully.

"She doesn't want to commit?"

I give a quick nod. "She doesn't know about the commitment part yet."

"She doesn't know? What are you waiting on? It's not like she has a choice. She's either going to have to commit or declare why she won't, but she has to know about it to do it."

"I tried to tell him." Perry dumps his plate into the trash and gets back up to check the grill.

"I know, but I'm afraid of losing her. When I was going over everything, I felt like if I told her one more thing, she would run for the hills. Now I feel like she's going to run anyway."

Admitting that out loud makes my fear palpable. I can taste it on my tongue and feel it knot up in my throat. If she runs, I don't know what I'm going to do. I'll lose everything. Literally everything.

"Well, I'm sure you'll find a way to make it right. If she runs, do what we do best and run after her. Eventually, she will have to come around, right?"

Ashe looks at me like I should know the answer. God, I wish I did, but he does have a point.

A squeal from the back of the yard breaks our attention away from our conversation, and suddenly we're all on full alert. As if in mass hysteria, all of the children under five are stripping out of their clothes. Mae, the obvious ring leader, is already naked and running like she's getting paid for it. I was afraid this was going to happen.

"*Lux I need you,*" I say gruffly, hoping to wake him up.

"*What?*"

"*We've got kids to round up and the tentacles could help with that.*"

He takes over just as I'm yanking my shirt off and he runs after May first. As soon as she sees she's being chased, she giggles that much harder and squeals that much louder.

All of the naked heathens follow suit. Now I have a yard full of frenzied naked kids with squeals so loud I'm sure it is only a matter of time before the entire neighborhood starts coming out to see what's going on. I hear the side gate open, and almost as one unit, I see their little eyes turn toward the gate. I know what they're thinking as soon as I see their little tentacles start flailing in the air. I didn't realize so many of our friends had kids under the age of five. If they were older, their tentacles would have already receded back into their bodies. I should have thought this barbecue through a little harder.

"Close the gate!" he yells, but it's too late. Three have already made it through. But it doesn't matter because the rest of them straight scale it like they were playing leapfrog.

Fuck me. The moms will never leave us in charge again. I run off toward the front yard trying to lay my hands on any kid at this point. But the little fuckers are slippery. I take a quick survey of the yard. All the grown folks look like we're trying to catch a bunch of chickens on steroids. I see the front door open across the street.

Here we go.

Chapter Eighteen

Mika

"What in the name of all that's holy?"

Angela, one of the nice ladies I just met, is standing at the window checking up on something outside.

Then I hear it.

It sounds like there's an amusement park out there. We all rush over to the window and the gasp is audible. There are kids everywhere. Naked kids and grown Brielarans chasing after them but having the hardest time catching them. Older kids are running around too, but thankfully, they left their clothes on. They appear to be taking advantage of the mayhem.

"Oh, my word! What are they doing over there? I'm going to kill Perry," Dyana exclaims.

She rushes to the door, yanks it open, and high-foots it across the street. The ladies are murmuring aloud and the nice party we were having is over just like that. Everyone follows Dyana across the street.

Everyone except for me.

Seeing them, all of them running around with their tenta-cles flailing about, is a sight I'm not prepared for. Their eyes are all glowing amber red. Their skin is all different hues. Their sharp, shiny teeth and taloned fingers glint in the sun. They are everywhere.

I can't move. My heart pounds and the air becomes thin. It suddenly dawns on me Lux isn't the only one with the power to hurt me. Not only that, but I have to create and carry one of these in my body for god knows how long. I've been surrounded this whole time by beings that could do the exact same thing he did. Burn me the way that I'd been burned before. I don't know why the thought never crossed my mind before now. I was consumed with Solomon and Lux. I never had a moment to think about it.

What I do know is I'm beyond terrified. I can hear my panting breath over the noise. I've only been concerned with Lux this entire time when I had an entire town to fear.

I lean against my front door and close my eyes. I count backward from fifty slowly. When I'm done, I don't open my eyes because I still hear the squealing laughter, which means everyone is still there. Everyone. There are so many of them.

So many.

Furiously trying to control my breathing as hot tears well up behind my eyelids, I feel silly and hysterical. As the scene plays out in front of me, the anxiety riding me bareback without a saddle is rough, raw and disrespectful. I want to leave. I don't belong here.

I attempt to calm myself down and place a hand on my chest. I swallow the tears that flow down the back of my throat and take a deep breath in through my nose.

I am safe.

I am unafraid.

I am in control.

Continuing to repeat the affirmations to myself with my eyes closed, I feel someone standing in front of me. Fear prickles the back of my neck and heat assaults the front of my body.

But the scent is calming and familiar. I take a deep breath of the calm scent that neutralizes my nerves without even trying. The prickly fears covering the back of my neck evaporate. My nostrils flair as I greedily inhale more of the aroma that is putting my frayed nerves to sleep. My chest expands as I breathe in deeply. I sigh in contentment. The feeling covering me is calming enough to stop the tears from falling. I'm at peace.

I open my eyes, and a shirtless Lux stands directly in front of me. So close I can feel his warm breath on my face.

From the corner of my eye, I can see his tentacles have me boxed in, but I don't feel fear. The question in my head must be clear in my eyes because he answers me without having heard the question.

"Since you have agreed to complete the Passage with us, I mean Solomon, and you have consummated, our scent has the ability to calm you; make you feel safe rather than fear.

"You were in distress so I came to check on you, but I think you would rather have Solomon here. I'll bring him back now." He takes a few steps back.

"No. It's okay. Please don't leave."

Holding my hand out to stop him, my words are rushed and desperate but I don't care. He watches me with skepticism. Yeah, I would be skeptical too, if I were him, but whatever the scent he has is working.

"Your scent helps." He nods and moves closer to me.

"Why are you upset?" His whispered words are tinged with the concern I see in his eyes.

I don't look anywhere else. Just at him. It's amazing I'm not afraid of him anymore. I'd thought I would always be. I've seen and felt the damage he's capable of. Yet, I feel comforted and safe being surrounded by him. For once, I want him to stay.

What a difference a day makes.

"There are so many of you in one place. I've only seen you. But all the running, screaming, and tentacles flying everywhere made me feel like I was in danger. I'm surrounded by beings that can hurt me. I have nowhere to run. I can't leave until we are done. I'm stuck. A single solitary prey in a town full of predators."

My words are not accusatory or said hatefully but more as a revelation to not just to Lux but also to myself.

Solomon nor Lux can stay with me all of the time. What is stopping someone else from coming after me the same way Lux did? I thought I'd dealt with the whole chase, probe, and aftercare nightmare. Unfortunately, that is not the case.

How ironic is it to find comfort in the very being who caused the fear and pain in the first place?

Lux rests his chin on top of my head and his appendages surround me snuggly, like a weighted blanket. He doesn't say anything. He continues to hug me and I continue to inhale his intoxicating scent. It has quickly become my salvation, my lifeline to safety and sanity. I can't get enough of it.

Without realizing it, I wrap my arms around him and lay my head against his chest. The fear that overwhelmed me moments ago starts dissipating and the madness across the street is nonexistent. I hear nothing except the beating of his heart and our synchronized breathing. I don't feel anything except the comfort of his arms and...heat swirling in my belly. My mouth waters and my core clenches.

I feel a low purr coming from Lux's chest, evidence that he also feels the sudden surge of heat. I grind my teeth together to keep from moaning out loud.

Lux reluctantly steps away from me; his appendages retract, and I miss them instantly.

"You are not in danger. And even if you were, I would not allow anyone to hurt you. You belong to me. You belong here because you belong to this town. Everyone knows that. No one wants to hurt you. They are excited to meet you and I'm excited to show you off." He leans in and lays a soft kiss on my neck, his teeth lightly grazing me. He leans away from me again. "I understand if it's too soon or you aren't comfortable with it. You are my only concern."

I feel the need to please him. "Only if you stay with me."

"I never planned to leave you in the first place." He grins, runs his thumb softly along my cheek, and kisses the other one. "Come. Let me introduce you."

He reaches for my hand and waits for me to take it. I don't miss how he asks permission and is concerned about my feelings. The fact that he's trying makes me want to try too. I put my hand in his and allow him to lead me across the street.

"Glad to see you've decided to join the party." A Brielaran with an opalescent skin tone, amber eyes and tight curls cut close to his head walks over to me. Even with that skin, I couldn't miss those deep dimples in his cheeks.

"Xens?" He picks me up off my feet in a bear hug.

"You got it. Sis. It's about time we officially met. Took you long enough."

My mouth opens in shock.

"Took me long enough? According to my timeline, this is happening way too fast, but I'm happy to finally meet you. I would know you anywhere. Those dimples give you away."

He smiles, leans down, and pulls a little boy in front of

him. This is what Perry must have looked like when he was a boy.

"I would like you to meet Perry Jr...or PJ. PJ, this is my sister, your aunt Mika. Say hello."

"Hi. If you're my aunt, where have you been?"

I smile at his bluntness.

"I only found out that I had a brother. You look exactly like your dad. It's uncanny."

"Everybody says that."

"How old are you PJ?"

"I'm seven," he says proudly.

"What is your Brielaran's name?"

"His name is Totu. He's shy. I always have to ask the questions that he wants to know."

"That's interesting. When will I get to talk to him?" I watch PJ stare blankly at nothing before he answers, which is also pretty interesting. I can only assume he and Totu are talking. I've never witnessed Lux and Solomon or Xens and Perry, for that matter, in a conversation before.

"He says soon but not today. He's not feeling it today. Maybe one day, when you come over to play, you can meet."

"Oh..." Apparently, the discussion is over because PJ runs off like we weren't speaking.

"Don't be offended. He has the attention span of a butterfly," Lux explains.

Something runs right into my legs and then proceeds to climb me like I'm a tree. Panic thumps in my chest, and Lux is aware because he pulls whoever climbed up my body off of me.

"This little rascal here is Mae. Perry and Dyana's baby girl."

All of Mae's tentacles are reaching to get back to me. Despite the tentacles, red alligator-like eyes and sharp teeth, it's obvious she is a child in every sense of the word. Maybe not a typical one but a child, nonetheless. My heart softens immediately, and my arms reach out to her. Lux spares me a quick glance before handing her over.

As soon as I have her in my arms, she hugs me tight. Her little head lies on my shoulder. I feel comforted by her aggressive hug and instinctively rock her back and forth, and within minutes, she is asleep.

"Did she fall asleep on you just that quick?" Perry reaches over and takes her from me.

"Looks like it."

Lux starts laughing. "She ought to be tired after the run she took us on. I'm exhausted."

"True. Let's hope she's out for the night because I don't have the energy for any more exercise. Besides, I already know that Dyana isn't done letting me have it tonight because of this barbecue Solomon insisted on having."

Lux shrugs. "Maybe groveling will help. I'm going to show Mika around. Why don't you lay Mae down in the house."

"Nah, I think I'm gonna round everybody up and head on home. You going to brunch tomorrow?"

Lux looks at me briefly and then shrugs his shoulders. "If Mika will agree to go with me, of course. If not, then no, obviously, I won't be able to make it."

"Is that your way of asking me if I want to go?" I smirk at Lux.

"Yes. I have no shame in admitting that." He reaches over and grabs my hand, pulling me toward him.

"Where is this brunch being held?" I ask Lux, but Xens answers instead.

"Every Sunday, Brielarans and their C.O.s are invited to have an all-white brunch at the palace. Only the chosen and their mates are invited to brunch. Usually, the Monarch makes an appearance, but it isn't always a guarantee. You should go. The gardens are something you should see."

"All white brunch?"

"Yeah, you're supposed to wear all white to the brunch. Classy and no club wear." Xens shakes his head. "Believe me, it has to be said. You wouldn't believe what some of the folks show up in."

I look at Lux who hasn't taken his eyes off me. "I would love to take you to brunch at the palace tomorrow. Xens is right. The gardens are beautiful. I think you would enjoy them."

"Is that the only reason why you want me to go? So that I can see the gardens?"

Of course, I want to see the gardens, but that isn't why I want to go to brunch with him. I want to know why he wants me to go. I know my motives. I haven't missed my sudden interest and wanting to learn more about him. And let's not forget that intoxicating scent I'm quickly becoming addicted to. I won't be admitting that to him, though.

"No. Any reason I can use as an excuse to spend time with you is a good reason."

"Hmm." I pretend to contemplate his request. "Are you asking for Solomon or for yourself?"

He looks uncomfortable for a few seconds before straightening his shoulders and looking me in the eye.

"For me. I want you to come with me. So, what do you say?" His eyes spark as he watches me.

"I'll take it under advisement," I respond nonchalantly. The sparkle in his eyes dims a little until he sees the grin I cannot hold back. He yanks me to his chest. His appendages wrap around my body and lift me until my feet leave the ground. My squeal, not unlike the ones of the children from earlier, surprises me.

"Okay! Okay! I'll go. I'll go."

I barely recognize my laughter. I stop when Lux smiles but no longer laughs, watching me intently. He lowers me until my feet are back on the ground.

"You should do that more often," he says quietly.

"Do what?" I ask, truly not knowing what he means.

"Laugh. You're always beautiful, but when you laugh, you are breathtaking."

Lux

Mika is surrounded by Becca, her twins, Jeana and her four. The smile on her face is one I always want to see. She scared me for a minute there. I felt her heart beating rampantly from across the street. As soon as I could, I rushed to her, praying to God she wasn't in danger. It never dawned on me she was panicking. And I for damn sure never suspected she wasn't over the whole chase thing.

I shouldn't be surprised. It was a traumatic experience for her and Solomon. Some of it wasn't my fault. The Passage is what it is. But my impatience made things worse. I'm sorry she was hurt. I meant the apology I gave her but I am not sorry for choosing her. We can work through anything, just as long as she is mine in the end.

"Ours and if she chooses to leave us, you may think differently. I will make you pay for it, I promise you."

"Solomon..."

"I'm not kidding. You're lucky she allowed you to stick around and she agreed to brunch tomorrow."

"*I know, Solomon. I said I would make this right and I will.*"

"*We'll see. We can't afford any more mishaps just because you feel vindicated by duty. Duty doesn't mean shit if she leaves us. Keep that in mind.*"

"*I will.*"

"*It was good to see her laugh. It's good to see her smile,*"

It's good to see her anything besides sad, afraid or mad. Almost anything else I can live with."

"*You have a point there. Looks like the barbecue is about over. What do you say we walk her home?*"

"*Do we have to? Any chance we can convince her to stay over?*"

Hope fills my heart.

"*Not a chance. Be happy you got her to agree to brunch. We gotta take this one day at a time.*"

"*Okay, but I'm warning you now. If I get wind she might think about me in her bed. I'm going to...*"

"*You're not going to do anything until she's ready. Now, go get our C.O. unless you want me to take over.*"

"*Wait your turn,*" I growl.

"*Yeah, thought you might say that. Get moving.*"

"*Alright, alright. I like this more assertive side to you. When dealing with women before, you didn't give a flying fuck what we did as long as it was fun. Now you're trying to school me on manners? I know how to treat a woman,*" I retort haughtily.

"*Mika isn't just any woman. She's our C.O. The only woman we will ever commit to. We can't afford to make any mistakes. Our future depends on it. So yeah, I'm going to watch you like a hawk to make sure you don't fuck up again.*"

"*You're never going to let that shit go, are you?*" I tug on my hair in frustration.

"*Not until she's ours for real.*"

"*Well, who am I to slow down the wheels of progress? Let's get this show on the road. God knows I'm sick to death of hearing you air my sins out like dirty laundry every chance you get.*"

"*If the situation was reversed, you would do the same,*" Solomon reminds me.

"*Damn straight.*"

I pick up trash and upright chairs that have fallen over as I make my way to Mika. She is now talking to Kim and her three. I'm so glad the fear she experienced earlier is gone. I hope it stays gone. I didn't enjoy seeing her that way.

When I get close to her, her eyes find mine. My breath catches in my throat and I stop moving, waiting for a sign she still wants me around. After a few seconds, she smiles at me and turns her attention back to Kim and I take a deep breath.

"*You got lucky again, mothafucker.*"

"*Shut the fuck up.*"

I stand next to her, close enough to touch her but I don't. She's the boss and in control of this whole thing. I move according to her direction. I half-ass listen to her and Kim chalk it up about a fundraiser for the school and I almost growl at her.

I don't care about this shit. I like Kim. She's an amiable woman, a wonderful mother, but damnit, I want Mika all to myself. She's already spent more time with her than I have. Hell, everyone has.

When Kim finally leaves, I can barely contain my relief. Mika turns to me with her hands on her hips.

"Impatient, aren't we?"

"What do you mean?" I pretend to not have a clue but come on, anyone who knows me knows I'm impatient.

"I heard you growling."

"Growling?" I didn't realize I was growling loud enough for anyone to hear me.

"Yes, growling. Why are you in such a hurry anyway? I don't want to keep you if you have somewhere to be. You can go whenever you're ready. Believe it or not, I can walk myself home."

"I'm not in a hurry to go anywhere. Besides, where you go, I go."

I knew the moment I said it that it was the wrong thing. The smile on her lips morphs quickly and her eyes narrow into slits.

"I didn't mean it that way. I promise. I don't always think before speaking. Please forgive me," I say quickly. She purses her lips at me and then releases a smile.

"It's okay, Lux. I'm going to have to loosen up and let some things go if I want to complete this, so don't feel as if you have to walk on eggshells and watch every word you say. Just be yourself. I'll let you know if I'm truly offended."

My shoulders relax as a cleansing breath leaves my body. "I can live with that."

"Good." She looks me over and then shakes her head. "So, do you plan on putting a shirt on sometime today? I'm positive I saw Solomon leave my house with one on earlier."

I'd completely forgotten that Solomon shed the shirt so we could chase down the kids.

"I, uh.." I run my hand down my chest. She smiles and shakes her head.

"Luckily you're easy on the eyes so I think I can live with it for a few more minutes."

"You like the way I look?"

The lascivious grin on my face cannot be helped. Is it possible she could be attracted to me too? She rolls her eyes and walks across the street and I follow her. Not that she isn't able, but I'm not ready to leave her yet.

To be in her presence and have her not angry or scared of me is still a novelty. I watch her from the corner of my eye, dying to know what's on her mind. It's obvious that something is weighing her mind down. The evidence is in the heaviness of her sighs and the wariness in her eyes.

We make it to her door and she sighs heavily, again.

"Well—" She bites her lower lip, dragging her teeth across it. A lump forms in my throat that I have a hard time swallowing.

"So—" I croak out.

Her eyes fly up to meet mine. I lean my shoulder against the door beside her and shove my hands in my pockets. Nerves are eating me up right now.

If I were Solomon, she would be inviting me in and probably stripping off her clothes. As a matter of fact, Solomon was supposed to come back tonight.

"What time should I be ready tomorrow for brunch?"

Okay, so I guess that shoots down my thought of possibly staying over.

"I can pick you up about ten thirty. Is that okay?"

"Sure. I can be ready by then." Her hand latches onto the door knob.

"Um—" I run my fingers through my hair again, and now I'm the one sighing heavily.

"I thought maybe you would like Solomon to say goodnight. I was going to—"

"Actually, it's okay. I'm a little tired and I know you have to be tired too, after the day you've had. Besides, isn't saying goodnight to you the same as saying goodnight to Solomon?"

"Yes. Solomon can hear you just as I can when we are human. I know you like the look of Solomon, so—" She shakes her head at me.

"What?"

"This morning, I would have agreed with you. But after this afternoon, I can honestly say things have changed. You made me feel safe and you calmed me. I saw another side to you I didn't think existed. Yes, I know Solomon is you and you are Solomon. You're one but not the same. I have come to that realization. At first, I thought it was impossible, but after today, I don't feel that way anymore."

"You don't? You can accept us in both forms?"

My heart is running a marathon in my chest. If what she's saying is true, we are closer to her being ours completely than we thought. We'll finally be able to fulfill our duty to Abrielara and experience what our ancestors wanted us to experience.

"Yes. I can. Now I don't feel like you're going to attack me every time I see you, I can eventually move past everything else from before."

I watch her eyes look over my face and for the first time, I feel naked and bashful about it. I duck my head, allowing my hair to hide part of my face. She reaches up and tucks some of my hair behind my ear. My eyes meet hers again. She crosses her arms and props her shoulder against the door.

"Did you think I wouldn't be able to?"

"Yes. I was positive after I accosted you in the pharmacy that you would never forgive me. Even after I apologized, I hoped but I didn't believe it would happen."

I step closer to her and her head moves up to maintain eye contact.

"I know Solomon told you already how much he wants this to work between us, but I want you to know that I want this to work too. If it doesn't, my existence here is pointless. The only reason why I'm even here is—"

"Don't even fucking say it Lux. She's not ready to hear it yet."

I clear my throat. The inquisitive look on her face pushes me to keep going, just not where I wanted to.

"Whatever you need from me, from us—you can have it. I don't care what it is, as long as it means we complete this together."

"Okay. Thank you for telling me." She steps back from the door and grabs the knob again but pauses for a second before kissing my cheek.

"Thanks for today. I'll see you tomorrow at ten thirty. Oh, and one more thing."

"What's that?" I'm not sure I want to know.

"I'm completing the Passage with you too. Don't forget it." She opens her door and closes it softly behind her.

I could never forget that.

I spend the rest of my evening cleaning up my yard from the barbecue. Didn't take long with the help of my tentacles, but it was hard to stay motivated. I found myself staring into space, thinking about her and the possibilities our lives could have.

I've never admitted to anyone that our biggest hang-up with choosing a human was having the human not choose us because of what I looked like. My insecurity always manifested in being overbearing or manhandling, exactly what I did to Mika.

My need for her and my insecurity about myself overwhelmed me. Even to the point of putting Solomon in jeopardy. The fact he fought the Passage and me so hard from the beginning was like another level of rejection. Yeah, I know Solomon's stalling had nothing to do with me. It still didn't stop my feelings of insecurity and inadequacy.

At one time, I thought the Passage would pass me by, that I was found unworthy of feeling, giving, and receiving love. Our own mother had rejected us on sight. The moment that I laid eyes on Mika, I knew she was ours. I pushed Solomon so hard because she was itching to leave. The fact that Solomon tried to get her to leave made me so angry. It felt like he was working against me.

I know he didn't want to hurt her but we had no choice. Her fear was needed to accelerate the adrenaline and push the probing DNA through her body. Can the probe be successful without adrenaline? Of course, but without it, there's a chance the probe would fail. It might miss something vital that could alert us to her incompatibility with our DNA. Risking her life was not an option.

I sit on the deck and stare into the woods. My mind goes to the moment her body burned and seeped with the probing DNA boiling her skin to death.

I hated myself. Truly hated myself enough to wish the insanity would take over my brain and kill me. I've never had a problem exerting my will over whomever to get what I wanted. The one time I should have, when it would have been warranted, I decided to be a punk and let her tell me what to do. In turn, her poor body was ravaged unmercifully. Possibly scarring her for life. Thankfully, she relented, letting us complete the aftercare. She's fully recovered. At least physically.

The fact she's able and willing to forgive me is more than I deserve. If given the opportunity, I'll spend the rest of my life repaying my debt to her. If she commits to us, I'll spend the rest of our lives showing her how much she means to us. How special she is to us. I hope to God I don't do anything else to fuck this up.

I'll make sure you don't. Just as long as you make sure I don't.

Deal.

Chapter Nineteen

Mika

I discreetly watch Lux clean his front yard. As discreetly as I can without curtains to hide behind until I remember I don't have anything to wear to brunch tomorrow and the day is slipping away from me. I call the one person I know is ready to shop at a moment's notice and then head upstairs to freshen up while I wait on her to show up.

My mind automatically goes back to what happened today, the sudden change in my relationship with Lux and his marvelous scent. I still smell it. Solomon has always smelled good the few times I've been around him, but it was different today.

I guess it's as Lux said. Since we have consummated, he smells different to me. Makes sense but still. My reaction is still crazy. I shake my head to vanquish the memory. Like most women, I have a real thing for how a man smells, but whatever Lux has going on is no ordinary musk. And I cannot allow it to influence me or my decisions. I've already taken an extreme detour as it is.

I haven't thought about my mother's diary or her motives since, well since before my date with Solomon.

Abrielara has completely taken over my life. I have to remember to keep my wits about me. I can't afford to even crush on them a little, much less fall in love with them. All they want is to for us to complete the Passage so they aren't overcome by insanity and die. Then they can go on with their lives as before. A logical incentive if you ask me.

I can't say I'm mad at that, but I know me and my romantic sensibilities. Nobody has time for a broken heart. I need all of this to end so I can go back home and proceed with my life as normal.

I turn my neck from side to side to look at my face and neck in the mirror. The bruising from the chase finally lightened up and now it's like it never happened. The rest of my body has also recovered remarkably. Now if I can get my mind to forget, then I'll be all good. Two quick honks spur me into action. I've got to find a nice white dress for a brunch with an alien tomorrow.

Definitely never saw that coming.

"This is the dress. Classy but definitely low-key sexy." Becca holds up a fitted white dress with capped sleeves and enough cleavage to make this dress unsuitable for church. Good thing I'm not going to church. She twirls it around, and I finger the sides where there is a slit of material missing.

"Looks like they ran out of material when they made this dress."

"Nice feature. I completely missed that. Now you have to try it on."

She shoves the dress toward me.

"I thought I was supposed to dress for a classy brunch?"

"You are but we don't know what this dress looks like

until we put it on you. Now scoot. I'm curious. With your skin tone, I bet it's going to look gorgeous."

She flops into one of the chairs outside the dressing room and I do as she bids. I slip the dress on and scrutinize my reflection. I turn from side to side, trying to check out the back. Well, it definitely fits. Looks like I've been poured into it. There'll be no bending down in this dress. The length is slightly below the knee and pencil-skirt straight. I don't necessarily have a problem with that, but the slits on both sides of the dress go from the armpit to the waistline. Showing a good amount of skin. No way anyone would miss that if they looked at me for any length of time. Overall, I like the dress. The slim fit definitely shows off my curves in the best way but I'm not sure if I'd label it classy.

I walk out of the dressing room so that Becca can take a look. Her grin is the widest I've seen without a drink in her hand. "Now that is a dress. Wow. You are a stunner in that one. Fits you perfectly."

I raise my arms and turn around so she can see the slit on each side.

"I like it even better with the slits. Adds to the sexiness of the dress."

"I thought this was supposed to be a classy brunch?" I remind her again. I mean, the dress is nice, and I like it and all, but it's tight as hell. Tight doesn't scream classy. I don't know. Maybe it's just me.

She rolls her eyes. "You keep asking and I'm going to keep saying the same thing. It is, honey. Haven't you ever heard classy isn't determined by what is worn but by who is wearing it? Or something like that?"

"No. I can honestly say I've never heard of it."

"Well, you have now."

I face the mirror again. I'm not quite sure this is the right dress.

"Do you think they'll like it?"

As soon as the words exit my mouth, I know it's my biggest concern. I want them to like it.

"Are you kidding? They'll be tripping all over themselves trying to get you out of it. Trust me, you have nothing to worry about."

The sales lady walks up at that moment and Becca barely spares her a glance. "Ring it up. We'll take it."

The next morning I'm looking myself over in the mirror again. This time with white sling backs and my braids pulled to the side in a bun. No jewelry except some pearl earrings that I found on our shopping trip last night. I also decided on eggplant-colored lipstick. Other than eyeliner and mascara, that's it for makeup.

Since we're going to brunch, I don't eat anything but I'm not sure it was a good idea. I'm hungry but my stomach is churning with nerves. Eating something might have settled my stomach.

I wonder if Lux is going to be the Lux I saw last night or the Lux I met the night of the chase or even in the pharmacy? I stop myself from pondering the subject. It doesn't matter. We have to get through this and for some reason, I trust him. I don't know what's come over him, over me, or if his scent caused the change, but whatever it is, it's making things easier. At least for me.

Two taps on the front door and I make my way downstairs. I grab my white clutch off the side table and open the door. I sweep him from head to toe slowly. He's dressed all in white, which complements his bronzed, iridescent skin. His hair flows freely, adding another contrast to his overall look. His short-sleeved casual linen shirt isn't tucked in and has one button unbuttoned at the top. His pants are wide-legged and his brown loafers appear to be ostrich leather. Shined to perfection. He looks nice. He takes his hands out of his pockets and holds one out to me.

"Wow. You look beautiful. Are you ready?" His eyes continue to drink me in. I guess Becca was right. The dress was a good choice.

"Thank you. You look nice too." I lock my door and I feel him step closer to my back. He doesn't say anything. I stand there, even after locking my door, waiting on him to say something or make some kind of a move.

He doesn't after a time, so I turn around. His eyes aren't quite red but aren't exactly brown either. I'm looking at Lux, but it's apparent that Solomon is close to the surface too.

"I missed you last night." His words are spoken low and softly.

"You did?" I'm surprised by his admission and even more surprised I'm happy to hear it.

"Yes. I didn't sleep well last night."

"Do you ever sleep well?"

I remember a few occasions when I saw him standing on his porch in the middle of the night. I still don't know what runs through his mind while he watches my house with such intensity.

"When I sleep with you."

My heart skips a beat. "You've only slept with me once."

"Not true. Just because I didn't sleep in the same bed with you doesn't mean I didn't sleep with you. During the after-care. I spent many nights sleeping next to your bed. Even when I started sleeping in the bedroom down the hall from yours, I still slept better there than I ever have anywhere else."

"I didn't know," I whisper.

"I wanted to be here. With you."

He leans in closer, his minty breath fans my face. I watch the warm flakes in his eyes flare as the edge of his irises glow gold.

The heat is there again, billowing like a cloud between us and sucking out all of the oxygen. The haze is back, covering my vision and the clarity in my brain.

The sound of a barking dog breaks up the fog and I step away, inhaling deeply. I look back into his eyes and they are warm again, not quite glowing but still red with gold flakes. I cross my arms, hoping to appear in control.

"Why didn't you say something before you left last night?"

"I didn't know how you would feel about it. I didn't want you to think I expected us to have sex just because you and Solomon had—"

I put my hand on his arm. "Lux, I already told you we're all in this together. In my mind, what Solomon and I do includes you. As you've plainly stated, you and Solomon are one. If you wanted to stay over, you just had to ask. I'm happy to know you don't have any expectations but I want us to be honest with each other. If you had asked, I would have let you stay."

I walk around him and stop short. "Whose car is this?" I look over my shoulder at him. With a pleased grin, he shrugs.

"It's mine."

I'm not a car girl. I know as much about cars as I know about what it means to be a Brielaran. But even I know this car is expensive. It looks nice but definitely not what I expected.

"I didn't know you had a car. I thought you only had the truck."

He walks toward me and opens the door to the sleek charcoal-colored sports car.

"Well around here, having a truck is imperative but there are those occasions, like today, when a car like this is the better choice. I prefer driving the car."

He helps me into the low slung car and closes the door after me. He gets in beside me and revs the motor a few times.

"A car like this is made to take a woman like you for a ride at least once."

I cut my eyes at him. "Corny."

He flashes a genuine smile my way. "I mean every word of it."

The ride to the palace is as smooth and quiet as the car we ride in. Lux and I don't talk much, and even though my nerves seem to have subsided, my mind is still cluttered with all of the little loose threads hanging around my life. I feel like a ribbon flailing in the wind.

I feel rootless, without foundation and without direction. At this point, I feel anyone could tell me anything and I would be remiss not take it into consideration. What would I know? I have nothing or no one to confer with to garner the facts. I have no more control over my life than my mother had over me when I was young.

Lux slows the car to take a curve and then suddenly a beautiful opalescent building comes into view. It glistens in the sun while rays of color run through it as if the building itself is alive. He stops outside a huge gate and rolls down the window to nod at the guard and proceeds on through.

"Nervous?"

I undo my seatbelt before looking at him.

"A little. Yes. I don't know what to expect. So, I'm going to follow your lead."

"Nothing to be nervous about. You're with me. You're one of us. Relax. You're going to have a good time. I promise."

"Okay."

He winks and then opens his door. "Don't move."

He walks around and opens the door, taking my hand to help me out of the car. His eyes look me over from head to toe with appreciation again.

"What is it?" I glance over my shoulder at him as he closes the door.

"May I speak freely?" He takes my hand and puts another hand around my waist. His taloned fingers immediately find the little strip of bare skin and lazily caresses it. Chill bumps cover my body from the heat of his touch. Maybe this dress wasn't a good idea after all.

"Of course."

He looks me over again and shakes his head slowly. "You, your body and this dress—perfection."

"Lux." I purse my lips at him.

"What? It's true. You know I think you're beautiful. I can't stop looking at you. And I want to tell you every chance I get. I hope you don't mind because that isn't going to change."

I realize Lux and Solomon share similarities I never noticed before. Even in the way they talk. Before, Lux spoke plainly, almost robotic. But now that we've consummated, he and Solomon sound a lot alike. The only difference is how they look and the vehicles they drive.

Interesting.

We walk through a set of tall wrought iron gates covered in honeysuckle, trumpet vines, and climbing hydrangeas.

"This is the garden?"

We walk the paved walkway that is surrounded by tables and chairs. The atmosphere is intimate. There are several tables already taken.

"Yes, part of it. We'll be eating a little deeper into the garden. Brunch is always held outside unless the weather doesn't permit it. Then, of course, the Monarch opens up the grand dining hall."

We stop at a table overlooking a large fountain, surrounded by tulips of every color I can imagine.

"I know tulips are your favorite, so I thought we could eat here." He pulls a chair out for me and pushes it in when I sit. I have to say I'm impressed with Lux. Who knew he had manners?

"Thoughtful of you, thank you. It's beautiful here."

"Yeah, it is, but I want to bring you at night. With the lights, the flowers, the water, and the music, it's fairytale-like."

"Oh yeah?" I can almost see it.

"Yeah. I must bring you back here. When I was a kid, I half expected to see Cinderella running across the courtyard."

I look around. The grounds are exactly what you'd expect a castle to have. An immaculately groomed expanse of space, with a representation of all the elements, peaceful and full of color.

"You're right. It's beautiful here and if Cinderella comes running around the corner, I won't be surprised. But I can't see you putting any thought into fairytales as a kid."

Lux and fairytales? Please. I don't believe it.

"Well, I didn't say I spent a lot of time thinking about it." He scoffs at me. "I spent a hell of a lot more time thinking about you. Long before I set eyes on you, I thought about you. I was always thinking about you."

Lux

Okay, so I might be coming on a little strong.

"You think?"

"Shut up."

Judging by the look on her face, I think it's safe to say she wasn't expecting me to be quite so frank and I should probably scale it back a little. But I've got everything to lose if I don't put all my cards on the table every chance I get.

Now that we are so close to fulfilling our purpose, I can't help but try to rush the process. I want to cement her into our lives before she has a chance to think about it for too long. But seeing her reaction makes me realize that overdoing it wouldn't be good either.

"She's the boss, remember? We go at her pace."

"I know, you're right. I'm just anxious."

"I get it. Just don't overdo it."

"I'm sorry. Sounded kind of creepy didn't it?"

Before she answers, the waiter comes and takes our order. I watch her do her best to avoid looking at me.

"That's not good."

"Nope. It isn't. Just give her a minute."

Her tongue is constantly rewetting her lips nervously. The waiter finally leaves and she still doesn't look at me.

"I can't."

"Your impatience is going to be the death of us."

"I guess the fact that you won't make eye contact with me answers my question."

"Don't be a smartass."

I shove my hair roughly from my face. I stuck my foot in it...again.

"I wasn't creeped out by what you said. It was heavy, you know? After learning what I have so far about the Brielaran race, I understand why. But I've orchestrated my entire life under the assumption no one ever gave a damn about me. It hit me some kind of way, you know?"

"I get it. Trust me. I get it."

Our lunch arrives and Mika digs in. I make quick work of cleaning my plate even though I've suddenly lost my appetite. Which is totally not like me. I'm always hungry. However, what sits across the table from me is far more appetizing than the food on my plate. I want to tell her again how beautiful she is when I hear the knocks. Her head pops up and she looks around.

Good. She hears them too.

Three knocks sound off again, and she looks around again.

"Do you hear that?" she whispers, looking under the table and behind her.

"Yes. We're being summoned. When we finish up here, we'll need to go inside."

"Being summoned? By whom? For what and why doesn't anyone else here it?" She looks around at the other tables.

"The Monarch. She requests our presence. We're the only ones hearing it because she knocks telepathically. Because you and I are connected, she is now fully connected to you." She cocks an eyebrow. "Think of it like this. Because you're an unknown hybrid, your connection to her was like an unpaved road overrun with foliage. The path was there but unknown and hard to maneuver. Now you're a chosen hybrid who has started the Passage. The road is now paved with lights and street signs. It's so much easier for her to find you and for you to hear her."

"Okay. Do we need to go now?"

"Only if you're finished eating."

She lays her napkin beside her plate. "I'm finished. Do we need to wait for the waiter?"

I stand and hold my hand out for her to take. "No. The Sunday brunch is free. The restaurant is open seven days a week for breakfast, lunch, and dinner. For all other days, we'll need to pay."

She lays her small soft hand in mine. I lead her back to the pebble-stoned path that takes us to the Queen. I can barely contain my excitement. Solomon has seen the Monarch several times but this is the first time the Monarch and I will meet face to face even though we've spoken many times. Now that I'm completing the Passage I'm finally able to come to here as the real me...the whole me I've waited my whole for this moment. I want her to be proud of me.

I run a talon over the top of Mika's hand. I'm in awe of how soft her hands are, how good and sweet she smells. How did I get so lucky?

Mika hasn't spoken a word, but when we step inside the Jewel of Abrielara, her mouth falls open in wonder. The beauty of the place is enough to shut anyone up. Words are not enough to describe the splendor displayed in every nook and cranny of this place.

I guide her up the gilded staircase to the enclosed balcony that overlooks the garden. The Monarch takes her brunch there. She likes to look over us all without being observed. She considers us her children. In some ways, we are. She is by far wiser than we are. She is most definitely older than any of us. And without her, we'd most likely perish.

At the top of the stairs are two heavily guarded ornate iron doors. Knowing that the Monarch has summoned us, the guards don't question us before opening the doors. I stop before entering and kneel in front of her.

"Lean on me. We'll need to remove our shoes before entering the Atrium."

I remove both of her shoes and then mine. Her hands shake a little so I hold both of hers in mine.

"Don't be nervous."

"Easy for you to say," she whispers back.

"Do you think I'd take you anywhere that would put you in danger?"

"Do you want me to answer truthfully?"

I shake my head at her.

"You're never going to let that go, are you? Between you and Solomon..."

"Don't bring me into this."

I don't finish the sentence because Mika is no longer paying me any attention. At her intake of breath, I know she is once again stunned by the beauty of the room.

"Beautiful, isn't it?" The entire room is made of glass. You can see the pebbled walkway and part of the garden through the floor. The room is decorated in the same style as the garden, full of beautiful flowers and foliage. There's even a huge floor-to-ceiling waterfall at the other end of the room.

"Yes, it is. You can't even tell this is here from the outside."

She walks to one side of the room and points outside. "Is that the table we sat at?"

"Yes. This part of the building is hidden on purpose. It's cloaked from the community for privacy."

"Lux. You made it. Finally."

I turn to the smooth sound of the Monarch's voice. She holds her hands out to me, and I walk toward her like a child would to a grandmother. I'm happy to see her. I bow my head before reaching her.

"Enough of that. Come here and greet me properly."

I stand and wrap my arms around her. She hugs me back and then steps away to take my face in her hands.

"My boy. I'm so happy to finally see this handsome face in person."

"But we speak often."

She waves her hand at me.

"True, but that is no different than picking up the telephone. Of course I love hearing your voice, but seeing your face is much better."

She smiles at me and then turns her attention to Mika, the sole reason we are here.

The silence is so loud as her eyes focus on Mika's face. I feel power radiate from the Monarch and I'm suddenly hit with fear. I don't understand what's going on and cannot do anything about it even if I did.

The Monarch's aura is bright with orange, golds and browns. This is unusual. The aura of the Monarch is usually deep red or purple. She holds her hand up in front of me and I find myself moving backward away from Mika. Now, this is not what I was expecting.

"What the fuck, Lux!"

"You got me. I don't know what's going on."

"She's not going to hurt her—"

"Calm yourself, boys." the Queen commands.

She stands in front of Mika now. Mika doesn't appear afraid at all. In fact, she looks a lot more relaxed than she did before we drove out here. The Queen puts her hands on each side of Mika's face as she did to me moments ago.

"Tell me who you are, child."

Mika blinks a few times and her eyes swing to me.

The pleading in them is apparent. She has no idea what's going on or what to say. Unfortunately, neither do we.

"My name is Mika Burris."

Her voice, calm and steady. Her eyes are back on the Monarch who smiles gently at her.

"No. Tell me who you really are."

Her eyes glow brightly now, almost all gold and no red. Mika's glow too, only not the beautiful electric blue we're used to seeing. Now they are green. Florescent green. Mika smiles back at her, her body rod straight, not from fear but something else.

"I am the Librarian." She bows her head to the Queen. "At your service."

The Monarch gasps and brings her hands to her face.

"Is it true?" She turns to look at me. "How long have you known?"

I open my mouth to speak, but she stops me before I can get a word out.

"Be honest, Lux, or I'll ask Solomon to speak instead. He'll have no problem telling me the truth." She points a long-taloned finger at me.

"We weren't sure. We took her to the crash site and she could read the hieroglyphics. We made an appointment for her with Brady to have some tests run. We wanted to be sure before we brought her to you."

Mika's head turns my way sharply. Her eyes grow darker. Her eyebrows and her lips pinch together. I obviously said the wrong thing.

"Don't be mad. We told you everyone visits with the Monarch after they are chosen. The difference with you is that we wanted to make sure we weren't mistaken. We had our suspicions. We honestly didn't think the Monarch would want to see us today. We thought it would be a little later. At least, we had hoped."

"Stop rambling, Lux," the Monarch says. "You're not in trouble. I'm too delighted to be angry that you kept such an important secret from me. You do know what this means for you don't you?"

I nod. I haven't quite dealt with it all myself yet. She turns back to Mika.

"I'm fully aware that you don't have any idea what it means to be the Librarian. I know that your experience here so far has been, shall we say...traumatic. So, I want you to keep your appointment with the doctor. Have your tests completed."

She turns back to me. "As soon as he has the results, I want him to send them to me. Of course, he must inform Mika also."

She turns back to Mika. "Although I don't need them to know that she is the Librarian." She walks to the far wall and looks over the garden. "We will have much to discuss, and I will tell you everything you need to know, but most of it will come to you. Especially now that you have been awakened to that side of yourself. It is never good to rush these things. I can be patient."

She smiles at us and the hold she has on my body releases. I walk to Mika, trying to judge her reaction or feelings toward me. I have no idea what she's thinking. Her face looks calm enough but I have been on the receiving end of her feelings when she appeared calm before. There was nothing calm about the result.

"I look forward to seeing both of you again soon. Now, if you will excuse me, I have an appointment that I must keep."

I bow my head and take Mika's hand and lead her out of the Atrium, but she stops us before we exit the room.

"Oh, and congratulations," she says to Mika. Her eyes float to me. "I'm proud of you. You've done well but you might want to tell her everything."

"Thank you." I have no idea what the congratulations are for other than for who I chose. I know for damn sure what she means by the rest of it. I wish she hadn't said it. Not now. Not when we are so close and not before I've had a chance to win her over.

I retrieve our shoes, putting hers back on her delicate feet. I refrain from saying anything until we get to the car. Now that we're out of the castle, anger radiates off Mika like solar flares, snappishly licking across my skin.

I open her door for her and lean in to buckle her seatbelt. She yanks it out of my hands and secures it herself.

Okay. So she is mad at me.

"Mad at us. Fix it."

"I don't know how. You're the one who decided not to tell her the whole truth."

"I had every intention of telling her the truth. Just not all at once and when I thought she was ready. Come on, you know this."

"Look where that got us."

"Just fucking fix it or let me take over."

"No. I'll fix it."

I walk around and slide into my seat and close the door. The car purrs like she always does when I turn her on, only this time, I get no joy from it.

"What the fuck does she mean by tell me everything? What the fuck is a Librarian? And if you tell me it's someone who works in a library, I'll gnaw your eyes out with my teeth."

Chapter Twenty

Mika

One thing I cannot stand is being lied to. Being kept in the dark is the same thing. Lying by omission. Knowing that I've been searching for answers about myself and my family since I got here should've been enough for him to do the right thing as soon as he suspected something. I understand he didn't know for sure but that's no excuse. I've been grasping and begging for answers this whole time. Anything would have been better than nothing.

"I'm sorry, Mika. I am. Perry, Solomon, and I thought you might be the Librarian—"

"Perry too?" I cover my head with my hands and lower it to my knees.

"Baby, we weren't sure. We didn't want to assume."

"Don't baby me. Since when do you use endearments? You suspected enough to talk with Perry about it but not with me. I felt like a lunatic standing inside the cave seeing pictures and words all over the walls, only for Solomon to tell me he didn't see them. He could have said something. Anything."

"Mika." His voice is calm, but his eyes are anything but calm. Red throbbing orbs, his eyes look like laser beams. His shouldered tentacles bulge against his linen shirt. Normally, I'd be intimidated but not anymore and definitely not now. He could puff up as much as he wants to. I don't care. I'm too pissed.

"What is a Librarian, Lux? What does that mean? What else are you keeping from me?" I know my voice is shrill, but all I feel is betrayed and angry.

He takes a slow deep breath. His jaw grinds slowly and the flaps on the bridge of his nose flare in time with his breaths.

"Let me get you home first. This is not a discussion I want to have in the car with you."

"Fine."

He speeds out of the parking lot and we don't say a word to each other all the way home. I don't want to hear shit but the fucking truth. That's it. Nothing else. If he tries to get out of it, then I have nothing else to say to him. I don't want anything else to do with him, either.

Meeting the Monarch was not what I thought it was going to be. She is beautiful. Ethereal. She put so much fear in me by being in the same room with her. The power she exudes is formidable.

There's no question she held some kind of power over me and probably anyone she wanted. Her presence was light and heavy at the same time. When she touched my face and asked me again who I was, something inside me clicked and then took over. It was like someone turned the lights on, and I woke up and suddenly knew who I was. She drew that out of me. How or why, I don't know. I'm just as confused as ever.

One thing I'm not confused about is how angry I am at Solomon and Lux. Perry too, when I think about it. The welcome committee. Did they know too?

Right before the party, the look on their faces implied they had thoughts about something. Maybe this was it. Again, they had the opportunity to tell me something I have a right to know and chose not to.

I can't bring myself to look at Lux. If he doesn't tell me what I want to hear...

"We're back."

I didn't notice that we had made it home already. I unlatch the seatbelt and unlock the door.

"Mika. Please don't be angry. I promise to tell you everything I know and everything I suspect. I don't want you to be upset with me."

His eyes aren't glowing red orbs anymore. Instead, the warm honey look is back.

Obviously, Solomon wants to speak his mind. I don't care who does the talking as long as I get some answers.

"I can't promise you anything."

I exit the car and head toward the house. Not even bothering to see if he's following. If he doesn't, so be it. I'll be banging on the judge's door next if that's the case. Either way, somebody is giving me some answers.

Today.

I open the door only to immediately close it and lean my back against it. I close my eyes because surely I'm imagining things.

"What's wrong." Lux runs his hands through his hair.

"The living room is full of people. Aliens and Humans. At least, I think they're people."

"I don't understand. What do you mean?"

"I mean, when I opened the door, there are people everywhere. All of whom I have never seen before."

"That's crazy." He moves me to the side, opens the door, and then closes it again.

"What the fuck?"

I roll my eyes at him. "Like I would know. You tell me. Nobody in this town tells me anything. Do you know those people and why do they look so—"

"Ghostly?"

"Yeah." That's it. I truly am losing my mind. I have slipped into the deep end of the pool and can't swim my way out.

"Well, no, and I don't know what they're doing here. Unless..." He looks around a little bashfully.

"Unless what?" I prod.

"Unless they're here so you can record their love story."

The anger leaves my body like a deflated balloon.

"Their what?" I whisper.

"Their love story. The Librarian is extremely important to us because the librarian records our love stories. Validates our existence. This is the reason why we're here in the first place. We haven't had a librarian since Dane's grandmother... Well, your great-grandmother died long before any of us were born. There are literally hundreds of stories that need to be recorded. And they can only be recorded by you."

"Me? But I—"

Lux shakes his head at me.

"Yes, by you and only you. You record, transcribe, keep track, and make sure our stories are guarded and accessible for generations after us to see. To prove to ourselves and the universe that even we can love and be loved. Even we are salvageable, although we are unworthy.

"Because I've chosen you, it solidifies my place beside you as your guardian. I'm the one who is tasked with protecting you and this library. It explains why we've always felt connected to it. I've always felt this place was special, particularly the library."

I step away from the door and sit on the porch swing. My

mind, again swirling with more questions. It's been nothing but one big tornado. As soon as I get used to one idea—whoosh—here comes something else to blow my mind to smithereens.

"Even if this is all true, why would the Librarian and the library need to be protected? Who would dare attack it with you all running around here?"

Lux bends down in front of me and takes my hands. "Back in the day, it was a different story. The natives were always under attack after this land was discovered. Our real story getting out into the wrong hands would mean certain devastation for us and possibly the human race.

"Of course, internal politics have played a part too. We've had our library burned down several times and had to start over. That's why no one knows what the hieroglyphs say. Besides the Monarch, the Librarian is the only one who can read the language and our last Librarian has long been gone. Other than the Monarch, the Librarian and her Guardian are also the only ones of our species with special powers. Powers like the ones you displayed in the pharmacy and in your closet. It's so we can continue to protect our legacy.

"We've had outsiders, like other beings from other planets, come with the intention of getting rid of us all. We want a record to show that we were here and that we flourished. The Librarian is the one to do that."

"But I thought this town had a Historian. Couldn't the historian do the job?" My heart begins to pound. I know what he's going to say. I just know it.

"No, sweetheart. The Historian knows our basic history, but all the information that the historian receives comes from the Librarian. The Historian can't read the language and definitely can't see or talk to those who have already passed on."

His voice remains calm. His scent washes over me in soft waves but isn't calming me down. Not like I wished it would.

The sound of his voice or his scent doesn't change the meaning behind his words. The one thing he has avoided saying is the only thing I hear loud and clear.

I'm never going to be able to leave this place. I'm stuck here. Of course, I'm sure I can travel but I will always be tied to Abrielara. I will always have to come back here.

Suddenly the weight of everything that's happened to me my entire life sits on my shoulders. It bears so heavily on me, my shoulders physically slouch. The pain in my neck bends it so forcefully that my head almost hits my knees. Hot, fat tears make a hasty escape and I don't even have the energy to stop or wipe them away.

I give up. I give in. She wins. Abrielara wins.

Everyone here wins except me. I have to pay the exorbitant price that I didn't even know I owed. I thought I was free after leaving the misery of my mother's house. I knew life would be better when she died because I could get to know my mother without her interference. But no, as usual, she has the last laugh. Even in death, she has the last word. The woman obviously harbored a hate for me so vicious that even impending death couldn't soften it.

I followed her instructions and found myself chosen. Not my choice, but okay, I bought into it with the understanding one day soon, I could go back home and resume the life I had actually chosen. Then I'm told I have to produce an offspring. Surprisingly, that didn't even cause me to blink an eyelash. I was resigned to it. Why wouldn't I be when the alternative was possible death? And now he's telling me all these people, living and dead, depend on me. They want me to stay because their story will remain unwritten and untold if I don't.

Talk about pressure. What kind of person would I be if I left here anyway, knowing what they needed?

I allow my head to lie on my knees. The tears make their path down my legs. I'm vaguely aware Lux is still crouched in front of me. I don't know what to say anymore. There's nothing else to say.

"Mika, since I'm telling you everything, there's something else I need to tell you."

His gentle words are said from soft lips that brush my earlobe. I know better, though. Those soft lips are about to tell me something I don't want to hear. Probably something that will hurt. At this point, I expect nothing less. I raise my head anyway, enough to look into his eyes.

"The Passage is not seven stages, it's eight. After the consummation is the commitment. As a hybrid, you must complete all of the necessary stages. Committing to me is not a requirement but voicing your decision about it is. Since I chose you, I'm obviously committed to you, but you're under no obligation to commit to me."

His eyes search my face, and I know he's waiting to see how I will react to his words. I have nothing left to give. I relax my back against the porch swing and look down at my lap.

His voice returns as a gravely, barely-there whisper.

"I'm assuming you are similar to the other female hybrids here. Once you're pregnant, you can do what you like, go where you want. You would have fulfilled the most important part of the Passage. However, if you choose not to stay, the baby will need to stay with me."

Again, I have no choice. Yeah, I could choose to leave my baby here, but I wouldn't want to do that. This brings a whole new meaning to the word stuck. Why he didn't tell me this before doesn't matter. But there is one choice I can make.

I stand slowly and move around him to the door. I don't bother looking behind me as I walk in and close it.

I'm brought up short by the ghostly beings still littering my living room. I forgot all about them. The hopeful look in their eyes doesn't lift my spirits.

I walk toward the stairs and they part the way for me. Their murmurings are quieted, I'm sure, by my solemn disposition. Unfortunately, I'm not in the hosting mood at the moment. I can't even bring myself to offer a smile.

I turn over for what feels like the thousandth time. Not able to sleep a wink. The damn moon shines high and bright through my windows. Any other time I'd bask in its luminescent beauty. Instead, I wish I could find a fucking switch to turn the bitch off. I should have bought those shades, at least for my bedroom windows. I grab a pillow and cover my face. Not that it would help any. Newsflash, it isn't the moon keeping me awake.

Lying here watching the numbers on the digital alarm clock keep time has helped me figure out one thing. The reason I'm so fucking angry isn't that there are decisions to be made. It's because all of the decisions have already been made. I can't make a single one for myself except deciding not to die or suffer the consequences. If my mother's greasy attorney had not insisted that I come here, I'd have gone on living my life in happy oblivion.

I think I know why my mother wanted me to come here. The only thing that makes sense is she wanted me to know about my family history. The kicker is she knew the restrictions I'd face once coming here. This was her way of letting me know she got the final say over my life.

She knew what coming here meant for me. She could have easily told the judge where to find me and sent Perry my way. She could have written it all down in her diary for me to read in the privacy of my own home. I didn't have to come here.

At the same time, if I hadn't come, I'd never find out the truth about me. I would have never met the welcome committee, the judge, Perry, Lux or Solomon. As angry as I am with Solomon, I can somewhat understand his line of thinking. Ultimately, he's always trying to protect me somehow, and I believe his heart is probably in the right place. I also can't forget how I feel when I'm with him. With them both.

What if they're my people? The ones I'm supposed to be with? Does it matter how we found each other as long as we did?

I climb out of bed and walk to the window overlooking the front yard. Lux stands on his porch, looking at my house. Just as I suspected he would be.

I pull on my robe and wade through the otherworldly crowd still inhabiting my living room. Evidently, there's no rest in the afterlife. Their eyes are still full of hope and what looks like concern. This time I offer a small smile as I pass.

I open the front door and watch him watch me. It's apparent he isn't sure what to do. He shuffles his feet and his talons are fidgety. He almost looks embarrassed at being caught staring at my house. I take mercy on him and wave him over. In less than a blink, he is standing in front of me.

"I'm sorry, Mika. We didn't mean to hurt you. Please forgive us."

"It's okay, Lux. I didn't wave you over to talk. I know you must be tired, and there's no point in both of us losing sleep."

I turn and walk back into the house, and this time, I make sure he follows me.

Lux

I admit seeing her standing in her doorway scared me at first. I couldn't imagine why she would want me to come over. I pulled the last straw when I told her everything. Well, almost everything. There's one major thing but I'm not sure I ever will. I guess it depends on if she decides to stay or not.

"At the rate we're going, we never will."

"You love pointing out the obvious, don't you?"

"Like you don't?"

"If you can't offer anything useful, just shut the fuck up."

"You should've taken your own advice in the pharmacy, dickhead."

"Again with the dirty laundry. When are you going to let it go?"

"Not until she's ours and maybe not even then."

"Good to know. I'll be sure and return the favor."

Solomon is finally silent. We're exhausted, cranky, and just fucking tired of being in limbo. I meant it when I said I didn't sleep well without her. Neither does Solomon. Before her, I never had a problem. Since the Passage started, I'm a mess.

I follow her past her unearthly houseguests and up the stairs. When we make it to her bedroom, I stand and watch her like an idiot. I'm honestly afraid to make any moves. What if I completely misunderstood or misjudged the situation? The last thing I need is to give her another reason for hating me.

After she removes her robe and turns to shut off the light, she looks over her shoulder at me.

"Are you going to get into bed, or are you going to stand there for the rest of the night? If you don't want to sleep here, you can always pick one of the rooms down the hall."

No other instruction is needed. I strip my clothes off and slide under the covers behind her. She clicks the light off and the urge to close my eyes hits me like a knockout punch. Before I drift off, I have the presence of mind to say one thing.

"Thank you."

I don't feel I've slept more than a couple of hours before the heat wakes me before the break of day. The reason for it snuggled against me. I evidently didn't fall asleep deep enough to change back into my human self because all my limbs surround her.

I slowly work on extracting them from her but she makes a sound of protest and snuggles closer to me if that's even possible. I stop moving because I don't want to wake her. She needs the rest. But more importantly, I don't want to move. I love how she feels in my arms. I love how she's naturally comfortable with me, even though I am most certainly not her favorite person.

"Don't overthink it. Just enjoy it."

I wrap my arms tightly around her. There isn't a breath of air between us. I lean my head down and lay a light kiss on her naked shoulder. Then I bury my nose into the crook of her neck.

Big mistake.

Her scent envelops me and I almost believe everything will be alright again. I inhale deeply and the cloud begins to drown me in more than peace. Heat lights up between us. My eyes close as I relish the feeling. I can't stop from rocking my hips into the globes of her ass. I want to get closer to her. I wish I could crawl inside her and zip her up like a garment bag.

This is crazy.

She is mine. She belongs to me. I don't know what I must do to convince her to stay, but I've got to figure it out. Whatever it takes, I'll do it.

"We'll do it and she's ours, not just yours."

"If you want me to enjoy this, be quiet."

I'm damn near shaking with want. It's like I'm having withdrawals or feigning for a hit. I take another deep inhale and the groan that escapes me is raw. Desperate. I want too much. I need her too much.

I take turns licking and kissing her shoulder and her neck. I can't help myself. I promise to stop if she tells me to or never wakes up. But until then, I need this time with her.

The moment she wakes up, her body goes still and her breathing pauses. I'm anxious and embarrassed, but then it completely lifts away like a veil. I have nothing to hide.

"I'm sorry. I didn't mean to wake you."

"It's okay. But you've got to stop apologizing so much. What's done is done," she says on a loaded sigh.

Guilt lays into me again. She's tired and feels some kind of way because of me. And probably a little because of her mom. But I'm responsible for most of it.

"I wish I could make it all better," I say more to myself. More than anything, I want her to be happy, and I want to be the one to make her happy.

"Some things are out of our control." Her voice is soft from sleep, but the scent of her arousal implies that she's anything but sleepy. My body responds with a heat wave and sends vibrations all through my body. I know she feels them too. We're too close for her not to.

The heat between us is not something that can be ignored. I don't know how she feels about it, but there's only one way to find out. I turn her in my arms so she faces me. Her eyes illuminate a low-frequency blue and my skin tingles at the recognition.

I pull her flush against me and attack her mouth with mine after shielding my teeth. Her hands find their way into my hair, holding my head so my lips stay on hers.

No problem there. I have no intention of letting up any time soon. I put my appendages to work, holding her to me, pulling her tank top over her head and ripping her boxers off. She sighs when I bring my lips back to hers after yanking off my boxers.

Suddenly it hits me. What if the chase is still a nightmare for her and she is reminded when I enter her body? Some things, some actions that come naturally to me, may frighten her. Scare her away. Some things about my alien body are vastly different from my human one. Those things will most likely turn her off.

"It might but what choice do we have? There is no us without you."

"Thank you for saying that."

"Be gentle and be kind. Ask permission before doing something you think she might not like. She'll be fine."

"You sure?"

Solomon's silence brings me to a full stop. I can't jeopardize what we've already gained. It would be stupid.

With that thought, I pull back a little. The heat between us turns from a thick fog into a light, airy breeze. I extract my limbs from her body and lay flat on my back, unable to meet her eyes.

What was I thinking coming in here? I came close to

ruining everything we've worked so hard for. I should've shifted back into my human before I got into bed with her.

"No, Lux. Since we're trying to be transparent with her, this is part of it. We can't hide you away forever."

"You're willing to risk losing everything? Just to include me?"

"Yes,"

"I'm not."

"What's wrong? Why did you stop?"

Can I even say what my problem is out loud? I know my hang-up. No point in weighing her down with it.

Solomon groans in my head. *"You can be so infuriating."*

"Nothing. I'm tired and you need to rest. I'm sorry I woke you."

Although she doesn't respond, I hear her breathing and feel her agitation. None of which can overcome the heat that's still permeating the air.

"Feel that? She wants you."

"I may have to go to another bedroom after all."

She snaps the light on and I blink the shield from my eyes so I can see her. She sits up and scrutinizes my face.

"You're right. You look exhausted. Your eyes are bloodshot. But I also know you aren't half as tired as you are turned on, so what gives?" She leans back on her hands. Her nipples are hard and pointed directly at me. I groan inwardly and close my eyes to temptation.

"Mika."

"Just tell me, and I'll let it go or don't, and I'll..." She shrugs her shoulders and looks away from me.

I can't take my eyes off the curve of her neck that meets the beautiful slope of her shoulders. My eyes sweep to her nipples, still peaked. My mouth waters for a taste. My tongue takes a leisurely tour around my lips.

"You're seriously gonna turn that down?"

"I know. I can hardly believe it myself."

"Or you'll what?" I manage to ask, not taking my eyes off her body. The heat is heavy again and the air around us is electrified.

"Oh, for Pete's sake."

She hops up and yanks the blankets off of my body. My main erection bears absolutely no shame and stands straight and proud.

I feel the other appendages in my body ready to extend. I look into her eyes, and the beautiful blue of her Brielaran is back, commanding me to answer the call she demands of me. The urge, the tendency, is there. But when she puts one leg on each side of me, all my doubts from moments ago evaporate like magic, and I have no idea why I second-guessed myself, to begin with.

"Looks like you can't turn her down after all. I knew you couldn't."

"If you aren't going to be quiet, I'm going to lock you out."

"Don't be scared. I don't bite." Her words are accented with the swift descent of her hips as she sinks down on me.

"Ah—sweet..." I can't groan out more because I don't remember the rest of the words. Her hot sweet body encapsulates me. Every fucking ridge on my dick has a home inside her body. She fits so fucking perfectly it cements the notion that she was made for me. She is mine.

She continues to ride me. No harsh, jerky moves. Smooth liquified movements like a sexy, soulful slow dance. Every nerve in my body sings and I'm ready to burst.

I allow two more of my appendages to extend, and soon another one can join but not before I enjoy her dance for a bit longer. I meet every dip and swerve of her hips with my own. My talons take a slow trip up and down her sensitized body.

She leans her head back and allows our bodies to naturally dictate the movements and speed. I sit up and finally take one of her nipples into my mouth and suck in time with the push and pull of our bodies.

"Oh, Lux!" She sighs my name drowsily and creams all over my dick. I'm so close to losing my shit. I'm strung up about as tight as I'll ever be but I don't want it to end yet. There's more I want her to experience with me. A hell of a lot more I want to experience with her.

I flip her over quickly. The shock in her eyes is enough to slow us down.

"You may not bite, sweetheart, but I definitely do."

I scrape my teeth across the skin of her shoulder before taking a nip without breaking the skin. I graze my talons over her erect nipples as she hisses and writhes underneath me. "You like how that feels, baby?"

"You know I do." She groans, threading her fingers in my hair.

I continue to rock into her with long deep strokes. "You want more?" I growl in her ear.

"Yes, oh yes." She sighs. She stretches her hands above her head and turns her head to look me in the eye. Her eyes are so bright, and for one moment, I'm tempted to tell her the secrets of my heart. Her pussy clamps down on me again, pulling me back to reality.

I allow my second erection to descend and lean in, sinking my dick deeper into her and allowing her clit to be massaged by the vibration from my lower abdomen. Two of my other appendages bend her knees and hold them apart for us. Two others grab her ass cheeks, gently spreading them and putting her at an angle best for what I have in mind. Her eyes grow large and then droop with desire when she feels it. It won't be long now. The sweet juices from her pussy seep down onto me.

"Do you trust me?" I ask because once I have her permission, there's no turning back. Her moan of agreement is confirmed with a shake of her head.

I don't wait for her to let me know she understands before I lather my second erection and her forbidden hole with her sweet juices. I command my second erection to thin down so the intrusion won't jar her. The vibrations from my lower abs have her on a high so potent that I could say anything and I don't think she'd care. But if I hurt her again, I would care.

My first erection is still pumping into her with the deep sensuous pace she set when she rode me. I kiss her lips and slowly push my second erection into her ass, taking small breaks. She's so deliciously tight. I don't take my eyes off her in case she wants me to stop but also because she is so beautiful. I could never tire of looking at her. Her pussy clamps down on me and I know she's almost ready to cum again. She's almost there, and fuck, so am I.

I allow my second erection to finally sink to the hilt. Her eyes are closed. I'm not sure she even realizes how deep I'm into her until I slowly expand in her ass. I allow it to grow just enough for her to feel it but not in pain. I hold still. Her eyes pop open and widen with the realization. I can't help but smile. I'll bet the farm that she has never had it like this before.

"Lux." She groans. Her face is painted with a look between pleasure and pain.

"Relax, baby. Just relax. It'll get better. I promise." I continue to watch her as I litter her face and body with soft kisses. I pulse my second erection to get her used to me and stretch her little by little. Her body gradually relaxes around me.

When she stops flinching, I allow it to thicken and harden at the size right at her comfort zone. I move just a little to make sure she's good.

Her moan melts me.

"How do you feel?" I groan in her ear. She squeezes me so exquisitely. A few seconds of patience are all I have left to give.

"I'm okay."

"Just okay?" I hoped for a sight better than okay.

"Full."

I pop up from her neck to search her glistening eyes. "How full?"

She cracks a small smile and contracts her body around me, and we moan at the sensation. "Deliciously full."

That's all I need to hear. I synchronize my movements. God, I've never felt anything as glorious as her. Chill bumps cover my body as I struggle to keep the pace. Her eyes drift closed and then open again when her pussy latches onto me so vigorously. Her juices wet me up so good again. So good.

"Mika," I growl, unable to control the euphoric desperation I feel.

I kiss her luscious lips, my tongue covering every delicious inch of her mouth. "Do you have any idea how much you mean to me?" I mumble. The depth of how much touches our soul. I open my eyes to see her eyes on me.

"I can't live without you. The only reason I'm here is to love you. The only reason."

"Lux," she whispers. Her tone implies she is shocked by my admission. I grind on her as my last attempt at maintaining my sanity and keeping my mouth closed. She throws her head back, bucking against me. She's going to cum again. I so wish I could lean down and lick up every last drop. However, my first orgasm is about to be quickly followed by a second, and this time, I won't be able to slow it down. I feel it cover me from head to toe like a blanket.

"Oh, Lux!" She pants and then drowns my dick in her sweetness.

"Oh shit, baby, you feel so fucking good."

My orgasm begins to smother me, and soon, I can't hold it off. The groan from the pit of my gut erupts from me as I spill into her body. She continues to wring me and my second orgasm follows right behind it, pouring my hot cum into her ass.

Even though I don't have anything else to give, my body acts on autopilot. Steadily pumping into her body, not wanting to lose the grip she has on me. It has become something I can't live without.

Chapter Twenty One

Mika

A ringing wakes me from a deep sleep. I curse it and bury my face into the pillow. I was enjoying the heaviness this kind of sleeping creates after the night I've had, especially when you need the rest so badly. After a few moments, I realize it's my cellphone, and I roll over to answer it. My hand meets nothing but sheets. Lux is no longer in bed with me. The alarm clock says it's after noon, explaining why he isn't here. I'm sure Solomon had to work today.

"Hello," I try to say after clearing my throat.

"Hello, is Mika Burris available?"

I sit up and attempt to wake up so I can remember this conversation later. "Speaking."

"Hello, Mika. This is Shawna at Dr. Merrick's office. You have an appointment with us tomorrow, but we were hoping we could squeeze you in today. The Monarch wishes us to put a rush on this."

At the mention of the Monarch, I'm awake-awake.

"Today is fine. What time should I be there?"

"Wonderful! If you could be here no later than two-thirty, that would be great. We do have some minor paperwork we'd like you to fill out. Just the usual family history stuff. We will see you then."

She disconnects the call without an official confirmation, but that's fine. It isn't like I have any real plans today. I check the clock again. It's already twelve forty-five. I've got to get my ass in gear if I want to make it there on time.

I shove the covers off and sprint to the bathroom to turn on the shower. I'm positive if I put one foot in front of the other, I'm sure I'll make it through the day just fine.

Dr. Merrick's office is in the medical building, but luckily, it's on the fifth floor and a lot quieter than Perry's floor. I grab the clipboard after signing in and proceed to answer the same stupid questions you always fill out at the doctor's office.

I wonder if they're required to make you fill out the same questions everywhere. What if you put down all the wrong answers then what? Is someone going to call and say, I'm sorry, but we feel you made a mistake on question number seven. According to the last time you filled this out, your great-great-aunt had breast cancer, not your grandmother.

I roll my eyes and fill out the stupid form. I've finally finished it when a statuesque redhead calls my name, and I follow her through the double doors. While she runs through the usual triage, I mentally replay my night with Lux.

He's literally a sex-toy shop inside of a living, breathing body. He has a built-in vibrator. Seriously, I could have never thought that up.

I wonder why he changed his mind at first? I'm glad I changed it for him, but I can't think of a reason he would suddenly change it in the first place. It was obvious he felt the same heat I did. His eyes were lit up like fireworks. If I couldn't feel the heat, I damn sure could see it in his eyes.

The nurse leads me to a room decorated nicely with pastels and leaves me alone with my thoughts. I wonder what he's thinking now? What did he think of our night together? I wish I was able to wake up to see him off.

My house has gotten even more visitors since last night. The backyard is full of folks who didn't make it inside. I don't know what I'm supposed to do. I hope the Queen is right and it'll come to me.

"Ms. Burris."

A tall, bearded man with dark auburn hair and sparkling green eyes opens the door and sticks his hand out.

"It's so nice to finally meet you. I'm Dr. Merrick, but you can call me Brady. I grew up with Solomon and your brother. I've heard a lot about you from them."

"Nice to meet you, Brady. Wish I could say the same. I seem to get information when it's deemed necessary."

Dr. Merrick nods in agreement and sets his chart down.

"Yeah, this town is like that. Can be a little unnerving and downright frustrating sometimes. I spoke to Solomon this morning, and he explained everything that has happened up to this point. He wanted to be here but had a last minute emergency. Is there anything I should know that he doesn't?"

"No. I can't think of anything. I'm sure he told you about the guests who showed up at my house?"

"Yes, he did. That's a sure sign you're the Librarian. They've come because they recognize your aura and you can see them. My main concern is you're an unknown hybrid. First, I need to confirm that you're Perry's full-blooded sibling. The judge is positive you are, but I would like to verify it before I jump into trying to determine what kind of hybrid you are. I'm a fan of Dr. Dane St. John and his work. I've studied everything he's recorded. There are some studies out there I can't find the complete records of, but I have faith I will one day. I think you could hold the key to a lot of the questions we've had. With your permission, I would love to delve right into those. This would not only help you but our community too."

"Sure. What would I need to do?"

The doctor sits in the chair in front of me and tells me about the number of tests he'll need to run. He should have the paternity results by the end of the day. But he shouldn't need to see me again for at least another three months.

The nice nurse who brought me in comes back and takes several vials of blood from me.

"We'll run some initial tests that we always do on our females and then proceed with the other tests. I'll run these right now. We should have our answers to the questions about your general health in about twenty minutes. You're welcome to go back out to the lobby. We'll call you back when we're ready."

The twenty minutes fly by, and before I know it, I'm back in the same room waiting on Dr. Merrick again.

"Your labs look great, Mika. Your blood test isn't quite done, but it shouldn't be too much longer. I'll give you a call when it is. I'd like you to set up an appointment with us in about three months to give a second round of blood. I'd also like you to keep a journal of any fluctuations you feel in your overall health, including mood swings. Now that you're going through the Passage, any insight you can lend on your experience would be helpful."

"Great. Thanks, Dr. Merrick."

"You're welcome. And I don't know if you know this already, but you're pregnant. Congratulations. I don't know if you have an OB yet, but here is a card for Dr. Camacho in case you don't. His office is upstairs. He'll need to see you as soon as possible. Abrielaran pregnancies are typically shorter than human pregnancies and the experience can be scary if you aren't prepared."

He hands me two business cards, his and Dr. Camacho's. I blindly follow him out of the room and to the appointment desk to set up my next appointment. I haven't said anything other than to answer some questions. I'm in shock. Solomon and I just had sex for the first time, what was that...four days ago?

Is this why the Monarch congratulated me? How is that possible? I thought you had to have a certain level of HCG in your blood to determine pregnancy. Wouldn't four days be too soon?

"Ms. Burris?"

I look down at the lady at the desk. "I'm sorry. What did you say?"

"I was asking if you wanted me to tell Dr. Camacho's office that you were headed on up?"

"Oh. Yes, I guess you'd better. Thank you."

"No problem. His office number is on the card. See you in three months."

Pregnant? I guess I shouldn't be shocked in the grand scheme of things. It feels sudden though, even if I do feel like I've lived a lifetime here already. I don't even know what to feel anymore. I'm stuck here, going through something I can't respond to because I don't know what's supposed to happen next.

What really stinks is how solitary this feels. I'm nothing more than a puppet. Decisions anyone on this planet should have the right to make for themselves have been taken from me under the threat of death. Dr. Merrick seemed happy to find out what may be in store for me, but I'd rather not know at this point. It's never good. Never.

The waiting room in Dr. Camacho's office is a bit livelier than Dr. Merrick's. Looks like I'm in the right place. The room is full of pregnant women. I grab a seat after signing my name to the list. Every eye in the room is on me and they're smiling. That's nice, but I'm sure that since the pharmacy drama has already run the gossip mill, now seeing me in an OB's office will add more grain to the pot. The news will be around town before I leave my appointment. I guarantee it.

I look at the clipboard in my hand. Yep, same questions. My God, we're in the same building. Can they not share information?

HIPPA.

Right.

"Suspicion or confirmation?"

The heavily pregnant lady sitting next to me leans over and not quite whispers in my space. Her shoulder-length mousy brown curls bounce with childlike excitement.

"Excuse me?" I lean back a little.

"Do you suspect your preggers, or do you already know and need the doc to confirm it?" Her eyes are wide with giddiness. Again, I'm quite positive it's because she'll be getting the firsthand account of what I know will be spread to every man, woman, and child in Abrielara before I leave here. No point in pretending I don't know what she's talking about. The doctor's office pretty much seals it for me.

"Neither. Another doctor confirmed it for me. I was told to come and, I guess, get more information." I shrug and go back to filling out the form.

"I'm Nina, by the way." She sticks her hand out to me.

"Nice to meet you, Nina. I'm—"

"Mika." She giggles. "Everyone knows who you are."

My mouth and eyes widen at her admission. Why, I don't know. I know this town knows all about me already. I shouldn't be surprised one bit, but somehow I am. I close my mouth, smile, nod, and return to filling out the paperwork.

"This is so exciting! Finally, Solomon is going to have a baby!" She squeals like a two-year-old. Literally. I think her feet even did a happy stomp or something. I look around the room, and every eye is on us.

Their faces are either brightened by their smiles or their hormones. I can't tell which.

I don't confirm nor deny her statement. It doesn't matter what I say. This town has already made up its mind.

Besides, it's true.

I'd only gotten halfway through the page when my name is called. I don't think I can take any more of the happy stares. By the looks of this waiting room, the Monarch has a lot of pull, apparently, and rightly so.

There's no way I should be ahead of any of these ladies. Surprisingly, they seem perfectly fine with it. I, on the other hand, would have been livid.

I'm one of those people.

This time a male nurse takes me back, and he fits the same profile as all of the other males I've seen around here. Tall, good looking and somewhat broody. No small talk whatsoever, but after the squealing in the waiting room, I'm okay with it.

While waiting for Dr. Camacho to show up, I eye the phone in the corner. Should I or shouldn't I? This is what he's been waiting for. The sole reason for this whole choosing chase thing. Maybe I should wait for Dr. Camacho to confirm, but then again, I'm sure that Dr. Merrick's test is accurate. Even if it has been barely four days since we did the do for the first time. Of course, he'll no doubt hear about it within minutes anyway.

Yeah. I might as well call him. I dial his office only to be told he's in surgery and will be most of the day. He has three of them.

I can't help but feel disappointed. For once, I'd like to be the one with all the answers and dishing out the tea. Instead, he'll probably hear it from someone else before he even leaves the O.R.

Not sure why I care. It's how things are done around here.

I lean my head back against the wall and close my eyes.

Pregnant.

Even though Solomon told me that adding to Abrielara's population was the goal, I'm still surprised. I've been avoiding the thought of this part of the Passage the second he mentioned it. Obviously, avoiding it only got me so far.

A nurse comes in and drops off a cup for me to pee in and then it's more waiting. More waiting with more questions without answers.

The room looks like any typical OB exam room. Walls covered with posters of women smiling gleefully at the thought of bringing a life into the world. Right alongside Mommy and Me ads. A model of the reproductive system sits on a table with several different pamphlets about what to expect when you're expecting. This is not a place I ever thought I'd be in. I have no idea how to be a mother. A good one.

Dr. Camacho finally breezes in. His dark hair playfully falls over his forehead and his dark eyes twinkle. His friendly smile relaxes me and I smile back when he squeezes my hand.

"Obviously, I'm Dr. Camacho. How are you, Mika? I've heard so much about you. I'm sorry I haven't had a chance to come around to introduce myself."

"From the looks of your waiting room, I don't know how you would have ever found the time."

"Yeah. It's pretty busy around here this time of year. All the babies made during our celebration of the treaty are ready to be hatched." He laughs but stops short when he sees my stern reaction. "Just kidding. Our babies don't hatch. Take a seat. I see that Dr. Merrick sent you here because your urine test confirmed your pregnancy. Congratulations."

"Thanks," I say without conviction. My eyes remain on the floor.

"You don't seem too happy about it. Want to talk about it?" He crinkles his eyebrows together.

"I...." I shrug my shoulders and take a deep breath and start again. "Everything is happening so fast. I don't have time to even catch my breath before something else happens. Not to mention, everyone in this town knows more about me and what's happening than I do now. According to Dr. Merrick, it isn't likely to change either."

"He's right, to a degree. It isn't. You're new in a town where there are no secrets from the citizens. Once you complete the Passage and things settle down, their interest in you will wane. I promise." He pats my shoulder reassuringly. "As far as your pregnancy goes. Abrielaran pregnancies typically last six to seven months tops. At the beginning of your sixth month, you'll need to be bedridden and stress-free before delivering."

"Did you say six to seven months?" I don't even get nine months to get acclimated.

"Yes. Seven months at most is all you get. The Brielaran gene accelerates the growth of the fetus and shortens the gestation period. Most pregnancies last about twenty-four, twenty-five weeks at most, if there are no complications. If it goes the full seven months, then it usually means that the mother has to be sedated before we deliver the baby for her safety."

For her safety.

So not only are you chosen, chased within an inch of your life, and burned to death on the inside out, but you also get pregnant, and the baby attacks you from the inside.

I don't know what to say or how to feel. At every turn, my life is being put in some kind of jeopardy. Is there ever going to be an end to any of this? Then what happens after I have the baby? What else do I have to do before I can enjoy a peaceful life? When can I do whatever the fuck I feel like doing because I fucking feel like it?

Not likely any time soon. All the stories I've heard about motherhood is it's all sleepless nights from here. With an Abrielaran baby, who knows how much worse it can be? A vein begins to throb in the middle of my forehead. I trace it with my finger as visions of what my life is soon to become plays like a movie trailer in my mind. No different than the barbecue at Solomon's I bet.

A throat clearing brings me out of my pity party interlude. Dr. Camacho leans forward and takes my hands in his.

"Are you okay?"

"I guess so. I don't suppose I have any other choice but to be okay."

He offers me a hopeful smile. "It's going to be fine. We will be in constant communication. We'll have a birthing plan in place long before you're expected to deliver. Unfortunately, natural births are impossible. Your human body won't be able to take the strain of birthing an Abrielaran baby with all of their limbs. You'll have to have your baby by C-section. But like I said, no worries. I have delivered hundreds of babies. You and your baby will be fine."

"I'm glad you're so sure. So what do I do now?"

"Well, thankfully, you're only a few days along, so we have plenty of time to get everything worked out. Just focus on keeping yourself healthy, happy and stress free. I'll write you a script for some prenatal vitamins. Be sure you take them every day and stay hydrated. That's all you need to do right now. Oh, and I would make sure that any business you need to attend to is taken care of sooner rather than later. You won't be able to do anything once you hit your twenty-second week."

"Thank you. Do you have any information that I can take with me?"

"Absolutely." He hands over several pamphlets. "Here is some reading material. Of course, you are welcome to call my office or me any time if you have questions. Okay? We'll reach out to you within a few weeks when you're a little further along."

"Okay. I'll see you then."

My mind keeps circling around the fact that I'm pregnant as I leave his office. Just one more thing cementing me to this place.

First is to call Solomon. He deserves to hear this from me. Maybe I can catch him between surgeries. I stop in the corridor and call him from my cell. His phone rings directly to voicemail which is full. I hang up and call his office.

"Dr. Christiansen's office. How can I help you?"

"Is Dr. Christiansen available?"

"No, he's currently in surgery. He's pretty booked up today and probably won't be free until early evening. May I take a message for him?"

I hang up without responding. He'll be told long before I'll have the chance to. It's something I'm just going to have to be okay with.

Solomon

I close the door to my office with an exhausted sigh. What a day. Three surgeries back to back. That last surgery took a lot longer than I thought it would. I slip my shoes off and lie down on my couch, throwing an arm over my eyes. I need a few minutes.

"Got a minute?" Perry peaks his head in without knocking.

"As long as that minute includes keeping my eyes closed. What's up?"

"Just coming by to congratulate you on a successful surgery. I heard one of the nurses saying that watching you was like watching magic happen."

I start chuckling. I love the compliment but I don't think clearing an obstruction is magical but maybe it is.

"Thanks. That poor mom was obviously in a lot of pain."

"Who was the OB?"

"Godfrey."

"What was wrong?"

"One of the baby's tentacles was wrapped around his lower intestine and then he had somehow knotted another tentacle around it."

Perry lets out a whistle. "Damn. No wonder the surgery took so long. Were you able to save all of his appendages?"

I remove my arm from my face and open my eyes. Doesn't look like I'm getting any sleep since Perry is in a talking mood.

"Yeah, believe it or not I was able to save them all. That's why the surgery took so long. I had to unwrap a few that he had wrapped around other things. The knot around his lower intestine was the worst."

Perry shakes his head.

"There was a minute when I considered amputating."

"I'm glad you didn't. Well, thank God everybody is doing well. Now that I know some of the details I understand why the nurses were saying it was magical. Please tell me you had the presence of mind to record it? This is something our medical school could use as a teaching tool."

"Yeah, I recorded it. But only because the mom asked me to. She said in case she or her baby died she wanted her husband to have something. Or if her baby died, she wanted to have something so I recorded all three hours of it." My stomach grumbles loudly and Perry hikes his eyebrows at me.

"Sounds like you need food more than sleep. How 'bout we head over to Lenny's? I could use a big ole greasy cheeseburger right now."

My stomach grumbles again at the sound of that. "Sounds good. Just let me take a quick shower first."

"No problem. I'm gonna run over and see if anyone else wants to come along. I'll be back in a minute."

I head to the bathroom and start removing my clothes. I check my cell and see if I have several missed calls from Mika but no voicemail. Probably because it's full. Damn it. I don't have time to listen to all of them now. I'll have to clean it out later.

I call her back but it goes to voicemail. I wonder what she found out from her appointment with Brady? It's getting on into the evening, so I'm positive her appointment was over hours ago. She could be out with the committee. Hopefully, I'll see her tonight but I'm so tired right now I'm not sure how much longer I'm going to be able to keep my eyes open.

As soon as I turn the shower on, my mind begins to run on

autopilot. Thinking of last night, I was so afraid that when Lux made love to her, she would be terrified. It's one thing to accept him walking around and staring at her house at night, but it is quite another to accept the one that hurt her into her bed.

She didn't seem afraid though. Not at all. I'm glad she forced him to see her side of things. I'm worried about the commitment. I want her to commit because she wants to and not because she feels coerced or anything else. I'd never be happy if she decided to stay and was miserable the whole time. I couldn't live with myself if that happened. I have no idea where her head is at. I know she is okay with having a baby. Maybe okay isn't the right word.

Resigned.

She's resigned to the idea, but I don't know if she would stay or be happy leaving the baby with me.

I turn off the shower and step out to dry off. At some point, I have to tell Mika how I feel about her. Preferably before she makes a decision one way or another. I don't want what I say to influence her but at the same time I can't have her leaving here not knowing either.

I'll tell her tonight. She may laugh in my face but at least it'll be off my chest. I pull my black t-shirt over my head and step into my shoes.

"Hey, you ready in there? We're starved so you need to get moving."

I roll my eyes. "Coming. Keep your panties on."

I grab my wallet and my cell and walk out to find Dyana, Becca and Michael there with him. Disappointment hits me and I have to work hard for it not to show on my face.

"Look who I found wandering the hallways."

"I see." I give Michael a quick nod. "Looks like you've recovered from the barbecue. Where are the kids?"

"With my mother thank God. I needed a break. Dyana and Becs decided to get some fresh air so I thought I'd tag along."

"Makes sense. I was lucky enough to be able to send everyone home with their parents." I chuckle. The barbecue was fun but it was a mess. Those kids really know how to tear up a yard.

"Yeah. I didn't miss that. The next time you mention a party without the wives, I will not so kindly decline."

"No way man. That was fun. The kids kind of got out of hand but it wasn't that bad."

"The next time you have a party, we'll be leaving the kids at your house and we will all go home," Dyana says.

"Well, there you have it folks. The end to my barbecues. It was fun while it lasted."

"It wasn't bad for you because you didn't have a wife breathing fire at the back of your neck all the way home afterward. Just you wait until it's your turn. I promise you'll be singing a different tune then. Now let's go. I'm ready to eat."

Lenny's is one of the oldest restaurants in Abrielara. This place is where my grandparents fell in love and where my dad brought us every Saturday afternoon for burgers and shakes. I hope to one day continue that tradition.

We find a booth and give our orders. No need for menus. Hell, I don't even think they offer them anymore. I pull out my phone to check for messages again and still nothing. Maybe she's out with Jeana and Kim.

"In case you're wondering, she wasn't home when we dropped by before coming by the hospital." Becca sits in front of me with a knowing smile.

"Oh yeah?"

"Yeah."

"Congratulations, Dr. Christiansen!" A group of teenage girls squeals at me on their way out the door.

"What's that about?" Michael asks.

"Solomon had a tough surgery today that turned out exceptionally well. I'm sure all of Abrielara has heard about it by now."

"Oh in that case, congratulations!" Dyana offers. "No wonder you look so tired. How long was the surgery?"

"Three hours. I had two other surgeries before, but they weren't nearly as long or as complicated."

"That explains the bags under your eyes."

I flip her my favorite finger but all she does is laugh. The waiter brings our food and drinks but before she leaves, she also congratulates me. Before I've gotten halfway through my meal, I've been congratulated at least five more times. I'm aggravated but the rest of the table thinks it's funny.

"I am not in the mood for this shit, so cut it out," I say to them as seriously as I can. I pull out my phone and start listening to messages so I can delete them. That way, if Mika calls me back, she can actually leave a message.

"It's funny is all. Every time someone comes over, your face turns beat red." Becca giggles.

"You're gracious though. I'll give you that." Dyana winks at me.

"Thank you." I wink back, picking up my beer.

"Congratulations, Dr. Christiansen!" Another group of kids run by on their way out.

"Damn it. Is there anyone in this town who doesn't know about that surgery?" At this point, I don't want to hear about it anymore. "I think we need to have another round of training regarding HIPPA laws and the importance of confidentiality.

This is insane." I throw some bills on the table and get up. Everyone else does the same.

"They can't help that you're such a rock star in the O.R.," Dyana chides and pats my cheeks. "I'm sure it also doesn't hurt that you're so cute."

I throw my head back to get away from her patting hands. "I haven't been cute since I was about six."

"That's not what those girls sitting at the soda bar were saying when I walked past them to the ladies' room."

"Whatever, Dee. I'm out. I'll talk to you all tomorrow."

Mika is all I can think about when I exit the restaurant. I haven't seen her since I left her bed this morning. I just want to wrap my arms around her so I know she's safe and sleep.

"Library," Lux says.

"What?"

"Mika's on her way to the library."

"Oh, ok great. I'll just meet her over there."

"Absolutely not. Go home," the Monarch interjects.

"Why?" I can't help asking.

"She and I need to talk without you being a distraction. Don't worry. She'll be home safe and sound tonight. So, go on home."

I can't argue with the Monarch even if I wanted to. I'm itching to drive by the library, just so I can lay eyes on Mika. Instead, I miss the turn I needed to make and am pulling into her driveway before I know it.

Chapter Twenty Two

Mika

The moment the late afternoon air hits my face, my intention to drive home from the medical building is forgotten. I walk without clear direction. Every moment of my life in Abrielara replays in my mind...again. It seems to be all I ever do. Watching my life happen to me has grown excessively tiresome. But yet, I'm still not used to it. Although I should be at this point.

I wish things were different. That momma hadn't died. Or that I could have made amends. I wish she'd told me about this place. What I was in for before I got here. I wish...for a lot of things, but considering that mercy wasn't granted before, I can only assume that wishes won't be granted either.

Knowing this does not stop me from thinking about every single mistake I've ever made. The words I said with passion but didn't sensor and didn't apologize for. The hateful actions I took for the hell of it. The spiteful way I did things just so that I could say I did what was asked, but begrudgingly. The hateful way I dug my heels in when I didn't have to because I knew I could make it hurt worse.

No. I can't blame myself for the mistakes I made as a kid. I also can't keep rehashing my past to make sense out of it. Sometimes sense has nothing to do with it, especially when family is concerned. I shouldn't continue to ask the why of the actions of a dead woman, either. Even though I know, I'll continue to do so. Rejection and regret give me no other choice. At least for now.

No one ever said that just because you gave birth to a child means you have to love them. As much as that hurts, there's nothing I can do about it. But I know when I'm wrong, and there were a lot of times when I was.

I wonder if there's any truth to the thought of someone payin' for their raisin'? If so, It would definitely apply to me. How can I be a good mother when I was such a horrible daughter?

With that thought, I realize I've stopped walking and now stand in front of the library. The warm glow from the light inside softly illuminates the grounds under the now darkening sky. My first day in Abrielara comes to mind. I said I would come here and look for answers, but I just never had the time. Looks like I've got nothing but time now.

The normal lift in my heart I usually feel at just the thought of a library falls flat. The whole initial Passage discussion with Solomon is regurgitated. The uneasiness floating around my throat since the word pregnancy entered the conversation sinks to my stomach like a cement block. I'm not sure I can take hearing or reading any more informa-tion. Anytime I've learned something new here, I've been the one to pay the price. Finding out something else may just kill me.

"Come in."

I look for the owner of the voice. I see no one. I'm ridicu-lous. The only idiot out here roaming the streets in the dark like they're not in a town full of aliens is me.

I face the library. I don't know what I'm doing out here. I need to go home.

"Come in. Straight to the back."

I've finally lost all of my marbles. None of this can be normal.

"This is your new normal. Come on back."

I'm not sure how I should take that but I follow the instructions anyway. Again.

I enter the library and walk straight to the back. My fingers caress the spines of the books as I pass. The earthy yet crisp smell of the pages brings a smile to my face. Maybe losing myself in this library isn't such a bad idea. I need the distraction.

"A distraction is the last thing you need."

The Monarch stands before me in jeans, a short-sleeved green top, and ballet flats. Her braids are down and she isn't wearing the jewelry she wore when I saw her last. She's dressed like any chick you'd see on the street.

Not quite sure what I should do next. Surely the Monarch doesn't walk around town unattended.

"As you pointed out, I am the Monarch. Which means I can do what I please. Even if what I want to do is sit in our library and wait for you."

"I didn't mean any harm..." Can she...

She holds up a hand. "It's okay. I know you didn't mean anything by it and to answer your question, yes I can read your mind. Now that we are connected, we can communicate telepathically."

Right. Lux mentioned that already. "How did you know I was going to show up here? I didn't have a clue where I was going when I left the hospital."

"I guided you here. Once I heard the news, I knew we couldn't waste another minute. I thought it was time you and I had a talk. I heard from Dr. Merrick that you're healthy and you are indeed the daughter of Dane St. John."

"What? No one told—"

"I told Dr. Merrick that I would tell you when I saw you tonight. Now you and I need to see how far you have progressed since beginning the Passage."

I can't imagine I've made any progress since yesterday.

The Monarch chuckles. "You may be surprised."

She stands in front of one of four large books sitting on podiums. I lean closer to one to get a better look. It's a ledger.

"These four books list every family that has made Abrielara their home. Every person listed has completed the Passage and decided to stay and raise their family here. Proving that the Brielaran race is not only salvageable but is civilized, thriving and worthy of love. Once you and Solomon complete the Passage, your name will also be added here. Provided, of course, that you build a life together here in Abrielara."

"What happens to Solomon if I don't?"

"Technically nothing. He completed the duty given to him. We cannot force you to stay if you don't want to and we cannot punish him for your decision.

"However, the Brielaran in him will see it as rejection and proof that he isn't worthy of love. He could give in to his Brielaran instincts and force me to put him down or Lux could dissolve into Solomon and never be seen or heard from again. Lux could also agree to continue to coexist with Solomon. If Solomon can convince him to. That would require Lux to still have the ability to think rationally. Solomon would have to work fast for that to happen.

"If Lux goes down one of the unhappy paths but leaves Solomon alive, I'll lose the telepathic connection I have with him since his Brielaran no longer exists. He'll be just like any other human on this planet. Ultimately it's Lux's choice how he plans to respond."

"If you have to put Lux down, what happens to Solomon?"

"It depends. If I can get to Lux in time, I can separate them. But if not, then Solomon will die when Lux does. Transitioning during the Passage merges their DNA, making it almost impossible to separate them without their consent. It isn't a decision I make easily. If Lux's behavior is harmful to himself or Solomon, I won't have a choice."

I can't imagine what that would look like for Abrielara, or me.

"If I don't commit to him, what does that mean for me?"

"Honestly, I don't know. If you were like all of the other Abrielaran females, nothing would happen to you. Since you are not, I can't be sure. It may mean nothing or it could mean the difference between life and death for you as well. Why don't you have a seat so we can talk?"

I sit beside her as she sets one of the books between us. She flips through the pages until she finds the one she's looking for.

"This page is dedicated to your family lineage. As you can see, it has your parent's signatures on the day they committed their lives to each other."

It feels strange seeing my mother's signature with a different last name. More proof she had an entirely different life than I thought she had.

"Your family can be traced all the way back to when the crash happened. The Brielaran who integrated into your family line was not in the original ship but was on the ship that came to retrieve them and decided to stay. As you can see with Dane and every male before him, the name of their

Brielaran is also listed. The Brielaran, the Abrielaran, the one they chose, and their offspring are all listed here."

As I read name after name, I begin to understand how important this entire process is for Abrielara. How proud they must have been to be able to write their names down in these books.

"You should be proud as well. What you should take away from seeing these names is how much you really do belong here. Abrielara is your true home. Your roots are here."

"It would seem so but why wouldn't my mother tell me about Abrielara?"

"As a guess, I would say it was to protect you. But I wouldn't dwell on it. If they're meant to be known, answers will show up when they're supposed to."

"Which, in my case, likely means never," I mumble under my breath.

"That's definitely possible. We all have questions that we'll never know the answers to."

"Even you?" It's hard to imagine that someone like her wouldn't have all the answers.

"Even me. I haven't always been the Monarch. I was young once. I had parents with histories and issues of their own. To this day, I can't tell you why they did some of the things they did. What I can say is that every living thing has their own experience that no one else can exactly relate to. Not every line or story is the same.

"No one is born knowing all the answers, and we make mistakes sometimes. Our parents included. Some things are none of our business. The best advice I can give you is to let it go and forgive yourself and your mother. You'll have a more peaceful life if you do."

I already resigned myself to never having all the answers, but having some insight would give me a little relief, at least.

"Did you know my mother? Meet her when she was here?"

"Yes, I did. Once Dane chose her, I met with her much in the same way that I met with you. She was a lot like you. Full of fire, heart, and curiosity."

"Was she happy?"

"Yes, I believe she was. For a few years at least."

Her smile, as she recounts the memory, again makes me wish I had known my mother better. Known her when she was happiest.

"I know people fear me. Especially humans who know our truth, but she lived here for several years. She understood our culture. I was disappointed when I found out she had left without speaking to me first.

"When you were about four, I realized you existed, but according to your mother, you showed no signs of carrying our DNA. It wasn't my normal process to take someone else's word on the subject. But I trusted her judgement so I had no cause to bring you here. I never understood why she never reached out when she realized you should be tested for the gene. Now that she's dead, I will probably never know."

"You knew about me?" Now that's something different than what I've been told.

"Yes, I did. And before you ask, let me say that thousands of people on this earth are descendants of a Brielaran but don't carry the gene. There's no need to introduce them to a culture that they wouldn't be able to participate in unless they were chosen."

"What is your normal process for confirming if someone has Brielaran DNA or not?"

"Well, if they're male and their Brielaran didn't notify me, they would be tested and sent to me to be double-checked. If they are anywhere else, then I would send one or two people from my council to confirm if they should be tested. If they believe they should be, they figure out the most humane and discreet way to make that happen."

She takes one of my hands in hers. "If I had known everything, your story would be quite different. Sometimes things happen the way they should. Of course, I would have loved for you and your mother to have stayed here. She was within her right to leave. All that matters is that you're here now." She pats my hand and then releases it. Leaving me with the feeling she isn't just talking about how I came to be here but also the life I lived in general.

I bow my head, recalling how I felt after finding out about this place and who I am. I blamed momma for knowingly keeping me from the truth. Come to find out, she wasn't the only one who could have done something. How many other people on this earth are connected to Abrielara but don't know it exists?

"What are the odds that there are people on this earth that carry the gene but they don't know it?"

"There's always a chance. Unless they were able to mutate the gene in a specific sequence that I can't detect, then the chances aren't likely. Not saying that your father was the only doctor who's tried to change our DNA but he had gotten the closest to succeeding."

A rough chuckle jingles in her throat. "Well, looking at you now, I would have to say he did succeed. Others could have done the same, but eventually, their Brielaran would notify me or guide them here if they were male.

"Even if their human didn't want them to?"

"What their human wants is not a priority when they are ready to begin the Passage. Anything that may stand in their way of completing that Passage is of no consequence compared to fulfilling their duty.

"If they are female, their gene wouldn't activate until it was time to complete the Passage. In order for that to happen, contact with another Brielaran would need to be made. Which means I would be notified. If they never met up with a male hybrid, then their gene would remain dormant."

Lux's ridiculous behavior since the moment I arrived and Solomon's agitation makes more sense now. Lux was, and is, compelled to complete the Passage. Solomon fought against it because he didn't want to hurt anyone. He didn't want to hurt me.

"Exactly. Most Abrielarans don't buck up against their Brielaran when it comes to the Passage because they know it's a part of the journey. It's inevitable. They're taught to surrender to it. Solomon is just as bullheaded as Lux. Only Solomon isn't ruled by his duty to Abrielara. He's ruled by his heart. But even he had to surrender. The duty to Abrielara is so much greater than any of our wants or needs."

She smiles softly and looks back down at the book again.

She's right of course. I've learned that first hand. Surrender to whatever is thrown at you is the motto around here.

"So, there are a couple of things I want to do," she says, rising from her chair. She grabs a book from the shelf behind her and hands it to me.

"Open it to any page. It makes no difference which one."

The leather-bound book is not as large as the four books behind us but it's obviously old. I don't read the title but I flip it open to the middle.

"What do you see?"

At first, I just see symbols on a page. I get ready to voice that fact but then the symbols begin to light up. Exactly the way the symbols in the cave did. They jump off the page like one of those pop-up books. The kind that scares the breath out of you.

"Symbols. Words."

She nods. "Read it to me."

I attempt to moisten my dry lips with my equally dry tongue. As if that's going to help me decipher the meaning behind these symbols.

I hate being put on the spot. Especially for something I can't wing without sounding ridiculous. After a few seconds of stalling, I calm down. The voice in my head becomes clearer and louder. I can read this. No winging necessary.

"Her land is bountiful and rich. Her skies are free of warships. Her waters run clear. Can her inhabitants offer us the same; a place to grow, flourish, and survive? Is this the place? Our new home?"

The Monarch's smile tells me I did not disappoint her. I sit back in my seat with a sigh of relief.

"You just proved to me that you are our Librarian. Only you and I can actually read the text and translate it without official training. Before we move on, there is one more thing I want you to do."

The intense beam from her eyes makes my chair more uncomfortable. My fingers fidget with each other.

"Read the same passage in our native Brielaran tongue."

"Oh, I don't think..." I don't think. I know. I know I have no business trying to read this. I can't possibly read that in a language I haven't even heard before.

"Don't think. Relax your mind and loosen your tongue." She nods toward the book and I reopen it. My stomach flutters furiously.

"Don't be nervous."

Easy for you to say.

She laughs at me.

I look at the passage again. The symbols light up in bright colors, the same as before. The voice in my head is silent. Where do I even begin?

"What if I can't?" My question is really not a question but a confession. There is no what-if about it.

"If you can't, it only means that we'll need to wait a little bit longer. It'll happen when it should. It could be because you haven't officially completed the Passage or because you're afraid."

I meet her eyes. I am afraid but I can't say those words. Maybe she can read them in my eyes.

"There's nothing to fear. You're safe here. No one is perfect and you have a lot to learn. But first, we need to see what kind of learning curve we're working with here. So just relax and do the best you can. Let it come to you naturally."

I review the passage again and do my best to do what the Monarch instructed. Relax my mind. Loosen my tongue. Don't try too hard. Let it happen naturally.

I reread the words so many times I now have them memorized. Just not in Brielaran. I close the book and my eyes. I sit in silence until the whispering begins. I strain to listen but stop because instinctively, I know I shouldn't.

Let it happen naturally.

Soon, the whispering is coherent, and I realize the voice isn't mine. It's the Monarch. She's speaking in what I can only assume is Brielaran. It sounds beautiful. The words are melodic and smooth and flow easily from her. I stop concentrating on the dialect and start listening to what she's saying.

"A Priest, a Rabbi, and a Minister walk into a bar...."

I laugh out loud and then cover my mouth when my voice echoes in the library. The Monarch is about to tell me a joke.

"I see you are familiar with this type of joke," she continues in the same tongue.

"Yes, I'm familiar," I respond in kind without thinking about it.

"Ah, see there? You did it. If you can speak the language telepathically, you can also speak it oracularly. You may need practice but that's okay. It will come."

Her smile fills me with pride.

"Let's move on. As you know by now, the Librarian is immensely important to our community. You are immensely important to our community. And not just because you're the Librarian. Every citizen is important. Having your name listed here is a big deal but there's more to it.

"For the last eighty years, our community has not had its stories recorded. That means their lives on Earth were not over when they died. As long as you are still in Abrielara, they will seek you out. When they've told you their story, they'll be able to move on."

"Record it how? I'm a shoe designer, not a writer." This is going to be a disaster.

"All you have to do is listen to them and write it down. Transcribe exactly what they say. No more. No less. In the library in your home, there's a row of thick, heavily bound books in the back. Those books are the recorded love stories of the citizens of Abrielara. Read them. You will understand more when you do."

"Are you sure there's no one else more qualified for this? What about the historian?" I've asked this question before, but I'm hoping for a different answer.

"The historian is also important but without you, the historian wouldn't have a history to tell. At least not much of one. Besides, the historian can't see or hear those who have passed on. I can't either. Only you and your guardian can. There is no one else who can do this."

"Can the guardian become the Librarian if I choose not to?"

"Unfortunately, no. His destiny is to be the guardian. If there is no Librarian, then there is no real need for a guardian."

"Oh. Why wouldn't they have their stories recorded before they died?"

"When we had a Librarian, they could if they wanted to. When your great-grandmother passed unexpectedly, we were left without a choice since a new one had not been named."

Although Lux already told me what the role of the Librarian was, hearing it from the Monarch after the news I received today reconfirms I'm not leaving here. Off top, no way would I leave Abrielara without my baby. I also don't want to be that person who can't think of others before themselves. And I have no idea what happens to me if I chose not to commit. It's a lost cause.

She reaches over and grabs my hands.

"It's not a lost cause. It's all in how you look at things. I know you haven't decided how you feel about Abrielara. I know you feel that you've been thrown into a situation that you didn't choose. But you are vital to this community. No matter how you got here or the reason why your mother decided to wait until she died to tell you about us, this is your home. You belong here. You have a purpose. It's up to you decide to walk into your destiny or run from it because of fear or uncertainty.

"The answers to your questions about your mother will not change who you are or your place here. At the same time, I want you to be happy. If you feel Abrielara is not the place for you or that you don't want to be the Librarian for our community, then I don't want you here either. Life is too short to be somewhere you don't want to be, doing something you don't want to do. Nobody will fault you for following your own heart."

She sits back after releasing my hands and I release the breath I'd been holding. My mind is just as cloudy as it was before. I'm still unsure how to be okay with all of this.

"I want you to think about why you're struggling with staying in Abrielara. What is it about being the Librarian that scares you? What needs to happen for you to be happy here? I think when you have those answers, you'll have a better idea of what your next steps will be."

"Thank you. I'm sorry I'm not..."

"Stop right there. Don't apologize. This is your life. I just wanted you to know how much we need you and that Abrielara is your home. However, it's your life. Keep that in mind when you answer those questions. Just don't take too long to come to a decision. I'm guessing you don't have that much time left."

It's not the first time I've been given that advice. I just don't get how I'm told I have a choice, but, in the same breath, prove to me why I don't. However, one thing is clear. It's too late to back out now. Whatever choices I think I have left have already been made. I want to live and being pregnant are two great reasons for my decision.

Does everyone who has Brielaran DNA struggle with this the way I have? Or is it just because I wasn't born into this community?

"May I ask you something?"

"Absolutely."

"Did you always know you were going to be the Monarch?"

"It would have been easier if I had, but no, I didn't. Believe it or not, I thought something had to be wrong with me. I was seventeen, unmarried, and without children.

Anywhere else in the world, I would have been considered an old maid. In Abrielara, I was a female who had not been chosen. I thought I would never be chosen, but we're taught to be patient. Our community has never functioned the way the rest of the world does, but we're still influenced by it. The community was good to me, for the most part. But it didn't stop me from feeling unworthy anyway."

"That must have been hard."

"Yes, it was, but I had to lean on my education and just be patient.

"One spring day, I was called to see the Monarch. The jewel looked a little different then. It was a lot smaller and the grounds weren't kept. It was still pretty wild out here."

"How long ago was this?" I ask without thinking. "If you don't mind saying."

"A little over a five hundred years ago."

"Oh, wow." I wasn't expecting that answer.

She chuckles and I wonder what she was like as a child.

"Much like most, I would say. To this day, I remember how scared I was to walk into her chambers. She was so tall and so beautiful. I'd never been anywhere near the palace before that. I had seen her before, but not up close or personal.

"She sat me down and told me she would not be with us the following year. I was scared. What would we do without a Monarch? I asked what the fate of our species was to be if she wasn't going to be here to lead and protect us. She told me I would be the one to answer that question because I was going to be the next Monarch.

"I'll be honest with you. I thought she had lost her mind. Me....the Monarch? No way. I told her she had the wrong person but then she asked why I thought I hadn't been chosen yet. I couldn't answer her question. She informed me it was because when I become the Monarch, I will be the one doing the choosing.

"At that moment, I thought of every reason why she was incorrect. I didn't have tentacles like she did. I didn't have an aura that everyone could see like she did. I wasn't wise or have all the answers. I could barely protect myself. There was no way I could protect a community. She said I would have all that and more when the time was right. She would teach me a lot of things, and some things I would have to learn on my own.

"I left the palace that day and never told a soul what I'd been told. Nor did I tell anyone I had seen the Monarch. But as time passed, I began noticing changes in myself and everyone around me. The first thing I noticed was how things seemed to be more enhanced in color and vibrancy. I felt changes inside my body that I couldn't see. I started hearing things. I thought I was losing my mind.

"Then one morning I was tending to the garden and the whispering turned into yelling. It was so loud I covered my ears with my hands. Today I'd say it reminds me of how one of those comic book heroes feels until he trains himself to quiet the noise." She shakes her head in wonderment. "So loud."

The Monarch stops talking and I can see she is replaying that day over in her mind. When was the last time she thought about her past?

"It's been a while." She smiles again and mindlessly taps the table with her finger.

"I'm just thinking about how I fought so hard against the idea of becoming the Monarch. I just couldn't believe that someone like me would be worthy of such a position. There were girls in our community that were more beautiful than I was. They commanded an audience everywhere they went.

They were educated, well spoken, and strong. The epitome of what you would expect the Monarch to be.

"I was none of those. I was educated, yes. But I was quiet. I did not command a room, much less an audience or a community. No one had chosen me and I had no real purpose. I had interests but nothing that put a fire in my belly. I was just existing. Just doing my best to be a good daughter to my parents and waiting to be chosen."

Her head leans a little as if a revelation just came to her.

"I felt much as I would imagine you feel today. Needing answers, questioning why, and looking for reasons why what you've learned can't be. I, more than anyone, understand why you feel the way you do. I won't bore you with my whole story. But I will say that once I accepted what was happening, the adjustment was easier to manage."

She pats my shoulder and stands.

"It's getting late and you've had a long day. Promise me one thing."

Her hand suddenly feels heavy on my shoulder.

"If you decide you don't want to be our Librarian, tell me before you tell Solomon. I want to be prepared just in case Lux's reaction is one I'll have to address."

"I will."

The concern in her eyes reminds me how much weight my decision has on the people of this community. It's not all about me. It never was.

My walk home is not as mindless as my walk to the library. The Monarch's words are heavy on my mind. I knew the answer to her questions before I left the library. I'm just not ready to say them out loud.

· · ·

Although all the lights are out in my house, it sounds like a party is going inside. The moment I open the door, the party like atmosphere quiets down to a murmur accompanied by wide smiles and hopeful eyes. It appears the number of my ghostly guests has doubled.

I smile in return and walk upstairs. The party commences and the noise level escalates. I'm not sure how much longer I can deal with this. I'm going to have to come up with some rules, a plan, or something. I understand their excitement but I'm not feeling quite as festive.

Yes, I've made my decision and you would think that would make me happy but it doesn't. I still have unanswered questions. The biggest and most important one is how do Solomon and Lux really feel about me? Sure, they talk a good game and they have a way of making me feel wanted. But are they really into me or are they wanting to complete the Passage and then go on with their lives; with our without me makes no difference.

"I can't live without you. The only reason why I'm here is to love you. The only reason."

Lux's words echo in my mind. Did he mean them or were his endorphins in overdrive? I'm trying not to romanticize them. He could literally mean that he can't live without me if we don't finish this. The Monarch as much as said so tonight. But I can't help but wish he wasn't referencing the outcome of the Passage.

I know there's a chance that I could still be affected by the Passage and all of its chemical reactions but it bothers me that this life decision isn't based on what my heart wants at all. Or even for them. From what I understand, they could choose anyone to complete the Passage with them. Why did they choose me? It's never been made clear. How do they know at first glance, I was who they wanted when it's apparent anyone will do?

In the end it doesn't matter, I guess. I have to complete the Passage myself, so their reasons for choosing me shouldn't matter but it does. I'm still going to do as I said, no matter their reasons, but I'm a realist. I want to complete this knowing exactly what this is. If it's just sexual for them then okay, I can live with that...or at least try to. If it's more, then I would love to know that as well. I want to tell them freely without fear of judgement that I have fallen in love with them both. I want the real thing with them. The romance, the truth in the everyday, the bad, the good, the ugly, and the magical. The most shocking part of it all, is I don't just want to belong. I want to belong to them.

I open my door and see Solomon's back facing me and I'm happy to see it. I missed him this morning. Missed him all day in fact. He turns over and his eyes are so bloodshot red, I know he hasn't slept a wink.

"When did you get in?"

"About an hour ago. I heard you were at the library with the Monarch. I wanted to stop by but I was advised not to."

He holds a hand to me but I ignore it and take my shoes off instead.

"I have to shower first. I've been out most of the day."

"Hurry."

As much as I don't want to, I rush through my shower. Solomon's eyes still look bad and his lids are at half-mast. The poor man is exhausted.

I slide in under the covers and his arms immediately latch on to me, pulling my back into his front and sticks his nose into my neck.

"Mmmm. You smell so good," he mumbles.

He's quiet and I suspect he's finally fallen asleep until he pulls me in tighter toward him.

"I'm beyond tired, but now I'm fucking horny and still can't sleep."

His hand rides up beneath my silk slip and sneaks beneath my lace panties.

"Mmmm. Already so warm and wet."

I feel him harden behind me and now sleep has escaped me too.

He rips my panties in half to remove them from my body and hooks and arm around my leg, raising it at the angle he wants.

"If you don't want this, tell me now."

His garbled words are said against my neck but I understand every one. I press my ass into him as a response and lean forward as much as he will let me. His groan is the only warning I get before he rams his dick inside of me.

A gasp is torn from me and I lean my head back against his shoulder. He stills inside of me and then begins to move in a way that belies the force in which he entered me.

I moan at the sheer sweetness of it. His languid movements are rich and fill me so completely that all of my misgivings from earlier have dissipated. All I can focus on is him and his movements, his kisses and his touches. His finger circles my clit slowly and my body hums as he plays mine so expertly.

He strums my clit and a shudder rains down on me.

"Solomon," his name whispers past my lips. His movements don't change speed but based on the growls I hear, he isn't far behind me.

His arm tightens around my leg, bringing it closer to my chest and his growl echoes in the room as he empties into me.

"Mine. All mine."

His words stop my drift into sleep but I can't help the wistful smile I feel on my face. He releases my leg and I know he's asleep. I close my eyes, willing my mind to forget his words until I feel tentacles surround me. Drawing me in closer to him.

"Mmmm. Lux," I whisper, and then I'm finally able to fall asleep. Just not before I remember that I needed to tell them something that would now need to wait.

Chapter Twenty Three

Mika

The sun's early morning hazy rays infiltrate my bedroom with warm peaceful light. I'm in no rush to leave it. I close my eyes and soak it in.

"Mika...Mika"

I snuggle deeper into the covers, then my breath stills. That voice...

"Mika..."

The breathy whisper forces my eyes open. There's something about that voice. It can't be who it sounds like. In the golden haze, a silhouette forms from a shifting shadow to someone I recognize.

"Momma." My heart rises then stalls and I'm overcome with so many feelings I'm not sure how to process any of them.

She smiles and waves at me. I sit up but before I say anything, she dissolves just as quickly as she came. I sit back slowly. My heart pounds. I'm drowning in so many emotions. She was here and gone so quickly...did I really see her? She looked and sounded like her. A younger version of her, but definitely her.

Could be more evidence I've lost my ever-loving mind. Then again, it could be a sign that I'm making the right decision. I don't know. I'm not sure if the reason matters. What I do know is I promised myself I would stop trying to make sense of why she chose to do things the way she did. This is probably my mind's way of rebelling against me.

If I can't control anything else, the least I can do is control my mind. I force it back to last night. The long walk home was the perfect opportunity to think. It's easy to get caught up in Solomon or Lux. Not noticing or minding that the days continue to pass by. It was good to clear my mind and finally make a decision on my own. I intended to tell them about my pregnancy this morning, but as usual they were gone before I even woke up. I have to tell them the first moment I see them today and I will vocalize my intent. They must not have heard yet or I'm sure Solomon would have mentioned it last night. They haven't asked whether I am going to commit to them or not yet, but it has to be on their mind. I've kept them waiting long enough.

I float the covers back with exaggerated flourish. For once, I'm motivated. I'm no longer weighed down with questions of why, when, or what if. My talk with the Monarch last night definitely gave me food for thought. And Solomon's words before he drifted off to sleep helped give me the clarity I needed. No matter their end goal or true feelings about me, I know how I feel about them. How I feel about Abrielara and my place here. I've always wanted to belong. To fit in. And even if I don't belong to them long term, I will have to be satisfied for right now. I'm honestly not sad about it. I can finally move on. If that isn't a reason to smile I don't know what is.

. . .

I decide to take another walk downtown. I figure an afternoon of sunshine and shoe designing is the perfect way to spend the afternoon. For once, I want to think about anything besides Abrielara, the Passage, or why momma wanted me here. It's time to get back to my real life.

Unlike my first or even second day in Abrielara, the people smile and wave at me. They ask how I'm doing and if I plan to attend the high school band concert in the park that afternoon. The vibe is so different than before. It's like I'm in a different town.

Another difference is that some ghosts who've been haunting my house and the grounds are venturing off the property. They're easy to spot with their dated clothing but they aren't quite as see-through as before. They are becoming more real in appearance to me. Pretty sure more of them have showed up but other than crowding me, they smile and keep walking. I smile back, no longer weighed down by my duty to them. Maybe now that I've made my decision, they feel less antsy. I don't know. I'll have plenty of time to talk to them in private and ask. They seem to understand. They smile, nod, and move on like any other citizen in this community with errands to run.

Except for one.

He smiles and waves like the others but he keeps his distance. I do the same in return and think nothing of it until I realize he's walking with me. He looks familiar, but I can't figure out where I've seen him before. I get the impression that he wants my attention but doesn't say anything. Nor does he come closer.

I find a seat outside a cozy café and order a lemon-lime refresher. And then it hits.

Dane.

I look around me but he's gone. He was definitely Dane. He wore the same clothes he had on in the photo with momma. He looks familiar because, aside from the dimples and his nose, Perry favors him.

When I realize he's truly gone, I sketch for a while. Sling backs, platforms, flats, sandals, stilettos, thigh highs, but eventually, my mind wanders back to the Passage. I force myself back to color and design but I guess my obsession over the past few weeks has become a habit.

Green. Pointed toe. Running through the woods.

Black. Thigh high boot. Lava burning a path through my veins.

Red. Open toe. Tentacles. Sharp teeth. Glowing eyes.

Purple. Lace-up stiletto. Pharmacy fiasco.

Yellow. Pumps. Ghosts.

I throw my pen down. Evidently, I can't go even one minute without thinking about the Passage or anything related to it. I'm sick of it. An unknown number lights up the screen on my phone.

Finally, a distraction.

"Hello?"

"Ms. Burris? This is Mercy Hospital. You're listed as the contact person for Brandi Mitchell."

"What's wrong? Is Brandi okay?" I'm ashamed of myself for not checking on my assistant more.

I grab my bag and chuck my tablet into it.

"Hopefully she will be once she gets through surgery. I'm calling to inform you she's having an emergency appendectomy."

"I'm on my way."

I was just asking for a distraction and now I have one. Brings a whole new meaning to be careful of what you wish for. I dial the hanger.

"Hello, Sandy? Is Bobby around? I need a ride to the airport."

Solomon

My ringing phone splits my head wide open. Groaning, I clench it between both hands. Hoping it'll stop soon, I try ignoring it, but the incessant ringing makes it impossible. I yank my phone off my desk.

"What do you want?"

"Wake up," Perry says.

"What do you want?" I grumble again.

"Where are you at?"

"At the hospital in my office. I have a patient I have to check on this morning."

The feel of Mika in my arms when I woke up made up for me not seeing much of her yesterday. She didn't stir when I got out of bed and I didn't wake her. I had every intention of going right back to her house but as per usual, things didn't go according to plan.

"I thought you were off today?"

"Technically but you know how it is once everyone knows you're here."

My quick check in on one patient turned into checking on all five. Then I agreed to work for Dr. Franks since his wife went into labor. I don't mind. Especially since he stood in for me when I started the Passage but it wasn't how I planned my day. I thought I could catch a little sleep until I had to make my rounds in an hour.

"I do. Unfortunately this isn't a social call. The judge is in the E.R. Melissa thinks he's having a heart attack. You might want to come down."

Perry disconnects the call. My pounding head is forgotten as I rush out the door. The judge hasn't been ill once my entire life. At least not that I can recall. The idea I could lose him, the one person who has always been here, humbles me to my bones. I don't want to know what life would be like without him.

The waiting room on the cardiac floor is full for a change. What's strange about it is it's full of women. I breeze past them to find his room. Perry is at the end of the ward, and I weave my way to him.

"He's flirting with the nurses." He shakes his head and rolls his eyes.

Boisterous laughter echoes from the room. My eyes bounce between the door and Perry.

"I thought he had a heart attack?" The judge is resilient but even he shouldn't be strong enough to laugh that heartily this soon after such a traumatic event.

"He had horrible indigestion and gas. His blood pressure was dangerously high as well. He seriously needs to change his diet or the next time could be the real thing. But for now he's fine," Dr. Jones informs us.

"Thank God."

"Yes, but can you boys do me a favor?"

"Sure," Perry and I answer in unison.

"When you take your father home, can you take his fan club with you? That waiting room hasn't been this full since they erected the building."

Dr. Jones walks into the judge's room and I thumb toward the waiting room.

"All of those women are here for dad?"

"Every last one. They beat me here and I was behind the ambulance."

"Wow."

"Yep. Wow. Tell the judge I'll be back after lunch to take him home. They're going to run a few more tests before they cut him loose."

"Alright then."

Dr. Jones leaves the room after a few minutes and I walk in to see the judge reviewing the hospital menu. I promptly remove it from his hands.

"After the scare you had, the last thing you need to do is read the menu."

"Melissa was just being cautious. I'm the picture of health."

"She may have jumped the gun, but you sir, are not the picture of health. You'll be following a heart-healthy diet. Starting now."

"Fine. I can follow that damn diet for a few days. Melissa is going on vacation anyway." His smug expression is infuriating. We've had this discussion before but he refuses to take his health seriously.

"No, Dad. Not just for a few days. From now on. I'll speak with Melissa when she returns about your diet. You've got to take better care of yourself."

"I know son, but you know how much I love food," he says, covering his heart with his hand.

"I know. The first step to change is admitting you have a problem. Now you have to take action. You've had one too many biscuits over the years. Time to cut back."

"Don't take my biscuits, son. I'll give up the pies if I can keep the biscuits."

I shake my head at him. "Pitiful. A biscuit sometimes isn't

too bad but you can't eat them every morning. The bacon and the daily cigars have to go too."

The judge clutches his chest. "You're killing me, son."

"You're ridiculous and you're killing yourself." I pat his shoulder. "I'm glad you're okay. I'm going to check on my patients before I go back home and get a little more sleep. Perry will be back for you after lunch."

The door to Mika's house is open when I pull into my driveway. Instead of walking back into my house, I walk across the street to hers. Maybe I can talk her into taking a nap with me. I just need a little more sleep. Who am I kidding. I need a lot more of her and that's all to it.

"At least you finally admit it. The first step is acknowledging the truth."

"Shut up. As usual, you like to but in when you're not needed."

"I'm always needed. Like last night. Her mind was obviously running wild. Instead of drifting off like you did, I snuggled with her so she could fall asleep."

"That was nice of you and the least that you could do since I put in all the work before I went to sleep."

"That wasn't work and you know it."

"True it wasn't but I exerted energy that I didn't have to spend. Why am I discussing this with you?"

"Because you're nervous. She makes you nervous."

"I know that but only because I don't want to lose her. You may have scared her off with your declaration the other night."

"What declaration?"

"Don't play dumb. When you told her you couldn't live without her, and the only reason you're here is because of her.

Did you see the look in her eyes after you said it? That was the look of fear my friend."

Lux is silent and even though I'm joking a little, I realize he may not see it that way.

"Hey. I'm kidding. You spoke your truth and I think she was in awe of it. I was joking."

"You sure? I don't want to lose her either. I was just trying to be completely honest with her. I want her to know how much she means to us."

"I understand. Let's see what her mood is today."

I knock before stepping in to find her putting clothes in a suitcase.

"Where are you going?" I lean against the door jam. My question came out harsher than I wanted but I'm shocked by what I'm seeing here.

"Home. I won't..."

"Weren't planning on telling me first?" My gut begins to burn.

"Telling you first? As in asking for permission?" She looks perplexed at the thought.

I shrug. "If that's how you want to put it."

"You're a bit of a smart ass today aren't you? Didn't get enough sleep last night?" She stops packing and stares at me with her jaw set. Her snarky comment puts my teeth on edge and Lux tries to push in.

"Not now."

The edge tapers off just enough for me to appear calm even though on the inside I'm being shredded. Was she really going to leave without telling me first?

"I didn't sleep as well as I could have until you got here. Then I slept like a baby but you know that. And what did you do all day yesterday?"

"Unless you forgot to tell me yet another thrilling fact

about the Passage, I don't believe I'm required to give you the play-by-play of my day."

"Doesn't look like I'm the only smart ass in the room."

She shrugs much the same as I did a few minutes ago. "If that's how you want to look at it." She resumes packing.

"I'm going to ask you again for the last time. Where are you going?"

Her pointed stare begins to change into a heated blue one.

"I'm going to tell you...for the last time. Home." She slams her suitcase shut and walks past me to the bathroom.

"Why?"

"Because I can." The defiant jut of her chin dares me to keep asking. I never back down from a dare. Even the subtle ones.

"Not good enough. Why are you going home, and why didn't you discuss it with me first?"

"Because I can and because I don't have to. Agreeing to complete the Passage with you does not mean you can dictate how and where I move around. I wouldn't be surprised if I had to explain that to Lux but not to you, Solomon." Annoyance flutters her eyelids.

She swings the suitcase off the bed at the sound of the honking horn and walks past me.

"I don't have time for this shit," she mutters to herself.

"If you leave, you'll regret it."

She stops and looks over her shoulder at me.

"Is that so?" She dresses me down and walks out the door. She gets in the truck with Bobby and doesn't look at me again. But my eyes follow the truck until it is out of sight.

"That didn't go well."

"No need to state the obvious, Lux."

"Evidently I do. What the fuck got into you?"

"Her attitude rubbed me the wrong way."

"That isn't it. You're upset because we don't know if she's coming back."

"Again, you're stating the obvious."

"Only because you won't admit the truth."

Before I can make it across the street, the truck is back. Mika hops out and runs toward me. The moment her arms wrap around my neck, my anger subsides. I hold her tightly. Not wanting to let her go.

"I'm sorry." Her voice is muffled but I can hear it's draped in tears.

"I'm sorry too. I was being stupid. I didn't mean to imply you have to have my permission to leave."

"I didn't like the fact that you were telling me I had to ask for permission. I don't like being told what to do," she chuckles. "I should have just told you that my best friend is having an emergency appendectomy and I want to be there. I'll come back."

I pull away from her just enough to see her eyes.

"You promise?" My eyes search hers for the truth.

"I promise," she says without hesitation.

"Then I guess you can go." I intentionally sound as if I'm giving in but the relief in my heart can't be adequately expressed.

Her laughter causes me to laugh too until I can't resist her lips any more. I kiss her as deeply and as sweetly as I can. I want to remind her what she has here.

"Solomon?" She asks, breaking away from my kiss.

"Yes, baby."

"There's something else. I wanted to tell you last night but you were so tired, I didn't have the heart to disturb you."

My heart pounds at the possibilities of what she could say that would tear my world a part. "What is it?"

"I'm pregnant," she admits with half a smile. "Congratulations. I know it's what you and Lux have been waiting for. And why ya'll have been fucking my brains out every chance you get."

Her laugh doesn't hide her nervousness like she probably hopes it does.

"Pregnant? Already?" My heart pounds faster. Lux is pacing a hole in my head.

"You're not happy?"

The uncertainty on her face pains me.

"Of course I'm happy. We both are. Just surprised." I look over her face, looking for signs of her true feelings about it but I can't tell. "Are you...how do you feel about it?"

"Honestly, I'm still coming to terms with it but I'm not unhappy about it," she shrugs.

Gradually, a smile grows on my face and the full scope of what she just told me settles in me. Seeing my smile causes her to smile too. I pull her toward me and rest my forehead on hers. I fall into the depth of her eyes and allow myself to enjoy the news for what it is. Even though I haven't heard what I really want to hear yet, it's one step closer. I can only pray it will come soon.

"Besides finding you, that's the best news we've had in a long time."

I kiss her softly, hoping she can feel what Lux and I have been trying to tell her all along.

"There's one more thing," she says as she breaks from me again. The anxiety in her eyes in unmistakable.

"*Fuck,*" Lux whispers.

"I have decided to commit to you and Lux, if you want me. I'll stay here and raise our baby here. I'll just run my business from Abrielara. Of course..."

"*Oh, thank God,*" Lux exclaims.

I cut her words off with my lips. There are no words I can say to adequately express how happy those words make us feel.

"Of course we want you. We chose you didn't we?" I chuckle at her, shocked that she would doubt how much we want her for a second.

"I wasn't sure." She looks down at her feet, shifting her weight between them. "I mean, I know you wanted to complete the Passage but I also know you don't love me. I just wasn't sure how this part of everything was supposed to work." The anxiety is back in her eyes and now I understand.

"We're fucking idiots. I knew we should have told her how we really felt about her."

"Obviously we aren't that smart where women are concerned. Especially this woman. Our woman."

"Fix it now. Before we lose our chance."

"Why would you think that we don't love you? Lux and I never fight but we fight over you. The moment we saw you, we knew you were meant for us. We just disagreed on how to make you ours. We guarded our words and our steps because we were afraid of losing you. Lux told you the other night that he can't live without you and that the reason for his existence was to love you. What he meant to say was we can't live without you and we exist to love you."

"I said it how I meant it asshole. Don't put words in my mouth."

"Shut up. I'm trying to win our C.O over. Besides, it's true."

"I thought it was just endorphins talking. I was afraid to believe it could be true."

I try to shake Lux from my thoughts and continue. "I can't sleep without you. Every other thought in our head is about you. You're ours, Mika. The moment you got out of Bobby's truck that first day, you were ours. I love you more than I love anything else on this planet. You belong here in Abrielara. You belong with us. You belong to us and we belong to you."

She's furiously working at trying to blink the tears from her eyes but I've already seen them. I pull her back to me, chest to chest.

"Look at me baby," I whisper to her. The moment her eyes meet mine, I continue. "We adore you. With everything we have and are. Even if you don't love us back, we're willing to take what you can give. For us, the Passage has never been about a baby. Yes, our ancestors want our race to go on and so do we, but for us the Passage has always been about you. It doesn't work or make sense without you."

"Really?" She asks in disbelief.

"Really. When did you finalize your decision?"

"After the brunch with Lux but I was too upset to say it out loud. After talking with the Monarch I knew I needed to stick with what I already knew. I just didn't know how this was supposed to work out if I loved you, both of you, but you didn't love me. I didn't know if we co-parent or what happens. We never talked about our feelings. We just talked about the Passage and how it was important that we complete it. I was afraid I was just a means to an end for ya'll."

"Never that, baby. Never that. You love me?" I want to hear her say it again.

"You heard her. She loves me too. Don't skip over that," Lux interjects.

"I heard her, dipshit."

She gives me a sassy smirk. "You heard me, but because you asked so nicely. I love you. Both of you. I'm so happy you chose me."

"Feels good to hear you say that Mika. Now I want you to

hear us. You are the beginning, the end, the in between, the question, the answer, and the why. You are everything." I take her chin between my fingers and force her eyes to look into mine. "You hear me? Everything."

I kiss her knowing she can taste the truth on my tongue and the love in my heart.

Epilogue

Mika

"How much longer, Dr. Camacho?" I'm tired of being in this bed. I am dying to walk around for longer than two hours a day.

Solomon, bless his soul is driving me crazy. He just wants to make sure I'm safe and healthy while keeping the baby calm and healthy. I get it, trust me. However, he's more agitated than usual. He never wants to talk about it, so I don't press him, but something has him worried. Whatever it is, he'll feel much better soon. Today we meet our baby girl.

"Almost there, momma. We're just waiting on her to calm down just a bit more. Her heart rate is a little too fast."

Dr. Camacho has been closely watching her heartbeat for the last hour. I've been watching Solomon. He's pacing the floor and talking to Lux. Not sure what the conversation is about, but it's a deep one judging by how long he's been doing it.

"Solomon, sweetheart, come sit by me." I pat the bed. He sits and grabs my hand. "What's wrong? What are you and Lux talking about over there? And don't say you're worried about the baby because it seems like it's more than that."

"Truth?" He asks hesitantly.

"Always."

"Remember what I said about the baby and what she'll look like if she takes after me?"

Oh, that's what it is. He's worried I won't want her and will leave them both. No matter how often I try to reassure him, he never believes me.

"I told you when we saw her and all of her little tentacles on the ultrasound that I'm not going to leave, and I meant it. Don't you believe me?"

"I'm just trying to prepare myself for the worst."

I rest my hands on his cheeks. "Relax. There's nothing to prepare for except to make sure she's fine. I need you to be strong for both of us."

"I just don't want to lose you." His face is layered with worry. His beautiful dark brows scrunch together while his lips pinch themselves thin.

"You are not going to lose me. I promise you I'm not going anywhere. I'm not your mother. Lux, help me out here."

Solomon's eyes flare with bright embers, turning his honey eyes red. Within seconds, Solomon is gone and Lux is sitting beside me.

"I'm trying but he won't listen. He worries too much."

"Try harder," I smirk at him. "So glad you decided to make an appearance. I was beginning to think you weren't coming."

"I'm always with you, even if you can't see me."

I run my fingers through his long hair. "I know but some-times seeing you calms me down."

He ducks his head. "I didn't think I would ever hear you say that. The scent helps, I know but seeing me...that's some-thing different."

"True, but we've come a long way since the chase. Don't you think?"

His half lipped grin gives me a small glimpse of his sharp teeth. "Yes, thank God. I didn't think we were ever going to get through that."

"Well we did. Now we just need to get through this. Help Solomon, okay?"

"Anything for you."

"I love you," I say.

He softly kisses me in response, coercing my lips apart so his tongue can play with mine. I recline against the pillows and he follows me down, applying more pressure to my lips. I cannot contain the moans filtering out of my chest, his harmonizing with mine.

A clearing throat breaks us a part.

"I just wanted to let you know it's time to go," Dr. Camacho's nurse informs us, but we don't pay her much mind.

I open my eyes to see Solomon is back.

"You make sure you come back to me," Solomon whispers and kisses me again.

"I don't want to be anywhere else."

Solomon

Xaria Ellita Christiansen was born on a beautiful December morning with my eyes and her mother's smile. We named her Xaria because it means the gift of love and Ellita because it means the chosen one. I never thought I could fall in love so fast but here I am, falling in love for the second time in six months. Watching Mika hold her for the first time put all of my fears to rest. She loves her too, but how could she not? Look at her. She has beautiful bronze skin and a mess of black curls on her head.

"I told you she wasn't going to leave. You should listen to me more."

"Maybe. I can't believe we made it here, Lux. Can you believe it?"

"Only because I witnessed it myself. With all your shenanigans, we almost didn't make it here."

"My shenanigans? How soon we forget the pharmacy incident."

"Okay, you may have a point, but you almost ran her off the first few days she arrived. We're lucky it turned out this way."

"Not lucky, Lux. Blessed. Tremendously blessed."

The End

Afterword

Thank You So Much For Reading!
Click the link to subscribe to my newsletter and receive a
bonus chapter to
The Chosen – The Interview
Keep Reading For A 2 Chapter Sneak Peek of
The Choice, Taliah's story. Available for preorder on Amazon

Sneak Peak: The Choice
Talia

"Mika needs you. Go to her now."

Whoever sent the enlightening postcard failed to inform us the simple directions would almost cost me my life.

Okay, maybe that's a bit of an exaggeration, but not by much. The tiny plane looked and sounded like it was on its last leg, engine or whatever. I honestly didn't think we were going to make it. I'm exhausted from the mental strain of contemplating my sudden death and the events that brought me to this point. Thank god we can land.

Breanna's bag hits the back of my thighs again for the umpteenth time as we attempt to disembark.

"Do you think you can manage to *not* break my legs before we get off this rickety plane?"

"I could if you would move a little faster. I would like to get off before it takes off again."

"Obviously, I can't do that."

The man in front of me looks over his shoulder quickly but makes no apologies for his slow movements. In fact, I think he walks slower just for the hell of it. He obviously has nowhere to go in his mustard yellow tweed jacket, which I would bet my life was not made in this decade or even the last three. He even had a hat to match with a little green feather tucked into a black ribbon on the side.

The tiny plane was filled with twenty passengers. Breanna and I were lucky to get a ticket at the last minute, with the Tulip Festival in full swing and all.

My little sister and I started this journey all because of a postcard with a picture of tulips on the front. Tulips are Mika's favorite flower, so it immediately brought her to mind when I saw it. The message was written in my mother's handwriting.

Nothing remarkable about that except my momma is dead and has been for over six months. The message is ominous and unclear except for the address on the card. *2121 Morningside Dr. Abrielara, Washington.*

We have never heard of Abrielara.

When I went to see that slimy lawyer, he informed us Abrielara was indeed the place where Mika went to claim her inheritance. To think back on the reading of the will, Breanna and I could not sit in on the portion pertaining to her. We thought it was odd, but then again Mika's and momma's relationship was odd.

My arm throbs from holding my carryon up instead of rolling it. It really should have been checked if I weren't afraid it would get lost. Although, I don't feel too bad. Breanna's bag is bigger and heavier than mine. I barely remember packing it.

Since receiving the postcard, I've done nothing but worry about Mika. Mika who needs no one. Mika, who's so smart, self-sufficient, and confident, now needs us.

In what way? How could we possibly help her? We just lost momma. We can't afford to lose her too, not this soon.

No need to think that way. Put those thoughts away right now.

I eject the handle so I can roll it now that we are actually moving. Brianna manages not to hit the back of my legs anymore and we can finally get off the plane. Now to find out how we can get to Abrielara.

Such a strange name for a town. I look around to see where we can rent a car. According to the lady on the phone, it was something new they were offering.

"There it is." Breanna points to a sign partially hidden by the exit sign.

"Thank God."

There's no line, so we can walk right up to the desk of Wilson's Creek Car Rentals. Shouldn't be too hard to get a car to rent.

"Good morning ladies. How can I help you?"

"Hello." I check her name badge. "Sally. We called and reserved a car yesterday?"

"Oh, yes! You would be Taliah and Breanna Burris, correct?"

"Yes."

"Wonderful, well believe it or not, we've had an influx of traffic within the last few hours. I'm sorry to say the four-door sedan you wanted is unavailable. However, we have a compact car I would be happy to rent to you for two extra days, no charge."

"At this point Sally, I don't care if it's a bicycle as long as it's motorized and can get us where we need to be."

"Speak for yourself," Breanna mumbles.

I ignore her. I'm tired and I want to get settled.

"Where do I sign?"

The car we rented isn't hard to pick out. It's the only neon yellow car in the parking lot.

"You expect me to ride in that shoe box?"

"Why not? We flew in one to get here."

I swear sometimes she can be such a child.

"Thank God I didn't bring the extra suitcase or we would be in trouble." Breanna huffs as she finally gets her suitcases in the back.

"*We* nothing. *You* would be in trouble. I told you I had no plans to stay here for more than three days. That should be enough time to find Mika and make sure she's okay. Yet you still insisted on bringing that big ass suitcase."

"I like to be prepared," she throws back at me.

"For what, though? Where do you think we're going? We're going to Abrielara. A town so small I had to magnify Google Maps six times before it showed up so I could see it." I yank my seatbelt on.

"Like I said, I like to be prepared and don't do that."

She wiggles her fingers at me.

"Do what?"

"Put on your seatbelt. I want to drive." She hops out of the car and walks around.

"Fine, but I'm warning you Breanna. If my head comes anywhere close to kissing the dash, I'm taking over. I'm not playing with you."

Breanna is a horrible driver. I'm surprised she's kept her driver's license this long.

"I will obey the driving laws of the land. Promise."

As soon as we're belted in and Breanna turns on the radio, I know I'm in trouble. If the lot were paved instead of gravel, she would have burned rubber leaving the parking lot. My head flings back against the seat. I don't have to worry about my head kissing the dash, because it's being pushed up against the headrest.

"Breanna!"

"Sorry."

She slows down, but I'm positive she still isn't going the speed limit.

Slow. Down." I want to get where we are going as quickly as she does, but I want to get there in one piece.

"Oh, come on. We're on a country road with no other cars around. It's the perfect place to floor it and see what this baby can do."

Is she out of her mind?

"What this baby can do? A few seconds ago you were calling this baby a shoe box. No. First of all, we're in the country and anything and anyone can dart out into the road and then it's lights out. If you want to floor it so bad, then you should find a closed track and floor it there. Preferably without me in the car."

"Party pooper." She sticks her tongue out at me.

"Call me what you want, but I want to live."

We ride in silence for a few miles. After receiving the postcard three days ago, I haven't slept much and I know Breanna hasn't either. Breanna and I aren't that close to Mika only because we were closer to momma.

Momma and Mika were too much alike and butted heads constantly. Once Mika moved out, it was easier not staying in touch than it was to maintain contact. With her career and living a totally different life than we do, the distance between us just got wider. But now I'm wishing I had tried harder. Wishing I had made some kind of effort to keep her in our lives.

We may not be close, but Mika is my sister. I've always admired her spunk, her fearlessness, and her creativity. I never told her any of that, but I wish I had. Momma dying was hard on all of us, but at least Breanna and I were prepared. As prepared as one can be for a death.

It wasn't a sudden death. But for Mika, it had to feel like it was out of the blue. Momma made us promise not to tell Mika she was sick. She didn't want to guilt her into visiting. So we didn't tell her.

I know momma loved Mika and I know Mika loved momma, even though both of them had a hard time showing it. Tears spring to my eyes. It hits me that if Mika is gone, she will have died never knowing how much momma loved her. How much she cared for her. How proud she was of her.

Breanna reaches over and squeezes my hand as I blink the tears away.

"We'll find her and she's going to be fine. Don't worry. Mika is tougher than both of us. Don't give up hope. We haven't even started looking for her yet."

"I know. I just feel bad. We should have done a better job of staying in touch."

"Yeah, I know. There's no excuse now. We have nothing keeping us from staying in Abrielara longer if we need to. I'm open to it. I'm sick of Atlanta, anyway."

"It's a thought. I don't have anything tying me down in Atlanta now, either."

Marlon demanding I stay home instead of looking for Mika, freed me from any strings I had in Atlanta.

"What about Marlon?"

"Marlon and I broke up yesterday."

"Ha! Good for you. I never could stand that good for nothing Uncle Tom. I'm telling you, Lia, he has a wife and kids somewhere. He looks like the type."

"Well, if he does, it's no longer my problem." I reach into my bag to grab some gum. I really should have had some breakfast this morning. I didn't feel like eating in Atlanta at the airport. It was too damn early.

"What happened? Give me some of that gum."

I cock an eyebrow at her and her bad manners.

"Please," she holds her hand out.

I hand her a stick. "He tried to forbid me from coming. He said Mika was a big girl and could take care of herself."

"No he didn't." She spares me a quick glance before returning her eyes to the road.

"Yes he did. He said I was an idiot to go to some podunk town that no one has ever heard of because I received a post-card. He thinks we're being set up."

"Set up? By whom? Momma? It's her handwriting on the postcard." She's just as flabbergasted as I was by the notion.

I shrug my shoulders in response.

"Not unless someone forged her signature." Breanna says softly. She turns to look at me, her eyes wide. "Oh, my god Lia. What if he's right? What if someone forged her signature to get us out here and, like idiots, we're walking right into a trap?"

"Brea, it's not a trap and even if it is, we still have to find Mika. We can't seem to get her on the phone and she hasn't returned any of our messages. So either something is terribly wrong, or she is extremely mad at us and has written us off. Either way, we need to find her so we can move on. At least I do."

Brea sits back in her seat with a heavy sigh. "You're right. We need to find her."

The rest of the ride is spent in silence until the Welcome to Abrielara population 3510 sign appears.

"Finally." I grab the postcard from my purse. Before we even think about checking into our hotel, I would like to find the address on the card. I punch the address into the GPS. It's been calculating for the last five minutes.

"Where am I supposed to go?" Breanna stops at the fork in the road.

"The address says 2121 Morningside Drive, but the GPS is trippin'. I'm not sure how to get there. I guess we're going to have to stop and ask someone."

"Wait, that street sign says Morningside Drive." Brianna points to the sign on her side of the road. We look at each other.

"Okay, so I guess let's look at the house numbers."

"Fingers crossed."

2121 is right around the bend from the street sign. A big, beautiful log cabin with windows for days. Of course, her yard would have tulips. Lots of tulips.

"This is it."

"Wow. I can see why she never came back to Georgia or went back to New York."

"Yeah. Let's see if she's home."

After several minutes of knocking on her door, no one answers. The doorbell seems to be out of service because nothing happens when I press it.

"Well, we tried." Breanna states, obviously just as disappointed as I am. To be so close to seeing her only to leave without so much as a glimpse.

"Maybe she's in town somewhere. We can at least check in, walk around, and see if we can find her. If not, we can always come back here." I walk back to the car but turn around when I see Brianna hasn't moved a muscle.

"Brea, come on. We'll come back. We're close. I'm sure we'll see her sometime today." I thread my arm thru hers, praying my words are true.

"Okay, lead me to the hotel. I think I need some coffee."

"Yeah, me too. I could actually use a nap." Seeing the address on the card was an actual address took a weight off my back. Now I feel like I could sleep until dawn.

"Directions say to take a left, stay straight until we come

to the town circle. It says we will know when we get there because there's an enormous fountain in the middle of the road. Then to take a right on Shipley and the hotel will be on the left."

"Sounds simple enough."

We pass more large log cabin homes which look like they should be a part of *Architectural Digest*. The streets are immaculate. Strange thing is no one is out and about. It's eight a.m., early but not too early and yet no one is on the streets. Like no one. We pass a bakery, a coffee shop, a barber shop, and none of them appear to be open.

"I don't think this is Abrielara. I think we're in Mayberry."

"You would be right except the address says Abrielara, and we found it, so I think that nixes the Mayberry theory. But I know what you mean. I would expect to see some people walking around. At least see some of these stores open."

We continue to drive thru until we come to a fountain in the middle of the road.

"Okay, so now take a right here," I direct her.

The hotel is exactly where the lady I spoke to on the phone said it would be. Only, I don't think we can call it a hotel.

"Uh, you sure?"

"Yeah, this is it. See the sign?" The sign was an old-fashioned one with *The Pettigrew* written in black fancy lettering.

"Yeah, I can read. But this looks like a B&B, not a hotel. Lia, you know how I feel about staying in people's homes I don't know." She crosses her arms and pouts at the notion of staying here.

"Breanna, we don't have a choice. It's either sleep here or in the car. This is the only place I could find that resembled a hotel. Come on. I'm sure it's nice."

"Well, it looks nice but if Norman Bates greets us at the front desk, I'm not saying anything. I'm just gonna turn right around and come back to the car. If you know what's good for you, you won't say shit. You'll just follow me."

"And here I thought you were the adventurous one of the two of us. Come on. Grab your stuff and let's get checked in. We need to figure out a plan so we can start looking for Mika."

The Pettigrew doesn't look bad at all. It looks cozy and friendly, with a beautifully landscaped yard and patio. It's also a log cabin home, but not as big as the ones we passed on the way into town. There wasn't a lady at the desk, but the man who was, wasn't exactly friendly. He was tall, broad shouldered, with eyes as dark as obsidian and lips shut so tight I'm not sure they were real. His hair is just as black as his eyes and with his firm jaw line, he would be handsome if he smiled just a little. His disposition though, was horrible and completely overshadowed what made him attractive in the first place.

I glance over at Breanna quickly and sure enough, she's wearying the hell out of that gum and her eyes are watching this guy as if she's waiting for him to do something. He hasn't reacted to us. He's indifferent and I believe if he didn't have to talk to us at all, he wouldn't have.

After providing our names, he hands us our keys and shows us to our room. He was nice enough to take our bags, even though we didn't ask and he didn't offer.

"Thank you?" My voice is polite but somewhat sheepish, causing my gratitude to come out as a question. He, of course, does not respond. He just walks away.

"Well. Alright then." Breanna puts her purse on the table. "Even if his attitude could use an adjustment, at least the rooms are decent."

Thank goodness Breanna and I could get a suite with a connecting bathroom. Breanna and I learned a long time ago we are better off sleeping in separate rooms. She likes the heat and I like it cool.

"True. From what we've seen so far, it shouldn't take us long to find someone who has seen Mika."

I grab the map of Abrielara that was left on the table. "We can unpack and maybe grab something to eat. While we're doing that, we can come up with a plan on how we want to approach this."

"Okay, but from what we saw when we drove in nothing looks open."

"You're right. This place is supposed to offer breakfast, though. Maybe they have a continental breakfast or something. It'll be better than nothing. From the looks of this map, the downtown area is only like ten blocks. We can cover that before lunchtime."

"We can cover even more ground if you take one side and I take the other," Breanna suggests, looking over my shoulder.

"Great idea. Let's unpack so we can get going."

For once, I'm feeling as if we will have answers sooner than we thought. Abrielara is a tiny country town. Surely someone has seen Mika at some point. I refuse to believe otherwise.

Breakfast at the Pettigrew is pleasant, but the coffee is outstanding. I have never tasted any coffee as good anywhere else. I'm hoping to purchase some online or at least take some home with me because the boutique brands of coffee I indulge in aren't going to cut it anymore.

"Okay, so how about I take the right side of the street and

you take the left? Did you grab your cellphone?" I pull mine out of the pocket of my jeans and hold it up.

"Yep, but I don't know how much good it's gonna do. I don't have a signal."

"Yeah, I don't either, but we are out in the woods. Could explain why a signal is hard to come by."

I slide my phone back into my pocket. "Well, at least we both know where we're staying. After you complete your side, just come back to The Pettigrew and wait for me. Hopefully, I won't be long behind you."

"Got it. This shouldn't take long. See you in a few."

Breanna crosses the street and I walk up the block to the Abrielara Coffee House, which now appears to be open. Looks like a good place to start. I feel my cellphone buzz in my pocket.

Maybe I've finally got a signal. No such luck. Just an alert to let me know I don't have a signal. Like I needed an alert for that. I continue to walk while checking my phone, hoping to find a pocket of service somewhere until I come in contact with something hard, hot, and then wet.

"Oh!" I step back as the hot liquid seeps into my light weight sweater."

"Are you okay?"

I look up into the green eyes of a tall, good looking man with dark auburn hair. His extended goatee is the same color as his hair, but his eyelashes are much darker. The most notable thing is the huge dark stain spreading across his white t-shirt.

"Oh my god, I got it all over you." Without thinking, I reach over to pull his shirt away from his body, as if the coffee hasn't already seeped thru it.

"It's okay. I'm fine, really." His light chuckle is a little raspy and deep. Not boogey man deep, but deep enough I know I am talking to a grown man.

"Are you okay?" He asks again. The quick sweep of his eyes over me warms me up in the chilly breeze of the morning. When his eyes return to mine, they reach right in and tug something inside of me. His tongue takes a leisurely trip from one side of his bottom lip to the other. His eyes never leave mine.

My mouth waters for something sweet, like tea, a cupcake, the sugar in the cream in his coffee left on his chest. I mean shirt. He winks at me and I'm reminded he asked me a question.

"I'm okay. I'm so sorry. I wasn't watching where I was going. Your shirt is ruined," I manage to say.

He shrugs with a small lift of the corner of his mouth. "It's just a shirt. It's fine."

"I feel horrible about it. Can I pay you for the shirt or for the coffee at least? I can't imagine there being anything left in the cup."

He turns the cup over and empties what few sips were left in it. God, now I feel terrible.

"How about you make it up to me by having a cup with me? I can order us another one and we can walk to my office so I can change my shirt. You can tell me all about you on the way there."

I hesitate. I don't know this man. Even if he is the first and only person to talk to me besides Brea and Lerch at *The Petti-grew*. But there's something about his eyes and the way he looks at me that makes me want to say yes.

"I don't know you. I'm not sure that would be such a good idea." Regardless of how he looks at me, going back to a strange man's office in a town where I don't know anyone isn't smart.

He wipes his hands off on a napkin he pulls out of his pocket. He puts his hand out between us.

"Hi, my name is Brady. Dr. Brady Merrick, if you want to be formal." The easy smile on his lips makes me smile, and I put my hand in his. His fingers wrap around mine quickly, as if they were eager for the touch.

"I'm Taliah. Taliah Burris, if you want to be formal, but I prefer just Taliah."

"Just Taliah it is then."

His easy going grin and bright eyes twinkle just enough for me to think he was probably a stinker when he was younger. Probably still is.

"Taliah, I think you're absolutely gorgeous and I would love it if you had a cup of coffee with me. We don't have to go to my office if you don't feel comfortable. Shirt's almost dry anyway, but I would love to get to know you better."

He hangs on to my hand and I'm in no rush for him to let go, but I'm here for a reason. I slowly remove my hand from his.

"I would love to except I'm looking for someone and I would like to find her quickly, if I can."

He dumps his now empty cup and dirty napkins into the trash can. "Who are you looking for? Wait, are you related to Mika? Mika Christiansen?"

My heart stops and then pumps faster. "Christiansen? I'm looking for Mika Burris. If that's the same person, yes, I am. I'm her sister. Do you know where she is?"

"Of course I do. She's at home. You passed her house on Morningside Drive on your way into town."

"We just came from there, but no one answered the door."

Maybe Mika saw it was us and decided not to answer the door. The thought hurts, but it wouldn't surprise me. I just need to lay eyes on her to feel better.

"She's probably deep in that library of hers and didn't hear the door."

He reaches out to grab my hand again. "Why don't we get some more coffee and you come with me so I can change my shirt? Then I will be happy to take you to her. What do you say?"

I eye him up warily. If he is lying to me, I don't know what my reaction is going to be. This is almost too good to be true. We haven't even been in Abrielara a full day yet and the first person who willingly speaks to me knows where Mika is. It's gotta be some kind of record on somebody's list.

"If you would rather, I can take you to my office and I can call Mika's house and tell her you're here. While we're waiting for her to show up, I can admire your beauty and have some coffee. You can tell me all about yourself."

I still hesitate. There are movies out there where women come up missing because they trust the wrong people. This man is a doctor. An incredibly good-looking doctor. Surely he's safe to trust. But I've seen so many shows where the doctor and the killer were the same person.

He bites down on his bottom lip before giving me another wink. Yeah right. This one is smooth. A little too smooth. He may not be a mass murderer, but he's definitely a lady killer.

"You know, my stomach and my chest are burning something fierce right now from the coffee." He pulls at his shirt only to let it go and it sticks back to his body. My eyes zoom in on the huge brown stain on his shirt. Even though he's obviously joking, I give in. I ruined his shirt and wasted his coffee.

"Okay, we can go back to your office so you can change your shirt." I look across the street. No sign of Brea. "I have another sister I brought with me. I don't see her, though."

"I'm sure she's around here somewhere. Where are you staying?"

"The Pettigrew."

"Good, I'm sure she'll turn up."

I take another look across the street. Kind of strange how I haven't seen her since she walked over there. You would think I would see her go in and out of the stores, but no, nothing. But then again, Breanna does have the attention span of a gnat. She's all over the place sometimes. I wouldn't be surprised if something grabbed her attention and she forgot why we were here in the first place.

"Did you want to go back in and grab another coffee?"

"No, I can just as easily make some, or we can go out after I change and grab a cup." He watches me for a few more moments. "As long as she knows how to get back to the Pettigrew, she'll be alright. I'll get you here in plenty of time to meet back up with her."

"Okay." I take another quick look behind me and step in line beside Dr. Merrick. I'm sure Breanna will come looking for me before lunch time rolls around.

"So, Taliah, tell me about yourself while we walk. My office is just a couple of blocks up."

"Not much to tell. I've spent most of last year taking care of my mother, who was in hospice until she died. Lately, I've been trying to figure out exactly how to spend my time."

"I'm sorry to hear about your mother. What did she succumb to?" His eyes are kind.

"Breast cancer. She had it years ago and it went into remission, but it came back with a vengeance."

"I'm sorry."

His hand touches the center of my back softly. A vision of him wrapping me in his big arms comes to mind. How nice that would be. Marlon was not the affectionate type.

"So, what do you do for a living?" He asks as a glass building comes into view.

"I was a nurse. Well, I still am a nurse. When the cancer came back, I had to quit so I could take care of her. I haven't gone back because I'm not sure what I want to do next. Nursing is always good, but the strain of the last eighteen months has taken a lot out of me. I'm kind of weighing my options right now."

"Nothing wrong with that." He holds the door open for me so I can walk in a head of him.

"What type of medicine do you practice?"

He punches the button for the elevator.

"I'm a geneticist."

"Hmm. Are you widely experimenting with DNA or are you looking for a cure for something specific?"

"I'm always experimenting with DNA but not in the way you're probably thinking. I am looking for a cure for a particular ailment not well known outside this area. I'm following up on a study that was done years ago, but not much documentation has been left to study. So, I'm kind of working my way backwards."

"Sounds interesting." We step into the elevator.

"It is." He presses the number five and then turns to look at me. "But not nearly as interesting as you."

All I can do is smirk at his comment. Like I said, trouble. His eyes seem to brighten and then dim. We aren't outside and the lights didn't fluctuate, so I'm not sure what caused the change. What I know is with the look in his eyes and the sexy smirk on his lips, it definitely got a bit hotter in here.

Brady

It takes considerable strength not to eat this girl up in this elevator. Not literally, but yeah, literally. The bone structure on this girl is incredible. My hands itch to sculpt, to immortalize her features, although I'm not an artist.

I would not be surprised if she said she modeled for a living. The high cheekbones, the full bow-shaped lips, the classically beautiful face with elegant eyebrows and long lashes. Long lean legs encased in dark wash skinny jeans which also show off an ass I'm having the hardest time not salivating over. This girl is a goddess and I've got to have her.

I choose her. Today. We claim her today.

A heavy breath leaves my body as the elevator dings to signal we've reached our floor.

You agreed to do things differently, Stev'ik. The Monarch has already signed off on it and given her okay. You can't back out now.

Someone else will claim her if we do not. I choose her now. We must claim her now.

No. I'm holding you to your promise. Now pipe down. Let's see what else we can find out about her.

"Here we are." I open my office door and hold it open so she can come inside. "Come on back here. I have a little living space here just in case I have a test that's taking a while and I don't want to leave it." I unlock another door to my onsite living quarters.

"Do you stay overnight often?"

She follows me in and I close the door behind us. "Not too often, but recently there have been a few developments that I've stayed late to review. Have a seat anywhere. I'll be right back."

I take off the vest I had on so I can rip my shirt off and

chunk it in the trash. It's an old shirt not worth saving. I wipe the sticky off my chest and rush to get back to her, not wanting to waste a minute of our time together. I grab a black Henley from the drawer and walk back into the living room.

"So, how long do you plan on staying in Abrielara?" I look up before pulling the shirt over my head and stop. Her wide eyes are quickly shuttered after taking several trips up and down my body.

"Um, three days."

It's apparent she likes what she sees, and I'm not above flaunting it for her enjoyment. Anything I can do to sell her on the idea I'm a good catch.

"Like what you see? You can come over here and touch the merchandise. You can try me out before you take me home."

I run my hands down my stomach, flex my pecs a few times, and watch her eyes follow my movements. I can't stop the chuckle from slipping past my lips.

Her eyes shoot back up to mine. She crosses her arms and tries her best to look indifferent, but her face already told me what she thought about me.

"No thank you. I'm good right here and rest assured, I won't be taking you home."

"No shame in admitting you like all this. Come on over here and cop a feel. I promise I won't mind. I'll even let you take a bite if you want to." The idea of her laying her lips or teeth on me is highly appealing.

"I can admit you have a nice body, but you know that already. So, no thank you. I will keep my hands to myself."

"Aww. That's too bad. Maybe later I can change your mind." I'm hopeful as I pull my shirt on and walk toward the kitchenette. "You want some coffee? I can put some on and then give Mika a call."

"Sure. If you get her on the phone, may I talk to her?"

She looks anxious, almost as if she expects me to say no. "Don't see why not. Hang on." I get the coffee started and grab my cellphone and dial Mika's house, placing it on speaker so Taliah knows I'm doing what I said I would.

It rings only for a second before it's snatched up.

"Speak." Solomon's gruff voice more than implies they haven't even gotten out of bed yet, or at least he hasn't. Not surprising for Solomon. He is not a morning person, at least not lately.

"Good morning to you too, Grumpy. Get your ass up. I was hoping to speak to your wife." I catch the surprise on Taliah's face. She evidently doesn't know about Solomon, which means she probably doesn't know about Xaria either.

"She's with the baby. What do you want?"

Taliah's eyes grow even wider. Yep, I was right. Poor thing is shocked beyond words.

"She's got a visitor, and I was going to bring her by your house or have you guys stop by mine. Whichever is easier."

Silence is the only beat heard for a few minutes. I'm sure this latest development is a surprise they hadn't planned for.

"Let me talk to Mika and see what she wants to do. I'll call you back."

Taliah shakes her head furiously. "Uh, is there any way you can just put Mika on the phone? Her sister was hoping to at least hear her voice."

"Alright, give me a second. She's in another room."

Taliah puts her hands together in prayer, thanking me silently. I wink at her to let her know it's going to be okay. I can see the stress in her body just about ready to manifest itself into tears. That's one thing I can't handle, seeing a woman cry.

"She's coming. Hang on."

"Thanks."

Taliah is chewing her bottom lip to death. Without thinking, I reach over and release her lip from her teeth with my thumb. I can't stop myself from caressing it, feeling its softness, and wondering what it tastes like. I release it when Mika's voice comes thru the phone.

"Hello?"

"Mimi? Is that you?" The tears are at the brim. I can see them. I grab a paper towel because I know coming next.

"Of course it's me, Tee. I haven't been gone so long that you've forgotten your own sister, have I?"

The tears she was holding back burst through like the damn broke. I give her the paper towel and I take over the phone call since it's obvious she can't speak any more.

"Mika, do you mind if we drop by? Or we can meet at my house?" I pull Taliah into my arms.

"Sure. We can meet at your house. I have to call the judge first."

"Okay, how about we meet in thirty? Your other sister is here too. We're gonna pick her up and head on over."

I hang on to Taliah awhile after the phone call has ended so she can cry it all out. I hold her securely in my arms and rub her back. She shorter than me but not so short I can't hold her just right. When she calms down, I step back.

"You okay, baby girl?"

"Yes. I'm just so relieved. You don't know how worried we've been. Not being able to reach her or contact her at all has been stressful. Then to receive a postcard telling us she needed us made the situation worse. Hearing her voice just lifted all of that."

"I can imagine."

"Thank you."

"No, thanks needed. So, next order of business is to find

your other sister so we can reunite you guys and then you and I can go back to getting to know each other better."

"I owe you at least that."

"No owing. We get to know each other because you genuinely want to. Not because you think you need to repay me for doing something as simple as making a phone call."

"Okay." She gives me a soft smile, which melts my insides into pure mush.

Claim her now.

"Good. Now let's find your sister. We'll take my truck because my house is more than a few blocks away."

I ignore Stev'k's prompting for now. However, I know it's only a matter of time before I will no longer have that option.

I wait in the truck as Taliah runs into the Pettigrew to see if her sister is waiting on her. Within minutes, they are running out, happiness all over their faces. I get out and open the passenger door for Taliah and the back for her sister. Her sister looks me over pretty good before getting in the truck. She's obviously younger than Taliah. Having seen Mika, seems like beauty runs in the family. Breanna is shorter than Taliah and Mika, but still has the same curves.

"Brea, this is Brady. Dr. Brady Merrick. He's taking us to his house and Mika is meeting us there. Brady, this is my sister Breanna, but we call her Brea."

I reach around and offer her my hand. "Nice to meet you Breanna. You can call me Brady."

She studies my face for a few minutes and then gives me a big grin. She lays her hand in mine. "Nice to meet you, Brady. Thank you for doing this."

"Just like I told your sister, no thanks needed. Alright. Sit tight, we'll be at my house in a jiffy."

"So, does everyone in this town live in a log cabin?" Breanna asks as soon as I pull up in my driveway.

"No. The homes built in the last ten years or less aren't. Not unless the buyer picks that style. Most log homes around here are about twenty years or older.

"They're beautiful," Taliah walks up the stairs behind me.

"Thanks. I've always thought so. You guys come on in. Make yourself at home. Mika should be here shortly. I'm going to make some coffee since I didn't get to drink the pot I started at the office."

"I seem to be making a habit of interrupting your coffee time. I'm sorry."

"Baby doll, stop apologizing. Nothing to be sorry for. You want a cup?"

"Love one."

I look over her shoulder at her sister. "How about you Breanna?"

"Coffee would be great. Thanks."

"Alright. Coming right up." I leave them to look around, but keeping my ears peeled. I want to hear what Taliah says about me to her sister, if she says anything at all.

Instead of eavesdropping, we should be claiming! We must make her ours now!

Are you saying you are going back on your word that you gave to the Monarch just two months ago? You know how she hates it when people don't keep their word.

No. I do not enjoy disappointing the Monarch.

Well then, we have to do this right. Trust me, I agree. I want her too, but in order for us to do what we agreed to do and get what we want, we have to think this though. A little patience is required.

Stev'ik is inpatient, and he has a right to be. We've waited a long time to find someone to choose, but this is the worst time for him to choose someone. The absolute worst. I have to put the people of Abrielara before my own needs.

Before I can even pour the first cup, I hear the front door open and then screeching or screaming. What in the hell? I put the carafe down and high tail it back to the living room.

I had nothing to worry about. The sisters are in the middle of a hug fest.

Solomon walks toward me while keeping his eyes on the women.

"How did you run into them?"

"I was getting some coffee and Taliah ran into me. Told me she was looking for her sister and here we are. Speaking of which, I still have yet to have a cup. Want some?" I turn and walk back into the kitchen.

"Sure. I haven't had any either this morning." He follows me and I hand him the first cup.

How's the baby?"

"Perfect, if she would just sleep through the night."

"The kiddie whisperer hasn't got her on a schedule yet?" Looking at him now, I see his eyes are baggy and bloodshot. He returns a look of pure exhaustion. "Ah, the joys of father-hood. Remember, you asked for it."

"You're right and I wouldn't trade it. We really need to get her on a schedule, though. Mika has been getting up with her during the week and I take over on the weekends."

I finally take my first sip of coffee. The rich liquid cruises down my throat and straight to my soul.

Taliah

Although I knew she was coming, I wasn't prepared for the release of emotions upon seeing her. Stepping back, I look her over to confirm she's fine.

"You look amazing, Mika. I'm so glad you're okay." I hug her again.

"Thank you, but am I missing something? I saw both of you at momma's funeral. Did something happen?"

Based on the puzzled look on her face, it's obvious she didn't send the postcard. I pull it out of my purse and hand it to her.

"I received this a few days ago. Brea and I have been trying to reach you, but you don't return our calls and your assistant is no help. I finally saw momma's attorney, and he told me you were here. So here we are."

Mika continues to look at the postcard. "I see."

"Can you please tell us what's going on? Who sent it? We've been worried about you. And in case you haven't noticed that postcard is written in momma's handwriting. How is that possible?" Breanna asks, tapping the postcard with her manicured fingernail.

"I'm not sure. I would assume that momma wrote this before she died and had someone mail it for her. She loved to plan things." She sighs heavily and sits in the recliner near the fireplace. "When I got here, she had written me a letter with instructions to follow. I don't know what her bottom line is with bringing you guys here, but I think you guys should leave. Like immediately. Before it's too late."

She hands back the postcard.

"Leave? Why? We just got here, like an hour ago. Why would we leave?"

"I will be happy to come see you guys in a couple of

months, but right now, it's best if you go. Before…" She looks behind me and I turn to see what has her attention.

Brady and the man she came in with, connect her unblinking stare with one of their own.

"What's going on? You're acting so weird right now." Breana's eyes widen and shrugs her shoulders at me. I can only shake my head. I don't know what's going on either.

After a few moments, Mika's head nods in apparent resignation.

"It's already too late. At least for you." Her eyes land on me and a feeling of dread covers me.

"Too late for what?"

"You will get all the details later, but we need to get Breanna out of here while there's still time."

"What are you talking about? You aren't making any sense."

"I can't explain everything right now Taliah, but Brady can later. Right now, we need to get Breanna out of town. Now." The urgency in her voice is clear even though her words are whispered. It scares me.

"No. I'm not leaving you guys here. If you're staying, then so am I." Breanna crosses her arms in defiance.

"You don't know what you're saying, what you're putting at risk. For once in your life just trust me, Brea."

The plea in Mika's voice makes me fear for myself. Why is it too late for me to leave? Why does Brady have to tell me the details?

Brea flounces down on the couch, her eyes glued to her lap.

"If you guys are staying, then so am I. Ya'll are the only family I have left. Why would I leave and go where? If Taliah has to stay and you are already here, there is no reason why I can't stay either."

"Taliah, talk some sense into her." Mika turns to me.

"I can't when I don't know what the danger is. Besides, you know how hard-headed she is. When she puts her foot down, that's it, there's no moving her."

Mika's eyes look over my shoulder again. I follow her gaze in time to see the man she came with shake his head slightly.

How strange. There's something going on here and whatever it is, he doesn't want her to say any more about it. The Mika I knew would never let someone else determine for her what to say or when to say it. Especially not a man.

Her shoulders drop with a sigh. "Well, I guess there's nothing left to say. You can't say I didn't warn you."

The silence that follows is ominous. I don't know about Breanna, but my mind is flooded with all kinds of questions. All of which I know Mika will not answer. I'm so happy to see her. Happy to see she's fine or at least appears fine, but there is something weird going on here.

"How long have you been here, Mika?" I ask softly.

"Since momma's funeral."

"You didn't think to call us at least once to let us know where you were?"

Breanna's quick accusing tone leaves a lot to be desired. Can't say I don't understand where she's coming from though. But we only have our side of the story to refer to. We know nothing about Mika's time here.

"Well, no. I was told I couldn't."

"By whom?" I implore. "Who would have the right to dictate that?"

"Momma's attorney. It was Momma's wish that I not tell you where I was."

"Why would she do that?" Breanna asks but Mika ignores the question.

"Besides, neither one of you paid me any mind at the

funeral. I tried multiple times to get your attention so we could talk but both of you were too busy. I honestly didn't think you would know I was gone."

"Mika, that's not true." We may have been drowning in our own grief but had we known she really wanted to talk we would have made the time.

"Oh, really Taliah? Look how long it took you to realize something may be up. It never would have crossed your mind to come looking for me if it weren't for the postcard. Admit it. Nothing wrong with it because we know that's just how it is, but at least be honest about it."

"You have a point. We have never been close enough to know if there was something big going on in your life that I didn't see on the internet. Definitely nothing personal. That's something we want to change. The only family we have is in this room. We care what happens to you and want to be a part of your life. We hope you want to be a part of ours too."

Mika opens her arms to me and I walk in them, wrapping mine around her.

"I'm so happy you're okay sis. I really am."

"I'm glad I'm okay too." She laughs and squeezes me before letting me go. "I'm happy to see both of you." She looks over her shoulder at Brea. "Even bonehead Breanna."

"Hey!" Brea chucks a pillow at her and jumps up to give her a hug. "Just promise you will stay in touch with us from now on. None of this moving across the country without a note. My sanity can't take it."

After the emotional morning we had, we decide to meet again for a late dinner. Mika and Solomon, who I learned was her husband and a doctor as well, had some errands they needed to run.

I was grateful for a little down time and looking at Brea's face, I knew she could use a nap as well. There was still a lot to discuss. The biggest question being why she wanted us to leave so bad.

She said that Brady would fill me in on the details and I intended to get them. However, I felt the need to ask when he and I could be alone. Whatever was keeping me here wasn't a factor for Breanna yet. I know she's insistent on staying no matter what, but sometimes knowing the details can change your whole outlook on things.

I honestly don't know what could be so bad that leaving would make everything better. Or could force me to stay but not Brea.

Although there is something weird going on here, I can't help feel elated that we found Mika and she's okay. It's all I can focus on at the moment. However, tonight at dinner, Brady and I are going to have a little talk. Minus all of the smooth talking, body rubbing, and eye winking from earlier.

Yeah, minus all of that.

The Choice is will be available for preorder beginning February 28th on Amazon!